Charles Tomlinson

A Rudimentary Treatise on Warming and Ventilation

being a concise exposition of the general principles of the art of warming and

ventilating domestic and public buildings, mines, lighthouses, ships, etc

Charles Tomlinson

A Rudimentary Treatise on Warming and Ventilation
being a concise exposition of the general principles of the art of warming and ventilating domestic and public buildings, mines, lighthouses, ships, etc

ISBN/EAN: 9783337392208

Printed in Europe, USA, Canada, Australia, Japan

Cover: Foto ©Andreas Hilbeck / pixelio.de

More available books at **www.hansebooks.com**

A

RUDIMENTARY TREATISE

ON

WARMING AND VENTILATION;

BEING A CONCISE EXPOSITION OF THE

GENERAL PRINCIPLES OF THE ART

OF

WARMING AND VENTILATING DOMESTIC AND PUBLIC
BUILDINGS, MINES, LIGHTHOUSES, SHIPS, ETC.

BY

CHARLES TOMLINSON.

THIRD   EDITION.

LONDON:

VIRTUE BROTHERS & CO., 1, AMEN CORNER,
PATERNOSTER ROW.
1864.

PREFACE TO THE THIRD EDITION.

THE art of warming and ventilating buildings in a manner most conducive to health, convenience, and economy, has been discussed during many years with an earnestness which has increased with the increasing interest of the public. The scientific Chemist, the popular Lecturer, the Engineer, and we may hope in some cases the Architect and the Builder, have not failed to convince their readers and hearers how and why it is that constant supplies of pure air are even more necessary to health than the artificial warmth by which the rigours of our uncertain climate are mitigated. More than one-half the diseases which afflict humanity have been referred to the breathing of impure air, and a large proportion of our ailments certainly originate in our imperfect methods of warming.

Admitting, then, the importance of the subject, it seems to be equally important to furnish the public with accurate information thereon, in a cheap and popular form. The art of warming and ventilating depends on natural principles of great beauty and generality, which have been clearly made out by the scientific chemistry of the last three-quarters of a century. These principles are expounded at some length in the following little work, now issued for the third time; but as their application involves a description of other men's inventions, and a compilation from other men's books, I have made free use of the labours of writers who have preceded me on the subject; but I am not aware of having taken a single line from any one without due acknowledgment, even though most of the books referred to have little more than a historical interest. Some valuable Parliamentary Reports, General Morin's recently published *Etudes sur la Ventilation,* and the general progress that has been made in the subject during the last ten years, have entailed considerable labour on me in preparing this New Edition. The object has been, not to produce a technical work, but to explain to the general reader, whether lady or gentleman, the vast importance of the art of warming and ventilating, and the principles on which the successful practice of the art depends, whether in one's own house, or in a public building. I have also introduced a number of historical details which are curious and interesting, not only as marking the slow growth of real improvement, and the difficulty men have in grasping a new idea if a change of habit is involved in its acceptance, but also as illustrating some of the varied phases of our common nature. It is hoped that these amusing details will not make the book less interesting to those who seek to become acquainted with the beautiful laws on which warming and ventilation depend; the principle of the latter art being, in fact, identical with that by which nature ventilates our globe—a hot ascending current from the warm regions, while the cooler air streams in at a lower level from the temperate regions.

King's College, London,
February, 1864.

ANALYSIS OF THE CONTENTS.

INTRODUCTION.

ON THE PHYSICAL AND CHEMICAL PRINCIPLES CONCERNED IN THE ART OF WARMING AND VENTILATION.

PART I.

CHAPTER I.

ON THE METHODS OF WARMING HOUSES BY MEANS OF OPEN FIRE-PLACES, ETC., BEFORE AND AFTER THE INTRODUCTION OF CHIMNEYS.

CHAPTER II.

ON THE METHODS OF WARMING BUILDINGS BY MEANS OF CLOSE STOVES AND HOT AIR APPARATUS.

CHAPTER III.

ON THE WARMING OF BUILDINGS BY MEANS OF STEAM AND HOT WATER.

CHAPTER IV.

FURTHER DETAILS ON WARMING BY MEANS OF THE OPEN FIRE-PLACE.

PART II.

CHAPTER I.

ON THE GENERAL PRINCIPLES OF VENTILATION.

CHAPTER II.

ON VENTILATION BY MEANS OF MECHANICAL CONTRIVANCES.

CHAPTER III.

ON THE VENTILATION OF BUILDINGS, SHIPS, MINES, ETC., BY MEANS OF ARTIFICIAL HEAT.

CHAPTER IV.

ON SPONTANEOUS VENTILATION.

CHAPTER V.

ON HOT WATER AND STEAM AS A VENTILATING FORCE, AND ON THE COMBINED METHODS OF WARMING AND VENTILATING.

APPENDIX.

WARMING AND VENTILATION.

INTRODUCTION.

ON THE PHYSICAL AND CHEMICAL PRINCIPLES CONCERNED IN THE ART OF WARMING AND VENTILATION.

An inquiry into the constitution and uses of our atmosphere in the economy of nature and art, is calculated to promote a solemn feeling of admiration and gratitude. This wonderful creation encloses within its capacious curves, like a vast dome, the widely extended kingdoms of nature, to which it ministers materials for growth, health, and enjoyment, and by its transparency reveals to intelligent beings a glimpse of other creations beyond its limits. At one time, it stands in simple grandeur as a vault of tender blue, displaying the glorious sun and the landscape smiling beneath; at another time, its surface is chequered with fleecy clouds,—"the beauteous semblance of a flock at rest,"—or alpine heights of more than silvery brightness, or huge piled-up masses, dark and frowning; all contributing to form wondrous variety and beauty in the aerial scenery, and giving to the landscape below the ever varying charms of light and shade. Again, the blue of this splendid ceiling becomes deeper and deeper, and bright golden points shine out here and there, increasing in number until the whole surface appears as if richly studded with gems.

If these great and glorious sights were of rare occurrence, or could only be witnessed from a few chosen spots on the earth's surface, they would stimulate our curiosity, and we should eagerly hasten to those spots, or read the descriptions and gaze at the pictures which travellers and artists had prepared for us. But their common occurrence causes them to be viewed with indifference. There are also many hidden wonders connected with the atmosphere equal in beauty to those which appeal directly to the eye, but requiring study for their due appreciation. The atmosphere is a scene of incessant restless activity. The heat of the tropical sun upon the earth sets the air in motion, rarefies and causes it to ascend; meanwhile the air from cooler regions rushes towards the equator to supply the impending vacuum, and it performs various useful offices on its way. Here it is the trade wind or the monsoon; there it is the sea or the land breeze; in a third place, it is the hill and valley breeze—all giving health and refreshment to places which otherwise might be uninhabitable. Meanwhile the heated ascending air of the equator proceeds on its useful mission in the direction of the poles, forming an upper current, descending in some places and mitigating the cold of temperate regions, as the under current tempers the heat of tropical climes. The heat, too, which gives force and activity to these aerial currents or vast natural ventilators, also raises the waters of the ocean and charges the air with moisture; this moisture ascends and forms clouds, those busy and active water-carriers which traverse the unobstructed regions of the sky, and pour down their treasures on the city and the plain, and on the desert where no water is, filling the mountain cisterns, whence gush out the springs and rivers; and these descend in a meandering course, and diffuse beauty and blessing on the lower lands long after the rain cloud has been dissolved. It is the resistance of the atmosphere that causes the rain to come down in gentle drops, and thus gradually to diffuse its refreshing influence, instead of falling in torrents and cataracts, as it otherwise would, without the retarding and separating influence of the air. It is the atmosphere which dispenses the white fleecy flakes of snow to the temperate regions, whereby the earth is covered and protected from the chilling influence of a low temperature; the air, too, is the region of mists and fogs, which bring moisture in a still more gradual manner; a cold current of air blowing over a warmer stratum of air, and cooling it, thereby rendering its moisture visible; or, after sun-set, the river may be warmer than the air, and the escaping vapour condenses into large rolling masses. But we especially notice the beneficial effects of differences of temperature between the air and the earth in the formation of dew; the moisture which the heat of the day had exhaled from the earth is deposited when a cloudless sky allows the earth to radiate its heat into space, and to cool down below the temperature of the air; the refreshing moisture is then condensed upon vegetation and upon surfaces where it is most needed.

Not only are we able to trace in the atmosphere those great and regular motions which bring about an interchange between the air of the equator and that of either pole, but there are other motions, apparently more fitful and irregular, in the winds, which blow from all points of the compass, and tend perpetually to restore the equilibrium of heat and moisture.

How wonderful, too, is the action of the atmosphere on light. By its means the sun's rays are diffused, and their influence extended from the sunshine to the shade. Were it not for the atmosphere, the sun would shine in an intensely dark sky, and no object would be visible unless the solar rays fell directly upon it. Sun-set would be a sudden transition from light to darkness; and sun-rise a painful change from intense darkness to intense light. But under the present wise and providential arrangement, the transition from day to night is calm and peaceful; the sun departs in splendour, like a monarch attended by a gorgeous court, leaving a mild and subdued scene of beauty behind; the soothing influences of evening gradually steal upon us, and new scenes of wonder and beauty gradually become unfolded. After some hours of peace and rest, the portals of the eastern sky slowly open, and one rosy messenger after another ascends to announce the advent of the king of day.

In addition to these complicated duties which the atmosphere has to perform, there are yet others still more wonderful. A large number of the operations of nature are, as it were, daguerreotyped in the air in such a manner, as to convey to sentient and intelligent creatures information of what is going on. The murmuring of waters, the tinkling of rills, the whispering of winds, the sound of the forest in the blast, the rush of the cascade, the roar of the ocean, and the roll of the thunder, are only certain motions among material bodies, which impress their own peculiar characters on the air, and form what are called *sounds*. Sounds are of so numerous and, at the same time, of so distinctive a character, that a large portion of every language is appropriated to their precise description. Thus, to define a few of the sounds emitted by certain animals, we speak of the lowing of cattle, the bleating of sheep, the cawing of rooks, the cooing of pigeons, the hissing of snakes, and many others. These sounds, expressive of certain wants and motions, feelings and sympathies, have, doubtless, an intelligent meaning among the respective species of animals to which they apply ; but both sound and its perception are alike dependent on the atmosphere. The phenomena of sound and of hearing, however, obtain their most perfect and exalted development in articulate speech, by which intelligent and responsible creatures are enabled to shape air into words, those swift and winged messengers by which we express our wants and feelings, by which we advise, instruct, or admonish others, share in their joys, their sorrows, and affections. Inferior only to articulate speech is the language of music, which, like the beauty produced by form and colour, is an invention calculated to promote the happiness of man.

The uses of the air in the arts of life are innumerable. It is the cheapest and most effectual prime mover ; we have merely to supply the tools, the machinery, and the work to be done, and it will labour with untiring activity. It wafts our ships over every sea, turns our mills, raises water in our pumps, accompanies the diver in the diving-bell, bears up the balloon, feeds our furnaces : but here we come to a distinct series of valuable offices performed by the atmosphere, if possible even more extensive and important than those already referred to. The chemical history of the atmosphere is even more wonderful than the physical,* and

* The physical properties of the atmosphere are investigated in " Rudimentary Pneumatics."

will now require, for the object of the present essay, a few details.

The atmosphere is composed essentially of two gases, in a state of mechanical mixture, named oxygen and nitrogen. In its pure state, oxygen is chiefly remarkable for its energetic properties in promoting combustion, combination, and various other chemical changes. A taper, with a mere spark of fire in the wick, will, when plunged into oxygen, burst into flame, and burn brilliantly; iron wire, made red-hot at one extremity, will burn away with the greatest ease in this gas. An animal, in an atmosphere of pure oxygen, suffers from excess of vital action; its pulses throb with increased rapidity and vigour; the vital spark, as it were, bursts into flame, and destroys the animal. Nitrogen (or, as it is sometimes called, *azote*) is apparently as inert in its properties as oxygen is active. It supports neither life nor combustion, and one of its uses, if not its principal use, in the atmosphere, seems to be to dilute the oxygen, and to subdue the wonderful energy of this vigorous element to the endless number of useful purposes which it has to perform in the economy of nature. The proportions in which these two gaseous bodies are mingled are very unequal; every atom or particle of oxygen in the atmosphere is accompanied by four atoms or particles of nitrogen; or, in other words, if we take a measure of any capacity, divided into five equal parts, and decant into it four parts of nitrogen and one part of oxygen, we get a mixture which, as regards the rougher tests of respiration and combustion, is identical with pure atmospheric air.

In the great chemical operations of nature which are dependent on the atmosphere, oxygen passes through various mutations, and enters into new combinations, which form the basis of grand and wonderful contrivances. Some of the most important of these operations depend on the process of combustion, of which the following is a simple illustration:—A piece of wax taper (Fig. 1), fixed in the centre of a cork, is lighted and floated on the surface of water in a shallow dish; if this be enclosed within a bell glass, the mouth of which dips into the water and rests on the dish, the air of the glass will be cut off from any communication with the external atmosphere. The flame of the taper will immediately diminish, and in a few seconds be extinguished. On examining the air left in the glass, it will be found incapable of supporting animal life or combustion: four-fifths of the original bulk of air is still nitrogen, and this is apparently unchanged; the remaining fifth is no longer oxygen, but a compound of oxygen with the carbon and hydrogen of the flame—oxygen and carbon producing carbonic acid, and oxygen and hydrogen producing water, which, in

Fig. 1.

the form of vapour, condenses on the inner surface of the glass.

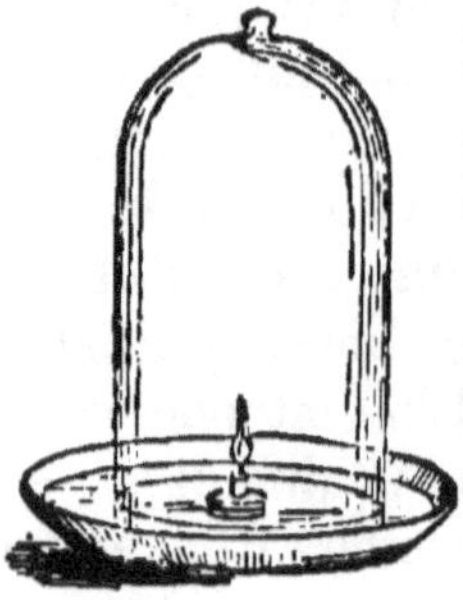

Now the product of combustion, called carbonic acid, is incapable of supporting life and combustion, and thus resembles nitrogen. But there are important differences between them—nitrogen is a little lighter than its own bulk of atmospheric air; carbonic acid is considerably heavier; nitrogen is an elementary or simple substance—that is, one which has never yet been resolved into two or more dissimilar parts; carbonic acid, on the contrary, is a compound capable of being separated or decomposed into carbon or charcoal, and oxygen. Moreover, pure nitrogen, shaken up in a bottle with a little lime-water, produces no change on the lime-water; carbonic acid renders it turbid, by combining with the lime and rendering it insoluble; nitrogen is scarcely absorbed by water, but water absorbs its own volume of carbonic acid; nitrogen has no taste or smell, carbonic acid has a sharp taste and an acid reaction. Hence, it will be seen that these two bodies, which have the common property of extinguishing life and preventing combustion, are marked by characteristic differences.

Some idea may be formed of the enormous demands on the oxygen of the atmosphere for supporting combustion, from the fact, that a single iron furnace burns or consumes, in the course of twenty-four hours, not less than three hundred and ten tons weight of atmospheric air, or as much as would be required for the respiration of two hundred thousand human beings within the same period.

Carbon, which forms the solid basis of most fuel, and in a minutely divided state renders flame luminous, is a simple substance, and exists in nature under a variety of forms. Its purest form is the diamond, as is proved by the formation of carbonic acid only, when it is burnt in pure oxygen. Charcoal and coke are other well known forms of carbon, the one obtained from wood and the other from coal. Coal is a compound of carbon, hydrogen, nitrogen, and oxygen, with a mineral and earthy residue. Wax, tallow, &c., are compounds of carbon, hydrogen, and oxygen.

Hydrogen, which is the source of all common flame, is the lightest substance that has ever been weighed: it is more than fourteen times lighter than its own bulk of atmospheric air at the same temperature; it supports neither life nor combustion. A lighted taper plunged into it is extinguished, but the hydrogen itself takes fire and burns at the mouth of the jar, where it is in contact with the oxygen of the air, with which it unites and forms water. One volume of oxygen combines with two of hydrogen to form water; or by weight, one grain of hydrogen unites with eight grains of oxygen, and as the hydrogen is sixteen times lighter than its own bulk of oxygen, it follows that one grain of hydrogen will occupy twice the bulk of eight grains of oxygen. Pure hydrogen burns with scarcely any light; in the flame of our lamps, candles, gas-lights, &c., the minutely-divided carbon, in rising up through the flame, becomes white hot, and presents innumerable luminous points; at the exterior of the flame the oxygen of the atmosphere seizes the minute atoms of carbon as they escape, and, by combining with them, forms invisible carbonic acid. A cold substance, such as a piece of glass or metal, held over a flame for a moment will condense a portion of the carbon in a minutely-divided state. If a lamp have a deficient supply of air it will smoke; that is, a portion of the carbon of the flame will escape without combining with the oxygen of the air. Lamp-black is formed by burning oil in a close chamber, with a deficient supply of air.

Hydrogen unites with nitrogen to form ammonia, for which purpose three volumes of hydrogen are required to one of nitrogen. This substance is pungent and acrid, but when diluted with air is an agreeable stimulant. It is very soluble in water, which at the temperature of 60°, takes up 727 times its bulk of the gas. Ammonia is an alkali, and combines readily with acids, producing an important class of ammoniacal salts.

Nitrogen and oxygen combine to form nitric acid, one part of nitrogen uniting with five parts of oxygen. Not only are these numbers different from those which represent the composition of the atmosphere, but the mode of combination is different. The oxygen and nitrogen of the atmosphere are mixed mechanically, just as a portion of fine sand diffused through water may be said to mix with it without combining. In either case, the bodies preserve their own peculiar properties; or the properties of the compound form a mean between those of its component elements. But in a chemical combination between two bodies, a third body is formed, the properties of which need not, and seldom do, resemble those of the component elements. Thus sulphur and oxygen combine chemically to produce sulphurous or sulphuric acid, substances the properties of which are quite different from those of the sulphur and oxygen which produce them ; the sulphurous has also different properties from the sulphuric. So with nitric acid : this compound has none of the properties of the constituents of the atmosphere, but a new set of properties peculiar to itself. This powerful acid may be formed artificially in various ways, but only one need here be mentioned. By passing a succession of electric sparks through a mixture of oxygen and nitrogen, this acid is formed; so also, during a thunder-storm, the lightning striking through vast masses of atmospheric air, produces nitric acid, which, combining with ammonia, also formed in the atmosphere, descends with the rain upon the earth in the form of nitrate of ammonia.

Now the object for which these details have been brought forward, is to enable the reader to take an enlarged view of the process of combustion, for this, in fact, constitutes the chief means by which nature accomplishes her annual cycle. An accurate knowledge of the homely processes of warming and ventilation depends upon a clear insight into the principles of combustion, and it is only an oft-repeated truism, that our useful arts become more efficient in practice, more economical, and more conducive to our happiness, in proportion to our knowledge of the principles upon which they depend. Now, according to the common acceptation of the term, combustion is the rapid union of a combustible with a supporter of combustion, whereby new compounds are formed, heat and light accompanying the formation. Thus a piece of iron wire or of phosphorous ignited and plunged into a jar of oxygen gas burns vividly, the metal falling in molten drops of oxide amid showers of scintillations, and the phosphorus emitting a flood of painfully vivid light. In this process, the oxygen and the iron unite to form a third substance, oxide of iron; the oxygen and the phosphorus also form a third substance, phosphoric acid. If, however, the iron be exposed long enough to the atmosphere, the oxygen will combine with it in precisely the same manner, and form oxide of iron; months or even years may be required for the completion of the process which in the jar of oxygen was accomplished in a few seconds; but the result is the same. The same amount of heat is evolved by the combination of the oxygen and the iron during the slow process of rusting, as in the rapid process of burning. So also with the phosphorus. A piece of this substance exposed to the air combines with the same amount of oxygen, and evolves precisely as much heat during the time that it slowly wastes away, and produces the same weight of acid as it would do if burnt in a jar of oxygen.

Now it must be evident, that if a process, rapidly brought about in one case and slowly in another, produce the same results, we do not add to our knowledge by associating different names and different trains of thought with the one as compared with the other; on the contrary, we disembarrass the subject by considering the processes as identical. Whether the combustion be rapid or slow, it is still combustion. Undoubtedly there are cases where slow combustion is not possible. A piece of coal and the oxygen necessary to its combustion may remain in contact for centuries without undergoing any change; but the moment a spark of fire is introduced, they begin to combine and soon disappear, with all the more obvious phenomena of combustion. In such a case, all we can say is, that a high temperature is necessary for the combination; but this case does not disturb the view we are endeavouring to impress upon the reader, that combustion may be a very slow process as well as a very rapid one.

Let us take another case of combustion. If a portion of the solid food of animals be placed in a red hot platinum crucible, it will burn away; its carbon will unite with oxygen from the air and form carbonic acid; its hydrogen will unite with oxygen from the air and form water; its nitrogen may escape free, or it may unite with a portion of its hydrogen, and form ammonia; and in this way all the gaseous volatile products will be expelled from the crucible, leaving behind only a small portion of ash, which consists of salts, some of which are soluble in water and others insoluble in that fluid.

Now, in a chemical point of view, the living animal frame is a real apparatus for combustion; it is a vital furnace, in which the carbon supplied by the fuel, which we call *food*, is burnt, and, combining with oxygen, escapes by the lungs and the skin into the atmosphere, under the form of carbonic acid. In this apparatus also the hydrogen of food is burnt, and uniting with oxygen, escapes as aqueous vapour; the nitrogen of the air, as taken into the lungs, is again exhaled by respiration, but the nitrogen and soluble mineral portions of the food are rejected, the one in the form of uric acid and urea, the other in the fluid form; while the insoluble mineral portions of the food are rejected in the solid form.

Now every portion of food which a person of mature age takes into his system, is thus dispersed from day to day. In infancy and youth a portion is retained to form materials for growth; in old age, the individual loses more than he receives, and, consequently wastes slowly away. But, in each case, the natural process is similar to the artificial one represented in the heated platinum crucible. We cannot, therefore, resist the evidence that the combustion of food, whether in the animal or in the crucible, is one and the same process; the only difference being, that in the crucible the heat is intense and the process rapid; in the animal, the heat is moderate and the process comparatively slow. That which is called animal heat (98° Fahr.), is in fact the heat of combustion, and the object of the domestic processes of warming and ventilation is to enable the animal to maintain this heat, and to convey away the gaseous products of combustion as fast as they are formed. The soluble and insoluble products of combustion are conveyed away by other natural means above referred to; and it will be our duty hereafter to show, that it is as unwise to neglect the means for clearing off our gaseous excretions, as it would be insane and unnatural to attempt to retain those of another kind.

Another proof of the identity of the two processes, is that nature disposes of the products of combustion in precisely the same manner, whether derived from ordinary combustion or animal respiration. The vegetable kingdom is the grand laboratory wherein these products of combustion are decomposed and elaborated into new combinations. Plants inhale or absorb carbonic acid, decompose it, retain the carbon as materials for growth, and return the oxygen to the atmosphere; plants absorb water or aqueous vapour, decompose it, retain its hydrogen, and also return the oxygen to the atmosphere; plants, it is imagined, sometimes take nitrogen directly from the air; they certainly take it indirectly from ammonia or its salts, including nitrates. Thus it will be seen that the chemical function of plants is directly the reverse of that of animals—the animal kingdom constituting an immense apparatus for combustion; the vegetable kingdom an equally grand apparatus for reduction, in which reduced carbonic acid yields carbon, reduced water its hydrogen, and in which also reduced ammonia and nitric acid yield their nitrogen, which is built up with the other elements into more complex organic products. The organic matter which constitutes the food of animals is destroyed by them, and rendered for the most part inorganic; this, in its turn, becomes the aliment of plants, the materials with which plants elaborate organic compounds, the atmosphere serving as the means of communication between the two kingdoms. Organic vegetable substances pass ready formed into herbivorous animals, which destroy a portion of them, and appropriate the remainder as materials for growth. From herbivorous animals these organic matters pass ready formed into the carnivorous, who destroy or retain some of them, according to their wants. The herbivorous animals are slaughtered for the use of the carnivorous, and when these, in their turn, cease to live, they decompose, and the atmosphere again takes up, in various ways and by various processes, the materials of which they were composed.

The great stimulus which gives motion to the wonderful machinery of the vegetable world is solar light. Under its influence, the carbonic acid yields its carbon, the water its hydrogen, the ammonia its nitrogen. It is not for the purpose of purifying the air that plants are especially necessary to animals. Their great use is to furnish a never-failing supply of organic matter, ready prepared for assimilation— fuel, in short, which animals can burn for their own use. The purification of the air by vegetation is a remote service ; the other service is so immediate, that if it were to fail us during a single year the earth would be depopulated.* The mean amount of carbonic acid in the atmosphere is scarcely one volume in 2,000, which is a surprisingly small quantity, when we consider how numerous and productive are the sources of this gas. Volcanoes, fires, animals, fermentation, and decay, are constantly producing it, nor will the quantity given off by a single individual appear insignificant, when it is stated that an adult man requires, for the purposes of respiration, during the twenty-four hours, about 12·66 oz., or 16·73 cubic feet of oxygen, producing 28,912 cubic inches of carbonic acid. As the volume of that gas is equal to 85 per cent. of the oxygen inhaled, it has been inferred (allowing 15 per cent. for the amount of oxygen fixed by hydrogen, &c.) that not less than 26·7 oz., or more than 1½ lb. of oxygen, are consumed daily by every adult ; and allowing 1·4 oz. of dry solid matter to be thrown off by the intestinal canal, and 2·2 oz. of solids by

* The chemical relations between the three great kingdoms of nature are stated at greater length in our "Essay on the Application of Chemistry to Agriculture," appended to Professor Fownes' "Rudimentary Chemistry ;" but the reader who desires to pursue the subject further, is referred to Liebig's "Chemistry in its Application to Agriculture," Professor Johnstone's "Elements of Agricultural Chemistry and Geology," and also to a Lecture by M. Dumas, on the "Chemical Statistics of Organised Beings."

the urine, the whole of the remaining portion of the food (exclusive of about $4\frac{1}{2}$ lbs. of water eliminated by the kidneys and the skin) must pass off in the gaseous form by the lungs.* These numbers vary with different individuals, and also in the same individual at different periods of the day; but limiting our attention for a moment to the carbonic acid, it is found that the more vigorous the circulation the greater is the amount of that gas exhaled: the greater too is the proportion in winter than in summer; after a meal than when fasting (varying too with the nature of the food); more of this gas is exhaled when awake than when asleep, in the proportion of 4 to 3 for the same number of hours; more carbonic acid is exhaled by children than by adults, in consequence of the greater activity of the vital functions; more by male adults than by females, unless of the same stature, and then the proportions given off by the two sexes are about equal. In fact, the amount of carbon exhaled in the form of carbonic acid from the lungs and skin of an adult man in the twenty-four hours, amounts to about $8\frac{1}{2}$ oz.; of which quantity the surface of the skin contributes only one-third of an ounce. In cold blooded animals the respiration through the skin is more extensive. Hybenating animals, such as the marmot, do not consume more than one-thirtieth of the oxygen that they require in the active state.

In the adult male about eighteen or twenty respirations are made per minute. The volume of air at each respiration may be taken at about 30 cubic inches, and this with twenty respirations per minute would require not less than 500 cubic feet of air to pass through the lungs in twenty-four hours. In this process the blood is exposed to the action of the atmospheric air, during which exposure it undergoes certain changes. "The blood from the right side of the heart, when it enters the lungs, is of a dark red colour; it is then dispersed in a state of most minute subdivision through the ultimate vessels of the lungs, and in these vessels is brought into contact with the atmospheric air, when it becomes of a bright red colour. In other words, the blood changes in the lungs its *venous* appearance and assumes the character of *arterial* blood. The blood thus

* Miller, " Elements of Chemistry," Part III.

arterialised, returns to the left side of the heart, from whence it is propelled through the arteries of the body. In the minute terminations of the arteries, the blood again loses its florid hue, and, reassuming its dark red colour, is returned through the veins to the right side of the heart, to be exposed, as before, to the influence of the atmospheric air, and to undergo the same succession of changes."—*Prout.*

On examining the respired air, it is found that a portion of its oxygen has disappeared, and a similar bulk of carbonic acid has been substituted. While oxygen gas is passing inwards through the membrane of the lungs, carbonic acid is at the same time passing outwards through the same membrane. In fact, the oxygen of the air is absorbed by the blood, and in some unknown state of combination reaches the extreme subdivision of the arteries, where it is united with a portion of carbon, and forms carbonic acid gas, which gas also, in some unknown state of combination, is retained in the venous blood, till in the lungs it is expelled, and oxygen is absorbed in its stead. Along with the carbonic acid, a quantity of aqueous vapour is separated from the blood, amounting to about 1 lb. from the lungs, and $1\frac{1}{2}$ lb. from the skin, in the twenty-four hours.

One great object of this process is the production and maintenance of animal heat. There is a gradual combustion of the carbon and of the hydrogen supplied by the food through the medium of the respired oxygen, as already stated. Now the carbonic acid which is the result of this process probably owes its noxious action rather to the mechanical obstruction that it offers to the escape of gas already in the blood than to any directly poisonous action. It acts, however, in destroying life if in sufficient quantity. Moreover the water given off by the lungs is not pure water, such as is liberated in the process of distillation or evaporation, but is contaminated with the most offensive animal effluvia. M. Leblanc states, that the odour of the air at the top of the ventilator of a crowded room is of so noxious a character that it is dangerous to be exposed to it even for a. short time. If this air be passed through pure water, the water soon exhibits all the phenomena of putrefactive fermentation. The water of respiration, thus loaded with animal impurities, condenses in the inner walls of buildings, and trickles down in fœtid streams. In the close and confined dwellings of the poor, this vapour condenses on the walls, the ceiling, and the furniture, and gives that permanently loathsome odour which must be familiar to all who take sufficient interest in the poor of large towns ever to enter their dwellings. Take up a chair, and it is clammy to the touch, and the hand retains the ill odour; and, if the poor people are remonstrated with, on the ground of want of cleanliness, they say that the supply of water is scanty, and what little they have must be dragged up-stairs from the yard or cellar below. The low state of health induced by such abodes produces a chilly sensation, even in summer, which renders the occupants averse to open windows, and in many cases, in consequence of the crowded state of the district, and the fœtid odours emitted from the sewer traps in the streets, an open window is a questionable remedy for bad ventilation.

We see, then, that there are many causes which render respired air injurious, if allowed to enter the lungs a second time. In proportion as the air of a confined space becomes vitiated by respiration, the quantity of carbonic acid increases, and as chemistry furnishes the means of determining this increase, while the other noxious products of respiration escape exact analysis, the amount of carbonic acid may be taken as the exponent of the degree of vitiation of the confined air. This method was adopted a few years ago, by M. Félix Leblanc, in an extensive series of experiments.*

The remedy for these injurious effects is efficient ventilation. In each act of respiration about 30 cubic inches, or $\frac{1}{8}$th of the quantity of air in the lungs is changed. The air that has passed through the lungs does not lose all its oxygen; it usually contains not more than about 4 per cent. of carbonic acid; but this expired air, by mingling as it escapes with several times as much, vitiates at least two cubic

* See Memoir read to the Academy of Sciences at Paris, 6th June, 1842 and inserted in the *Annales de Chimie et de Physique.* Third Series, vol. v. p. 223.

feet of air. Now the removal of this impure air, and the bring-ing in of a constant fresh supply, have been provided for by nature in the most perfect manner, and it is by our ill-con-trived artificial arrangements that the provision is defeated. The vitiated air, as it leaves the chest, is heated to very near the temperature of the body, viz., 98°, and being ex-panded by the heat, is specifically lighter than the sur-rounding air at an ordinary temperature; it therefore ascends and escapes to a higher level, by the colder air pushing it up, as it does a balloon. The place of this heated air is con-stantly supplied by the colder and denser air closing in on all sides. In the open air the process is perfect, because there is nothing to prevent the escape of the vitiated air; but in a close apartment, the hot air rising up to the ceiling, is prevented from escaping; and gradually accumulating and becoming cooler, it descends and mingles with the fresh air, which occupies the lower level. We thus have to inhale an atmosphere which every moment becomes more and more impure and unfit for respiration; and the impurities become increased much more rapidly by night when lamps and candles or gas are burning, for flame is a rapid consumer of oxygen. Under these circumstances our only chance of escape from suffocation is in the defective workmanship of the house-carpenter; the crevices in the window frames and doors allow the foul air a partial exit, as may be proved by holding the flame of a candle near the top of a closed door, in a hot room; it will be seen that the flame is powerfully drawn towards the door in the direction of the outgoing current; and on holding the flame near the bottom of the door, it will be blown away from the door, showing the direction of the entering current. If we stop up these crevices, by putting list round the windows and doors, so as to make them fit accurately, we only increase the evil. The first effect is that the fire will not *draw* for want of sufficient draught; if the inmates can put up with a dull fire and a smoky atmosphere, they soon become restless and uncomfortable—young people get fretful and peevish, their elders irritable, respiration becomes impeded, a tight band appears to be drawn round the forehead which some invisible hand seems to be drawing tighter and tighter every moment; the eyeballs ache and throb, a sense of languor succeeds to fits of restless impatience, yawning becomes general, for yawning is nothing more than an effort of nature to get more air into the lungs; under these circumstances the announcement of tea is a welcome sound, the opening and shutting of the door necessary to its preparation give a vent to the foul air, the stimulus of the meal mitigates the suffering for a time, but before the hour of rest, the same causes of discomfort have been again in active operation, and the family party retires for the night indisposed and out of humour.

But in the bedroom, the inmates are not free from the malignant influence. The closed doors, the curtained bed, and the well-guarded windows, are sentinels which jealously warn off the approach of fresh air. The unconscious sleepers at each respiration vitiate a portion of air which, in obedience to the law of nature rises to the ceiling, and would escape, if the means of escape were provided; but, in the absence of this, it soon shakes off those aerial wings, which would have carried it away, and becoming cooler and denser, it descends, and again enters the lungs of the sleepers, who unconsciously inhale the poison. When the room has become surcharged with foul air, so that a portion must escape, then, and not till then, does it begin to pass off up the chimney. Hence many persons very properly object to sleep in a room which is unprovided with a chimney; but it is evident that such a ventilator is situated too low down to be of much service. If there be no chimney in the room, a portion of the foul air escapes by forcing its way out of some of the cracks and crevices which serve to admit the fresh air.

That this sketch is not overdrawn, must be evident to any one who, after an early morning's walk, may have returned directly from the fresh morning air into the bedroom which he had left closely shut up an hour before. What is more disgusting than the odour of a bedroom in the morning? Why is it that so many persons get up without feeling refreshment from their sleep? Why do so many persons pass sleepless nights? The answer to these and many other similar questions may be frequently found in defective ventilation.*   How much disease and misery arises from this cause it would be difficult to state with any approach to accuracy, because the causes of misery are very complicated. Among the poor, the want of sufficient nourishment, neglect of temperance and cleanliuess, and excessive labour, all act with aggravating effect upon want of ventilation and drainage.   Among the middle classes, mental anxiety, overtasked powers, insufficient out-door exercise, are also aggravating causes ; but there is a similar want of attention to ventilation and drainage.   The rich suffer least, because they pass much of their time in the pure air of the country, and, are relieved from a good deal of anxiety, by being independent in circumstances; their rooms are also larger and less crowded than those of the other classes ; but still there is a neglect of ventilation, and they often breathe a poisonous atmosphere for hours together in the crowded and heated ball-room, the

* An attempt has been recently made to show that very much less air, or air of less purity, is required during the sleeping than the waking hours.   M. Delbruck, in a communication to the Academie des Sciences, at Paris, which has been made the subject of an article in the *Cornhill Magazine* for March, 1863, supports this idea, by referring to the behaviour of the lower animals. The dog retires to sleep in his kennel or corner, and, curling himself up, buries his head beneath his paws or his body; birds bury their head under their wing, with their beak in soft down ; hybernating animals are always sheltered from the air; the schoolboy buries his head under the clothes; non-scientific persons surround themselves with bed-curtains; soldiers camping out cover their heads to sleep, and railway travellers close the carriage windows.   In all such cases it is contended that science teaches one thing, instinct another, and that instinct is right.   It is urged that as plants by night absorb the oxygen they exhale during the day, so, by analogy, animals at night absorb some of the carbonic acid they exhale during the day.   In answer to this it is stated that only the woody parts of plants absorb oxygen by night, but they do so also by day, and that in excessively small quantities. The green parts of plants absorb carbonic acid by day, and when the stimulus of sunlight is removed they are inactive.   Animals, on the contrary, are not like plants, seeing that the blood never absorbs carbonic acid from the atmosphere.

All that can be said in favour of M. Delbruck's theory is that less oxygen is required during sleep, because the vital functions are then all depressed, and consequently less animal heat is generated.   The sleeper should be covered, so as to keep up the animal heat ; if the body be exposed to cold, it will not only prevent or destroy sleep, but may lead to more serious consequences.   Hence the open window at night, or other means of ventilation, may interfere with the necessary warmth and prevent sleep ; but this is not very likely if the bed-clothes are in sufficient quantity.   I often find it impossible to sleep on account of the closeness of the room ; but on lowering the top window sash an inch, or setting the door a little on the jar, the air of the room has been improved, and refreshing sleep the consequence.

theatre, the fashionable assembly, and even in church ; so that fainting, headache, and sickness are the not uncommon results.

A poisonous atmosphere! The expression will not be found too strong when we examine the ingredients of the air of an unventilated room. The products of combustion, whether they be those of the respiration of human beings, or the burning of artificial lights, consist of—1, carbonic acid ; 2, nitrogen ; 3, vapour of water, mingled with various animal products of a very offensive nature. Gas also often contains a minute portion of sulphuretted hydrogen which escapes or burns into sulphur compounds, and a minute portion of the gas itself (carburetted hydrogen) also escapes unburnt.

Carbonic acid gas acts as a poison. If we attempt to inhale it by putting the face over the edge of a beer vat, the nostrils and throat are irritated so strongly, that the glottis closes, and inspiration becomes impossible. In its pure state, then, it is impossible to breathe carbonic acid gas ; but when this gas is largely diluted with air, it can be breathed, and the symptoms resemble those of apoplexy. Professor Christison quotes a case related by M. Chomel of Paris, of a labourer, who was suddenly let down to the bottom of a well containing carbonic acid diluted with air, where he remained three-quarters of an hour. On being drawn up, he was first affected with violent and irregular convulsions of the whole body, accompanied by perfect insensibility ; fits of spasm, like tetanus, then came on. During the second day, these symptoms went off, and he continued afterwards to be affected with numbness. It is especially to be noted, that contrary to general popular belief, these effects may be produced in situations where the air is not sufficiently impure to extinguish the flame of a candle ; nor does the lurking danger display itself to the sense of taste or of smell.

The danger of using charcoal as a fuel will be noticed further on ; but we may here remark, that the proportion of carbonic acid necessary to produce a poisonous atmosphere is very small ; so much so, that in attempts at suicide by burning charcoal in an open room, the people who have entered the apartment have found the air quite respirable, and the choffer burning, although the person they sought was in a state of deep coma, from having been long exposed to the noxious influence.

Now as no person would consent habitually to swallow a small portion of liquid poison, knowing it to be such, though diluted with a very large portion of pure water, so it is equally unwise to consent habitually to inhale a small portion of gaseous poison, knowing it to be such, though diluted with a very large portion of pure air; and yet this is what the majority of persons actually do who occupy apartments unprovided with proper ventilating apparatus.

Nitrogen gas, which constitutes four-fifths of our atmosphere, will not support respiration or combustion, simply from the absence of oxygen. An animal plunged into an atmosphere of nitrogen would die, because this gas is incapable of oxygenising the blood. A flame is extinguished in this gas, because there is no affinity between it and the incandescent hydrogen and carbon.

The vapour given off by the lungs and the skin is charged with offensive animal effluvia, which greatly promote the contamination of the air of a crowded apartment. Dr. Faraday expressed his opinion to a parliamentary committee in 1835, on the subject of ventilation, that—" Air feels unpleasant in the breathing cavities, including the mouth and nostrils, not merely from the absence of oxygen, the presence of carbonic acid, or the elevation of temperature, but from other causes, depending on matters which are communicated to it by the human being. I think that an individual may find a decided difference in his feelings when making part of a large company, from what he does when one of a small number of persons, and yet the thermometer give the same indication. When I am one of a large number of persons, I feel an oppressive sensation of closeness, notwithstanding the temperature may be about 60° or 65°, which I do not feel in a small company at the same temperature, and which I cannot refer altogether to the absorption of oxygen, or the evolution of carbonic acid, and probably depends upon the effluvia from the many present; but with me it is much diminished by a lowering of the temperature, and the sensations become much more like those occurring in a small company. The object of a good system of ventilation is to remove the effects of such air."

The effects of air, vitiated by animal effluvia, is evident in the diseases of the lower animals when crowded together in confined places. The glanders of horses, the pip of fowls, and a peculiar disease in sheep, all arise from this cause; and it is stated that, for some years past, the English nation has been saved many thousand pounds a year from the diminished mortality of horses, in consequence of the army veterinary surgeons adopting a simple plan for the ventilation of the cavalry stables.

Our systems of artificial illumination have even a greater deteriorating effect upon the air of an apartment than the respiration of human beings. The leakage of a gas-pipe, or the imperfect combustion of the gas itself, in an apartment, would cause the inmates to inhale a portion of the gas. Sir Humphry Davy found, that when he breathed a mixture of two parts air and three of carburetted hydrogen, he was attacked with giddiness, headache, and transient weakness of the limbs; but common gas is often contaminated with sulphuretted hydrogen, as the blackening of the white painted wainscoting of rooms proves, in spite of the purifyiny processes adopted at the gas-works. This gas is one of the most deleterious of all the aerial poisons. It has been found by experiment, that air, impregnated with a 1,500th part of the gas, kills a bird in a short space of time; and that with about twice that proportion, or an 800th, it will soon kill a dog. This gas is emitted by cesspools and sewers, and has been a frequent cause of death when breathed in a state of concentration. Dr. Hallé says, "the individual becomes suddenly weak and insensible, falls down, and either expires immediately, or if he is fortunate enough to be quickly extricated, he may revive in no long time, the belly remaining tense and full for an hour or upwards, and recovery being preceded by vomiting and hawking of bloody froth." When the noxious emanations are less concentrated, the symptoms are still very alarming ; and in the dilute form, as in the emanations from the gully holes of the sewers of London, persons inhaling them have often been attacked with sickness, colic, imperfectly defined pains in the chest, and lethargy.

The emanations arising from the imperfect or slow combustion of oil and tallow are most injurious to health. The vapour of a smoky lamp, if disengaged in small quantities, excites intense headache. The fumes of the burning snuff of a candle are probably of the same nature, and are very poisonous, and every one must have remarked their penetrating nature; they fill the room the moment a candle is blown out, and their disgusting odour pervades the whole house in a very short time. Dr. Christison quotes a case in which they proved fatal : a party of ironsmiths, who were carousing on a festival day at Leipzig, amused themselves with plaguing a boy, who was asleep in a corner of the room, by holding under his nose the smoke of a candle just extinguished; at first he was roused a little each time, but when the amusement had been continued for half an hour, he began to breathe laboriously, was then attacked with incessant epileptic convulsions, and died on the third day.

In addition to all these contaminating agents, carbonic acid, nitrogen, animal effluvia, carbide and sulphide of hydrogen, &c., to which the air of an unventilated apartment is liable, there is yet another cause of injury to health in the disturbed electrical condition of vitiated air. This is a subject on which science has hitherto thrown but little light. All that we can do is to record the fact, that pure air, such as is fit for respiration, is *positively* electric, while the air which has become impure, and consequently unfit for respiration, is *negatively* electric.

The effects of breathing an impure air have frequently been insisted upon by medical and other writers. In the evidence taken before the committee of the House of Commons, on the health of towns, in the year 1840, the medical witnesses stated, that scrofulous diseases were a common result of bad ventilation,* and that, in the case of silk weavers,

* Mr. Carmichael, in his " Essay on the Nature of Scrofula," accounts for the extreme prevalence of the disease in the Dublin House of Industry, at the time he wrote (1810), by mentioning that in one ward of moderate height, 60 feet by 18, there were 38 beds, each containing *three* children, or more than 100 in all. The matron remarked, that there is no enduring the air of this

who pass their lives in a more close and confined air than almost any other class of persons, their children are peculiarly subject to scrofula, and softening of the bones. Dr. Arnott stated, that an individual, the offspring of persons successively living in bad air, will have a constitution decidedly different from that of a man who is born of a race that has inhabited the country for a long time; that the race would, to a certain extent, continue degenerating. Defective ventilation deadens both the mental and bodily energies, it leaves its mark upon the person, so that we can distinguish the inhabitants of a town from those of the country. This witness, in alluding to the want of knowledge among all classes on the subject of ventilation, states that he had heard at the Zoological Gardens of a class of animals where fifty out of sixty were killed in a month, from putting them into a house which had no opening in it but a few inches in the floor. " It was like putting them under an extinguisher; and this was supposed to be done upon scientific principles."

Some of the details in this Report refer to diseases consequent on the habitual breathing of air vitiated by a number of human beings, crowded together in a badly drained and ill-ventilated part of London; they are so frightful, that it is impossible to quote them here. No doubt these details refer to extreme cases among the poor and destitute; but no one will contend that the science and legislation of the day should be exerted only for those who have influence to command, or means to purchase their aid. Every one who has knowledge or wealth at his disposal, is bound to exert it as much for the benefit of his ignorant and poorer brethren as for his own pleasure and profit. There is not only a moral law requiring us to do so, but there is also a natural law, and both have this distinguishing proof of their divine origin; they are self acting; they confer the reward of obedience, and inflict the penalty of transgression, with a precision and certainty

apartment when the doors are first thrown open in the morning; and that it is in vain to raise any of the windows, as those children who happened to be inconvenienced by the cold, close them as soon as they have an opportunity. The air they breathe in the day is little better; many are confined to the apartments they sleep in, or crowded to the number of several hundred in the school-room.

which find no parallel in mere human laws and institutions. The fevers and contagious diseases, arising from our neglect of the poor, find their way into our own dwellings; the miasma of our courts and alleys enters our lungs, and casts us on a bed of sickness. If, through the mercy of God, we are permitted to rise again, ought we not to practise the lesson which the penalty has been seeking to convey to us?

But not only are our dwelling-houses badly ventilated, but those buildings on which the architect has lavished all his art and skill are often entirely destitute of special means for ventilation, and are so constructed as to render the application of such means extremely difficult, or even impossible. Such a contrivance seldom enters the mind of the architect. A building capable of holding from 800 to 1000 persons, whether it be a church, a lecture room, an assembly room, or a concert room, is, in consequence of this neglect, the too frequent scene of much painful suffering. When such a room is crowded, and the meeting lasts for some hours, especially in winter, the consequences are sufficiently marked; "either such a multitude must be subjected to all the evils of a contaminated and unwholesome atmosphere, or they must be partially relieved by opening the windows, and allowing a continued stream of cold air to pour down upon the heated bodies of those who are near them, till the latter are thoroughly chilled, and, perhaps, fatal illness is induced; and unfortunately, even at such a price, the relief is only partial, for the windows being all on one side of the room, and not extending much above half way to the ceiling, complete ventilation is impracticable. This neglect is glaringly the result of ignorance, and could never have happened, had either the architects or their employers known the laws of the human constitution." *

The same intelligent writer remarks, that in churches fainting and hysterics occur more frequently in the afternoon than in the morning, because the air is then at its maximum of vitiation. Indeed, in a crowded church the effects of deficient air are visible in the expression of the features of every one present—"either a relaxed sallow paleness of the

* Dr. Andrew Combe's "Principles of Physiology."

surface, or the hectic flush of fever, is observable, and, as the necessary accompaniment, a sensation of mental and bodily lassitude is felt, which is immediately relieved by getting into the open air." Some persons, however, do not find this relief; the headache often lasts for hours, and ends in a bilious or nervous attack.

Our school-rooms are often also sadly defective in respect of ventilation, and we have known cases where, with all the windows open, a proper supply of air could not be introduced into the crowded apartment. When the weather did not allow of open windows, the atmosphere of the room was most loathsome to a visitor entering it from the fresh air. All the inmates complained of a sensation of fulness and tightness in the forehead, and headache more or less acute. Command of temper on the part of the teachers, and mental progress on the part of the pupils, are of course next to impossible under such circumstances. The writer would appeal to the experience of teachers in general, whether the slow comprehension and listlessness of children in school, who are sharp and clever in the playground, may not be traceable in a great measure to the vitiated air which they are compelled to inhale?

In curious contrast to the defective arrangements of many of our public buildings, with respect to ventilation, are our public theatres and music halls. These are, for the most part, well ventilated, or at least an intelligent attempt is made to procure ventilation, and the managers do not fail to parade the fact in their play-bills. They are practical men; they know that for some years past the attention of the public has been directed to the subject of ventilation, and that a studious attention to the comfort of the house is as likely to bring people to it as attractive performances. They know, too, that people are more likely to enjoy and applaud the business of the stage when they can breathe freely, than when the head is aching and the senses are steeped in the drowsiness of a mephitic atmosphere. Some of the methods of ventilating theatres are clever and efficient, as will be noticed hereafter, and could easily be applied to those far more important buildings, the church and the lecture-room.

C

The traveller, in pursuit of health, business, or pleasure, is everywhere exposed to inconvenience and suffering from want of ventilation. In our coaches, railway carriages, and steamboats, the means for ventilation are inefficient. Some of my readers will probably be able to call to mind their nights of suffering in the heavy coaches of thirty or more years ago. I have frequently travelled inside the Salisbury coach in winter, which left London at 5 P.M., and arrived in Salisbury next morning at about 7 A.M., thus performing a journey of 85 miles in 14 hours; such a journey, with six inside (and I have sometimes formed one of eight), with windows closed at the special request of some lady or gentleman, who seemed capable of breathing without the usual supply of fresh air, was a protracted torture of greater magnitude than that endured now-a-days.* Yet it must be confessed that our railway carriages are not much better when the windows are closed and the travellers are numerous. A second-class carriage often contains from twenty-four to thirty, and even forty persons, and the air, under such circumstances, is intolerable. The first-class carriages are better, because there is less crowding, but even these are seldom provided with efficient means for the escape of the vitiated air. The sleeping cabins of our steamboats though fitted up with general attention to comfort, are entirely without any special contrivances for ventilation. I have travelled more than once from London to Hamburg, and have slept, or endeavoured to sleep, two nights in the cabin of one of the steam company's magnificent boats. The eagerness with which I have exchanged the fœtid air of the cabin for the pure air of the deck, even in rainy or boisterous

---

* In illustration of this part of our subject, I venture to relate the following anecdote, which, as far as I know, has never before appeared in print:— Some years ago an elderly gentleman, well known in the west of England, was travelling in the night coach from London to Salisbury, when he requested permission to have one of the windows down : this was stoutly refused by one of the five other passengers, and an altercation arose, which was suddenly cut short by a young midshipman thrusting his fist through the glass window, and, turning to the supplicant for fresh air, inquired whether he should break the other also. This was declined; the obstinate traveller sat in silence during the rest of the journey; but the old gentleman, interested by the bold and original conduct of his young friend, invited him to his house, and afterwards became the means of greatly advancing his prospects in life.

weather, will be understood by all who have undertaken such a voyage. The horrors of the crowded fore-cabin are happily known to me only by description.*

In our naval and merchant service much disease and mortality are the direct consequences of defective ventilation. The lower decks and close cabins of ships are often crowded with people engaged in cooking, eating, drinking, and sleeping. Their condition is bad enough in fair weather, but in a gale of wind, with the scuttles closed and the hatches fastened down, and no means provided for the admission of fresh air below but what can find its way by an opening of a

---

* I once took my passage in a steamboat from Cologne to Rotterdam (at that time a voyage of nearly forty hours), and found, when I had got on board, that there was no sleeping accommodation. This was of no consequence during the daytime, and not of much consequence, in fine weather, during the night, to an old traveller; but on this occasion, as night advanced, a cold drizzling rain compelled the passengers to seek refuge in the small cabin, the only one the vessel afforded. When tea and supper were fairly over, and nightcaps of various descriptions had been distributed among the guests, the low bench round the cabin was completely occupied. Those who could sleep did so; those who could not, tried a variety of postures, looked wistfully at the four comfortable corners occupied by envied sleepers. Some had slid down upon the floor; others found a hard pillow by leaning forward on the table before them; and those who still kept awake had an opportunity, by the faint gleams of a lamp, to study this odd, and not over cheerful, grouping. One of my companions, not being able to sleep, went on deck and resigned his place to me. I thus got a rest for my head, and with my great coat for a pillow, managed to pass, in a kind of restless sleep, the most dreary portion of the night. Early in the morning, an hour before daybreak, I went on deck; a moist fog rested sluggishly on the water, and rendered the shore barely visible. At this time an incident occurred which animated every one. A poor Dutch family was on board, consisting of a man, his wife, and four children, and it was suddenly proclaimed that the eldest boy had fallen overboard during the night, and was lost. "A man overboard" is a startling subject on every kind of water, and in every description of craft, and we were all busy with inquiries as to when and where and by whom he was last seen; search was made in every corner of the vessel, but all to no purpose;—the boy was certainly drowned, and there was no help for it. The father seemed to receive the condolence of the passengers with characteristic Dutch phlegm; he lit his pipe and received in silent resignation a long and apparently angry discourse from his wife. We were all very sorry for him and for her, when, lo! the black tarpaulin, which covered a large collection of goods on deck was seen to move, and from under one of its folds a large, round, sleepy face appeared, and crawling forth, with a yawn and a stretch, the object of our solicitude stood before us! The parents expressed their joy in rather an odd manner,—the mother scolded, the father quietly put down his pipe and began to cuff the boy rudely, and, but for the interference of some of the passengers, he would probably have received a sound thrashing for venturing, as it appeared, without leave, to sleep in certainly what seemed to be the most comfortable part of the vessel.

few feet square—when the vitiated effluvia from the healthy, the sick, and perhaps the dying, come steaming up the same aperture down which the fresh air is struggling to find its scanty way to the miserable inmates, how can we wonder at the mortality of seamen, especially in tropical climates. In troop or transport ships, the constitutions of the men are frequently enfeebled, instead of being strengthened by the voyage. Moreover, the evils arising from want of ventilation are aggravated by the horrors of sea-sickness; the sense of smell becomes morbidly sensitive; the bilge-water, or that stagnant corrupt water which lodges in the bottoms of tight vessels, emits the offensive odour of sulphuretted hydrogen and other gases; and these, combined with the closeness of the cabins in sailing vessels, few can endure with impunity. All this' is even made worse in steamboats by the odour of the hot, rancid tallow used for greasing the engines.

Mr. Robert Ritchie, in a paper on the ventilation of ships,* quotes a letter from a naval friend on the African coast, who says :—" On the lower deck of our little craft were stowed away one hundred persons, ship's stores, cook's coppers, &c. Never did I before feel so much the importance of a thorough ventilation. To sleep in such an atmosphere is next to impossible, and when exhausted nature sinks into repose, it awakes with that sickly and feverish sensation which betokens the derangement of your physical system, and that you have been inhaling a poison which is slowly but surely preying on the vitals' of your constitution. That disease and death should be frequent is only what every rational and scientific person would expect. Climate is blamed for every disease that appears in foreign stations, but I have not the slightest doubt that the want of a thorough method of ventilation on ship-board has, in very many cases, laid the system open to disease, which, in more favourable circumstances, could have been easily removed. The man who could improve the present wretched system would be justly entitled to the thanks of every humane and benevolent individual."

Such is the condition of a small, crowded sloop of war. In

* Jameson's *Edinburgh Philosophical Journal.*

large men-of-war the evils are less, on account of the ventilation of the lower decks by the gun-ports. These, of course, do not exist in merchant vessels; and in the lower, or orlop deck of all ships, there is great difficulty in establishing a constant uniform current of fresh air.

In these introductory remarks, we do not insist upon the necessity of warming our rooms and other enclosed spaces, for that is an art which is practically well understood, and will receive a share of attention in this little work. But if warming is easy and well understood, ventilation is also easy and badly understood; that is, it is very easy to ventilate a room or a building, but the necessity for doing so is not generally admitted by the great mass of the people, nor even by those whose duty it is to teach them and to provide for the practice. But to combine the two arts—to warm a room sufficiently, and at the same time to ventilate it thoroughly—is not easy, for the very means employed to ventilate a room must necessarily dissipate and carry away the heat employed in warming it. Something, however, may and ought to be done to combine the two methods, as we shall endeavour to show; but before entering upon practical details, it is necessary to invite attention to such of the laws of heat as are more immediately connected with our subject. We can scarcely do more, in our limited space, than bring together a few of the results of scientific principles, and refer the reader to larger and more comprehensive treatises for their verification.

In the process of warming and ventilating a building the laws of heat receive abundant illustration. Heat is one of those great natural forces that is always seeking an equilibrium which it can never attain. In doing so it influences surrounding objects in three ways:—First, by *conduction*, in which the heat travels from particle to particle, raising the temperature as it creeps along. Secondly, by *convection*, which refers to liquids and airs, in which the particles nearest the source of heat becoming warmed, ascend and impart their heat to surrounding particles, while the colder ones descend and take their place. Thirdly, by *radiation*, by which the rays of heat dart out in all directions from a central source.

Every one is aware that bodies conduct heat very differently.

The poker left in the fire soon becomes too hot to handle, while a short stick of wood may be burning at one end, and be scarcely warm at the other. A piece of marble and a piece of flannel, of the same temperature as indicated by the thermometer, will feel to the hand, the one cold and the other warm, because in the one case the marble conducts the heat freely from the hand, and the flannel scarcely at all. One, in fact, is a good, and the other a bad, conductor of heat. The metals, however, are the best conductors; but these differ greatly among themselves in conducting power. By exposing similar bars of metal to a uniform source of heat, acting at the end of each bar, and measuring the increase of temperature along the bar at intervals of 2 inches by means of a thermo-electric pile, the conducting power of metals for heat has been found to follow the same order as their conducting power for electricity. Of all the metals, silver is the best conductor, and taking this at 1,000, the number that represents the conducting power of gold is 981; of gold alloy (991 gold and 9 copper), 840; rolled copper, 845; cast copper, 811; aluminium, 665; rolled zinc, 641; cadmium, 577; bar-iron, 436; tin, 422; steel, 397; platinum, 380; cast-iron, 359; lead, 287; antimony, 215; and bismuth, 61. It is remarkable how greatly the conducting power of a metal is disturbed by the presence of small portions of impurities. Gold alloyed with 1 per cent. of silver, loses nearly 20 per cent. of its conducting power; while the carbon of steel and of cast-iron greatly diminish their conducting power, as seen by the above figures.

Different woods show very unequal conducting powers. In the same specimen wood conducts best in the direction of the fibre; density has but little effect on the velocity of transmission. American birch, a comparatively light wood, had a higher transmissive power than thirty-one other woods experimented on by Professor Tyndall.* Iron-wood, which has a specific gravity of 1·426 has a low conducting power; oak and Coromandel wood, the latter very hard and dense, stand near the head of the list; while Scotch fir and other light woods stand low. Professor Tyndall expresses

* "Heat Considered as a Mode of Motion," 1863.

the law of molecular action as regards the transmission of heat through wood in the following terms :—

" At all the points not situate in the centre of the tree, wood possesses three unequal axes of calorific conduction, which are at right angles to each other. The first, and principal axis, is parallel to the fibre of the wood ; the second, and intermediate axis, is perpendicular to the fibre and to the ligneous layers ; while the third and last axis is perpendicular to the fibre and parallel to the layers."

It is remarkable also that certain crystals vary in conducting power according to the position of the optic axis of the crystal. In quartz, for example, the heat travels more easily along the axis than across it, as may be proved by taking two plates of that substance, one of which is cut parallel to the axis, and the other perpendicular to it. Each plate is pierced with a small hole in the centre, in which a wire is inserted capable of being heated by connection with a voltaic battery. The plates are coated with a layer of white wax mixed with olive oil. On heating the wire the wax retires, as if it ceased to wet the crystal's surface, and accumulates in the form of a liquid ring ; on the line of demarcation it separates the melted from the solid wax. But there is this remarkable difference in the two cases. In the slice taken across the axis the wax is melted in the form of a circle, of which the wire is the centre ; while in the other plate the wax is melted in the form of an ellipse, the long axis of which coincides with the optic axis of the crystal, showing that the conducting power is greater in that direction than in the one at right angles to it.

Liquids and gases are very indifferent conductors of heat, probably on account of the mobility of their particles ; for no sooner is heat applied to a fluid body than the particles in immediate contact with the source of heat become warm, and, specifically lighter than the surrounding particles ; hence they ascend until they reach a stratum where they are in equilibrium with neighbouring particles. Thus air and water tend to arrange themselves in layers, the lighter and warmer upon the heavier and denser. We may notice this in lakes. In the month of July, Saussure examined the lakes of Thun and

Lucerne; the one at the depth of 370 and the other at that of 640 feet : both had the temperature of 41° Fahr., while the water at the surface indicated 64° and 68·5° respectively. Lago Maggiore, on the Italian side of the Alps, at the depth of 360 feet, had a temperature of 44°, while the surface was nearly 78°.   Mr. J. Jardine found, in September, that the surface of Loch Lomond, Scotland, over the deepest part, marked 69·3°; at the depth of 15 fathoms, 43·7°; at that of 40 fathoms, 41·3°; and from that to about 3 feet from the bottom, 100 fathoms, it decreased only the fifth part of a degree. Observations of this kind justify the popular notion that deep lakes never freeze, since convection may take place, of course, downwards as well as upwards; the particles at the surface, being chilled by cold, become heavier and descend, while the lighter and warmer particles rise to the surface, to be in like manner made heavier by cold, and to descend; but this process can only go on to 40°, since at this point water undergoes a remarkable molecular change, whereby it no longer contracts and becomes heavier by cold, but lighter, so that in sinking from 40° to 32° it occupies the same bulk that it did in sinking from 48° to 40°.   When the superficial water has reached 40°, it is at the point of maximum density by cold; any further reduction of temperature causes it to expand, and to send it to the surface until it reaches 32°, when it crystallises into ice, and in doing so undergoes a further expansion.

Before, then, a deep lake can freeze, this process of convection must proceed until the whole of the water has reached the point of maximum density by cold, and then, and not till then, can the surface sink in temperature from 40° to 32°, the freezing point.   While this process is going on the winter is passing away, and before the whole lake has reached 40° spring has arrived.   But as water is so bad a conductor of heat as scarcely to transmit it from the surface downwards the surface water may in summer mark a temperature of 70° or 80°, while the lower strata are at or about the temperature of maximum density which the cold of winter had impressed upon them.

After sunset similar phenomena, may be observed in the layers of the atmosphere.   Pictet found, at the end of the last century, that thermometers, placed, the one 5 feet from the ground, and the other at the height of 75 feet, marked different temperatures ; sometimes before sunset the lower thermometer was colder than the upper one, the difference increasing rapidly till sunset, and, indeed, during the night in calm weather.*

Convection may be illustrated by boiling water in a large tube or flask, by means of a spirit-lamp placed beneath it. If the water contain a little powdered amber or cochineal, which is of about the same density as the water, the particles will show in a striking manner the direction of the current. A strong current will ascend up the centre or axis of the tube, slackening as it ascends, from the giving off of heat to the colder particles ; while the colder particles form descending currents at the sides of the vessel, returning to the source of heat to obtain a fresh supply. In this way the water gradually rises in its temperature from that of the surrounding air to the boiling point, 212°; at which point the water, being equal in force to the atmospheric pressure, bubbles off in the gaseous or aeriform state. But even here there is a difference in temperature between the bottom and top layers. If a thermometer be placed with its bulb close to the bottom of the tube, while the bulb of a second thermometer be plunged just beneath the surface of the water, the lower thermometer may be 214°, and upwards, while the upper is only 212°. If the lamp be removed, boiling will of course cease, but the convective current will continue active for hours ; the hotter and lighter portions will arrange themselves nearer the surface, and in the process of cooling there may be a difference of 20°, and upwards, in favour of the upper thermometer, and that in a column of only six or seven inches in height. Even a column of cold water, exposed to the ordinary temperature of a room, will often be 2° warmer at or near the surface than at the bottom.

We have described the convective currents in water under the influence of heat. Were the air visible similar currents

* A number of interesting observations of this kind will be found in a volume of this series entitled "Experimental Essays." See Essay III., "History of the Modern Theory of Dew."

would be noticed streaming up on the outer surface of the heated tube, and from the surface of the hot water ascending to the ceiling, spreading and descending in colder parts of the room. This process would go on not only during the heating, but also during the cooling, of the liquid column, and not rest until equality of temperature had been attained. But such equality never can be attained, since a human being, or any warm-blooded animal, were it only a mouse, entering a room, at once disturbs the relations of temperature, and sets in motion convective currents. A lamp or a candle does so still more powerfully; a lump of ice would produce an inverted convection; in short, there is no such thing as rest in the air; everything in that region is in unceasing activity, and perpetual motion; which should be met by intelligence on our part. Convection points out the true principle of ventilation; the poisoned air, as it leaves our lungs—the poisoned products of combustion, as they leave our lamps and candles, are furnished, by heat, with wings, which cause them to ascend, and they would ascend and escape, and be useful in the vegetable world, where they are wanted, were it not for our ill-contrived domestic arrangements, where every room acts as a condenser, and brings the aerial poison down upon our heads to be breathed again. The grand process by which nature ventilates our globe should regulate our proceedings. The sun on the equator raises a powerful current, which ascends and spreads on either side towards the pole; while the colder air from the temperate regions streams in as an undercurrent to supply health and refreshment to living creatures.

Arrangements for warming are, for the most part, beyond the control of individuals; these are settled by the house-builder or architect according to ancient rule, and are adapted to our feelings or prejudices in favour of open fire-places; but the ventilation of our rooms depends in great measure upon ourselves, and we may be fairly charged with a presumptuous neglect of natural laws, if we fail to make use of some of the simple means for obtaining ventilation which we are about to describe. Before science had discovered the pernicious effects of impure air, it was not surprising that people did not ventilate. No plans for ventilation could be laid down on a proper basis, until the composition of the atmosphere had been properly defined : no definite meaning could be given to the word *ventilation* until the nature of the air itself was known, and the products of respiration and combustion had been proved to be poisonous.* But no sooner had the beautiful experiments of Priestley, Cavendish, and others, made an impression on the scientific minds of the day, than means were contrived for ventilation. Thus Cavallo, in his "Treatise on the Nature and Properties of Air," (4to., London, 1781), quotes from an older work a method of ventilating a room by means of a small tube opening into it, in or near the ceiling, which might either be carried to the top of the building, or be made to communicate with the external air by a small perforation through the wall at the roof of the room, by which means a proper circulation would be established, and the foul air be carried off. In order to admit fresh air into the room, another opening was made in the ceiling, having a communication with a small pipe that led from thence to the outside of the wall, where it was bent and conducted downwards till it reached the ground, being left open to communicate with the external air. The cool air would thus be forced in at the lower opening of the tube, and made to ascend into the apartment in proportion to the quantity that escaped towards the higher regions by means of the ventilator.

Here we have a plan of ventilation at least seventy years old, and yet, at the present day, ventilation is still discussed and quarrelled over, as if it were some new thing. The proper supply of fresh air is denied to the great mass of

---

* Ventilation was probably first practised in mining districts, as a work of necessity, in consequence of the rapid conversion of the oxygen of the air into carbonic acid, by the respiration of the miners, the combustion of their candles, and the large quantities of irrespirable gases liberated by the gunpowder used in blasting. Mr. Henwood has given a summary of the analysis of eighteen samples of air taken from the mines of Cornwall and Devon, from which it appears that the proportion of oxygen was only 17·067 per cent., while the carbonic acid was 0·085 ; the nitrogen 82·848 ; and in one instance the proportion of oxygen was reduced to 14·51 ; and in another, the carbonic acid was 0·23 per cent. These results show a diminution in the proportion of the vital ingredient of the atmosphere from its usual per centage of 21, and an increase of the poisonous ingredient, carbonic acid, from 0·05, its usual amount, calculated to produce great injury to persons exposed to the breathing of such a fluid for hours together.

the population, because builders, who ought to be perfectly acquainted with these things (who ought also to be able to construct chimneys that will discharge their smoke into the air instead of into the room), too often neglect to study the natural laws which chemists and physiologists have placed on a sure basis. We are told that the native porters of Canton are accustomed to balance the load which they carry on a pole upon their shoulders, by means of a large stone at the other extremity of the pole, and that they deemed the suggestion of an Englishman an impertinent interference, who wished them to balance one package by means of another. " Our ancestors," they said, " were very wise men, and they never carried more than one package at a time, and this they balanced by means of a stone; shall we be wiser than our ancestors ?" So may a large proportion of our modern builders exclaim, " Our ancestors were very wise men ; they never thought of providing special means for ventilation in rooms and public buildings; shall we be wiser than our ancestors ?" Many a powerful satire on the modern practice of house-building is afforded by the stifling effects of ordinary dwellings. For example, Dr. Macculloch, in his "Account of the Hebrides," remarks, that while the inhabitants had no shelter but huts of the most simple construction, which afforded free passage for currents of air, they were not subject to fevers ; but when, through the good intentions of the proprietors, new dwellings were erected, and were made close, *comfortable*, and *commodious*, the stagnating air, and other impurities, joined to the want of cleanliness in the inmates, generated febrile infection. Now, we think, it must be admitted, that had these new dwellings been properly ventilated, by special means contrived for the purpose, there is no reason why they should have been more unhealthy than the old ones.

The third mode by which heat seeks to attain equilibrium is by *radiation*. A grate of burning coals warms a room by this method—the rays of heat proceeding from it are evidently not brought by currents of air, for they set in towards, and not from, the fire ; nor is the heat brought by convection, since heated currents ascend ; nor by conduction, for that in gaseous bodies is very slow. Radiation is the force by which the heat of the sun reaches the earth; the heat of a fire warms the room; and the heat and light of a lamp or candle become diffused. From these sources the heat proceeds in radial lines as from a centre; and in common with all central forces, the intensity diminishes inversely as the square of the distance from the radiating point. For example, the heating effect of the candle, Fig. 2, is nine times less at 3 feet than at 1, and four times less at 2 feet than at 1. If a board, 2 feet square, be held with its centre 2 yards from the candle, and another board, 1 foot square, be held parallel to the first board, half way between it and the candle, it will intercept the whole of the light that would

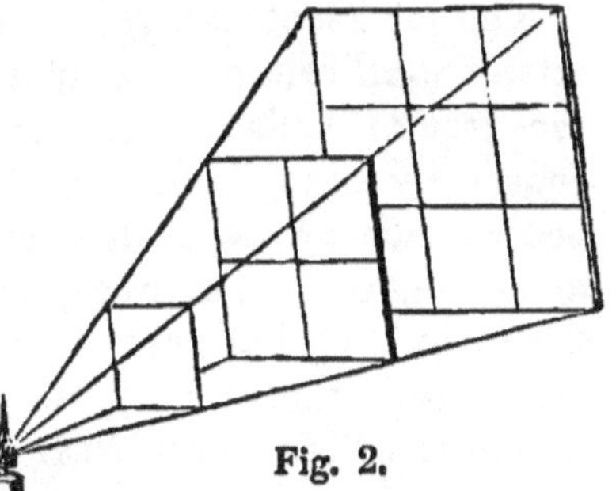

Fig. 2.

have fallen on the first board. The same board, 1 foot square, would also intercept, exactly, all the light that would have fallen on a third board, 3 feet square, three times as far from the candle. This is what is meant by the law of inverse squares; the first board at the distance indicated by 1, from the candle, receives a quantity of light and heat indicated by 1; the second board, however, at the distance 2, has the same quantity of heat and light spread over a surface four times larger, and, consequently, has only one-fourth the intensity of the first board. The third board, at the distance 3, has only one-ninth the intensity, since it is spread over a surface nine times larger than that of the first board.

Radiant heat has many of the properties of light. It moves with the same velocity, and is subject to the same laws of reflection, absorption, refraction, transmission, &c. The heating rays may be reflected or transmitted without disturbing the temperature of the bodies which reflect or transmit them; but if the rays be absorbed or arrested in their course, so as to become wholly or partially extinguished as rays, the body absorbing them immediately rises in temperature.

The radiation of heat is a very different process from conduction; the one being instantaneous, and the other slow. Conducted heat raises the temperature of the conducting bodies; radiant heat may not disturb the temperature of the bodies that transmit it. Gaseous bodies are not only the worst conductors, but the worst transmitters of heat; while the metals, which are the best conductors, do not transmit radiant heat at all.

The incessant struggle that is going on among bodies to attain equilibrium of temperature is strikingly illustrated in the case of radiant heat. All bodies, in whatever state, are constantly engaged in radiating heat. When a number of bodies radiate to each other equally, so that each, in proportion to its size, receives as much as it gives, the temperature remains the same. If, however, a body of a higher temperature be introduced among them, they radiate their heat to it; but it radiates to them more heat than it receives, so that its temperature falls, while their temperature rises until equilibrium is attained. If a colder body be introduced, they radiate to it as before; but as it radiates to them less heat than it receives, its temperature rises, while theirs falls. The chilling effect which a ship's crew feel on approaching an iceberg arises from the fact that they radiate towards it more heat than they receive.

A ray of heat, or of light, proceeds in a straight line until it meets a reflecting surface, from which it rebounds in another straight line, the direction of which is determined by the law, that the angle of incidence is equal to the angle of reflection.

. It must also be noticed that the plane of reflection, or that imaginary plane which contains both the incident and reflected ray, is perpendicular to the reflecting surface at the point of contact. In curved surfaces a perpendicular, or *normal*, can be erected at any point, which in such cases acts as a tangent plane, touching the curved surface at such point; hence, if a speculum have the form of a paraboloid, any number of rays proceeding from a point called its focus will be reflected into parallel lines, and if such parallel lines or rays fall upon such a surface they will all be reflected so as to meet in its focus.

Two such specula are shown in Fig. 3, with their axes in the
same straight line. If a hot body, such as a flask of hot water,
be placed at c, in the focus of the mirror, A, all the rays
which it sends to that mirror will be reflected in parallel
lines, and so reaching the other mirror, B, will be reflected so as
to meet in its focus, D, where a thermometer will be affected
more than at any other spot, even though such spot be much
nearer the hot body, c.   If a screen be placed either between

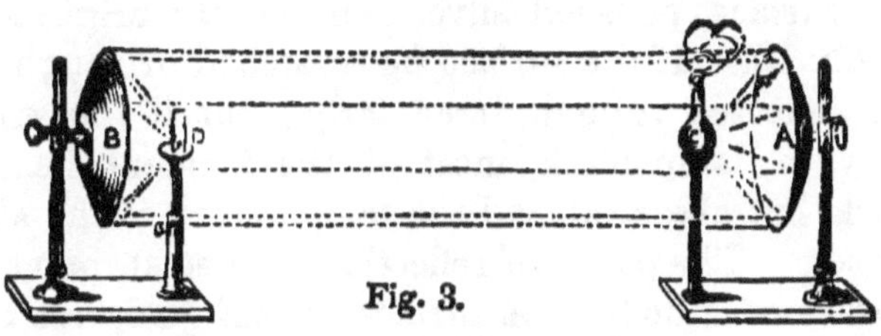

Fig. 3.

c and A, or between B and D, the effect on the thermometer
instantly ceases.   A red-hot iron ball, placed in the focus of
one mirror, will fire combustible bodies placed in the focus of
the other mirror, at the distance of 10 or 15 feet, or more. If
a ball of ice be placed in one focus, a thermometer in the other
will be observed to fall.*   It was once supposed that this arose
from the radiation of cold ; but bearing in mind the theory
of radiant heat, already given, it will be seen that the thermometer sinks, because it radiates heat to the ball of ice.
Indeed, if one of the parabolic mirrors be turned with its
axis towards the blue sky, a thermometer in its focus will
sink some degrees by day, and it has been known to sink as
much as 17 degrees by night. If one of the mirrors be
turned to the sun, the rays of which may be considered as
physically parallel, they will be collected in the focus of the

* This experiment is commonly referred to M. Pictet, of Geneva, and is
described in his *Essais de Physique*, published in 1790. The experiment,
however, is spoken of by Oldenburg, in a letter to the Hon. Robert Boyle, dated
Dec. 19, 1665. He says—" I met the other day, in the 'Astrological Discourse'
of Sir Christopher Heydon, with an experiment which he affirms to have tried
himself, importing that cold accompanies reflected light, by employing burning spherical concaves, or parabolical sections, which he saith will as sensibly
reflect the actual cold of snow or ice, as it [they] will the heat of the sun."—
Boyle's Works, 1744.

mirror, and illustrate the origin of the word "focus" by its powerful heating effect.

The mirrors used in the above experiments are of speculum metal, or of copper silvered on the concave faces. Such a surface, being the worst kind of radiator, absorbs the least proportion of the rays impressed upon it, and, consequently, reflects the greatest number. Surfaces differ greatly in reflective power: metals are the best reflectors; but in very different degrees. Out of every 100 heating rays that fall upon a surface, polished silver reflects 90; bright lead, 60; glass, only 10. If the surface be scratched or roughened the heat is reflected from it irregularly; but if the surface be coated with lamp-black, most of the incident heat is not reflected, but absorbed, and the temperature of the absorbing body rises. The power of reflection resides at, or very near, the surface of a body. A surface of leaf gold, less than the 200,000th of an inch in thickness, reflects heat nearly as well as a mirror of solid gold. The best reflectors are the worst absorbents, and *vice versâ*.

The absorbing and radiating powers of the same substance are directly proportional to each other. Sir John Leslie formed a cubical vessel of tinned-iron plate, and covered one of its sides with lamp-black; a second with writing-paper; a third was roughened by scratching; and the fourth was left bright. On filling the cube with hot water, and placing it in the focus of one of the mirrors, with a thermometer in that of the other, a different temperature was obtained as each side of the cube was presented to the mirror. The largest amount of heat was radiated from the lamp-black, less from the paper, still less from the scratched surface, and least of all from the polished surface. Details of this kind have a great practical value; for we see that a hot liquid in a blackened vessel will cool down more quickly to the temperature of the air than if it were in a bright vessel; and hot-water pipes, intended for warming a building, should be blackened in places where the heat is to be distributed, and kept bright in the approaches where the heat is not wanted.

The increased radiating power of a surface roughened by emery, by the file, or by drawing streaks or lines with a graving tool, arises, according to Melloni, from increasing the density of the surface. In support of this view, he took four plates of silver, two of which, when cast, were left in their natural state, without hammering, and the other two were planished to a high degree under the hammer. All four plates were then finely polished with pumice-stone and charcoal, and after this, one of each of the pairs of plates was roughened, by rubbing with coarse emery paper in one direction. The quantity of heat radiated from these plates was as follows :—

Hammered and polished plate . . . . 10°
Hammered and roughened plate . . . . . . 18°
Cast and polished plate . . . . 13·7°
Cast and roughened plate . . . . 11·3°

Thus it appears that the hard hammered plate was increased in radiating power four-fifths, by roughening its surface, while the soft cast plate lost nearly one-fifth of its power by the same process.

Melloni made the remarkable discovery that the amount of absorption depends a good deal on the nature of the heating source. If we take the naked flame of an oil-lamp, a platinum wire heated to redness in the flame of the spirit-lamp, a piece of sheet copper heated to between 700° and 800° in a current of hot air rising from a lamp beneath it, and, lastly, a copper canister filled with boiling water, we have four distinct sources of heat. If one of the balls of a differential thermometer be blackened, it may evidently be placed at such distances from each of these sources as to indicate the same temperature in each case. If the ball of the thermoscope, instead of being coated with lamp-black, be covered with another substance, the distances observed in the former case will now no longer apply in order to get the same temperature. If, when the ball was covered with lamp-black, the heat absorbed in each case were 100°, it will, if coated with white lead, and placed at the same distance from the naked flame, as before, only indicate 53° ; at the same distance from the red-hot platinum, only 56° ; from the heated copper, 89°; from the copper cube of boiling water the result is the same as when the ball of the thermoscope was covered with lamp-black.

given in the following table : the results of a few of which are
Other substances were tried,—

Absorbing Surface.	Naked Flame.	Incandescent Platinum.	Copper at 750°. Fahr.	Copper at 212° Fahr.
Lamp-black	100	100	100	100
White lead	53	56	89	100
Isinglass	52	54	84	91
Indian ink	96	95	87	85
Shell-lac	43	47	70	72
Polished metal . . .	14	13·5	13	13

It will be seen from this table that lamp-black absorbs all
the heating rays from whatever source, and that the absorptive
power of a metallic surface, though small, is uniform in every
case. It will also be noticed that the less intense source of
heat, viz., that of boiling water, a greater amount is absorbed
than in the other cases. It is an old observation by Franklin,
that pieces of cloth of the same size and texture, but of different
colours, placed on newly-fallen snow, absorb heat in different
proportions, as indicated by the greater or less rapidity with
which the snow melted under them. The absorption was
greatest in the case of the black cloth, less with the blue, still
less with the green, and diminishing in the order of purple,
red, yellow, and white. Melloni also found that bodies varied
considerably in their transmissive power for heat. Such as
are transparent to heat are called *diathermanous*, or *diathermic*,
from $\delta\iota a$, " through," and $\theta\epsilon\rho\mu o\varsigma$, " hot," while bodies that
are opaque to heat are termed *athermanous*, or *adiathermic*
(the Greek *a* signifying " without "). Bodies that are transparent to light may stop the rays of heat more or less completely.
Pure water, for example, transmits most of the rays that it
does not reflect ; the addition of a few drops of indian ink will
greatly diminish the transparency of a large quantity of water,
but still the light transmitted is of the same kind as that
transmitted by pure water. It has the same order and
arrangement of colour, when passed through a prism, as that
transmitted by pure water. If, however, the water be made
turbid by means of indigo, the transmitted light is no longer
the same, some of the luminous rays having been more com-

pletely absorbed than others. The heating rays may be supposed to undergo a somewhat similar change; but while a vast number of bodies, solid, liquid, and gaseous, are transparent to light, there is only one known solid that is diathermanous, or transparent to heat, and that is rock salt. Atmospheric air, oxygen, nitrogen, and hydrogen in a pure and dry state are almost perfectly diathermanous; but several transparent gases, especially olefiant gas, and also vapours, have been shown by Professor Tyndall to be powerful absorbers of heat. Liquids also absorb varying proportions of the heating rays.

Heat, like light, admits of being refracted, as may be seen by the action of a burning-glass, which converges the sun's rays to a point. The solar spectrum has its heat very unequally distributed, the maximum temperature being just below the red ray. If, however, other sources of heat be used instead of the sun, the position of maximum temperature is found to vary. In the spectrum from the flame of a naked lamp, the maximum intensity is about the middle; in that from ignited platinum it is nearer the red; in that from copper at 750°, it is still nearer; while the heat radiated from a surface at 212° contains a few only of the more refrangible heating rays. It appears, then, that a pencil of invisible heat consists of rays of different refrangibility, and such a pencil, in passing through certain substances, becomes altered in character, as light does in passing through coloured media. We know that the sun's rays pass through glass and other media without being absorbed, so that a burning-glass may produce a focus of intense heat and light, and be itself quite cool; while if held before an ordinary fire it will produce a focus, indeed, but one containing very little heat and light, while the glass itself becomes warm. Glass, then, transmits the heating rays of the sun with ease, but such rays exist in very small quantities in incandescent bodies. A glass screen is used for looking into a highly heated furnace, and this can be done without inconvenience, since the glass absorbs the heated rays and transmits the luminous ones. If the sun's rays be transmitted through water, and then through green glass, coloured by means of oxide of copper, a beam of greenish light is obtained, which, when concentrated by lenses, has considerable intensity but no heat, the heating rays having been separated during the filtration.

The properties of radiant heat vary, as we have seen, according to the source; but when heat, from whatever source, has been once absorbed and radiated again, it has lost the distinctive character of its source.

If the reader will turn to our "Introduction to the Study of Natural Philosophy," he will find some remarks on the distinction between heat and temperature. Bodies of the same temperature may contain very different quantities of heat although the thermometer may show no difference. Two flasks of equal size, one containing a pound of olive oil and the other a pound of water, left for some time in a room at 40°, will both mark that temperature on a thermometer inserted into each; but if the flasks be taken into a warm room at 70°, the thermometers will be seen to rise slowly from 40 to 70°, but not with equal paces—the thermometer in the oil will rise much more quickly than that in the water; hence it is a perfectly fair inference that less heat is required to raise the oil from 40° to 70° than so to raise the water. If the flasks be taken back into the cold room the oil will cool more quickly than the water. That the water contains more heat than the oil at any given temperature, may be proved by placing the flasks in boiling water, and then in funnels containing equal quantities of ice. The water, in cooling down to the temperature of the ice, will melt twice as much ice as the oil. It is evident, then, that bodies of the same temperature may contain unequal quantities of heat; that the quantity of heat required to raise pure water 1 degree, as from 32° to 33°, must be varied in order to produce the same effect on other bodies; which quantity of heat required to raise a body 1 degree is called its *specific heat.* Pure water is the standard of comparison, and its specific heat is said to be equal to 1·000.

One of the methods of ascertaining the specific heat of bodies is the *calorimeter,* which consists of three concentric metal vessels, s, o, e, Fig. 4, enclosed one within the other, and connected by as few supports as possible. The instrument must be in a room where the temperature is not over 40° nor under 32°. The two outer compartments, s o, and also the cover, are filled with broken ice, which, being in a melting state, preserves a constant temperature of 32°, only receiving heat from the external air as well as from the innermost vessel, E. When, therefore, the substance, the specific heat of which is to be examined, is placed in E, all the heat that it gives out is employed in melting the ice which immediately surrounds it, and the water thus obtained passes by the pipe, *d*, into a vessel

beneath, in which it is weighed; and it is thus ascertained how much ice has been melted without raising its temperature, or how much water might be raised 142° (a number that will be explained presently, p. 48) by the cooling of the substance examined through a known number of degrees, since no heat can penetrate to this ice from the external air, because all the heat that enters the calorimeter from without is absorbed in melting the ice of the outer vessel, and the water

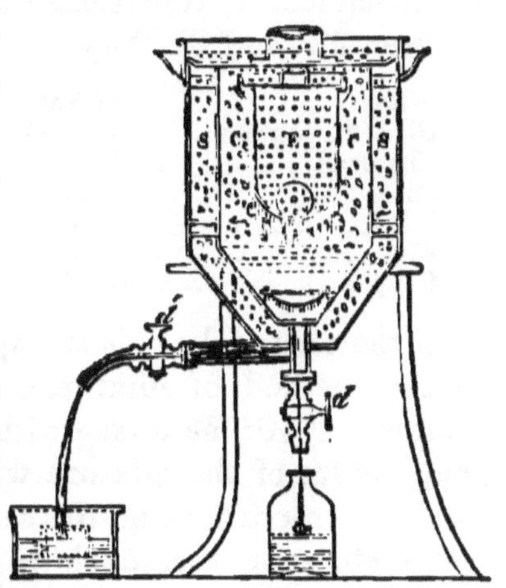

Fig. 4.

thus formed drains away to waste through a separate pipe, *d'*, and is not allowed to mix with the drainage of the inner ice.*

* Similar contrivances have been used for measuring the relative quantities of heat evolved by the combustion of different kinds of fuel. The following table contains a few such results:—

Fuel of which 1 lb. is burned.	lbs. of oxygen consumed.	lbs. of ice melted.
Hydrogen	8	320
Light carburetted hydrogen	4	88
Heavy carburetted hydrogen	3·5	85
Carbon	2·66	40
Wax	3·14	126
Tallow	3·1	111
Ether	2·6	107
Naphtha	3·33	97
Olive oil	3	93
Alcohol	2·1	58

In fact, as long as the two outer vessels are kept constantly supplied with melting ice from the top, they form a perfectly insulating wall, through which no heat can pass, for as ice cannot exist above 32°, whatever heat enters it must be employed in melting the first layer, and can proceed no further if that layer be renewed. By means of the calorimeter, tables of specific heat have been constructed, of which the following is a specimen. It represents the specific heats of equal weights between 32° and 212° :—

Water	1·00000	Brass	0·09391
Oil of turpentine	0·42593	Silver	0·05701
Charcoal	0·24150	Tin	0·05623
Glass	0·19768	Mercury	0·03332
Iron	0·11379	Gold	0·03244
Zinc	0·09555	Platinum	0·03243
Copper	0·09155	Lead	0·03140

In the case of liquids the specific heat may be ascertained by the method of mixtures. If a pound of mercury, for example, at 40°, be mixed with a pound of water at 156°, the temperature of the mixture will not be the mean, as in the case of two portions of the same kind of liquid of different temperatures, but as much as 152·3°; the water having lost 3·7°, while the mercury has gained as much as 112·3°. If these numbers be compared, we find that as 112·3° is to 3·7°, so is 0·03332, the specific heat of mercury as given in the above table.

The specific heat of gases is found by conducting them from a vessel at 212°, through a spiral tube surrounded by cold water, which is thus raised in temperature ; and in this way, by operating with different gases, different results are obtained.   In order to raise 1 lb. of water from 32° to 212°, the same quantity of heat is required as will raise 4 lbs. of atmospheric air the same number of degrees; hence the specific heat of air is one-fourth, or, more exactly, 0·02669 that of water. So, also, a pound of water in losing 1 degree would raise 4 lbs. of air 1 degree. On comparing equal volumes the result is more striking ; water is 770 times heavier than air, and a cubic foot of water, in losing 1 degree of temperature, would raise 770 × 4 = 3080 cubic feet of air 1 degree. The very much greater capacity of water for heat over all other bodies, solid, liquid, or aerial, is of considerable importance to the well-being of this globe. The ocean thus acts in mitigating climate, since the heat of summer is slowly given out during winter, so that islands and the shores of continents enjoy a milder climate than the remoter inland. The small specific heat of mercury allows it to become quickly heated and quickly cooled, and thus renders the thermometer sensitive. The mobility of air and its susceptibility to heat render it liable to frequent change. When air is suddenly compressed it gives out its heat, while its sudden expansion produces cold. As the air ascends from the earth it expands, its capacity for heat is increased, so that it cools itself and surrounding bodies. Cold air, on the contrary, descending from the upper regions, has its temperature raised by condensation as it approaches the earth, without obtaining a supply of heat from any other source. In this way parts of the earth are rendered habitable, as on mountain slopes in the equator, where the air from the burning sands below becomes cooled by expansion in ascending, while the cold winds from the snow-clad summits above become condensed and warmer in descending.

When heat is added to a solid body, the first effect which marks the increase of temperature is *expansion ;* that is, the cohesive or attractive force becomes more and more opposed by the repulsive force of heat ; the particles are consequently separated to greater distances, and the temperature rises. At a certain point, however, the temperature, as marked by the thermometer, becomes stationary, and although the heat be continually applied, the temperature does not rise. The solid is now undergoing a change of state ; it is passing from the solid into the liquid state ; and no rise in temperature will be observed until the whole of the solid has become liquid. The point at which a body begins to fuse or melt, is called its *fusing point,* or *point of liquefaction,* and is different in different substances. The quantity of heat absorbed by the body, and unaccounted for, as far as the thermometer is concerned, is called *latent heat.* When the body is liquefied, the temperature again begins to rise, until another point is attained, when it again becomes stationary, and the liquid begins to pass off in the form of vapour or steam. This point is called the *boiling point*, and is also different in different substances. The heat absorbed during the process of boiling or vaporisation is also called latent.

If, for example, a quantity of snow, at the temperature of zero, with a thermometer in it, be placed in a vessel on the fire, the temperature will be observed to rise to 32°; the snow will then immediately begin to be converted into water, and the thermometer will become stationary at 32°, until the whole of the snow is melted. This temperature, is, therefore, the melting or fusing point of snow or ice, and the heat absorbed or rendered latent during the process, being that which is necessary to produce liquefaction, is hence called also the *heat of liquefaction*.

The amount of heat thus rendered latent may be ascertained by placing in the calorimeter a pound of water at any given temperature, and observing what weight of ice it dissolves in falling to some other temperature. In this way we can ascertain that a pound of hot water, in falling through about 142°, will melt a pound of ice; and in general, any given weight of water, in falling through 142°, gives out sufficient heat to melt its own weight of ice. When, therefore, ice is liquefied it absorbs and renders latent as much heat as would be sufficient to raise its own weight of water from $32°$ to $32° \times 142° = 174°$. This large quantity of heat is necessary to the liquid condition of water. It cannot exist without it any more than ice can exist without giving it up. To prove this, let a flask of water at 60° be immersed in mercury at 30° below zero F., *i.e.* at—30°; a thermometer, No. 1, in the mercury will gradually rise, and a thermometer, No. 2, in the water will fall until it reaches 32°, the freezing point of water; No. 2 will remain stationary while the water freezes; but No. 1 will go on rising, showing that the water while freezing is giving off heat to the mercury. When all the water has become ice, No. 2 again begins to fall; but No. 1 still rises, until its temperature is the same as No. 2. The latent heat of the water is thus gradually made apparent, and is given out during the freezing; and as the temperature of the ice is the same as that of the water before it was frozen, or when

No. 2 became stationary, the heat thus liberated must pass to the mercury.

This liberation of heat during freezing mitigates the winter's cold and diminishes the thickness of the icy layer produced by one night's frost, for as the water freezes on the surface, one portion of the heat of liquefaction is given off to the air, and another portion to the water below. So also during a thaw, the ice in melting slowly absorbs its proportion of latent heat, and the accumulated ice and snow of winter gradually disappear. If ice were rapidly to absorb its latent heat, the snow and ice would liquefy too quickly, and terrible floods would be the consequence; but as the latent heat of water is greater than that of any other body, it undergoes its changes more slowly. The latent heat of water is 142·65°; that of zinc is 50·63°; of silver, 37·92°; of tin, 25·65°; of sulphur, 16·85°; of lead, 9·65°; and of mercury, 5·11°.

When all the ice or snow in a vessel over the fire is melted, the thermometer will rise from 32°, through 180°, until it reaches 212°, which is the boiling point of water under ordinary atmospheric pressure. The thermometer again remains stationary while the water is passing off in the form of steam. This change of state from the liquid to the gaseous form requires a large amount of heat to be absorbed and rendered latent. If we note the time required to raise water from the freezing to the boiling point, or from 32° to 212°, through an interval of 180°, and then note the time required to boil away the whole of the water, it will be found to be $5\frac{1}{2}$ times that of the former; that is, if it require 5 minutes to raise the thermometer 180°, or from freezing to boiling, it will require $27\frac{1}{2}$ minutes to boil away the whole of the water without any rise of temperature. It is obvious, therefore, that during this time, the water, in passing into steam, must have absorbed $180° \times 5\frac{1}{2} = 990°$, which is the latent heat of steam.

On condensing steam, the latent heat becomes apparent, just as the latent heat of water does when it becomes solid. It is this large amount of latent heat in steam which renders it important as a heating agent: 1 gallon of water converted into steam contains sufficient heat to raise $5\frac{1}{2}$ gallons from 32° to 212°. Hence, steam made to circulate in pipes through a building is an efficient and economical source of heat: 1 square foot of radiating surface in a steam-pipe being, in general, sufficient for warming 200 cubic feet of space. No other vapour contains nearly so much latent heat as steam: 990° is perhaps in excess, but taking 966·6 as the more probable number at the boiling point of water, the latent heat of an equal weight of alcohol at its boiling point is 374·9°; that of ether, 162·8°; and that of oil of turpentine, 133·2°. Equal bulks of different liquids give very different volumes of vapour; a cubic inch of water at 212° becomes very nearly a cubic foot of steam at the same temperature, expanding as it does into 1,696 times its volume. Alcohol boils at 173°; a cubic inch of the liquid at 60°, expands into 528 cubic inches of vapour at its boiling point; ether boils at 95°, and gives 298 cubic inches of vapour; oil of turpentine boils at 214°, and gives 193 cubic inches of vapour. It is this marvellous expansive force of steam, due in great measure to the large quantity of vapour from so small a quantity of liquid, that renders it so admirable a prime mover in the steam-engine. Alcohol boils at a lower temperature, and requires much less heat in becoming vapour, yet, were it as cheap as water, it would not be so economical in the steam-engine, on account of the comparatively small volume of vapour produced by the liquid.

The sum of the latent and sensible heats in a body is very nearly constant. For example, if water at 212°, in changing its state from the liquid to the vaporous, absorbs 950° of heat, water at 262° would absorb only 900°, and water at 162° would absorb 1,000°, the sum in all three cases being the same, viz., 1,162°.

The quantity of vapour given off by different liquids at a given temperature bears relation to their boiling points, the most volatile liquid giving off the largest quantity of vapour. The difference of volatility in different liquids may be measured by sending a few drops of each liquid into tubes filled with mercury, and standing in a cistern of that metal. As soon as the liquid reaches the Torricellian vacuum it instantly evaporates, and fills the space with vapour, which, by its elasticity, depresses the mercurial column, and measures the elastic force, or the pressure of the vapour in question, at the observed temperature : for high temperatures the barometer tube can be enclosed in a wider tube filled with water, which can be raised to the boiling point. The quantity by which the mercurial column descends represents the length of the column that the vapour would support. Thus, at 50° the vapour of ether will support a column of rather more than 11¼ inches of mercury; while the vapour of alcohol will support less than 1 inch; and the vapour of water not much more than ¼ of an inch. At 212° the vapour of water supports 30 inches of mercury; or, in other words, is equal to the atmospheric pressure. Beyond this temperature it becomes high-pressure steam, which at 230° will support a column of mercury 42·45 inches high. In the following table, the first column represents the temperature, and the other columns the height of mercury in inches supported by the vapour of the substance at the head of each column.

Temp. Fahr.	Ether.	Alcohol.	Water.
Degrees.	Inches.	Inches.	Inches.
— 4	2·725	0·131	0·036
+ 14	4·356	0·256	0·082
32	7·176	0·501	0·182
50	11·278	0·948	0·361
68	17·117	1·732	0·686
86	25·078	3·086	1·245
104	35·971	5·159	2·168
122	49·920	8·673	3·631
140	68·121	13·776	5·874
158	90·92	21·228	9·201
176	116·03	32·000	13·998
194	153·50	46·800	20·740
212	193·72	66·330	30·000
230	246·02	92·590	42·450
240	—	—	49·670
250	—	—	58·210
260	—	—	67·730
270	—	—	77·850
290	—	—	100·200
300	—	—	111·810
320	—	—	135·000

It will be seen by this table that water and other volatile liquids throw off vapour at very low temperatures when exposed to the air : this process is called spontaneous evaporation. The liquid fills the space above it with vapour of a fixed density and elasticity, depending on the temperature. When the space can contain no more vapour at a given temperature it is said to be saturated. The density of the vapour at the given temperature has a certain fixed pressure, which is measured by the column of mercury which it will support. No more vapour can enter the space unless the temperature be raised, and should the temperature fall, a portion of the vapour will be condensed, and the remaining vapour will expand so as to fill the original space and have a density and elasticity due to the altered temperature. During evaporation the vapour is supplied from the surface only of the liquid. During ebullition or boiling, steam is formed at every part of the liquid. In boiling, the vapour maintains the same temperature, provided the pressure remain the same; but evaporation may go on at all temperatures and pressures, the quantity of liquid evaporated depending on the temperature and the amount of surface exposed ; or the pressure may be increased or diminished, or removed altogether, without affecting the result, or that quantity of vapour which can exist in a given space at a given temperature ; the saturation of that space requiring a longer time in proportion to the density of the air contained in it; while in a vacuum the saturation is instantaneous ; this is the only difference.

The amount of evaporation, however, is greatly influenced by the motion of the air, which carries off the vapour from the surface of a liquid as fast as it is formed. A strong wind will cause twice as much vapour to be discharged as a still atmosphere. Dalton ascertained the number of grains weight of water evaporated per minute from a vessel 6 inches in diameter, for all temperatures between 20° and 212°, when the air was still, or in gentle or brisk motion. When the water was at 212°, the quantity evaporated was 120 grains per minute in a still atmosphere ; 154 grains per minute with a gentle motion of the air, and 189 grains per minute with a brisk motion of the air. The following is an extract from his table between the temperatures of 40° and 60° :—

Temp. Fuhr.	Force of vapour in inches of mercury.	Evaporating force in grains of water.		
Degrees.		Still.	Gentle.	Brisk.
40	0·263	1·05	1·35	1·65
42	·283	1·13	1·45	1·78
44	·305	1·22	1·57	1·92
46	·327	1·31	1·68	2·06
48	·351	1·40	1·80	2·20
50	·375	1·50	1·92	2·36
52	·401	1·60	2·06	2·51
54	·429	1·71	2·20	2·69
56	·458	1·83	2·35	2·88
58	·490	1·96	2·52	3·08
60	·524	2·10	2·70	3·30

The amount of spontaneous evaporation is also greatly influenced by the quantity of vapour already existing in the air. In order to find this, we must ascertain the *dew point* of the air, or the temperature at which the vapour in the air begins to condense, and then, by referring to the table, the quantity of vapour in the air at the time can be found, and this, deducted from the quantity shown by the table to be given off at the ascertained temperature of the evaporating liquid, will give the quantity of water that will be evaporated per minute. In finding the dew point, the wet and dry bulb thermometers may be used, with reference to the Hygrometric Tables issued by Mr. Glaisher, which give the dew point when the temperatures are known. The principle of the hygrometer is to bring some colder body into the air, or have the means of cooling some body to such a point as shall just condense the vapour of the air upon its surface. Dr. Dalton, adopting Le Roi's method,* used a very thin glass vessel, into which he poured cold water from a well, or cooled down the water by adding a small portion of a freezing mixture. If the vapour were instantly condensed, he poured out the cold water, and used some a little warmer, and so on, until he could just perceive a slight dew upon the surface. The temperature at which this took place was the dew point. In

* See " Experimental Essays" in this series—Essay iii.

Daniell's hygrometer, the cold is produced by the evaporation of ether. Now, suppose the dew point of the air to be 40°, and the temperature of the air and of the evaporating liquid to be 60°, with a still atmosphere, the vapour in the air, as shown by the table at 40°, is 1·05 grains, which subtracted from that at 60°, or 2·10, gives 1·5 grains per minute as the quantity of vapour given off from a surface 6 inches in diameter.

During the spontaneous evaporation of wet surfaces, a considerable degree of cold is produced by the quantity of heat rendered latent by the formation of the vapour, and the heat is mostly derived from the liquid itself, or the surface containing it. By proper contrivances, water may be frozen, in consequence of the abstraction of heat during the rapid formation of vapour. When a person takes cold from wearing wet clothes, the vapour from the clothes obtains its heat from his body, and the chilling sensation is often the greater the warmer the air. A person with damp clothes, entering a room filled with hot dry air, is very likely to take cold, on account of the powerful effect of warm air in abstracting moisture.

In a badly ventilated room, the moisture from the' breath of the inmates, and from the combustion of lamps and candles, accumulates nearly to the point of saturation. This is well shown by an experiment of the late Professor Daniell. The temperature of a room being 45°, the dew point was 39°; a fire was then lighted in it, the door and window were shut, and no air was allowed to enter; the thermometer rose to 55°, but the point of condensation remained the same. A party of eight persons afterwards occupied the room for several hours, and the fire was kept up; the temperature rose to 58°, and the point of condensation rose to 52°. Now, if this room had been properly ventilated, the vapour would have been removed as it was formed, and with it the effluvia and impure air.

We have given in this Introduction a few of the leading phenomena and laws of heat, which we think must be sufficiently impressive for every thoughtful reader, without reference to the nature or cause of heat. Science is most efficient in investigating the laws of phenomena rather than the causes of things; but still it is impossible to repress speculation as to the nature of the forces with which we are constantly dealing, and this speculation, with minds of a high order, may sometimes take the place of induction, and lead to very important results. Thus, heat has been supposed by some to be a very subtle fluid, capable of penetrating and combining with matter so as to produce latent and sensible effects; while heat has been supposed by others to be a kind of molecular motion, which may be generated by friction, percussion, compression, combustion, &c.

Let us examine this dynamical or mechanical theory of heat a little more closely. Philosophers suppose matter to be everywhere penetrated by a highly elastic ether which fills all space, and connects star with star, as well as atom with atom. The atoms which form a mass of matter are held together by cohesion, while at the same time they vibrate across their positions. Such vibrations are communicated to the elastic ether, and the vibrations of the ether are also communicated to the atoms. Friction or percussion, or the contact of a heated body, increases the amplitude of the vibrations of the atoms, and the body expands, while the ether which fills the interatomic spaces is also in a state of vibration, and resists the force of attraction on the part of the atoms of matter. Regarding heat as a mode of motion, temperature may be raised or lowered by increasing or diminishing the rates of vibration of the particles. A cold leaden bullet, on a cold anvil, struck with a cold sledge hammer, becomes heated; " and could we gather up all the heat generated by the shock of the sledge, and apply it without loss mechanically, we should be able by means of it to lift the hammer from the height to which it fell."

Heat, then, as a mode of motion, is but an illustration of that great principle of the *conservation of force* which pervades modern science, based on such ideas as these—namely, that the amount of force in the universe is fixed and definite; that the creation of force by human agency is as impossible as the creation or destruction of matter; and that all forces are mutually convertible—heat passing into motion, and motion disappearing, to appear again as heat, or light, or electricity.

We cannot better illustrate this theory than by stating the experimental facts and the reasoning by which the *equivalent of heat* was determined, or, in other words, how much heat is represented by a given amount of motion, and how much motion can be produced from a given amount of heat. For the following details we are indebted to Professor Tyndall's charming volume already referred to.

It is known that a gaseous body expands $\frac{1}{490}$th of its volume for every degree of Fahrenheit, or $\frac{1}{273}$ for every degree of Centigrade; so that a cubic foot at zero C., on being heated to 1°, becomes 1·00367 cubic feet, or, expressed in other language—

1 vol. at 0° C becomes 1 + ·00367 at 1° C.
   „   at 2° „   „   1 + ·00367 × 2
   „   at 3° „   „   1 + ·00367 × 3

and so on. The constant number ·00367 is the fraction of its own volume which a gas at 0°, or the freezing point, expands on being heated 1°; it is the coefficient of expansion of the gas. If Fahrenheit's scale be used, the coefficient will be smaller, in the proportion of 9 to 5.

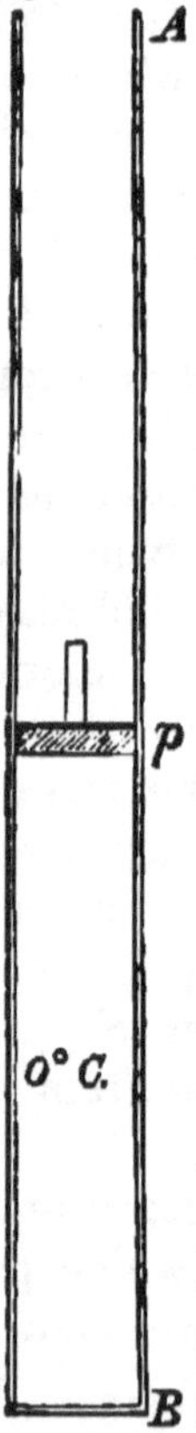

Let A B, Fig. 5, be a tall cylinder, 1 inch square, filled with air, closed at the bottom and open at the top, with a piston, p, moving in it, air tight and without friction; which piston it is supposed shall weigh 2 lbs. 1 oz. Suppose the piston at p to be 273 inches above the bottom, B, of the cylinder. Let the air beneath the piston be at the temperature of 0° C.; on heating the air from 0° to 1° C., the piston will rise 1 inch, and will now stand at 274 inches from the bottom. If the temperature be raised 2°, the piston will stand at 275 inches; if 3°, at 276; if 10°, at 283; if 100°, it will stand 373 inches above the bottom. If the temperature were raised to 273° C., 273 inches would be added to the height of the column; or, in other

Fig. 5.

words, by heating the air to 273° C., its volume would be doubled.

In this experiment the gas evidently does work. In expanding upwards it has to overcome the atmospheric pressure of 15 lbs. on the square inch, together with the weight of the piston, which is 2 lbs. 1 oz. The section of the cylinder being 1 square inch, the gas, in expanding from p to A, does an amount of work equivalent to raising a weight of 17 lbs. 1 oz., or 273 oz., to a height of 273 inches. The effect, indeed, is the same as if the air above the piston were abolished, and a piston weighing 273 oz. were used.

Now, suppose that instead of allowing the gas to expand by heat, its volume be made constant by increasing the pressure; suppose the initial temperature to be 0° C. as before, and the pressure also the same as before—that is 273 oz.; if we heat the gas from 0° to 1° C., a weight of 1 oz. additional is required at p to keep the pressure constant; this augmentation of $\frac{1}{273}$, then, is the measure of the elastic force of the gas. If we heat it 2°, 2 oz. additional are required to keep the volume constant; and so on up to 273°, when an addition of 273 oz. is requisite; in short, the original pressure must be doubled, in order to keep the volume constant.

In both these experiments the quantity of matter heated is the same, and the temperature to which it was raised was in both cases the same; the quantities of heat, however, are very different. Suppose that in order to raise the temperature of the gas at a constant *volume* 273°, 10 grains of combustible matter were required, then, in order to raise the temperature of the gas, the *pressure* of which must be kept constant, an equal number of degrees would require $14\frac{1}{4}$ grains of the same kind of fuel. The heat produced by the additional $4\frac{1}{4}$ grains in the latter case is entirely consumed in lifting the weight. Now, the quantity of heat applied when the *volume* is constant is, to the quantity applied when the *pressure* is constant, in the proportion of 1 to 1·421. From this fact the mechanical equivalent of heat was first calculated. Its value may be determined somewhat in the following manner:—Let c, Fig. 6, be a cylindrical vessel with a base 1 square foot in area; let $p\,p$ mark the upper surface of a cubic foot of air at the temperature of 32° Fahr. or 0° C.   The height A p will then be 1 foot. Let the air be heated until its volume is doubled.

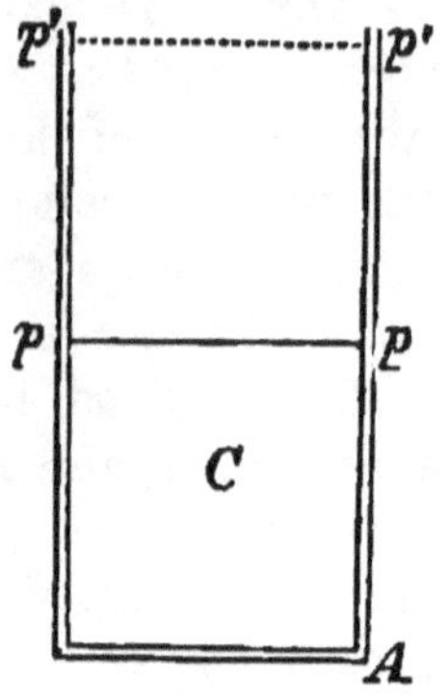

Fig. 6.

It will require it to be raised 203° C., or 490° Fahr. in temperature, and when expanded its upper surface will stand at $p'p'$, 1 foot above its former position; but in rising from $p\,p$ to $p'\,p'$, it has forced out the atmosphere, which exerts a pressure of 15 lbs. on every square inch of its upper surface; in other words, it has lifted a weight of 144 × 15 = 2,160 lbs. to a height of 1 foot.   The capacity for heat of the air thus expanded is 0·24, water being unity.   The weight of the cubic foot of air is 1·29 oz., hence the quantity of heat required to raise 1·29 oz. of air 490° Fahr., would raise a little less than ¼ of that weight of water 490° Fahr.   The exact quantity of water equivalent to the 1·29 oz. of air, is 1·29 × 0·24 = 0·31 oz.; but 0·31 oz. of water heated to 490°, is equal to 152 oz., or 9½ lbs. heated 1°.   Thus the heat imparted to a cubic foot of air, in order to double its volume, and enable it to lift the weight of 2,160 lbs. 1 foot high, would be competent to raise 9½ lbs. of water 1° Fahr. in temperature.

The air has been heated under a constant pressure, and we have seen that the quantity of heat required to raise the temperature of a gas under constant pressure a certain number of degrees is, to that required to raise the gas to the same temperature when its volume is kept constant, in the proportion of 1·42 to 1; hence we have the statement— 1·42 : 1 = 9·5 lbs. : 6·7 lbs. This shows that the quantity of heat necessary to augment the temperature of the cubic foot of air of constant volume 490°, would heat 6·7 lbs. of water 1°; deducting 6·7 lbs. from 9·5 lbs., we find that the excess of heat imparted to the air in the case where it is permitted to expand is competent to raise 2·8 lbs. of water 1° in temperature.   As already explained, this excess has been employed to lift 2,160 lbs. 1 foot high.   Dividing 2,160 by 2·8, we find that a quantity of heat sufficient to raise 1 lb. of water 1° Fahr.

in temperature is competent to raise a weight of 771·4 lbs. a foot high.*

Quitting this part of the subject, it will be instructive to show how the doctrine of specific and latent heat is taught by the new theory.

Take a piece of metal—lead for example—and apply to it a certain amount of heat. The heat is disposed of in two distinct ways—one of which is to impart that kind of motion to the particles by which the temperature is raised, and which is sensible to the thermometer; while another portion of the heat is expended in forcing the atoms of the lead into new positions, and this portion is lost as heat. In thus moving the particles into new positions, a portion of the heat is expended in performing *interior work;* and as the body cools,

---

* According to Dr. Tyndall, this method of calculating the equivalent of heat was first indicated by Dr. Mayer, a physician at Heilbronn, in Germany, in the spring of 1842. In August, 1843, Mr. Joule communicated a paper to the British Association at Cork, in which he describes a series of experiments on magneto-electricity, executed with a view to determine the mechanical value of the heat. In 1849 he obtained the following number for the mechanical equivalent of heat:—

772·692 from friction of water, mean of 40 experiments.
774·083   „   mercury „   50   „
774·987   .   „   cast-iron „   20   „

For reasons assigned in his paper, Mr. Joule fixes the exact equivalent of heat at 772 lbs., which is almost identical with Mayer's equivalent. In adjusting the claims of Mayer and Joule, it must be remembered that if Mayer started the theory, it was Joule who did the work, and established the theory on an experimental basis. The idea, however, that heat is not a fluid, but only a motion, is at least as old as Bacon and Locke; while Rumford and Davy showed, by experiment, that motion is convertible into heat. Carnot, Grove, Clausius, Helmholtz, Holtzmann, Rankine, and Thomson, may all be named as worthy labourers in the field; but the discovery of the exact equivalent of heat—that is, how much heat is represented by a given amount of motion, and how much motion can be produced from a given amount of heat—must we think, be shared between Mayer and Joule. Professor Tait, however, expresses his opinion that most of the results obtained by those who have worked at the dynamic theory of heat must rest on hypothetical grounds until we know more of the intimate structure of matter and the kind of motion to which heat belongs. " The general principle of the conservation of energy is founded on the exact determination of relations of equivalence betwee 1 the various forms of energy, and especially between heat on the one hand and each of the others in succession. This was begun by Joule in 1840, and had already produced a vast amount of important results before the appearance of Mayer's first paper." Professor Tait denounces the analogy as false between the falling together of material masses by gravitation, and the condensation of a gas by the external application of mechanical force. See *Philosophical Magazine,* 1863.

the forces which were overcome in separating the particles to a greater distance again resume their sway, and act by drawing the particles nearer together.

In gaseous bodies it is probable that the elementary atoms, whether different in size and weight, if of the same temperature, possess the same amount of energy called *heat*, the lighter atoms making good by velocity what they want in mass. The atomic weight of hydrogen is 1, that of oxygen by the new theory 16 ; so that a pound of hydrogen would contain sixteen times the number of atoms that a pound of oxygen would, since the number of atoms in a pound weight is inversely proportional to the atomic weight. Hence, in order to raise a pound of hydrogen 10°, say from 50° to 60°, sixteen times more heat would be required than to raise a similar weight of oxygen 10°. So also a pound of hydrogen, in falling through 10°, would yield sixteen times more heat than a like weight of oxygen in falling 10°. But in gaseous bodies there is no interior work, since there are no molecular attractions to be overcome. In solids and liquids, on the contrary, not only are there more atoms present in a given weight, but there are differences, due to the consumption of heat in interior work, and these differences represent the *specific heats* of bodies, or their *capacity for heat*, as it was formerly expressed, under the idea that some bodies were capable of holding a greater store than others of heat, considered as a fluid.

The nature of this interior work is further illustrated in the case of water just above and just below its point of maximum density, when it occupies the same bulk, though containing very different quantities of heat. " Suppose a pound of water heated from $3\frac{1}{2}°$ C. to $4\frac{1}{2}°$ C.—that is 1°—its volume at both temperatures is the same ; there has been no forcing asunder of the atomic centres, and still, though the volume is unchanged, an amount of heat has been imparted to the water sufficient, if mechanically applied, to raise a weight of 1,390 lbs. a foot high.* The interior work done here by the heat can be nothing more than the turning round of the atoms of water.

* 772 foot pounds being the mechanical equivalent for 1° Fahr., 1,390 lbs. will be the equivalent for 1° C.

It separates the attracting poles of the atoms by a tangential movement, but leaves their centres at the same distance asunder, first and last."

This interior work, then, may not consist in producing expansion, or pushing the atoms further apart, but may actually draw them closer together, as when they are thrown into that condition of polarity in which we suppose them to be when it separates two surfaces highly charged with opposite electricities, or when the particles of the magnet show equal and opposite forces at their extremities, or when the particles of a saline solution become built up into some regular crystalline form ; that is the kind of interior work which we may suppose is here referred to.

When a body changes its state, as when ice melts, as much heat enters it as would suffice to raise the same weight of water 143° Fahr. in temperature ; and when a pound of water at 212°, becomes a pound of steam at the same temperature, 967 times as much heat is required as would raise a pound of water 1° Fahr. in temperature. The heat thus lost, as far as the thermometer is concerned, is said to have become latent. Professor Tyndall says : " The fiction was invented that it was rendered latent :" but we cannot help remarking that such an expression as " internal work," is quite as much a fiction as that of " latent heat." Professor Tyndall's ingenious explanation of some of the phenomena which we have been discussing in this Introduction is briefly as follows. Referring to latent heat, he says :—

" The fluid of heat hid itself in some unknown way in the interstitial spaces of the water and of the steam. According to our present theory, the heat expended in melting is consumed in conferring potential energy upon the atoms. It is virtually the lifting of a weight. So, likewise, as regards the steam, the heat is consumed in pulling the liquid molecules asunder, conferring upon them a still greater amount of potential energy ; and when the heat is withdrawn, the vapour condenses, and the molecules again clash with a dynamic energy equal to that which was employed to separate them, and the precise quantity of heat then consumed now reappears.

"The act of liquefaction consists of interior work—work expended in moving the atoms into new positions. The act of vaporisation is also, for the most part, interior work; to which, however, must be added the external work performed in the expansion of the vapour, which makes place for itself by forcing back the atmosphere."

Note (page 43).—It was until lately supposed that all gases were equally diathermanous or transparent to the heating rays—for such distances, at least, as were under control in ordinary physical experiments. Thus Melloni found no sensible interception of heat in a distance of 18 or 20 feet of atmospheric air. It is very different with compound gases and vapours, as has been recently shown by the experiments of Tyndall. When the source of heat is a cube of copper filled with boiling water, and the column of gas 4 feet in length, the absorptive power of different gases is expressed by the following numbers :—

Air, oxygen, nitrogen, and hydrogen—each . . .	1	Nitrous oxide	355
Chlorine	39	Sulphuretted hydrogen .	390
Hydrochloric acid . . .	62	Marsh gas	403
Carbonic oxide and carbonic acid—each . . .	90	Sulphurous acid	710
		Olefiant gas	970
		Ammonia	1195

The absorptive power of vapours for rays of obscure heat is also remarkable, and the results have thrown a new light on certain cosmical phenomena. For example—it has been supposed that organic life could scarcely exist in planets most distant from the sun, on account of the low temperature prevailing there, the heat diminishing according to the law already explained (page 37). In such a surmise, however, the influence of a gaseous and vaporous envelope surrounding the planet has not been taken into account. The sun's rays, passing into such an atmosphere, would be partly retained by absorption, and thus prevent the cooling of the planet by radiation into space. The absorbent effect of the vapour in the earth's atmosphere is such, that its removal, for a single summer night, from the atmosphere which covers England, would be attended by the destruction of every plant which a freezing temperature could kill. The perfumes of many flowers have a remarkably high absorbent action for the obscure rays of heat. An atmosphere scented by the essential oil of patchouli had an absorbent action expressed by 30; with lavender it was 60; with cassia, 109; with aniseed, 372; so that the perfume of a flower-bed absorbs a large proportion of the radiant heat of low refrangibility that falls upon it.

Regarding the earth as a source of heat, at least 10 per cent. of its heat is intercepted by the aqueous and other vapours within 10 feet of the surface. Tyndall has also shown that the most powerfully absorbent gases are also the best radiators—a law which has long been established in the case of solids.

PART I.

CHAPTER I.

ON THE METHODS OF WARMING HOUSES BY MEANS OF OPEN
FIRE-PLACES, ETC., BEFORE AND AFTER THE INTRO-
DUCTION OF CHIMNEYS.

SOME instructive results may be obtained from the inquiry, how far the physical structure and mental characteristics of men are influenced by the comparative scarcity and abundance of some of the prime necessaries of life. The unequal distribution of solar heat over the earth is the cause of marked differences in national character; and where an artificial in-door climate is required, the ease or difficulty with which fuel is procurable has a great effect in promoting or interfering with the health and personal comforts of nations; and these, by a reflex action, contribute much to the formation of character. It has been remarked, that formerly the county of Buckingham being overgrown with wood, it was thought necessary to clear it away, on account of the refuge it afforded to the numerous robbers who infested the district. The people being thus deprived of fuel, became in the course of time stunted in growth and dulled in intelligence; until, by the extension of inland navigation, fuel became cheap, and then the inhabitants began to improve. In the county of Lancaster, on the contrary, the great abundance and cheapness of fuel were extremely favourable to health and comfort, and hence, according to Sir Gilbert Blane, the Lancasterians, especially the females, have become noted for their well-formed persons and handsome faces. In Yorkshire, and other parts of England where fuel is abundant, the people are generally well-grown, healthy, and intelligent, and their average height is said to exceed that of the inhabitants of other parts of England where fuel is scarce. The Norwegians are generally well lodged, each house being furnished with glass windows, and an iron *kakle* or stove; and on this account they are a better grown race than the North-Western Highlanders of Scotland, who procure their fuel with difficulty, and consume it in a rude and unthrifty manner. In France, where fuel is scarce, the average height of a man does not exceed 5 feet 4 inches; in the Netherlands, where fuel is more abundant, the average height is 5 feet $6\frac{1}{3}$ inches; and in England, where fuel is cheap and abundant, the average height is upwards of 5 feet 9 inches; in Sweden, where wood is as abundant as our coal, the peasants are tall, vigorous men, notwithstanding their uncleanly habits and the rigour of the climate.

I think it is Dr. Franklin who remarks, that where fuel is dear, working people live in miserable hovels, and are ragged, and have nothing comfortable about them; but where fuel is cheap, or managed to advantage, they have decent habitations, and are well provided with necessaries. The obvious reason is, that the working hours of such people are the profitable ones, and they who cannot afford sufficient fuel have fewer such hours in the day than those who have it cheap and plentiful; for much of the domestic work, whether of women or men, that requires but little bodily exercise, cannot well be performed when the fingers are numbed with cold. Poor people, therefore, in cold weather, go to bed earlier, and lie longer in the morning than they would do if they had good fires to sit by; so that their hours of work are not sufficient to produce the means of comfortable subsistence.

The comparative scarcity or abundance of fuel will, of course, greatly determine the method of creating an artificial climate within doors. In some parts of China, where fuel is scarce, the people secure themselves from the cold of winter by warm clothing, and this is probably a safer method even than our own, because with them the defence is constant and uniform, while our in-door clothing is thin, and we rely for warmth upon an atmosphere heated to the temperature of summer. If the person be well clothed, the coldest atmosphere can be breathed with safety, and its effect is often highly exhilarating, as in skating on the ice or in walking briskly. We often enjoy the warmth of a bed while breathing an atmosphere cold enough to freeze the water in the ewer. Hence it is better, as Dr. Arnott remarks, to clothe so as to feel comfortably warm in a room heated to 60°, or 62°, as a steady temperature, which it would not be dangerous to enter or to leave, than to dress lightly in a room heated by a common fire to 70°, or more, and which is liable to sink to 50°, or less.

In Normandy, where the cold of winter is severe, and fuel expensive, the lace-makers, in order to keep themselves warm, and at the same time to save fuel, agree with some farmer, who has cows in winter quarters, to rent the close sheds. The cows are tethered in a row on one side of the shed, and the lace-makers sit cross-legged on the ground on the other side, with their feet buried in straw. The cattle, being out in the fields by day, the poor women work all night for the sake of the steaming warmth arising from the animals. An analogous practice is recorded of the Nottingham lace-makers, who are said at one time to have been in the habit of crowding together in a small room for the sake of the heat engendered by their breath, in spite of the poisonous atmosphere thus produced.

The Laplander, during eight months of the year, inhabits a little hut with a small hole in the centre of the roof for the admission of light and the escape of smoke, and obtains heat from a smoky lamp of putrid oil, as the Esquimaux does in his hut of snow. The effect of this arrangement is, that the Laplanders are commonly afflicted with blear eyes. The Greenlander builds a larger hut, and contrives it better, but it is often occupied by half a dozen families, each having a lamp for warmth and for cooking, and the effect of this arrangement, according to the remark of a traveller, " is to create such a smell, that it strikes one not accustomed to it to the very heart." It is to be feared that a similar effect would be produced on any one of our readers were he to enter the huts of some of the Irish and Scottish peasantry, or even the rooms of the poor in our large towns.

The method of obtaining warmth in Persia is scarcely an improvement on the smoky lamp of the Laplanders and Green-landers. A large jar, called a *kourcy*, is sunk in the earthen floor, generally in the middle of the room. This is filled with wood, dung, or other combustible; and when it is sufficiently charred, the mouth of the vessel is shut in with a square wooden frame, shaped like a low table, and the whole is then covered with a thick wadded quilt, under which the family, ranged around, place their knees to allow the hot vapour to insinuate itself into the folds of their clothing; or when they desire more warmth, they recline with the quilt drawn up to their chins. The immovable position necessary for receiving the full benefit of the glowing embers is inconvenient; and the effluvia from the fuel is nauseous and deleterious. Headache is produced, and, from the number who sleep entirely under the quilt at night, suffocation is not an uncommon accident. The kourcy also serves for an oven, and the pot is boiled on its embers. This rude and unwholesome method is adopted in the noblest mansions of the cities, as well as in the dwellings of the poorer classes; only, in the former, a more agreeable fuel is burnt, and the ladies sit from morning till night under rich draperies spread over the wooden cover, endeavouring to overcome the soporific influence of the foul air by occasional cups of coffee, or the delightful fumes of the *kalioum*.

The burning of fuel in the midst of an apartment is by no means confined to nations whom we are in the habit of calling barbarous and uncivilised. In Seville and other parts of Spain, preparations for winter are made about the middle of October. The lower summer apartments are stripped of their furniture, and the chairs and tables are removed to other rooms on the opposite side of the court. The brick floors are covered with thicker mats than those used in the warm season. A flat and open brass pan, about 2 feet in diameter, raised a few inches from the ground by a round wooden frame, on which those who sit near it may rest their feet, is used to burn a sort of charcoal, made of brushwood, called *cisco*. The carbonic acid given off by this fuel is injurious to health; but such is the effect of habit, that the natives do not refer their ailments to the stifling fumes of their braziers.

The charcoal brazier is a very ancient method of warming

an apartment; the Greeks and other nations commonly used it, and sought to correct the deleterious nature of the fumes by burning costly odorous gums, spices, and woods.

The braziers of the Romans were elegant bronze tripods, supported by satyrs and sphinxes, with a round dish above for the fire, and a small vase below to hold perfumes. A kind of close stove was also used : but, in either case, the smoke was so considerable that the winter rooms were differently furnished from those appropriated to summer use. The former had plain cornices, and no carved work or mouldings, so that the soot might be easily cleared away. In order to prevent the wood from smoking, the bark was peeled off, and the wood kept long in water, and then dried and anointed with oil. It is not, however, evident how this plan should prevent the smoke of the burning fuel.

The great convenience of the brazier, and the apparent cleanliness of the fuel,* are arguments in favour of its continued use even in our own day. A visitor to some of our beautiful cathedrals in winter, during the time of divine service, Salisbury Cathedral for example, will be astonished to see on the floor of the choir two or three enormous braziers full of live charcoal; a peculiar odour arises from them, and pervades the building; a pleasing sensation creeps over the whole frame, and the tendency to sleep is often irresistible; persons troubled with cough cease to cough, and an unusual effort is required when the service is over to rise and quit the building.† The enormous size of the enclosure prevents any fatal effects from the abundant evolution of carbonic acid, nor have we ever heard of any well-authenticated case of injury to any one;

---

* Charcoal has this advantage over gas, alcohol, oil, and every kind of fuel that contains hydrogen, namely, that the products of combustion are dry; whereas, if hydrogen is present in the fuel, water is always formed in considerable quantity, every 1 part of hydrogen producing 9 parts of water. This is of importance in some cases, as in lecturing on a subject requiring dry apparatus, such as electricity, in the presence of a large audience, in a spacious theatre. Under such circumstances a small pan of live charcoal, resting on a large tile, and covered with a plate of copper placed under the prime conductor, will allow experiments to be performed with success even on a rainy day. A similar arrangement with a small gas stove is not so effectual, for the reason above stated. Some further illustrations of this kind will be given when we come to speak of the ventilation of lighthouses.

† This description applies as forcibly now as when it was written thirteen years ago, in the first edition of this work.

but a very little consideration will show that, in a smaller space, such as a room, this primitive method of obtaining warmth might lead to dangerous consequences. A single pound weight of charcoal consumes in burning $2\frac{6}{10}$ lbs. weight of oxygen, which is the quantity contained in between 13 lbs. and 14 lbs. weight of atmospheric air. Now, a good-sized room, 20 feet by 13 feet, and 10 feet high, does not contain more than about 200 lbs. weight of air, and as the combustion of 1 lb. of charcoal produces $3\frac{6}{10}$ lbs. of carbonic acid, which, by mingling with the rest of the air of the apartment, renders, at least, 36 lbs. weight of air unfit for respiration, making in all about 50 lbs. weight of air, it follows that, in such a room, the air will require, for healthy respiration, to be renewed many times an hour.

The fatal effects of the charcoal brazier, in a close room, are too frequently illustrated in the deaths of suicides, and sometimes in accidental deaths, as recorded in our newspapers. Some years ago, a picture dealer, near Hanover Square, availed himself of this means of destruction. We have been told of a case where two servants, who slept on the ground-floor, took a pan of charcoal into their bedroom one cold night, and were both found dead next morning. But, perhaps, the most remarkable case of self-murder, by this means, is that of the promising son of Berthollet, the celebrated chemist, seeing that the fatal act was conducted with all the method and precision of a scientific experiment. This young man became affected with great mental depression, which rendered life insupportable to him. Retiring to a small room, he locked the door, closed up every chink and crevice which might admit fresh air, carried writing materials to a table, on which he placed a seconds' watch, and then seated himself before it. He now marked the precise hour, and lighted a brazier of charcoal before him. He continued to note down the series of sensations he then experienced in succession, detailing the approach and rapid progress of delirium, until, as time went on, the writing became larger and larger, more and more confused, and at length illegible, and the writer fell dead upon the floor.

In many trades the workmen are habitually exposed to the

fumes of burning charcoal: bookbinders, engravers, cooks, &c., suffer much in health from this cause; and it is rare to find that any means are taken to ventilate the places in which they work. The use of gas is, however, in many cases superseding that of charcoal, and the change is most desirable.

In addition to the brazier, the ancient Romans were acquainted with flues for warming rooms and buildings; but as these were costly contrivances, their use was confined to the wealthy. These flues, forming what was called the *hypocaustum*, were conducted below the floor of the room intended to be warmed. The hypocausts were of two kinds—the first, constructed with flues running under the floor, and heated from a fire-place on the outside of the building; and the second kind formed like a low chamber, having its ceiling supported by small pillars or by dwarf walls, and sometimes with flues, leading from them to other apartments. The hypocaust discovered at Lincoln, of which Figures 7 and 8 are a ground plan and a section, will explain this construction.

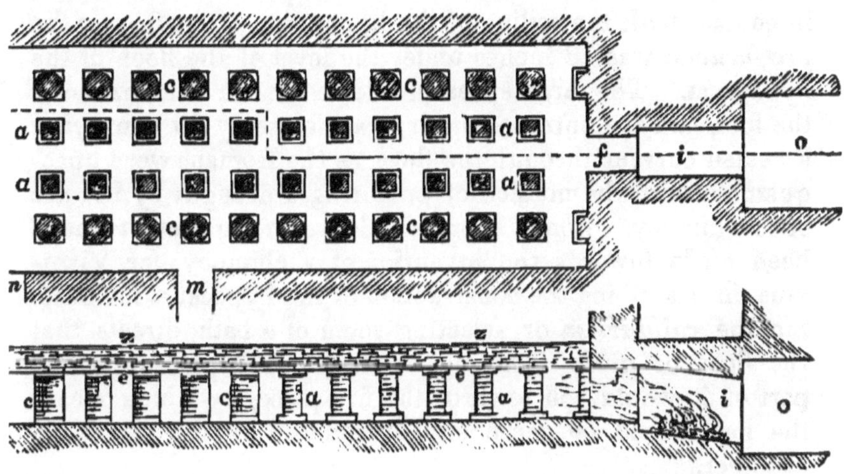

Figs. 7 and 8.—Ground plan and section of ancient hypocaust at Lincoln.

This hypocaust was 24½ feet long and 9½ feet wide; it contained four rows of brick pillars, *a a*, *c c*, two of which were square and two circular. The square pillars, *a a*, were

8 inches on the side and about 9 inches apart; the circular ones, *c c*, were 11 inches in diameter. Each pillar rested on a brick or tile for its base, and another tile formed its capital; thus making its height, which was that of the heating chamber, about 26 inches. The ceiling of the hypocaust was formed of large bricks; on them were placed courses of tiles, bedded in mortar, and on them a layer of stucco, to form the floor of the room *z* to be heated; the entire thickness of the floor being about 10 inches. The fire-hearth was at *i*; and the flame and smoke passed through the arched cavity or throat of the furnace *f* into the hypocaust. Two flues, *m n*, opened into the hypocaust; the flue *m*, which probably conducted the smoke and hot air under some other apartment, was about 6 inches high and 14 inches inside; its bottom was raised about 2 inches above the floor of the hypocaust. The flue *n* was about 6 inches square, and placed as much under as above the floor of the hypocaust; this seems to have been a smoke flue. The position given to these flues was probably intended to retain at all times the hottest portion of the vapour in contact with the ceiling of the hypocaust. The floor of the *præfurnium* was 18 inches under the level of the floor of the hypocaust. The large space provided for the combustion of the fuel, and the entrance of air, was necessary for conveying a heated current through the flues, as the Romans were unacquainted with the method of procuring a draught by the use of a chimney. Some approach, however, appears to have been made towards the invention of a chimney, for Vitruvius, in describing the construction of the hypocaust for heating the *calidarium* or sweating-room of a bath, directs that the floor be made inclining, so that a ball placed on any part of it would roll towards the fire-place, by which means the heat would be more equally diffused in the sweating-chamber.

The hypocaust is well known to the Chinese, and is in common use about Pekin, where the winter climate is severe. The houses of the better class are built with double walls and with hollow flues extending beneath the floors. The fire-place is constructed either against the exterior wall of the apartment to be heated, or in an inferior room adjoining; by which means the annoyance from dust and smoke are avoided, as well as the inconvenience of servants entering the room to attend to the fire. From the fire chamber proceeds a main flue, which is connected with the horizontal flue, *a b*, (Fig. 9). From this another flue, *c d*, proceeds at right angles to about three fourths of the extent of the room ; these flues are perforated with holes at proper distances, in order to give out the smoke and heated air equally over the whole area of the flooring. Two horizontal flues are built in or attached to the side walls, as at *f g*, in order to carry off the smoke into the external air. The flooring of the apartment consists of flat tiles or flagstones, neatly embedded in

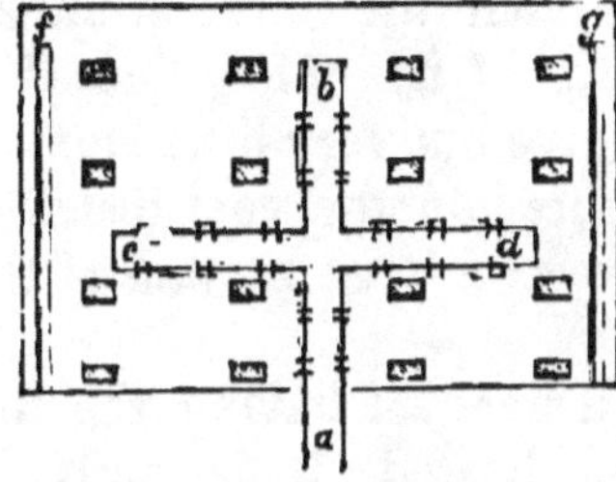

Fig. 9.—Chinese hypocaust.

cement, so as to prevent the escape of the smoke or heated air from the flues beneath into the room; these stones or paving tiles, resting on blocks of stone or bricks, may be of any thickness required for the extent of the air flues which are employed. By this contrivance, the heat, coming in contact with every part of the floor, is uniformly diffused over the apartment. The floors, also, being very imperfect conductors of heat, being once sufficiently heated by the flues, and the apertures of the main flues outside being stopped, retain a sufficient heat for domestic comfort during many hours. The paving tiles of the rooms are often made of ornamental porcelain ware of considerable thickness. Even the benches and sleeping places are warmed by this contrivance. These are built hollow, with bricks, in the form of a square bench, or oblong bed; and communicating with the flues, or having their own separate flue, are thus heated. Those who dislike lying on the hot bricks, or on the felt mat that is spread over them, suspend from the ceiling over the heated bench a kind of hammock, made of coarse cloth ; and thus they enjoy warmth and repose. In the morning, the bed places are covered with carpets and mats, on which the inmates sit.

The ingenious economy of the Chinese (from which we

might often borrow a useful lesson) prevents the flues from becoming choked by soot. Instead of employing pit coal of good quality, they make use of the inferior or small refuse coal for this purpose, and mix it with a compost of clay, earth, cow-dung, or any refuse vegetable matter; and then form it into balls, which are dried in the sun or open air. This method is not adopted on account of any scarcity of fuel, for coal is abundant in China; but the Chinese, unlike the English, know how to take care of it. They find that their fire-balls, during combustion, give out very little smoke; and they are extensively manufactured in the coal districts, and distributed by canal carriage over a large portion of the empire.

In the inferior class of houses, instead of having the fire outside the house or room to be heated, it is built in the corner of the dwelling room. A pit is dug for the body of the fire chamber and draught-hole; and the top, or head of the stove, is used for the different operations of cooking.

That no portion of heat may be lost, or escape into the room directly from the fire, beyond what is necessary to maintain a given temperature, vessels of water are placed on the head of the stove, and thus the heat, which would otherwise be lost, is absorbed and economised; while it affords, by its evaporation, the necessary supply of moisture to preserve the atmosphere of the room in a healthy condition as to moisture.

The Chinese call a stove which is heated by a furnace, a *kang*; the *ti-kang* is a furnace of which the flue runs under the floor or pavement of a room; and the *kao-kang* is that used for heating benches and beds. There is yet a third variety, the *tong-kang*, which is formed in the wall, and this differs from the *ti-kang* only in being perpendicular instead of horizontal. In the *tong-kang*, the heating flue is carried along the floor, with openings from it, at which the heated air and smoke ascend into the spaces of a hollow wall, thus nearly approaching the principle of the chimney. A *tong-kang* was erected by Sir William Chambers, in 1761, for heating the orangery at Kew Palace. In imitation of the Chinese method, he introduced heated air through an air pipe or flue in contact with the heating flues. In Fig. 10, the flue from the furnace is shown at *a*, the *tong-kang* flues at *c*, and the hot air flue at *e*.

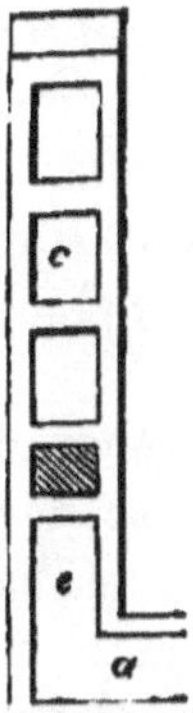

It is scarcely possible to improve upon these refinements of the Chinese, except by the introduction of the chimney, the origin of which has been the subject of much learned discussion. Among drawings of Saxon dwellings we look in vain for that necessary feature of the house. " The Saxon thegne built his hall from the woods on his demesne, by the labour of his bondmen : it was thatched with reeds or straw, or roofed with shingle. In plan it was little more than

Fig. 10. its name implied, a capacious apartment, which in the daytime was adapted to the patriarchal hospitality of the owner, and formed at night a sort of stable for his servants, to whose accommodation their master's was not much superior in a small adjoining chamber. There was as yet but a slight perception of the decencies of life. The fire was kindled in the centre of the hall; the smoke made its way out through an opening in the roof immediately above the hearth or by the door, windows, or eaves of the thatch. The lord and his " hearth-men," a significant appellation given to the most familiar retainers, sat by the same fire at which their repast was cooked, and at night retired to share the same dormitory, which served also for a council chamber." * During the wars of that early period, the traces of Roman occupation, so far as dwellings were concerned, seem to have gradually disappeared, but there is every reason to believe that there were no chimneys in ancient Roman houses. And if the Roman houses in Britain were unprovided with chimneys, the Saxon dwellings were not likely to be supplied with them; indeed, all the descriptions tally with that already given of the rude hall, with its central hearth. Above this hearth, on the roof, was a turret or *louver*, filled with boards, which partially excluded wind and rain, and allowed the smoke to escape. This turret was often a great improvement to the

* " Some Account of Domestic Architecture in England from the Conquest to the end of the thirteenth century." By T. Hudson Turner. 8vo., Oxford, 1851.

external appearance of the building. The windows of this hall were placed high, and filled with oiled linen or *louver* boards. The heavy doors were opened by latches, and the walls were either rough, or coarsely painted, or hung with arras, which was suspended from hooks at the distance of three or four inches from the walls. The floor was of stone or earth, with a raised platform at one end, where were placed the massive table and benches.

The houses of small landholders and farmers were generally one story high, and if of two stories, the roof was so deep as to shut out the light from the upper rooms. The hall and kitchen formed one apartment, which was open to the timbers of the roof, and, in some cases, was furnished with a *louver* and a window, that could be closed with a shutter. When these houses had a separate sleeping apartment, old and young occupied it, and several reposed in one bed. Servants slept on the kitchen floor. Cottages had neither *louver* nor *loupe*, and the inmates slept round the fire.

The strongholds which were built about the time of the Conquest were several stories in height, and their roofs being used as a terrace for defence, the central hearth and *louver* were impracticable. The necessity of providing some exit for the smoke seems to have stimulated invention, and, accordingly, we find the germs of the modern fire-place and chimney in one of these strongholds. In the great guard-room of Conisborough Castle, erected in or near the Anglo-Saxon period, is a large fire-hearth. The mantel is supported by a wide arch, with two transom stones running under it; the back of the fire-place, where it joins the hearth, is in a line with the walls of the room, and the recess at the mantel is formed by the back of the fire-place sloping outwards, as it rises into the thickness of the wall, until it reaches a loop-hole on the outside, where the smoke finds an exit. Fig. 11 is an elevation and section of this fire-place, in which A is the floor of the room, E the mantel, and O the loop-hole.

In other castles erected about the same period, the hearth was formed in the thickness of the wall, and the conical smoke-tunnel ended in a loop-hole, as at Conisborough Castle. Fig. 12 is another elevation and section of these ancient contrivances for carrying off the smoke.   It is from Rochester Castle.   In the old palace at Caen, which was inhabited by the Conqueror while he was Duke of Normandy, the great guard-chamber contains two spacious recessed fire-hearths in the north wall, still in good preservation, from which the smoke was carried away in the same manner as in the above examples.

The transition from these contrivances to the common chimney would seem to be easy; but history has failed to record the inventor, or to define the place where the chimney was first used. It has been well remarked by Mr. Hudson Turner, that in seeking to ascertain the degree of antiquity which should

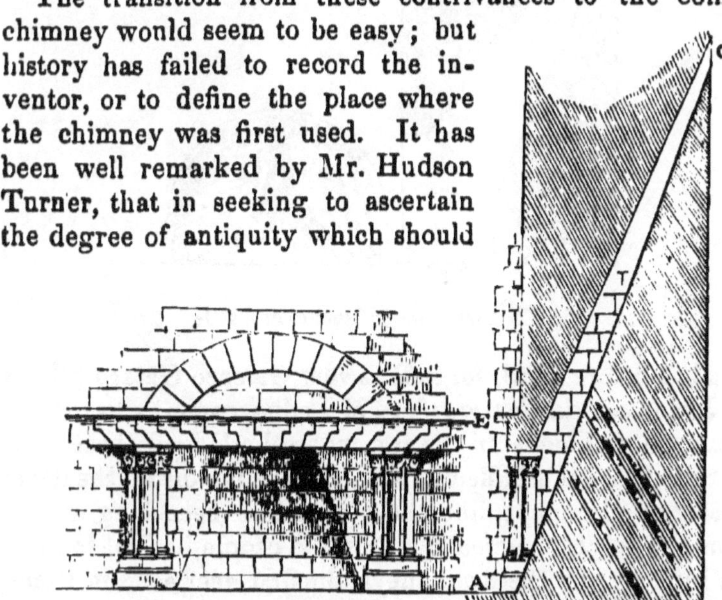

· Fig. 11. Elevation and Section of Fire-place in Conisborough Castle.

be assigned to the chimney, facts are often strangely contradictory of the statements of respectable writers. Existing remains prove that perpendicular flues were constructed in this country in the twelfth century, yet Leland, in the sixteenth century, speaks with surprise of a chimney in Bolton Castle. We can only suppose that the principle of the modern chimney was understood long before the practice of constructing it became general.* Chimneys seem to have been common at Venice before the middle of the fourteenth century. An inscription over the gate of the school of *Santa Maria della Carita* states, that in 1347, a great many chimneys were thrown down by an earthquake, a fact which is

* "Domestic Architecture," pp. 17, 18.

confirmed by John Villani, who refers the event to the evening of the 25th of January.　Chimneys had also been in use

Fig. 12. Fire-place in Rochester Castle.

‚at Padua before 1368, for in that year Galeazo Gataro relates,
that Francisco da Carraro, lord of Padua, came to Rome, and
finding no chimneys in the inn where he lodged (because at
that time fire was kindled in a hole in the middle of the floor),
caused two chimneys, like those that had been long used in
Padua, to be constructed by the work-people he had brought
with him.　Over these chimneys, the first ever seen in Rome,
he affixed his arms, which were remaining in the time of
Gataro.　Winwall House, in Norfolk (which has been described as the most ancient and perfect specimen of Norman
domestic architecture in the kingdom), has not only recessed
hearths, but flues rising from them, carried up in the external
and internal walls.　Now, if Winwall House really be an
Anglo-Norman edifice, its chimneys must have been built
in the twelfth century, and, consequently, the claim of the
Italians to the invention cannot be supported.　The chimneys
at Kenilworth and Conway were also probably erected anterior
to the date of those on which the Italians rest their claim.
Leland, also, in his account of Bolton Castle, which he says
was " finished or Kynge Richard the 2 dyed," notices the
chimneys.　" One thynge I muche notyd in the hawle of
Bolton, how chimeneys were conveyed by tunnells made on

the syds of the walls betwyxt the lights in the hawle, and by
this means, and by no covers, is the smoke of the harthe in
the hawle wonder strangely conveyed." Even when some
form of chimney was adopted, it sometimes happened that
only one of the private apartments was so provided, namely,
the chamber next the hall on the upper story. The
chimney-piece varied little from the twelfth to the fifteenth
century. We have seen that the fire-place at Rochester
Castle has a semicircular arch with zigzag ornaments, and
that at Conisborough shafts and jambs, and what is called a
straight arch, that is, the mantel-piece, is of several stones
joggled together. The chimney was not always carried
up to the top of the wall, the vent for the smoke being
sometimes merely pierced through the wall. At the same
period, namely, the twelfth century, the kitchen seems to have
had an open roof, cooking being performed at an iron grate
in the middle of the apartment.

Wooden lattices and shutters continued in use in the thirteenth century, although linen and glass were also partially
used. Church windows were occasionally covered in with
canvas, as is proved by the fabric accounts of Westminster
Abbey, and other churches. Fire-places differed little, except in
being of lighter construction. Flues were ordinarily cylindrical
shafts of masonry carried above the ridge of the roof. Orders
to raise the chimneys of the king's houses are frequent in the
time of Henry III. The mantels of such fire-places were sometimes elaborately carved or painted, with such designs as the
twelve months of the year, the figure of Winter with sad visage
and contorted body, &c. One flue sometimes carried off the
smoke from two fire-places. But flues were not always used
even in royal apartments; hearths of stone in the centre of
the room, and *louver* roofs, were still employed. Fire-places and
flues were, however, sometimes made of plaster, so that they
may have existed in buildings which preserve no trace of
them.

In the fourteenth century the hearth in the middle of the
hall still existed as a general custom. Huge logs were piled
on andirons, and the smoke escaped through the *louver*.
" This custom had its advantages. The heat was greater and

more generally diffused, which in a room of such size was of importance, while the smoke from wood or charcoal, when well ignited, is not considerable. Many *louvers* remain in halls of the fifteenth century. There are also frequent ex- amples of fire-places and chimneys in the fourteenth century, even in the hall, though they are more usual in the smaller apartments." *

It is not our duty to trace the further history of the chimney, nor to notice the methods by which the chimney shaft became so prominent and beautiful a feature in buildings during the reigns of the Tudors. It is sufficient to remark, that when once introduced in England, the merits of chimneys were soon appreciated, for we find it stated, that in the reign of Queen Elizabeth, apologies were made to visitors if they could not be accommodated with rooms provided with chimneys, and ladies were frequently sent out to other houses, where they could have the enjoyment of this luxury, for such it must be called, at this period, when the poorer class of houses was not yet furnished with it.

Wood was the ordinary fuel till the seventeenth century, and this was burnt on the capacious hearth, the logs being

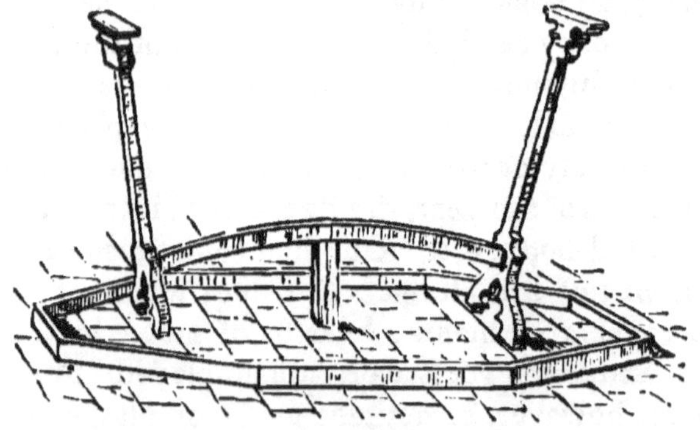

Fig. 13. Andiron.

confined within the two standards (Fig. 13) of the andiron,† their ends resting on the billet bar, for the purpose of admitting

* "Domestic Architecture," vol. ii. pp. 39, 40.
† Probably a corruption of the Anglo-Saxon *brand-isen* or brand-iron. Some say it was *hand* or *end* iron.

the air below them, and thus promoting combustion. For the large kitchen fire, the standards and billet bars were very strong and massive, but usually quite plain. In the hall, that ancient seat of hospitality, they were also strong and massive, to support the weight of the huge logs; but the standards were kept bright, or ornamented with brass rings, knobs, rosettes, heads and feet of animals, and various grotesque forms. In kitchens, and in the rooms of common houses, the andiron, as its name implies, was of iron; but in the hall the standards were of copper or brass, and sometimes of silver. The spacious receptacle was furnished with seats on each side of the hearth, and the snug chimney corner was the post of honour. When the whole family assembled to enjoy a leisure hour, it was round the hearth that they sat; with it was associated their ideas of domestic comfort and conviviality, and the word *hearth* became synonymous with *home.* In some of our rural districts the custom is still retained of the whole family sitting under the capacious chimney-breast, and it is an honoured custom which we hope may long continue to exist.

In smaller rooms, where the fire was made in a wide and deep recess, each standard was fixed into the back of the hearth by a lateral bar. Thus in Fig. 14, which represents the andirons in the hall at Vicar's Close, Wells, will be seen the standards, the billet bar, and the *reredos* or back of the fire-place, which in deep recesses brings the fire into the room. When the hearth was of moderate size, the andiron, as well as the *reredos,** was movable.†

So long as wood existed in abundance coal was not sought after for the purposes of domestic fuel. It was supposed that the fumes of coal had a peculiarly corrupting effect upon the air, and were most injurious to health. Its value, however, was appreciated by brewers, dyers, smiths, and others, whose occupations lead to the consumption of a large quantity of

---

* Also called *rere-dorse.* Hollinshed says—" Now haue we manie chimnies, and yet our tenderlings complaine of rheumes, catarhs, and poses. Then had we none but rere-dosses, and our heads did never ake."

† On the mantel-shelf is a scroll, bearing an inscription, which solicits the prayers of the vicars in favour of Sir Richard Pomroy, and expresses solicitude for the safety of his soul.

fuel, and towards the close of the thirteenth century coal was imported into London from Newcastle for the use of those trades. In 1306, however, parliament petitioned the king to prohibit the use of the noxious fuel in the city. A royal proclamation was accordingly issued prohibiting the use of coal, and as this failed in its effect, a commission was issued

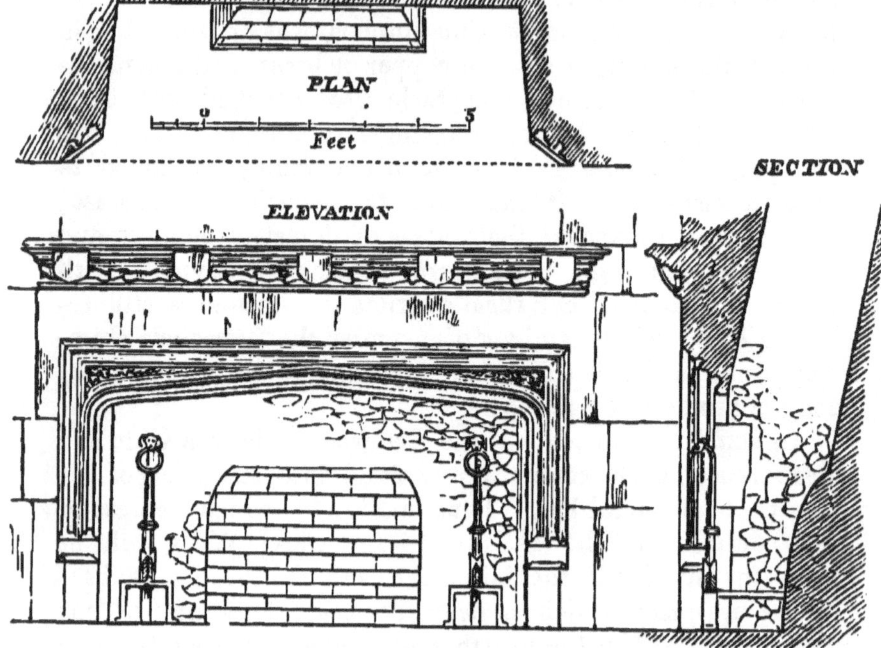

Fig. 14. Fire-place in the hall at Vicar's Close, Wells.

for the purpose of ascertaining who burned sea-coal within the city and its neighbourhood, and to punish them by fine for the first offence, and by the demolition of their furnaces if they persisted; but even these severe proceedings failed to put down the nuisance. A law was therefore passed making the burning of sea-coal within the city a capital offence, and permitting its use only in the forges of the neighbourhood. In the reign of the first Edward a man was tried, convicted, and executed, for burning sea-coal in London.* Even in districts

* Sir Gilbert Blane, in his "Select Dissertations on several subjects of Medical Science" (London, 1822), relates this circumstance in a note, p. 127, on the authority of "the late Mr. Astle, keeper of the records in the Tower:"

where coal abounded, it was not used as a domestic fuel; for we read that in 1349, in the religious house at Whalley, peat, with a very little wood, was the only fuel used.

So deeply rooted was the prejudice against coal, that it was not until the commencement of the seventeenth century that its use became more general. Ladies had an idea that a coal fire injured their complexions, and they would not even enter a house or room where the obnoxious fuel was used ; * nor would they even partake of meat which had been roasted at a coal fire. When Ben Jonson had to entertain a party of guests at his house, he warmed his room with a charcoal fire; but, on ordinary occasions, he used coal; for we find that, on more than one occasion, his flue caught fire from an accumulation of soot.

In an inventory, dated 1603, of the goods of Sir Thomas Kytson, at Hengrave Hall, in Suffolk, mention is made of " a cradell of iron for the chimnye to burne sea-cole with," and also " j fier sholve made like a grate to seft the sea-cole with." The cradle here mentioned was probably nothing more than a few bars bent into a semicircle, and fastened into the upright wall over the hearth.

There was, doubtless, good reason for the objections of our ancestors to the use of sea-coal, for the chimney fire-places were usually made in the form of a large square recess, and the breast of the chimney was of the same size as the recess itself. In order to rid sea-coal of its noxious sulphurous vapour, Sir John Hacket and Octavius de Strada proposed, in 1626, to convert the coal into coke, and thus make it as agreeable a fuel for chambers as wood and charcoal. A

among which " he had discovered a document importing that a person had been tried, convicted, and executed, for burning coal within the city in the reign of Edward I."

* This prejudice existed among French ladies until recently, when scarcity of wood fuel has somewhat mitigated it. It is related that an ambassador at Paris had issued cards for a large assembly, when, on the appointed evening, no ladies appeared, but gentlemen only—a report having been circulated that his lordship's rooms were heated by means of coal fires.

Another prejudice on the part of the French is, that our island is constantly enveloped in the smoke of our coal fires, so that we never see the blue sky. I was rambling one fine afternoon on the French coast, when, getting into conversation with a Frenchman, he looked towards England, then at the blue sky, and remarked, with a look of inquiring pity, " *Il ne fait jamais beau comme cela en Angleterre ?*"

patent was obtained for the purpose, but the speculation did not succeed, as the vapour given off by the coke was found to be nearly as unpleasant as that from coal.

About this time a great improvement was made in France in fire-places by Louis Savot (born 1579; died 1640), a licentiate in the Faculty of Medicine at Paris. He was early impressed with the maxim of Vitruvius, that it is quite necessary for an architect to have some acquaintance with medicine, and he saw no reason why a physician should not have some knowledge of architecture. Accordingly he studied architecture from a sanitary point of view; and in 1624 published a work on the subject, and which, as will be seen by the note below,* passed through several editions. Savot pointed out the means for curing that domestic plague —a smoky chimney; and, like a true physician, set about investigating the causes of the disease. He saw the evils of large chimneys, and the necessity for a due supply of air to the fire. The fire should be proportioned to the size of the chimney, and *vice versâ*, and smoke may often be prevented by lowering the mantel. " In small rooms," he says, " the chimney often smokes unless the door or window be open, not only because the fire devours and carries off a large quantity of the air of the room, but also because the fire requires a continual supply of air for its support; so that, if a proportional quantity of air which the fire consumes and sends up the chimney does not enter the room (which it cannot do in small rooms with a large fire), the fire languishes, and the smoke increases, since flame is nothing more than a kindled smoke, and smoke is only an extinguished flame, or, at least, not yet kindled." He also points out how the chimney may be too long for the fire, or how one large chimney may draw upon another smaller one ; and he recommends that the flue be smooth on the inside, to diminish friction. To improve the draught of the fire he raised the hearth about 4 inches, and lowered the mantel so as to make the opening of the fire-place about 3 feet high. The width

* " *L'Architecture Françoise des Bastimens particuliers.*" *Composée par M. Louis Savot*, 1624. There were also editions in 1642, 1673, and 1685, this last *augmentée de M. Blondel.*

between the jambs was reduced to 3 feet; the jambs from the mantel were to be carried up sloping to the waist, or where the flue begins to be of uniform width, and the opening of the fire-place was formed like an arch. But, where the fire-place could not be conveniently altered, Savot perforated with small holes a plate of iron, the width and length of which were nearly equal to the hearth, and this was fixed 3 inches above the tiles of the common hearth. On this perforated plate he placed a *grill de fer* of the same length as the billets to be burned, and raised 9 inches above the plate; the wood was placed on the grate, the charcoal on the perforated plate, and the hearth received the ashes; the air, rising through the small holes, made the charcoal burn briskly, and this so much assisted the burning of the wood, that a rapid draught up the chimney was established, and smoke prevented.

In Savot's description of the fire-place used to heat the *Cabinet des Livres*, at the Louvre, we have the first recorded

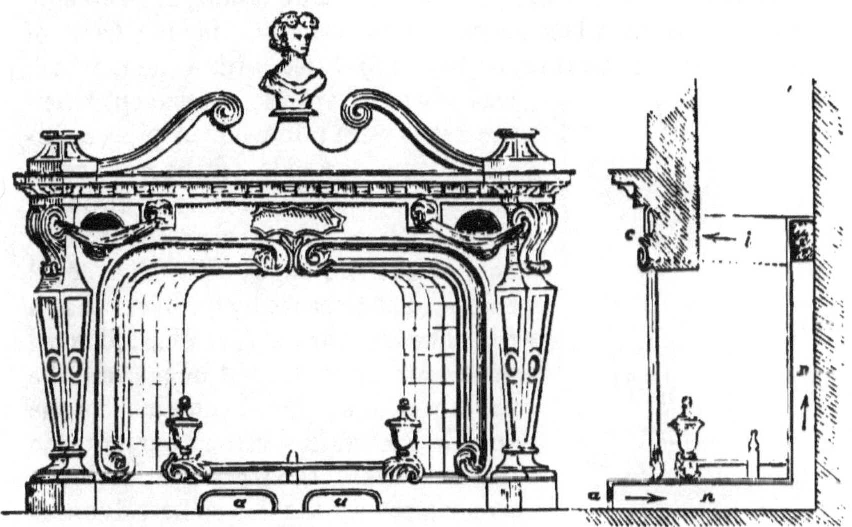

Fig. 15. Savot's Fire-place in the Louvre.   Fig. 16.

attempt at combining the cheerfulness of an open fire with the economy of an enclosed stove. Fig. 15 is a front view, and Fig. 16 a vertical section of this ingenious contrivance.

The hearth was a thick iron plate placed above the old hearth, with an interval, *n*, of 3 inches between them. The two sides, or covings of the fire-place, were also formed of thick iron plates, placed 3 inches from the jambs. The space, *n*, at the back, and the spaces at the sides, communicated with the space, *n*, under the hearth ; two pipes, or channels, *i*, communicating with these hollow spaces, opened into the room at *c*, as shown by the dotted line in the section ; these spaces could be closed at pleasure. When the fire was burning, the iron hearth, and the plates which formed the sides or covings, and the back, became very hot. The cold air at the floor, entering by the openings at *a*, into the space, *n*, was heated by the hearth, and rising into the spaces at the back and sides, had its temperature further increased ; it then entered the channels, *i*, and escaped at *c*, thus diffusing an agreeable warmth over the whole room.

About the year 1658, the project for burning coke, instead of coal, was revived by Sir John Winter, who invented an improved fire-place for the purpose. The cradle, or fire-cage, was placed on a box about 11 inches high, in the front of which was an opening, *o* (Fig. 17), fitted with a door, which was always kept closed, except when the ashes were removed. A pipe, *a*, intsered into the side of the box, communicated with the external air, at a level of 2 or 3 feet below the bottom bars of the fire-cage ; this pipe could be closed at pleasure by a valve. When the coke or *charked* (*i.e.*, charred) coal in the fire-cage did not burn well, the valve was opened, and the air from the outside rushed in a strong current into the box, and, by its powerful blast, soon roused up the fire ; the valve was then closed, and all communication with

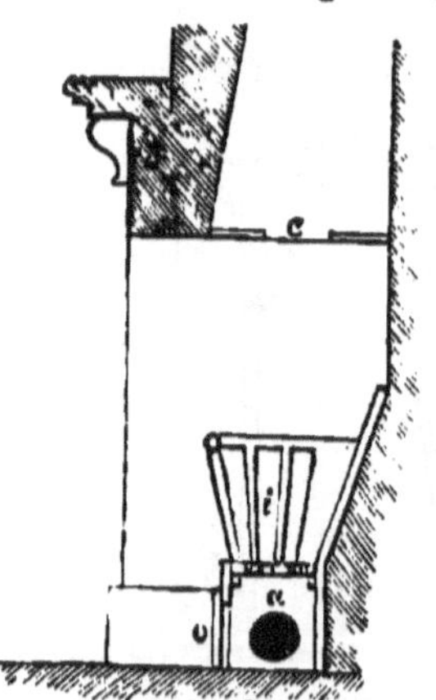
Fig. 17. Winter's Fire-place.

the external air was thus cut off. The flue was closed with an iron plate or *register*,* that moved on a hinge. It had an

* Savot's book is the first in which we have seen the *register plate* mentioned. He states, on the authority of Scammozzi, that it was customary in

opening, *c*, 8 inches square, for carrying the smoke into the chimney, and this was found large enough for a fire-place of any dimensions. This ingenious contrivance does not seem to have succeeded, although both it and the arrangement described by Savot have, with slight variations, been brought forward several times within the last three-quarters of a century, and patented as notable inventions.

In 1678, Prince Rupert invented a fire-place, so contrived that the draught took a downward direction before entering the flue, as shown in Fig. 18, in which *a* x is a wall built at a distance of 10 inches from the back of the hearth recess, and carried up to the mantel, where it is terminated by the wall x, thus completely closing all communication between the flue and the room. An opening, *a*, is made in this wall, 10 inches high, and of the same width as the length of the grate, and its sill is 2 inches above the top rib of the grate. Fixed within the chimney is a plate of iron, *i*, placed perpendicularly, so as to divide it into two equal parts. To the upper edge of this plate is hinged an iron door, *c*, as long as the chimney is wide, and this door can be brought into the position *c*, or

Fig. 18. Prince Rupert's Fire-place.

into that indicated by the dotted lines at *e*. The fuel grate stands on the hearth, and is placed nearly in a line with the wall of the room. At the back of the ash-pit is a brick that closes the aperture through which the soot is removed. When the fire is first lighted, the smoke door, *c*, is pushed back, and

England, when a brazier full of fuel was well lighted, and had ceased to smoke, to pass an iron plate (*porte de fer legère*) across the chimney, and so confine the heat to the room. This plate appears to be the same as the *damper*, but the term *register* is much older. In the furnaces of the alchemist, openings left for the supply of air, which could be contracted or closed by means of clay, were named registers. Thus, Ben Jonson says:—

> " Look well to the register,
> And let your heat still lessen by degrees."

when the draught is once established, this door is drawn forward, and the smoke being thus prevented from flowing upwards, reverberates downwards, and passes the lower edge of the division plate, *i*, and rises between it and the back of the hearth into the chimney flue. In boisterous weather, or with such a fire-place, in an upper room, where the chimney is short, another iron door, *r*, is hung under the edge of the mantel, in front of the fire-place, and extending the whole width of the opening. Its breadth varies according to circumstances, but it is made so as to reach within 2 inches of the upper bar of the fire-grate, when hanging in the position shown by the dotted lines at *s*. This converts the fire into a furnace, and the room will, in such case, be " warmer than it would be with a fire four times the size made in a common cradell." When the smoke flows regularly through the aperture, *a*, this door is thrown back out of use, as at *r*. In some cases, the ordinary fire-board or *fire-cloth* was used instead of this door.

" The fire-cloth," says Mr. Bernan,* " was a common appendage to a fire-place, particularly where wood was burned, for then the flue was large, the hearth wide and low, and the mantel high ; when the chimney smoked in certain winds only, the cloth was suspended, when wanted, from each corner of the mantel-piece. But when the disease was unremitting, the curtain was fixed by rings, running on a rod that went across the fire-place; when not used, it was drawn to one side, like the curtain of a cottage window; very often the fire-cloth was contrived to be drawn up like a modern Venetian blind, and made so deep as to reach from the mantel to the hearth, and serve the office of a fire-board, when there was no fire in the yawning chimney. The first variety of smoke-cloth was seldom more than 15 inches deep, and was frequently made of painted leather ; but in good houses, the suspended fire-cloths were usually of damask and tapestry. None of these contrivances are yet extinct."

In 1680, a stove was exhibited at the fair of St. Germains, near Paris, in which the smoke not only descended, but was

* " History and Art of Warming and Ventilating Rooms and Buildings," 2 vols., 1845.

also consumed. It is formed of hammered iron, and stands on the floor of the room. The fuel, wood, or coal, is contained in a vase, c (Fig. 19), with a grating at o, and this vase is

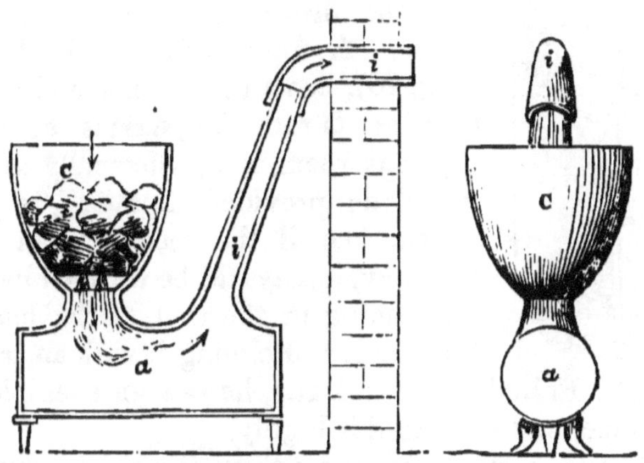

Fig. 19. Smoke-consuming Stove.

placed on a box or cylinder, a, from which a pipe, i, is carried into a flue, which has no communication with the hearth recess, nor with the air, except at the top, above the roof. The vase being filled with fuel, some dry brushwood is placed upon it. The upper part of the pipe, i, is then heated by a lamp, or hot iron, in order to establish a current of air from the cylinder, o, which current passes down through the fuel in the vase. A piece of lighted paper is then placed on the brushwood, and the downward current carries the flame downwards, first igniting the wood, and then the coals, and consuming the smoke in descending. The products of combustion thus carried into the cylinder, a, rise through the pipe, i, into the chimney. The descending current may be made evident by holding a flame over the vase, when it will be drawn downwards.   Justel, who described this arrangement to the Royal Society in 1681, says, that " the most fœtid things, matters which stink abominably when taken out of the fire, in this engine make no ill scent, neither do red herrings broiled thereon. On the other hand, all perfumes are lost, and incense makes no smell at all when burned therein." An improved edition of this stove was made by Dr. Franklin, as will be noticed further on.

An economical method of heating two rooms by one are is described by Savot.   A plate of iron is made to sepa-rate the fire-places of the two adjacent rooms.   A fire made on the hearth, *a*, (Fig. 20), heats the plate, *n*, and this, in its turn, by its radiation, warms the air in the adjacent room, *e*, as effectually as a stove would do, provided its flue, *i*, is properly closed.   Or if the second room have no chimney, it may still be warmed by making an opening in the wall, at the back of the fire-place, and closing it with an iron plate.

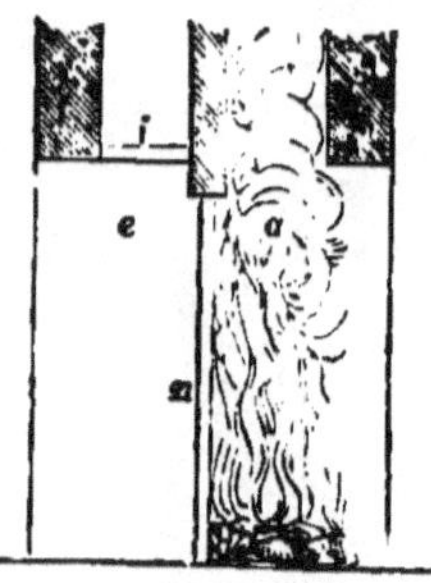

Fig. 20.

When Dr. Franklin was in Paris, he saw an example of this contrivance, and estimated it highly.

In all these early contrivances there is much ingenuity, and we bring them forward thus prominently, because they are really the legitimate ancestors of many reputed modern inventions, whose authors are either ignorant of, or have failed to acknowledge, their descent therefrom.   Patentees would often be spared much anxiety and expense, if they would condescend to study the subject to which their invention refers, before they introduce to the public a contrivance which may have been as well, if not better, done a long time before.   Discoveries in science and inventions in the useful arts, require genius often of a high order; and although it is not expected that all inventors should have the genius of Watt, it is at least required that they should possess some of his method of patient research.

But there is one writer, whose inventions have especially served as the type of many a modern fire-place, and at the time of their introduction in 1713, showed a great and sudden advance in the art of warming apartments.   It has been said, with what authority will be seen in the Appendix, that the author of the treatise referred to was no less a man than the Cardinal Polignac, who, under the assumed name of Gauger, published a treatise, entitled "*La Mechanique du Feu, ou l'Art d'en augmenter les effets et d'en diminuer la dépense, contenant le Traité de Nouvelles Cheminées qui echauffent plus que les Cheminées ordinaires, et qui ne sont point sujettes à fumer.*"   This treatise was reprinted at Amsterdam in 1714, and a translation of it, by Dr. Desaguliers (from which we are about to quote), was published in London in 1716.

In the preface the author has some sensible observations on the subject of warming and ventilation.   After remarking that persons who judge of the value of machines by their complication, will not find his inventions to their taste, he bestows a compliment on those who estimate " such devices from the simplicity of their construction, and the facility of their execution," and then proceeds thus : " A plate of iron or copper bowed or bended after such a manner as is not at all disagreeable to the sight ; a void behind, divided by certain small iron bands or partition plates, forming several spaces that have a communication one with another ; a little vent hole in the middle of the hearth, a register plate in the upper part of the funnel ; and for some shafts, a capital on the top, make up the whole construction and workmanship of our modern chimney.   Now, can there be anything more simple or plain, or more easy to execute ? "

" To be able to kindle a fire speedily, and make it, if you please, flame continually, whatever wood is burning, without the use of bellows ; to give heat to a spacious room, and even to another adjoining, with a little fire ; to warm one's self at the same time on all sides, be the weather ever so cold, without scorching ; to breathe a pure air always fresh, and to such a degree of warmth as is thought fit ; to be never annoyed with smoke in one's apartment, nor have any moisture therein ; to quench by one's self, and in an instant, any fire that may catch in the tunnel of a chimney ; all these are but a few of the effects and properties of these wonderful machines, notwithstanding their apparent simplicity. Since I used this sort of chimney, I have not been troubled one moment with smoke, in a lodging which it rendered before untenable as soon as a fire was lighted ; I have always inhaled, even during the sharpest seasons, a fresh air like that of the spring.   In 1709, water that froze hard everywhere else very near the hearth, did not congeal at night in my chamber, though the

fire was put out before midnight; and all that was brought
thither in the day soon thawed; neither did I ever perceive
the least moisture in winter, not even during thaws."

The treatise opens with the following remark: "It seems
that those who have hitherto built or caused chimneys to be
erected, have only taken care to contrive in the chambers
certain places where wood may be burnt, without making a
due reflection that the wood in burning ought to warm those
chambers, and the persons who are in them; at least, it is
certain that but a very little heat is felt of the fire made in
the ordinary chimneys, and that they might be ordered so as
to send forth a great deal more, only by changing the dispo-
sition of their jambs and wings." The methods by which a
fire may communicate its heating effect to a room, are cor-
rectly stated to be by *radiation*, by *reflection*, and by *conduction*. Now, as radiant heat is reflected according to the same
law as light, *i.e.*, the angle of incidence is equal to the angle
of reflection, it follows that, in a fire-place with straight
jambs very few of the rays are reflected into the room. Thus,

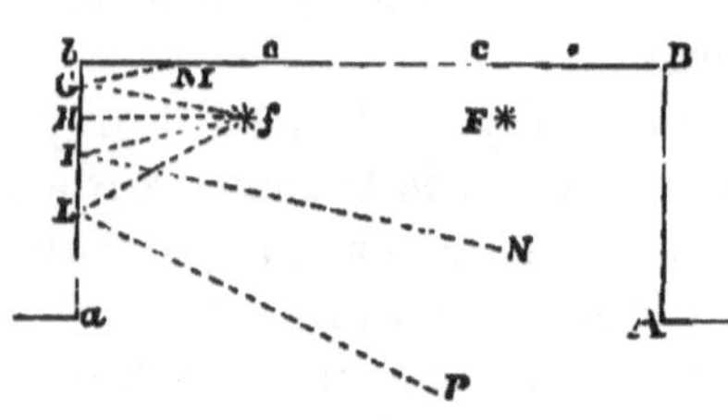

Fig. 21.

suppose a fire, *f* (Fig. 21),
to be made in an ordinary
chimney, A B, *b a*, of which
the jambs, A B, *a b*, are parallel, the ray of heat, *f* G,
will be reflected back in M;
the ray *f* H upon itself in *f*;
the ray *f* I in N; and the
ray *f* L in P; and this is the only ray that can be reflected
into the chamber, the others being to the back, or up the
chimney, or among the fuel, and contribute in no way to the
useful heating effect of the fire. In cases, however, where
the jambs are formed of plaster, there is not even this reflection, for the heat, falling upon the dull surface, is absorbed.
The author then describes what ought to be the correct form
of the jambs: "Geometricians," he says, "are sensible that
all radiuses which set out from the focus of a parabola and
fall upon its sides, are reflected back parallel to its axis. If,
therefore, you take on the bottom of a chimney hearth, A B,
b a (Fig. 22), a length, *c c*, equal to that of the wood designed

to be burnt, for example, of half a log or billet, which, at Paris, is 22 inches; from the points c c, let fall the perpendicular c D, c d, which may be the axis of two semi-parabolas, whereof c c are the vertices and A a (the distance between which is the breadth of the chimney), each of them one of their points; that done, you are to line

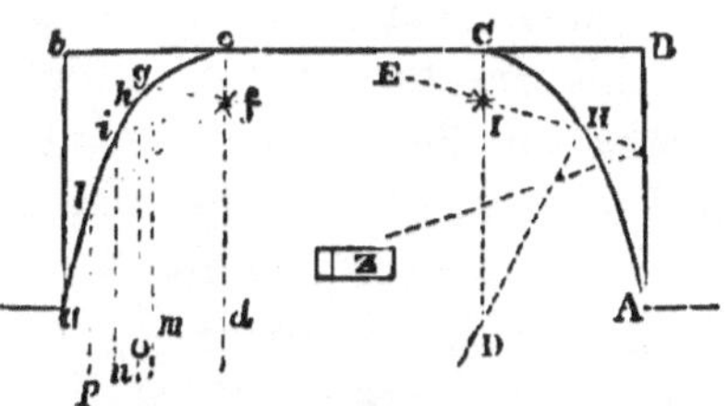

Fig. 22.

with iron or copper plates the two parabolical sides, A c, a c, of the chimney, and make the lower part of the concave parallel to the horizon, and as large as it can be, only leaving 10 or 12 inches for the aperture of the chimney funnel. By this arrangement as much of the heat as can be will be reflected, for all the rays of heat from the focus F f of each semi-parabola, as $f g$, $f h$, $f i$, $f l$, &c., will be reflected back parallel to the axis c d in m, n, o, p, and consequently, pass into the room. So also, all those rays, E H I, which are not reflected back parallel to the axis, will nevertheless be reflected into the chamber or very nearly so. Besides this, the jambs being so much nearer the fire than is usual, will soon become heated, and reflect a large number of rays."

All draughts in the room towards the fire were avoided, by introducing a *soufflet*, or blower, already described in Savot's and Winter's stoves (Figs. 15 and 17). Its opening was situated at z (Fig. 22), in the centre of the hearth, 10 or 12 inches below the plate on which the fuel was burned, and communicated with the open air by a channel from 4 to 6 inches square. The opening in the hearth was furnished with a metal frame, on which was hinged a trap door, or valve, opening upwards; the upper surface of this valve was furnished with a button, which could be grasped with the tongs, and a small bolt beneath could then be drawn back, or closed with the button with which it was connected. The sides of the valve were formed by two thin sectors of iron, which guided the current of air through the channel, and confined it within narrow limits. Two springs in the frame pressed against the sector sides, and kept the valve open at any desired angle, of course, when the valve was shut and bolted there was no current.

Several varieties of Gauger's fire-place are described in this treatise, all of which are furnished with parabolic jambs and the *soufflet*; but the back, the jambs, the hearth, and the mantel, were also made hollow, for the purpose

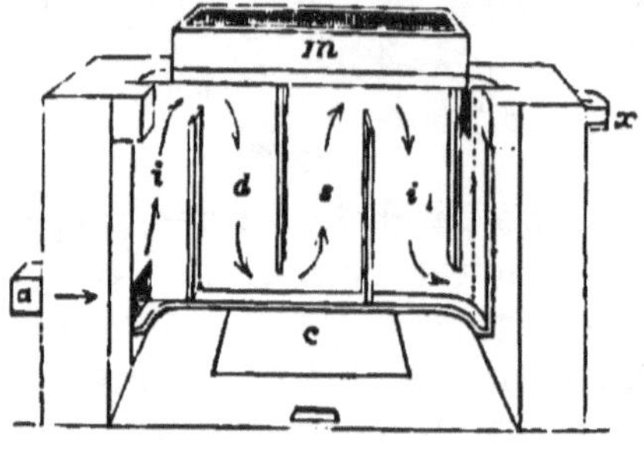

Fig. 23.

of pouring a copious supply of heated air into the apartment. These hollow spaces, named *caliducts* or *meanders*, are in one arrangement (Fig. 23) formed by perpendicular divisions. In another variety (Fig. 24) they are horizontal. In this variety the hearth is also hollowed out, and divided into a series of square spaces. The cold air entering at *a*, follows the direction of the arrows, and escapes into the room at *x*; *c* is the hearth, *m* the smoke flue, and *d s i* the caliducts.

The supply of hot air into the room was regulated by a valve in the air-channel, formed on the principle of Papin's four-way cock. A small cylin-

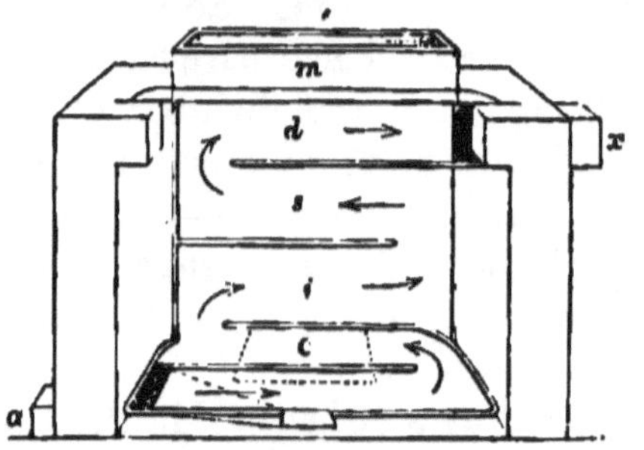

Fig. 24.

der, *x* (Fig. 25), moved within another cylinder, which was fixed. The revolving cylinder had two apertures, *o o*, and the

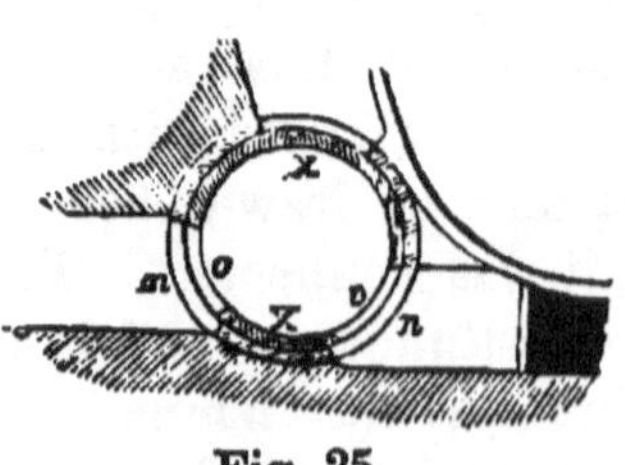

Fig. 25.

fixed cylinder three apertures, *n n*, The axis of the revolving cylinder passed through the cover of the fixed cylinder, and had a small lever or needle attached to it, by means of which the cylinder was turned by the hand into certain positions marked on a small dial. When the apertures, *o o*, in the revolving cylinder coincided with those in the fixed cylinder, *n n*, the external air from the channel was admitted into the caliducts in the chimney back: by turning the revolving cylinder into another position, the cold air was excluded from the caliducts, and admitted directly into the apartments.

The cylinder could also be placed so as to shut off the cold air both from the caliducts and from the room. In this way the air of the room could be tempered according to the wants and feelings of the occupants.

The arrangement to which the inventor gave his decided preference is represented in the following figures. Fig. 26

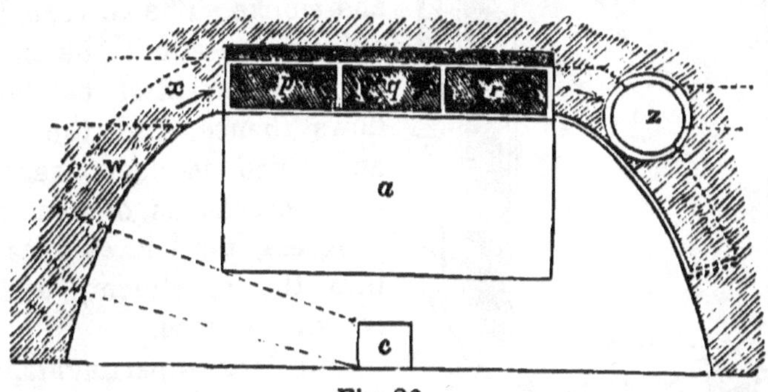

Fig. 26.

represents a horizontal section of the fire-place, and Fig. 27 a vertical section. The hollow metal case forming the back of the chimney is divided into three or more caliducts, *p q r*, each 4 inches wide and $6\frac{3}{4}$ inches broad, placed about an inch from the back wall of the hearth recess, with its lower edge, *m*, about 2 inches above the surface of the iron bottom plate or hearth, *a*. The jambs, *w*, lined with iron or brass plates, are formed in a parabolic curve, and solid at the back. The channel, *x*, conducting the external air into the caliducts, is 9 inches on the side; and the blower, *c*, furnished with its valve, forms an aperture 3 inches long and $2\frac{1}{2}$ inches wide, but instead of being supplied with air from the outside by a separate channel, the air is derived from the channel, *z*. The air valve, *x*, is placed at the junction of the cold air channel, with the caliducts; and the aperture, *z*, through which the warmed air enters the room, is fitted with a sliding valve, to close the warm air aperture.

The action of this apparatus is simple. The small wood on the hearth being lighted, and the valve of the *soufflet*, *c*, lifted up, the logs soon begin to kindle into a good fire; the smoke

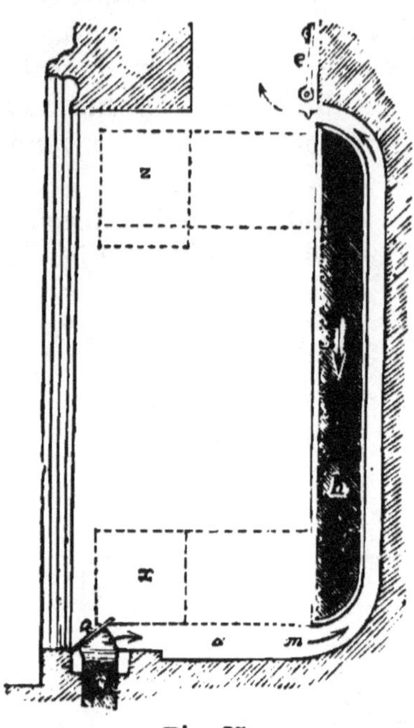

Fig. 27.

and flame rise into the space between the back, *p q r*, and the wall of the hearth, and, after heating the iron back of the caliducts, escape into the flue. In the meantime, the other face towards the room is also quickly heated by the flame and smoke. The valve, *o*, being adjusted to admit the external air into the first caliduct, it flows thence into the second and third caliducts, receiving fresh accessions of heat in its progress, until it escapes at *z*, into the apartment, which it speedily warms.

For large apartments, these fire-places may be erected in the middle of the room, and two may be set back to back, with one series of caliducts for both, so that the air will be heated, whether the fire be kindled in one or both. When kindled in both, the heating effect will, of course, be greatly increased. So, also, two adjoining rooms may be heated by one fire, provided the hearth recesses are placed back to back; for, by making a fire in one room, the heated air from the caliducts may be discharged into the other; or by carrying a pipe from the caliducts through the wall into an adjoining room, or through the ceiling into an upper room, an agreeable and a sufficient warmth may be distributed.

All subsequent writers of repute have acknowledged the great merits of Gauger's treatise. Franklin admitted the great assistance it had afforded him; and some of the improvements in stoves so successfully introduced by Count Rumford are similar in principle to those suggested in this book. It will be obvious how very superior is this *fire-place* to those on the common construction, from the following remarks by Mr. Bernan :—"The external air, in passing through the caliducts, being raised to a temperate heat, and spreading itself throughout the chamber, a person in the coldest weather is surrounded with warm air, and heated, without going near the fire, on all sides at once ; while, from the construction of the hearth, he enjoys the radiant heat in greater perfection than in the common chimneys. The large body of air, constantly flowing into the room from the caliducts, prevents all *chink winds* or dangerous disease-bringing currents ; and as there is as much impure air withdrawn as there is fresh warm air admitted, an unceasing salutary ventilation goes on, from the time the fire is lighted until it is extinguished ; so that a person may always remain in a room thus warmed, and breathe as pure an air as if he were in the fields."

The Gauger fire-places were constructed for the combustion of wood fuel. Dr. Desaguliers modified them so as to admit of coal being burnt, and, in conjunction with an architect, manufactured them, and erected a considerable number in London. For a time the comforts and convenience, as well as economy of these fire-places, were appreciated, and they were rising rapidly into favour ; but, unfortunately, an outcry was raised against them by Mr. Hauksbee and some other scientific opponents of Dr. Desaguliers, who declared that these fire-places "burnt the air, and that burnt air was fatal to animal life." This was a death blow to the Doctor's new fire-places, and many years afterwards, when referring to the subject, he mournfully remarks :—" As I took so much pains and care, and was at some expense to make this management of air useful, I can't help complaining of those who endeavoured to defeat me in it."

In 1745, Dr. Franklin introduced a fire-place, which he named the *Pennsylvanian*, in which Prince Rupert's descending flue was ingeniously combined with Gauger's caliducts. This invention was described in a pamphlet written and printed by Franklin himself. The following is a copy of the title-page :— "An Account of the new-invented Pennsylvanian Fire-places ; wherein their construction and manner of operation is particularly explained; their advantages above every other method of warming rooms demonstrated; and all objections that have been raised against the use of them answered and obviated. With directions for putting them up, and for using them to the best advantage. And a copper-plate in which the several parts of the machine are exactly laid down from a scale of equal parts. Philadelphia: printed and sold by B. Franklin, 1744."

The following is from Franklin's Autobiography:— "Having, in 1742, invented an open stove for the better warming of rooms, and at the same time saving fuel, as the fresh air admitted was warmed in entering, I made a present of the model to Mr. Robert Grace, one of my early friends, who, having an iron furnace, found the casting of the plates for these stoves a profitable thing, as they were growing in demand. To promote that demand I wrote and published a pamphlet, entitled, 'An Account of the new-invented Pennsylvanian Fire-places, &c.' This pamphlet had a good effect. Governor Thomas was so pleased with the construction of this stove, as described in it, that he offered to give me a patent for the sole vending of them for a term of years; but I declined it from a principle, which has ever weighed with me on such occasions, viz., *That, as we enjoy great advantage from the inventions of others, we should be glad of an opportunity to serve others by any invention of ours; and this we should do freely and generously.*

"An ironmonger in London, however, assuming a good deal of my pamphlet, and working it up into his own, and making some small changes in the machine, which rather hurt its operation, got a patent for it there, and made, as I was told, a little fortune by it. And this is not the only instance of patents taken out of my inventions by others, though not always with the same success, which I never contested, as having no desire of profiting by patents myself, and hating disputes. The use of these fire-places in very many houses, both here in Pennsylvania, and the neighbouring states, has been and is a great saving of wood to the inhabitants."

The following is a description of the Pennsylvanian stove

from Franklin's pamphlet:—"M, Fig. 28, is the mantel-piece or breast of the chimney, c the funnel, B the false back and closing, E the true back of the chimney, T top of the fire-place, F the front, A the place where the fire is made, D the air-box, K the hole in the side plate through which the warmed air is discharged out of the air-box into the room—H the hollow filled with fresh air, entering from without at the passage, I, and ascending into the air-box through the air-hole in the bottom plate near G, the partition in the hollow to keep the air and smoke apart; P the passage under the false back and part of the hearth for the smoke. The arrows show the course of the smoke. The fire being made at A, the flame and smoke will ascend and strike the top, T, which will thereby receive a considerable heat. The smoke finding no passage upwards, turns over the top of the air-box, and descends between it and the back plate to the holes in the bottom plate, heat-

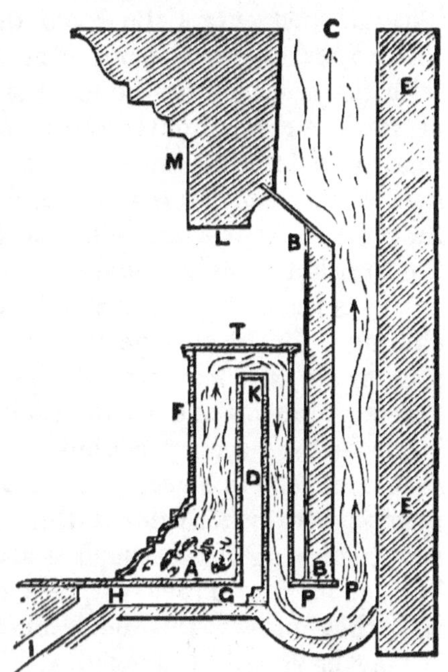

Fig. 28. "Profile of the Pennsylvania Chimney and Fire-place."

ing, as it passes, both plates of the air-box, and the said back plate; the front plate, bottom and side plates, are also all heated at the same time. The smoke proceeds in the passage that leads it under and behind the false back, and so rises into the chimney. The air of the room, warmed behind the back plate, and by the sides, front, and top plates, becoming specifically lighter than the other air in the room, is obliged to rise; but the closure over the fire-place hindering it from going up the chimney, it is forced out into the room, rises by the mantel-piece to the ceiling, and spreads all over the top of the room, whence being crowded down gradually by the stream of newly warmed air that follows and rises above it, the whole room becomes in a short time equally warmed. At the same time the air warmed under the bottom plate and in the air-box rises and comes out of the holes in the side plates, very swiftly, if the door of the room be shut, and joins its current with the stream before mentioned, rising from the side, back, and top plates. The air that enters the room through the air-box is fresh, though warm ; and, computing the swiftness of its motion with the areas of the holes, it is found that near ten barrels of fresh air are hourly introduced by the air-box ; and by this means the air in the room is continually changed and kept at the same time sweet and warm. It is to be observed that the entering air will not be warmed at first lighting the fire, but heats gradually as the fire increases. A square opening for a trap-door should be left in the closing of the chimney, for the sweeper to go up ; the door may be made of slate or tin, and commonly kept close shut, but so placed as that, turning up against the back of the chimney when open, it closes the vacancy behind the false back and shoots the soot, that falls in sweeping, out upon the hearth. This trap-door is a very convenient thing. In rooms where there is much smoking of tobacco, it is also convenient to have a small hole, about 5 or 6 inches square, cut near the ceiling through into the funnel ; this hole must have a shutter, by which it may be closed or opened at pleasure. When open there will be a strong draught of air through it into the chimney, which will presently carry off a cloud of smoke, and keep the room clear; if the room be too hot likewise, it will carry off as much of the warm air as you please, and then you may stop it entirely or in part, as you think fit. By this means it is that the tobacco smoke does not descend among the heads of the company near the fire, as it must do before it can get into common chimneys."

The Pennsylvanian fire-place was constructed for burning wood, but in 1753 Mr. Durno adapted it for the burning of coals, and sent one of his stoves to London as a model. The fuel box was 15 inches wide, $5\frac{1}{2}$ inches deep, from the grating to the top bar, $5\frac{1}{4}$ inches from front to back. This kept a room, 14 feet square, at a temperature of between 60° and 64° during 13 hours, with the consumption of only one peck of coals, at a time when the external temperature was 28°, or 4° below freezing.

A simple, but highly ingenious grate, in which the burning fuel is made to consume its own smoke, was also one of the many original contrivances of Franklin. It consists of a circular fire-cage (Fig. 29), about a foot in diameter, and from 6 to 8 inches wide from front to back ; the back is of plate iron, and the front filled with bars, of which the three middle are fixed, and the top and bottom movable, and either one may be drawn out for the purpose of filling the grate with fuel. The fire-cage turns upon axes, supported by a crotchet, fixed on a stem, which revolves upon a pivot fixed to the hearth. The fire is lighted by with-

Fig. 29.

drawing the upper bar and then placing wood and coals in the cage, as in a common grate; the bar is then replaced. So also in adding fresh fuel, the upper bar is removed and then replaced. When the grate is first lighted a quantity of thick smoke is emitted by the fuel ; but as soon as it begins to burn well, the cage is turned round on its axes, so that the burning coals at the bottom shall occupy a position at the top. The whole is then turned round on the pivot, so as to bring the bars again in front ; by this arrangement the fresh coals below the lighted fuel will gradually ignite, and their smoke, having to pass through the fire above them, will be entirely consumed. In this way the combustion is perfect, or nearly so, and this economy of fuel is accompanied by a much greater heating effect ; little or no soot is deposited, for all the combustible matter of the fuel is converted into heat. For want of some such contrivance, a very considerable portion of our fuel is wasted by our open fires under the best management. Soot is very inflammable, and a pound of it gives as much heat as a pound of coal; and the quantity of soot which lines our chimneys is very inconsiderable, compared with that which escapes unconsumed at the chimney top, and fills the neighbourhood with *blacks*, and, returning into our houses through the open windows, makes the furniture dirty, or, entering our lungs, offers an impediment to free respiration. Another advantage of the revolving grate is, that it may be turned into any position, so as to radiate its heat in one direction rather than another, and, by placing the bars in a horizontal position, a teakettle, or other cooking utensil, may be set on it.

We cannot part with Franklin without some notice of the services rendered by him in the cure of smoky chimneys. But first as to the chimney itself. We have seen that the invention of chimneys was not a scientific result, but an act of necessity. The first object proposed to be accomplished by them was to discharge into the air the products of combustion, instead of allowing them to spread over the apartment. With the huge wood fires of our ancestors, the large hearth recess and the capacious flue did not interfere with the accomplishment of the object proposed ; but as circumstances changed—when fire-places were introduced into small rooms, and coal was substituted for wood—the arrangements which were not altogether ill-suited to the baronial hall or kitchen did not apply. Science was unable, or did not condescend, to investigate the subject, and thus the defects of chimneys continued to exist through many generations. One great defect arose from the great capacity of the flue in proportion to the extent of the fire, the heat of which was often insufficient to determine an upward current for carrying off the smoke. It is now a matter of everyday experience, that the force of the draught in a chimney is so much the greater as the column of air which passes up it is longer or more heated, or, in other words, the taller the chimney, or the hotter the fire, the more rapid will be the draught. The ascentional force of this current is the difference between the weight of the column of heated air in the chimney, and a column of the surrounding atmosphere of equal height. Air and gases expand almost equally and very nearly in proportion to the increase of temperature. From 32°, the freezing point, to 212°, the boiling point, of water, they increase in bulk more than one-third, 1,000 pints at 32° becoming 1,366 at 212°. This is $\frac{11}{30}$ths of the volume at 32°, or about $\frac{1}{490\cdot9}$ for each degree of Fahr. Now, suppose when a chimney is *drawing*, the temperature of the ascending air in the average of its length is 25° above that of the outer air, which we may suppose is at 41°. The expansion of air for each degree is $\frac{1}{500}$th of its bulk at 41°, so that the column of air in the chimney will be dilated $\frac{25}{500}$ths, or $\frac{1}{20}$th. A column of such heated air in the chimney, 21 feet high, would balance a column of only 20 feet in height at the temperature of the outer air, and the ascentional force of the heated air (or draught of the chimney) would be that due to the difference in weight between the 21 feet of heated air and the 21 feet of colder air, and this would be equal to the pressure of a column of the colder air 1 foot in height. It is obvious from this that the draught is increased by increasing the perpendicular height of the chimney. Its length in a horizontal direction does not increase, but diminishes the draught, by cooling the air before it gets into the effective part of the flue. The draught is also increased by making all the air which enters the chimney pass through or very near the fuel ; for when much air gets into the chimney above the fire, by having a high mantelpiece, the mass of air in the chimney cannot get sufficiently heated. The shape and structure of the chimney may also assist or retard the draught. The chimney should be as small as possible ; only just sufficient to discharge the smoke and assist the ventilation of the apartment. The circular form is preferable to the square, on account of the resistance being equal on the internal surface, and double currents are less easily established. According to Peclet,* the horizontal section of the circular chimney-shaft of an ordinary apartment need not be more than 15 to 20 centimetres in diameter (6 or 8 inches), or an area of from 3 to 4 square decimetres (12 to 16 square inches), but it will be remembered that these estimates are for wood fires. Where coal is used they must be somewhat extended.

---

* *"Traité de la Chaleur considerée dans ses applications."* 2nd Ed. 1860. The reader interested in the subject in a technological point of view should consult vol. i., book 3, " On Chimneys " (*Des Cheminées*), from page 184 to 249.

In the cure of smoky chimneys there are practical difficulties and special cases which usually come under the pathological treatment of the smoke-doctor; these may all be resolved by reference to well-known scientific principles, but, unfortunately, the smoke-doctor is not always, indeed very seldom, a man of science. The following cases of smoky chimneys and the method of cure, will include as much as need be said on this subject to the intelligent reader.*

The most prolific cause of smoky chimneys is the want of a sufficient supply of air to the fire. This is sometimes the case in a new house, where doors and windows fit tightly and accurately, so that scarcely a chink is left for the admission of air. Or if the house be not new, the windows and doors are often listed, sandbags are placed over the junction of the two window-frames, and a thick mat closes the bottom of the door, and even the key-hole is often stopped. It is no wonder that, under such circumstances, the chimney should smoke; for the air necessary to support the fire must come down the chimney (the only way left for it) instead of passing through the fire and up it. Dr. Franklin's method ol ascertaining, in a rough way, how much air is required per minute to make the fire burn well without smoking, is to set the door open until the fire burns properly, then gradually to close it until smoke again begins to appear: next open it a little wider, and hold it in such a position as will admit the necessary supply. Now observe the width of the open crevice between the edge of the door, and the rabbet into which it would shut. Suppose this distance to be half an inch in a door 8 feet high; the room would, in such case, require for the entrance of the air an aperture equal to 48 square inches, or a hole 6 inches by 8 inches. This, however, would be more than is usually required. Dr. Franklin found that a square opening of 6 inches to the side was a good medium size for most chimneys. But now comes the

* The following references to Dr. Franklin are to a pamphlet "On the Causes and Cure of Smoky Chimneys," dated "At sea, 28th August, 1785." It is in the form of a letter addressed "To John Ingenhousz, at Vienna." It first appeared in the Transactions of the American Philosophical Society. It was read October 21, 1785, and afterwards published as a separate pamphlet in England and America.

difficulty (at least in English houses, where no air-duct is provided by the architect and builder, as in the Gauger fire-place), where to make this opening. If made in the door, it would not only interfere with the privacy of the room, but admit a cold draught to the back and feet of those sitting near the fire ; if made in the window, it would bring a cataract of cold air down upon the heads of the inmates.

It has been proposed to cut a crevice in the upper part of the window-frame, and to place below this a thin shelf, sloping upwards, in order to direct the air towards the ceiling, where, mingling with the heated air of the apartment, it would mitigate its temperature, and bring it down again to feed the fire. The objection to this plan is, that it condenses the products of respiration and combustion, and causes these aerial poisons to be breathed over again. An old-fashioned contrivance for kitchens was to place in one of the spaces of the window-frame a circular tin plate, containing a wheel mounted on an axis, the radii or vanes being bent obliquely ; these, being acted on by the entering air, forced it round like the vanes of a windmill, and at the same time dispersed the air to a certain extent, and prevented a distinct draught from being felt. Another method was to take out a pane of glass, and substitute a tin frame, giving it two springing angular sides ; and being furnished with hinges below, it could be drawn in more or less above, so that the incoming air might be directed upwards, and regulated as to quantity. A somewhat similar contrivance has been introduced for ventilating rooms, but when there is a fire in the room, it must serve the purpose of introducing air instead of letting it out. It consists of a number of strips of plate glass, arranged after the fashion of a Venetian blind, occupying the position of one of the panes of glass in the upper window-frame. By a little adjusting motion, the strips can be separated more or less apart, to regulate the supply of air, or closed entirely, so as to exclude it. Perforated panes of glass have also been introduced as ventilators, but they must also bring air into the room instead of letting it out, when a fire is burning. The best plan of all is the air-duct, described in Gauger's fire-places.

A second cause of smoky chimneys arises from the size of

the fire-place ; it may be too wide or too high. Dr. Franklin recommended that the openings in the lower rooms should be about 30 inches square and 18 deep ; and those in the upper rooms only 18 inches square and not quite so deep ; the intermediate openings diminishing in proportion to the height of the funnel.

But the funnel itself may be too high compared with the size of the fire. The hot air, ascending to a certain height, may distribute its heat to the air in the upper part of the flue, so that the whole may cool down, and the column within the flue be nearly of the same weight as an equal column on the outside. In such a case, there will be little or no draught to carry off the smoke, and it will, therefore, enter the room.

But it more frequently happens that the funnel is too short. The remedy in such case is to contract the opening of the chimney, so as to make all the air that enters pass through or very near the fire.

In some houses, instead of having a separate chimney for each room or fire-place, the flue is bent or turned from an upper room into the flue of another fire from below. In such a case, the upper chimney is too short, since the length can only be estimated from the place where it enters the flue of the lower room ; and this, in its turn, is also shortened in efficient length by the distance between the entrance at the second funnel and the top of the stack ; for all that part being supplied with air from the second funnel, adds no force to the draught ; and if there is no fire in the second chimney, it cools the hot current of the first, and so diminishes the draught. The remedy in this case is to close the opening of that chimney in which there is no fire.

Chimneys often overpower each other, and so produce smoke in the room. If, for example, there are two fire-places in one large room, with fires in each, and the doors and windows closed ; if the two fires do not burn equally well, either from not being lighted at the same time, or not equally supplied with fuel, or from any other cause, the stronger fire will overpower the weaker, and draw the air down its funnel to supply its own demand, bringing the smoke with it. Two chimneys in different rooms, which communicate by a door, may also act in this way whenever the door is opened; so, also, in a house where all the doors and windows fit tightly, a strong kitchen chimney on the lowest floor may overpower any other chimney in the house, and draw air and smoke into the rooms as often as a door communicating with the staircase is opened. Dr. Franklin mentions the case of a nobleman's house in Westminster afflicted with this troublesome complaint. It was a new house, and after the owner had paid for it, and discharged all claims, he had to expend £300 more before the smoky chimneys were cured. Of course, the only remedy for this disorder is, to provide each room with the means of furnishing the fire-place with a sufficient supply of air for the combustion of the fuel. When will architects and builders be convinced of the fact, that fire-places, as well as human beings, require constant supplies of fresh air, and that it is their duty to provide every room with air channels, placed so as to feed the fire without annoying the inmates ?

Another fruitful source of smoky chimneys is, when their tops are commanded by higher buildings, or by a hill, so that the wind blowing over them, falls like water over a dam, sometimes almost passing over the tops of the chimneys, and beating down the smoke. If the funnels cannot be raised, so that their tops may be of the same height or higher than the eminence, the only remedy is to mount one of those ugly contrivances with which the chimney-doctors delight to satirise the architect and builder, and which are thus enumerated in an amusing article in *Chambers's Edinburgh Journal*:— "The simplest of all consists in the well-known revolving bonnets or cowls, with wind-arrows on their summits ; which, by the way, were once called ' Bishops ' in Scotland, while a friend assures me, that in the west of England he has heard them styled ' Presbyterians.' The philosophy of this contrivance is sufficiently simple—in whichever direction the wind blows, the mouth of the chimney is averted from it. This principle has its development in a thousand devices— some looking like Dutch ovens come up to see the world, some like half sections of sugar-loaves, some like capital H's, and sundry other pleasing objects. The red chimney-pots,

too, have contrivances of a similar intention, in the diverging
spouts and cavities and twists which some of them delight in.
A different species is the perforated whirling variety, which
seem perpetually whizzing round for the mere fun of the
thing, since any good they do is extremely apt to escape
detection. They are a lively-looking apparatus; but on squally
nights, and when the pivot becomes a little rusty, the musical
sounds they give forth can scarcely be considered agreeable.
Among the more ingenious of smoke-curers, an invention of
recent origin, named the ' Archimedean screw ventilator '
deserves a place.   It consists, as its name implies, of wind-
vanes attached to the extremity of a revolving screw.   When
the wind strikes these vanes, it produces a rapid revolution
of the screw, which is thus supposed to *wind up* the smoke or
vitiated air from below. Perhaps it serves the proposed end ;
but whether the positive advantage thus gained is not lost
by the obstruction of such apparatus to the free passage of
smoke in calm weather, is a point in my estimation more
than questionable.   For the relief of such chimneys as only
smoke in windy weather, perhaps this and other forms of
external apparatus are best adapted.   Another invention of
equal merit is a chimney-cap of metal externally grooved in
a series of spiral curves up the pipe, which end in a kind of
mouth-piece, from whence the smoke issues. The wind, when
impelled against this apparatus, is supposed to take somewhat of the direction of the spiral grooves, and thus to form
an upward current to assist the emission of the smoke."   One
of the most recent of this class of inventions is " Day's wind-
guard," which consists of an octagonal metallic chimney-cap,
having four slits in it, which are protected by projecting
pieces or slips of metal.   When a current of air strikes in
any direction against the cap, it reflects or turns the air in
such a manner as immediately to produce a draught up the
pipe.   " In casting one's eye down the long streets of the
smoky city, in taking a survey of the roofs and their tormented chimneys, the infinity of other contrivances is so great,
that it is scarcely a poetical hyperbole to say our pen starts
back from it.   Here is patent upon patent, scheme after
scheme, each doing its best, no doubt, to obtain the mastery

over that simple thing—smoke; and each with a degree of success of a very hopeless amount. There appears to me something intensely ludicrous in these struggles against what seems to be an absurd, but an invincible foe; the very element of whose success against us lies in our not strangling him in his birth. Many obstacles are in the way, no doubt; there are obstacles in the way of every good; but I have little doubt, that had the perverted ingenuity which has misspent itself upon the chimney-pots been directed to the fire-place, we might have now had a different tale to tell. The smoke nuisance is laughed at as a minor evil, by a great practical people like ourselves, who heroically make up our minds to put up with it; but when it is considered as an item in the comfort, cleanliness, and health of a whole nation, it assumes, or should assume, a different position."

We do not by any means affirm that cowls and similar contrivances are always effectual in the cure of smoky chimneys; for it is easy to imagine cases where chimneys will, or rather must smoke, in spite of the whole host of caps, cowls, and vanes. For example, when a commanding eminence is farther from the wind than the chimney commanded, the wind would, as it were, be dammed up between the house and the eminence, and force its way down the chimneys in whatever position the turn-cap or other contrivance might be situated. Dr. Franklin mentions a city in which many houses were tormented with smoky chimneys by this operation, for their kitchens being built behind, and connected by a passage with the houses, the tops of the kitchen chimneys were thus lower than the tops of the houses, and thus, when the wind blew against the backs of the houses, the whole side of a street formed a dam, and the obstructed wind was forced down the kitchen chimneys, and passed along the passages into the houses, and so into the street. This was especially the case when the kitchen fires were burning badly. In summer, the annoyance assumed a different form, for the smoke was wafted from the kitchen chimneys into the chambers of the upper rooms.

Chimneys, which otherwise draw well, will often smoke from the improper situation of a door. Thus when the door and the chimney are on the same side of the room, and the door being in the corner, is made to open against the wall, as is usually done, to have it more out of the way, it follows that, when the door is partially opened, a current of air rushes in and passes along the wall into and across the opening of the fire-place, and whisks the smoke into the room. This happens more frequently when the door is being shut, for then the force of the current is increased, and persons sitting near the fire feel all the inconvenience both of the draught and of the smoke. A remedy may be found by an intervening screen, projecting from the wall and passing round a great part of the fire-place; or still better, by shifting the hinges of the door, so as to throw the air along the other wall.

A room with no fire in it is sometimes filled with smoke from the funnel of another room, in which a fire is burning. This arises from changes in density of the air in the cold funnel, from changes in temperature by day and by night, as well as from changes in the direction of the wind. It is found that when the temperature of the outer air and of that in the funnels is nearly equal, the air begins to ascend the funnels as the cool of the evening comes on, and this current will continue till nine or ten o'clock next morning; then, as the heat of the day approaches, it sets downward, and continues to do so till evening; it then changes again, and continues to go upwards during the night. Now, when the smoke from the tops of neighbouring funnels passes over the tops of funnels which are drawing downwards, the smoke is also drawn down, and descends with the air into the chamber. The remedy proposed by Dr. Franklin was, to contract the opening of the chimney to about 2 feet between the jambs, and to bring the breast down to about 3 feet of the hearth. An iron frame is then placed just under the breast, and extending to the back of the chimney, so that a plate of iron may slide horizontally backwards and forwards in the grooves on each side of the frame; this plate, when thrust quite in, fills up the whole space, and shuts up the chimney entirely when there is no fire. But when there is a fire, it can be drawn out, so as to leave between its further edge and the back a space of about 2 inches, which is sufficient for the smoke to pass; and so large a part of the funnel being stopped by the rest of the plate, the passage of warm air out of the room up the chimney is in great measure prevented, as is also the cold air from crevices to supply its place. The effect is seen in three ways:—1. When the fire burns briskly in cold weather, the howling or whisking of the wind, as it enters the room through the crevices when the chimney is open, ceases as soon as the plate is slid in to its proper distance. 2. Opening the door of the room about half an inch, and holding the hand against the opening near the top of the door, you feel the cold air coming in against your hand, but weakly if the plate be in. Let another person draw it out, so as to let the air of the room go up the chimney with its usual freedom in open chimneys, and you immediately feel the cold air rushing in strongly. 3. If something be set against the door, just sufficient when the plate is in to keep the door nearly shut, by resisting the pressure of the air that would force it open, then, when the plate is drawn out, the door will be forced open by the increased pressure of the outward cold air endeavouring to get in, to supply the place of the warm air that now passes out of the room to go up the chimney. "In our common open chimneys," says the Doctor, "half of the fuel is wasted, and its effect lost; the air it has warmed being immediately drawn off."

The form of the chimney-pot has also an influence on the free passage of the smoke. Many of those fancy chimney-pots ornamented, singly or clustered together, will cause the chimneys to smoke in strong winds; the ornaments serving as points of resistance to the wind, after reflecting it down the chimney; and the clustered arrangement presenting a broad resisting surface, so that the wind, in blowing against them, rises up along the surface, and blows strongly over the mouths of the pots, so that the smoke cannot force its way through the blast. In Venice the top of the flue is rounded into the true form of a funnel, and this is often found to answer the purpose; but, at present, we do not know of any remedy except a turn-cap, or one of the many inelegant contrivances, already referred to, which give such wonderful variety to the sky line of most of our houses and public buildings.

Cases of smoky chimneys may arise, which may puzzle

the science of the most accomplished smoke-doctor. We borrow two such from Franklin. "I once lodged," he says, "in a house in London, which, in a little room, had a single chimney and funnel. The opening was very small, yet it did not keep in the smoke, and all attempts to have a fire in this room were fruitless. I could not imagine the reason; till at length, observing that the chamber over it, which had no fire-place in it, was always filled with smoke when a fire was kindled below, and that the smoke came through the cracks and crevices of the wainscot, I had the wainscot taken down, and discovered that the funnel which went up behind it had a crack many feet in length, and wide enough to admit my arm; a breach very dangerous with regard to fire, and occasioned, probably, by an apparent irregular settling of one side of the house. The air entering this breach freely, destroyed the drawing force of the funnel. The remedy would have been, filling up the breach, or rather rebuilding the funnel; but the landlord rather chose to stop up the chimney."

The second case occurred at the house of a friend near London. "His best room had a chimney, in which he told me he never could have a fire, for all the smoke came out into the room. I flattered myself I could easily find the cause, and prescribe the cure. I opened the door, and perceived it was not want of air. I made a temporary contraction of the opening of the chimney, and found that it was not its being too large that caused the smoke to issue. I went and looked up at the top of the chimney; its funnel was joined in the same stack with others, some of them shorter, that drew very well, and I saw nothing to prevent its doing the same. In fine, after every other examination I could think of, I was obliged to own the insufficiency of my skill. But my friend, who made no pretension to such kind of knowledge, afterwards discovered the cause himself. He got to the top of the funnel by a ladder, and looking down, found it filled with twigs and straw cemented by earth, and lined with feathers. It seems, the house, after being built, had stood empty some years before he occupied it; and he concluded that some large birds had taken the advantage of its retired situation to make their nests there. The rubbish, considerable in quantity, being removed, and the funnel cleared, the chimney drew well, and gave satisfaction."

It has been remarked, that chimneys situated in the north wall of a house do not draw so well as those in a south wall, because when cooled by north winds, they are apt to draw downwards. Hence, chimneys enclosed in the body of a house are more favourably situated than those in exposed walls. Chimneys in stacks often draw better than separate funnels, because those that have constant fires in them warm those in which there are none.

We have been tempted by Dr. Franklin's amusing letter to enlarge somewhat on the subject of smoky chimneys, forgetting that the history of the Englishman's palladium, the open fire-place, is by no means complete. It is astonishing how little impression Dr. Franklin's labours in the art of warming rooms seem to have made, for when towards the end of the century a more influential, if not more zealous, labourer in the same department appeared, he found abundant defects to cure, waste of· fuel to remedy, and much discomfort to get rid of.

Count Rumford may be considered, in many respects, as a public benefactor. It is scarcely possible to overestimate the amount of good effected by means of his homely inventions and familiar Essays. He was equally at home in improving a chimney fire-place or a coffee-pot, a private bath or a public kitchen ; he showed equal zeal in investigating the laws of heat and the condition of the poor ; and even now, after a lapse of seventy years, we find his Essays * very pleasant reading. But the Essay that most concerns us here is the fourth, " Of Chimney Fire-places, with proposals for improving them, to save fuel; to render dwelling-houses more comfortable and salubrious, and effectually to prevent chimneys from smoking." Essay XI. is entitled, " Supplementary of Chimney Fire-places." Essay VI. is also " On the Management, Offices, and the Economy of Fuel." The fire-places which Count Rumford proposed to improve were large square cavities with the back of equal width with the

* " Essays, Political, Economical, and Philosophical."   By Benjamin, Count of Rumford. 4 vols. 8vo. London, 1796—1802.

opening in front, with the sides or covings parallel, so that the heat from the fire could not be reflected into the room from them, and the large open corners occasioned eddies of wind, which frequently disturbed the fire, and prevented the smoke from ascending, and even whirled it into the room. The Count very properly defines the object of a chimney fire as being simply to warm the room. He then, with naive formality, proceeds to say that it is necessary, *first* of all, to contrive matters so that the room shall be actually warmed ; *secondly*, that it be warmed with the smallest expense of fuel possible ; and *thirdly*, that in warming it the air of the room be preserved perfectly pure and fit for respiration, and free from smoke and all disagreeable smells. The quantity of heat that goes off, combined with the smoke, vapour, and heated air, is at least three or four times greater than that which is radiated from the fire.* All the combined heat escapes up the chimney, and of the radiant heat only a small portion escapes into the room. If the smoke and combined heat were made to pass by a winding flue into the room above, such heat might be turned to account instead of being thrown to waste into the atmosphere. Alluding, in another part, to the plague of smoke, he says, " I never view from a distance, as I come into town, this black cloud which hangs over London, without wishing to be able to compute the immense number of chaldrons of coal of which it is composed ; for could this be ascertained I am persuaded so striking a fact would awaken the curiosity and excite the astonishment of all ranks of the inhabitants, and *perhaps* turn their minds to an object of economy to which they had paid hitherto little attention."

The *Rumford* stove (as it is incorrectly called) has made the Count's name familiar among all classes, and is so well known, that a description is scarcely necessary. The Count's essential improvement consisted in contracting the area of the fire-chamber, and placing a flat surface in each interior angle, as in the plan Fig. 31, so as to reflect that portion of heat into the room which in the old square

---

* In his Sixth Essay, Count Rumford states that not less than seven-eighths of the heat generated is carried up the chimney and is lost.

chambered grates escaped up the chimney. The throat of the chimney was also greatly reduced in size, and the breast-work, *a* (Fig. 30), rounded off, in order to afford less obstruction to the ascent of the smoke. When the chimney required sweeping, the plate or flagstone, *b*, could be removed so as to open the throat, and be replaced after the operation. According to Rumford, in order to obtain the greatest effect from the fuel, the sides of the fire-place ought to be placed at an angle of 135° with the back of the grate, or, which is the same thing, at an angle of 45° with a line drawn across the front of the fire-place. (See Fig. 31.) These angular covings were not to be of iron, but of some non-conducting substance,

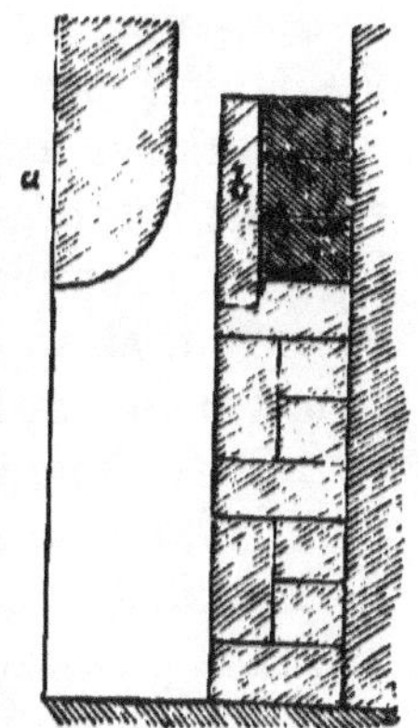

Fig. 30.

such as fire-clay, and polished with black-lead. He objected to circular covings, on the ground that they produced eddies or currents, which would be likely to cause the chimney to smoke; and he also objected to the old form of registers or metal covers to the breast of the chimney, for the same reason; and also because by their sloping

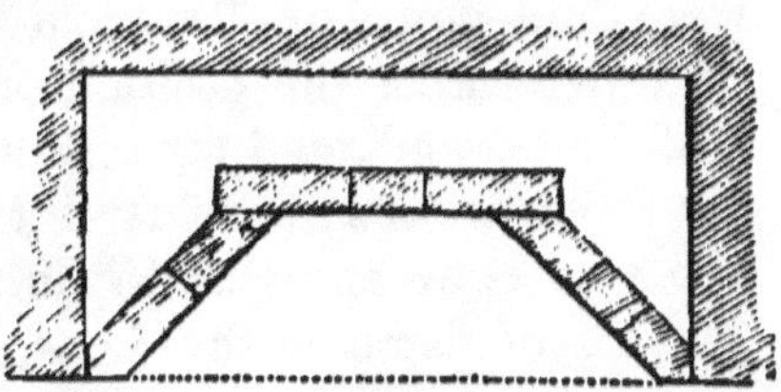

Fig. 31.

upwards towards the back of the fire-place, they caused the warm air from the room to be drawn up the chimney, and thus interfered with the passage of the smoke. These registers are now arranged so as to be lower at the back than at the front of the stove, but they are usually placed too high up. If brought down lower, and placed at an angle of 45°, much of the heat of the fire would be reflected into the room. The Count also greatly diminished the size of the fire-grate, and considered the best proportions for the chimney recess to be when the width of the back was equal to the depth from front to back, and the width of the front or opening between the jambs three times the width of the back.

Count Rumford was very enthusiastic about his fire-places,

and he communicates his enthusiasm to his Essays. There is, indeed, a charm about them which belongs to a man who is in earnest in his pursuit. He returns again and again to the point in hand, recapitulates, reiterates, gives directions for laying out the work; wood engravings with separate descriptions; lists of persons who have adopted his plans with success; lists of workpeople who execute the work; and, following the example of Dr. Franklin, he requests everybody to observe that, as he does not intend to patent any of his inventions which may be of public utility, all persons are at full liberty to imitate them and vend them for their own emolument, and those who wish for further information will receive gratis all the information they can require, by applying to the author, who will take pleasure in giving them every assistance in his power.

Count Rumford's improvements so evidently led to a saving of fuel and an increase of comfort that they made a permanent impression. His register stove has continued in use to the present day. The principles of its construction were laid down by Tredgold * in the following manner :—
" To determine the position of the covings, H H, so that they shall be best adapted for reflecting the heat of the flame into the room, we may consider F to be the focus of the fire, then if D A be at an angle of 45° in respect of D E, the heat from a portion of flame at the focus, F, would be reflected into the room in a direction perpendicular to the line D E, which here represents the front of the grate, the angle of incidence being equal to the angle of reflection, which is the condition required to be fulfilled. The same will be true of a portion of flame at any other part of the fire.

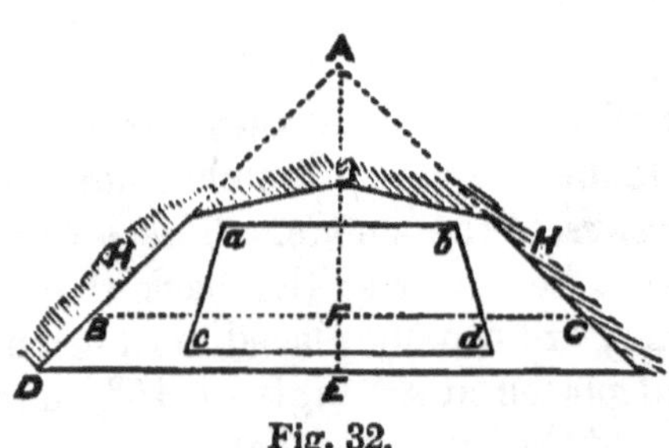

Fig. 32.

Therefore, to set out the covings so that they will reflect the heat with advantage into the room, make E the middle of the front of the grate, and E D half the width which is convenient for the opening, and make A E perpendicular, and

* " Principles of Warming and Ventilating Public Buildings." 1824.

equal to D E; then join A D, and it is the direction in which the coving should be placed. A greater obliquity would be still more effective, because it would spread the rays more into the room, but is not convenient in other respects. The back of the fire is usually straight; but, unless the fire be small, it is an advantage to make the back in two parts, forming an obtuse angle at *e*; in this angle the smoke collects and ascends with less obstruction than when it is dispersed over a flat surface. It is not necessary that the form of the fire should be regulated by the position of the covings, because its form does not affect the reflections; on the contrary, acute angles should be avoided, and the fuel kept in mass as much as possible. The form for the fire marked *a b c d*, in the figure, is drawn with the angles as acute as they ever should be made."

Passing over numerous modifications of the register stove as not involving any new principle, we come to the year 1815, when Mr. Cutler took out a patent for a register stove with a chamber or magazine beneath the grate for containing sufficient fuel to last a whole day. The following description is from the article "Stove" in *Rees's Cyclopædia:*—"The bottom plate of the chamber is movable, and by means of a wheel and axle the fuel contained in the chamber can be raised so as to bring a portion of it into the grate at the lower part or from beneath, and thus from time to time replace the fuel that is consumed without the trouble of throwing on coals. To make the fire burn, the flue must be so constructed as to produce a strong draught through and across the top of the fire. Introducing the fresh coals from beneath causes the smoke therefrom to be consumed in passing through the superposed hot coals. Another improvement is to reduce or extinguish the fire; the fire is lowered into the chamber beneath the grate, and is thus deprived of a supply of fresh air, and is consequently soon extinguished; moreover, sparks cannot fly out, so that the fire may be left with safety. By burning the smoke the full effect of the fuel is obtained; and were this generally practised in London the air would be as free from smoke as in Paris, and other Continental cities; chimney sweeping would be unnecessary; there would be no danger of soot in the flue catching fire, and smoke would not descend from chimneys into rooms. The saving the trouble of putting on coals; the continually bright and cheerful fire, and the easy and safe means of extinguishing the fire at night, are matters of importance; especially the last, considering how many fires occur in the night, doubtless occasioned by fires left unextinguished. The machinery for raising the bottom of the stove is simple. The chamber consists of iron plates screwed together, with a movable bottom fitted to it. A bar is fixed across beneath the bottom, the ends of which pass through slits in the side plates. To the extremities of the bar are attached the ends of two chains, which are made to wind upon the ends of a horizontal axle which extends over the top of the stove, so as to be out of sight in the chimney. The axle is turned by a crown wheel, which turns a pinion, the axis of which appears through the iron-work of the stove; in this end is a square hole for receiving a winch handle; thus, by means of the axle and chains, the bottom plate is raised, and fresh fuel is added to the lower part of the fire."

Cutler's arrangement does not seem to have met with much success, probably on account of the small amount of extra trouble required to feed the fire from below, instead of the off-hand plan of throwing the coals on the top. Cutler's plan was also wanting in simplicity. Dr. Arnott has effected the same object by somewhat simpler means, in an invention which he calls "The Smokeless Fire-place." This is described by him in a work* from which we gather the following particulars:—Fig. 33 shows the arrangements of this fire-place. The fire-box, *e f g h,* con-

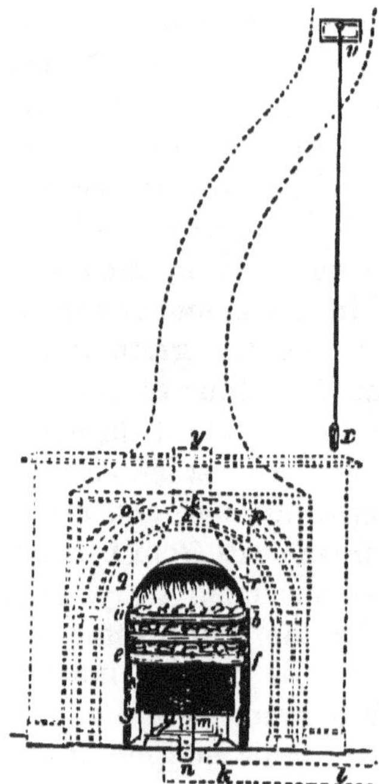

Fig. 33.

* "On the Smokeless Fire-place, Chimney-valves, and other means, old and new, of obtaining healthful Warmth and Ventilation." By Neil Arnott, M.D., F.R.S., &c. London, 1855.

taining the charge of coal for the day's consumption, has a movable false bottom or piston, *s s*, supported by a piston-rod, *m n*, furnished with notches in which the catch, *i u*, engages so as to support the piston at any required height. By placing the poker in one of these notches, and resting its point on some fixed support, it may be used as a lever of the second kind for raising the piston, and bringing a fresh supply of fuel into the grate.   Should it be required to replenish the coal-box while the fire is burning, as when the piston is on a level with the bottom bar of the grate, *e f*, a broad flat shovel or spade, of the shape of the bottom of the grate, is pushed in over the piston, which being let down to the bottom of the coal-box, the spade is raised in front by its handle, when the two front bars of the grate, yielding upwards to the pressure, expose the mouth of the coal-box, and a new charge of coal being shot in, the spade is withdrawn.   In lighting the fire the wood is laid on the upper surface of the fresh coal in the box, with a thickness of 3 or 4 inches of cinder or coked coal from the fire of the preceding day; when the wood being lighted, ignites the cinder above, and distils some of the pitchy vapour from the fresh coal below, and rising through the wood, flame, and cinders, burns with a flame.   When the cinder is fairly ignited, the volatile portions of the coal, passing through the fire, will be decomposed and resolved into invisible products of combustion, and the fire will remain smokeless. Of course it is not necessary to let the fire go out every day. If the coal-box be filled once or twice a day, according to the requirements of the grate, it will go on smouldering during the hours of the night, and can be quickly brought into full activity in the morning by raising the piston rod. It is a point of importance that the piston shall fit accurately in the box, to prevent the ingress of air from below, or in other words, to limit the combustion to that part of the fire which is visible from the room. If, however, it is required that the fire shall give out heat during the night, a small opening is made at the bottom of the coal-box for the admission of air, so that the combustion may be somewhat quickened. This opening also admits of enlargement for the purpose of removing the coal dust and ashes before lighting the fire.

I am not able from personal experience to speak of the success of this grate.* Its success as a smoke consumer must depend on the proper action of the piston and ratchet bar : I have heard of one or two cases where the piston has become fixed by a foreign body, such as a nail in the coal, and also by the fusion of matters in the coal : the ratchet-catch and bar may now and then get out of order, but the chief source of failure in this grate is the impatience which servants display on having to raise the fire so as to feed it from below. With them, the quickest and most natural method of feeding a fire is by discharging upon it an avalanche of coals from the scuttle. I have known even the mistress herself thus convert the smoke-less fire-place into an eminently smoky one. Besides, it is not certain that the so-called " combustion of smoke " produces so many advantages as the public suppose. It is true that the smoky atmosphere of London entails great labour and expense on its inhabitants in maintaining cleanliness. Dr. Arnott states that the cost of washing the clothes of its inhabitants is greater by $2\frac{1}{2}$ million pounds sterling a year than for the same number of families resident in the country, to say nothing of the injury of such articles as carpets and curtains, female apparel, books and paintings, decorations of walls and ceilings, and even the stones and bricks of the houses themselves, from the same cause. Then again, the frequent washing of hands and face leads to an increased consumption of soap. Many flowering shrubs and trees either cannot live or do not thrive in a London atmosphere. These and many similar charges have been brought against the smoke of London, by which

* A scientific friend writes of this stove as follows :—" It is rather trouble-some to manage, because I keep it going night and day in the winter time ; but I find the comfort of it to be well worth the trouble, as the room is warm in the morning, and I have merely to work the piston up two or three pegs, and get into bed again ; the fire then burns up of itself. In the day time it is allowed to smoulder in the box, and is worked up a little at night. It burns one small scuttle-full of coals in twenty-four hours in cold weather, and when only just kept alight it has gone for forty-eight hours with one scuttle-full, which just fills the box of the stove. It is a great acquisition for a person with delicate lungs. The chief trouble is in filling the box while the fire is alight. If, however, the fire is allowed to go out, and is lit again each day or night, there is not much trouble with it; in fact less than with an ordinary fire-place, if we reckon the trouble of stirring and putting on coals at intervals during the day. The keeping-alight-all-night-without-touching property, is what I bought it for."

is meant that portion of the fuel which has escaped combustion, and is discharged from chimneys in a minutely divided form, constituting the soot or visible smoke of a coal fire. The combustion of smoke, in its truest sense, can only get rid of this visible portion of the products of combustion, which is so obvious as to offend the eye, and contaminate the houses and their inhabitants. We cannot, however, agree with those who imagine that by getting rid of the visible carbon, we should greatly improve the health of the metropolis. Smoke is really a complicated product; the coal which is burnt in an open fire resolves itself into carbonic acid and water far greater in weight than the weight of the fuel originally burnt, together with small quantities of ammonia and sulphurous acid, flakes of pitchy bituminous matter, soot, dust, and ashes. Some injury is no doubt caused by inhaling the soot; but by passing the smoke through the fire or setting in operation some smoke-consuming apparatus, we convert the visible into an invisible smoke, cleaner, it is true, but scarcely more wholesome than the murky cloud which hangs over our city. We increase the quantity of carbonic acid, and do not get rid of the sulphur compounds; and it is these latter which are so inimical to vegetable life, and prevent the growth of that minute vegetation on the surfaces of stone buildings which, while clothing them in picturesque tints, protects them from the disintegrating effects of the weather. The sulphurous acid has also a directly corrosive action on the stone itself, on vegetation, furniture, and most objects that it comes in contact with.

But Dr. Arnott's fire-place has other merits in addition to that of consuming its own smoke. Under ordinary circumstances, the smoke of an open fire consists, not only of the pure products of combustion, but of the air of the room, which constantly streams into the open space above the fire, mingles with the smoke, dilutes it, and sets in motion the numerous chink draughts which render the open fire-place objectionable. Now, the quantity of pure smoke given off by a fire is comparatively small, consisting as it does of the air which actually passes through the fire to maintain the combustion, and the consequent combination of the oxygen of such air with the carbon, hydrogen, &c., of the fuel. The air which streams into the chimney from the room above the fire is a wasteful expenditure of the heat of the fire. To prevent this, Dr. Arnott places over the fire a cover or hood of metal, $y\,a\,b$ (Fig. 33), or, which he prefers, the space over the fire is similarly contracted by brickwork. The effect of this is, according to him, a saving of from one-third to one-half of the fuel required to maintain the desired temperature. The narrow part of the hood or brick channel is furnished with a throttle valve or damper, t, to regulate the current of air which passes into the chimney. This valve should not be opened more than enough to let the transparent smoke pass through. The size of the front opening of the fire-place admits of being contracted by means of a movable plate or blower, $o\,p\,q\,r$, so as to be able to raise the fire into activity in a few minutes. By the above arrangements, chink draughts from doors and windows are diminished, and they may be stopped altogether by making a special provision for the supply of air to the fire. This is done by means of the channel, $k\,l$, under the floor, leading directly from the external atmosphere to the hearth. The air coming in contact with the hot fender becomes tempered before it spreads into the room, while the products of respiration and of the combustion of lamps and candles are got rid of by means of the balanced valve, v,* which can be shut or left free to open by regulating the screw at x.

A skilful combination of the air-tube and caliducts of Gauger's fire-place has been made by Mr. Francis Lloyd, and described by him in the pamphlet mentioned below.† On considering the structure of an ordinary register stove, it occurred to him, that a considerable portion of the hollow space behind it might be turned to useful account, by substituting for the mere shell of cast-iron one horizontal and two upright tubes or caliducts, and by connecting them with

---

* This valve will be more particularly described further on. It is a happy adaptation of Dr. Franklin's suggestion as applied to the Pennsylvanian fire-place, page 98, *ante*.

† "Practical Remarks on the Warming, Ventilation, and Humidity of Rooms." London, 1854.—Mr. Lloyd has also published " A Description of Improved Hollow Bricks and Brickwork, intended to facilitate the Ventilation of Rooms." December, 1855.

one beneath the hearth-plate, to form a continuous tube round the fire, for the purpose of warming the air which passed through it. The air thus warmed was next to be admitted to the room in such a way that the inflowing current should not incommode the occupants. The upper part of the mantel seemed well adapted to this purpose, and supposing the upper horizontal tube to have an opening or slit extending along the top, and the stove being set sufficiently forward to place this slit beyond the line of the chimney-breast, the upper mantel, and mantel-shelf, could be formed so as to continue the passage-way from this tube, and thus the warm air would be discharged upwards into the room at about 4 feet above the level of the floor. The plan was adopted with success in Mr. Lloyd's house in town, and a second, and still more successful, experiment was tried at his country residence.

" The dining-room of a house, a few miles from town, was rendered scarcely habitable in consequence of the chimney smoking. The room (which was about 16 feet square and 8 feet high) was on the ground-floor, with no basement-story beneath. It was a few inches below the level of the garden in front, and had a provision for the circulation of air beneath the floor. The house was old, with doors and windows fitting but indifferently. The stove was of modern make ; but the fire invariably burnt dull, and the room was scarcely ever well warmed. As the room was required for daily use by the family, alterations to the old stove would have caused inconvenience ; a new register stove, of the ordinary dining-room kind, was therefore selected, with a view of trying how such an one could be fitted with air-tubes. The *plan* of the new stove is shown in Fig. 34. To the cheeks and the back of the face, *a a*, of the stove, were riveted two strips of sheet-iron, bent in the form

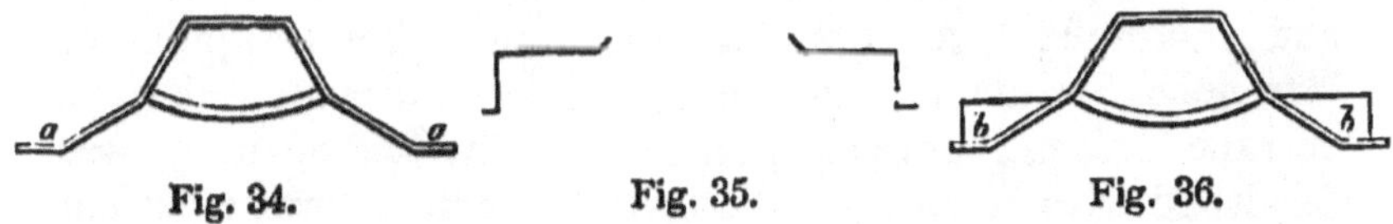

Fig. 34.   Fig. 35.   Fig. 36.

shown in Fig. 35. The plan then appeared as in Fig. 36. Two side chambers or tubes, *b b*, being thus obtained, the back of the upper face of the stove was fitted with a rectangular tube,

also of sheet-iron, which was connected with the two side
tubes, making uninterrupted communication between them.
The old stove was set very far back in the chimney shaft,
and was fitted with a large marble mantel, the displacement
or altering of which was on many accounts objectionable; it
was therefore determined, in this instance, to admit the air
into the room immediately under the mantelpiece, and afterwards to adopt means for preventing any inconvenient rush
of air in a horizontal line into the room. The area of a
section of each of the side tubes exceeded 18 inches, while
that of the horizontal tube was about 40 inches. The width
of the face of the stove was 3 feet; and to furnish the means
for the admission of the air into the room, an opening of 1
inch in width was left at the top of the horizontal tube, in its
vertical face, extending its whole length. A hearth-plate of
cast-iron was then provided with openings corresponding to
the horizontal section of the side tubes as shown in the plan.
The hearth-plate was then set with a chamber beneath,
extending in the middle as far back as the line of the front
firebars. From this chamber a zinc tube, 6 inches square,
was carried under the marble hearth beneath the floor,
through the front wall into the garden, where it was carried
up to the height of 14 inches, and was furnished with a
cap having sides of finely perforated zinc. A passage way
of 36 inches area was thus obtained beneath, around, and
above the *front* part of the stove, while there was a corresponding ingress for the air from the garden, and egress from
the upper part of the stove into the room. The stove was set
in the ordinary manner; and within twenty-four hours of the
removal of the old stove, a fire was lighted in the new one,
and the room was in occupation. It was at once evident that
the tendency to smoke was remedied, and the fire burnt freely
and cheerfully. As it was felt to be an important point to
introduce the air into the room in such a direction that its
entrance should not be perceptible, the air-opening was
furnished with a metal plate bent in such a form as would
direct the air-stream towards the ceiling, and also admit of
the supply·being diminished, or stopped entirely, as might be
found desirable. The complete and agreeable change in the

character of the air of the room was at once apparent to every one; and instead of the room being barely habitable in cold weather, it was found to be the most comfortable in the house. This stove was fixed at the latter end of December, 1850, and has been in use ever since, without the slightest difficulty of management, and with entire satisfaction to the inmates of the house. During the first winter careful observations were made on its action, and the results are in many respects remarkable. Within an hour after the fire is lighted, the air issuing from the air-passages is found to be raised to a comfortable temperature; and it soon attains a heat of 80°, at which it can be maintained during the day with a moderate fire. The highest temperature that has been attained has been 95°, whilst the lowest on cold days, with only a small fire, has been 70°. The result of twenty observations gave the following temperatures :—On two occasions the temperature was 95°; the fire was large, and the door of the room was left open, so that the draught through the air-tubes was diminished; on five occasions the temperature was below 80°, averaging 75°, the remaining thirteen gave an average of 80°. The mean temperature of the room at the level of respiration was 61°, while the uniformity was so perfect that thermometers hanging on the three sides of the room rarely exhibited a greater difference than 1°, although two of the sides were external walls. As might be expected, there was no sensible draught from the door and window. On observing the relative temperatures of the inflowing and general air of the room, it appeared that there must be a regular current from the ceiling down to the lower part of the room, and thence to the fire. The inflowing current being of a temperature nearly approximating to that of the body, was not easily detected by the hand; but on being tried by the flame of a candle it was observed to be very rapid, and to pursue a course nearly perpendicular towards the top of the room, widening as it ascended. It was also noticed that the odour of dinner was imperceptible in a remarkably short time after the meal was concluded. In order to trace the course of the air with some exactitude, various expedients were made use of. It was felt to be a matter of great interest to ascertain if possible the direction of air respired by the lungs. The smoke of a cigar, as discharged from the mouth, has probably a temperature about the same as respired air, higher rather than lower, and was therefore assumed to be a satisfactory indicator. On its being repeatedly tried, it was observed that the smoke did not ascend to any great height in the room, but tended to form itself into a filmy cloud at about 3 feet above the floor, at which level it maintained itself steadily, while it was gently wafted along the room to the fire-place. In order to get an abundant supply of visible smoke of a moderate temperature, a fumigator charged with cut brown paper was used. By this means a dense volume of smoke was obtained in a few seconds; and it conducted itself as in the last-mentioned experiment. On discharging smoke into the *inflowing air-current*, it was diffused so rapidly that its course could not be traced, but in a short time no smoke was observable in the room. Another experiment was made with a small balloon, charged with carburetted hydrogen gas, and balanced to the specific gravity of the air. On setting it at liberty near the air-opening, it was borne rapidly to the ceiling, near which it floated to one of the sides of the room, according to the part of the current in which it was set free; it then invariably descended slowly, and made its way with a gentle motion towards the fire. The air has always felt fresh and agreeable, however many continuous hours the room may have been occupied, or however numerous the occupants. It is difficult to estimate the velocity of the inflowing current; but if it be assumed to be 10 feet per second, there would pass through the air-tubes in 12 minutes as much air as will equal the contents of the room. And as it appears that the air so admitted passes from the room in a continuous horizontal stream, carrying with it up the chimney the rarefied air, the exhalations from the persons present, the vitiated air from the lamps or candles, and all vapours rising from the table, it is by no means surprising that the air should always be refreshing and healthful. Since this stove has been fixed, others have elsewhere been fitted up on the same principle, and have been found to exhibit similar satisfactory results."

The tubular stove is shown in vertical and horizontal section at Figs. 37 and 38, in which *a* is a flue 6 × 9 inches, for conducting the external air from the outer wall to the under side of the hearth-plate, *b*; *c c* are openings in the hearth-plate, *b*, communicating with two upright tubes of similar form, which conduct the air entering at *a* upwards to the horizontal tube, *d*. This tube is fitted to the two upright tubes, and has an opening extending along its whole length. If the width of the stove be 3 feet, this opening should be 1½ inch wide. The stove should be set 1¾ inch forward from the chimney-breast; *f* is the upper mantel, standing forward from the chimney-breast, *e*, 1½ inch; *g* is the mantel-shelf, with a portion of the back next the chimney-breast cut away, in order to continue the air-passage; *h* is a thin slab of marble, 1½ inch deep, built into the chimney-breast, and extending to the width of the mantel; it serves as a support for a chimney-glass, and also to divert the current of air from flowing directly up the chimney-breast; *i* is a strip of metal or marble, which serves to guide

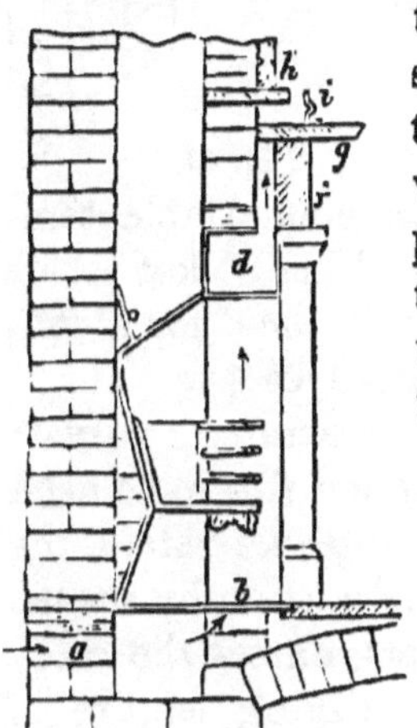

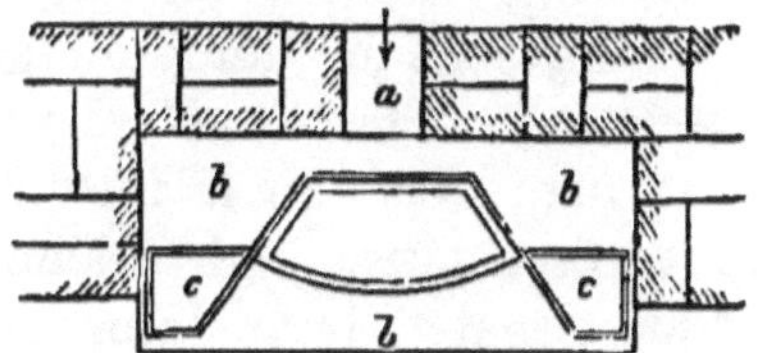

Fig. 37. Section.   Lloyd's Tubular Fire-place.   Fig. 38. Plan.

the air-stream upwards. By moving *i* to *h*, the supply of air may be regulated; or *i* may be fixed, and a thin strip of metal fixed on centres at the extremities be placed between *i* and *h*, so as to act like a throttle-valve. The opening between *i* and *h* need not be more than 1 inch.

Mr. Lloyd has also shown how hollow bricks may be employed so as to afford cheap, simple, and effectual means of ventilation, well adapted to the humbler class of dwellings. Fig. 39 is a brick of ordinary dimensions, containing two perforations, each about 2 inches square; Fig. 40 is a similar brick with pieces of the sides cut away; and Fig. 41 is an arrangement of these bricks, in which the dotted lines mark

air-channels intended for the back of the fire-place and chimney-shaft.   These air-flues may be carried to any height, and
to the right or left, as required, so that the heat at the back
of the fire-place and of the chimney may be distributed to

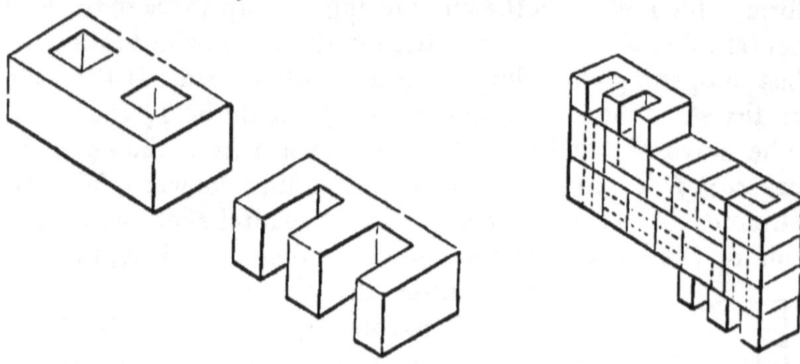

Fig. 39.   Fig. 40.   Fig. 41.

every room in the house, and maintain a comfortable temperature at the expense of only one fire.   The hollow brick
shaft being warmed by contact, will retain its heat for a considerable time, and warm the air in the air-flues.

Among the various contrivances for warming private
dwellings, the prejudices in favour of the open fire have been
respected.   Pierce's *Pyro-pneumatic Stove-grates* retain the
open fire: fresh air is introduced from the outside by means
of earthen pipes, and passing into caliducts, enters the room
at an elevated temperature.   The distinguishing feature of
the invention is, that the heating surfaces are formed of fire-
loam, so that the air is not burnt by contact with iron.   In
Jobson's *Stove-grate* the open fire is surrounded by a circular
parabolic reflector, which reflects the rays of light and heat
into the room in parallel lines.   The reflector turns upon a
hinge at the side, and can be brought out like a door for the
purpose of cleaning the grate or lighting the fire.   There is
a concealed ash-pan, which requires to be emptied only once
a week.   As the parabolic casting surrounds the grate, there
is little or no passage for the air into the chimney, except
through or close over the fire ; but the reflector can be made
to act as a ventilator by drawing it out an inch or two, so as
to allow the air to flow in around it.   Griffin's *Cottager's Stove*
appears to be judiciously arranged for the purposes of warm-

ing and ventilating. Fig. 42 is an external elevation, and Fig. 43 a vertical section. It has an open fire-place in the centre; a draw-shelf at the bottom of the grate; a drop-shelf at the top, which forms a blower when raised; a hot

Fig. 42. Cottager's Stove.

Fig. 43. Section.

plate for an ironing stove; an opening at the top for the escape of warm air; two ovens, or one oven and one hot closet; also a damper, a sweep-door, and a boiler. In the flange of the oven and closet are side doors for sweeping when required. The oven is equally heated all round by means of a flue, and when cooking is over, a fire of wet small coal, cinders, and ashes will last for several hours. Air is supplied from without by means of a pipe, which feeds the hot-air chambers at the back and side of the fire-place, and it escapes by an opening at the top. Even in the application of gas as a source of in-door warmth, attempts have been made to imitate the open fire. In Mr. Goddard's *Gas-stove*, the sides fold down so as to form a box of moderate dimensions, capable of being carried from room to room. When required for use, the sides are opened, and a flattened coil burner is supplied with gas by means of a flexible tube. When not intended to shut up, the fire-chamber is coated internally with porcelain, within which a tubular burner is set at an angle of 45°. A quantity of asbestos shavings being spread over the burner, the effect is something like that of a common fire.

In Ward's gas-stove the jets burn within a frame of thin sheet iron, which is fitted into an ordinary fire-place, after the manner of a fire-board.

In concluding this long chapter, we may remark that the open fire-place is so intimately connected with au English-man's ideas of domestic comfort, that it can never be expected, while coals are plentiful, that a more economical method of warming our rooms will become very common; it is, therefore, the duty of scientific men, to make the open fire-place as comfortable as it certainly is wholesome; and if a better method of supplying air to the fire than the present chance arrangement were adopted; if caliducts were led round the fire, so as to discharge warm air into distant parts of the room, and even over the house; if the various parts of the fire-place were of the proper shape and dimensions—there seems to be no good reason against retaining our cherished open fire, and converting it from a troublesome, uncertain, smoky, and expensive companion, into a source of health, pleasure, and economy.

CHAPTER II.

ON THE METHODS OF WARMING BUILDINGS BY MEANS OF CLOSE STOVES AND HOT-AIR APPARATUS.

ONE of the most intelligent advocates* in the cause of the CLOSE-STOVE *versus* the OPEN FIRE-PLACE, has preferred a very serious bill of indictment against the defendant. It consists of no less than eleven counts, of which the following is a summary. I. *Waste of fuel.* Of the whole heat produced from the fuel used, about seven-eighths ascend the chimney, and are wasted. The loss of heat is first, more than half, which is in the smoke as it issues from the burning mass. Secondly, that carried off by the current of the warmed air of the room, which is constantly entering the chimney between the fire and the mantelpiece, and mixing with the smoke. This is estimated at nearly two-eighths. Thirdly, the soot, or visible

* Dr. Arnott. "Warming and Ventilation, with Directions for making the Thermometer Stove, &c." London, 1838.

part of the smoke, is unburned fuel, and if more than half the heat produced be in the smoke, and nearly a fourth of it in the warm air from the room which escapes with the smoke, and if about an eighth of the combustible pass away unburned, there is a loss of at least seven-eighths of the whole. Count Rumford estimated the loss at fourteen-fifteenths. These estimates must of course be supposed to refer to the open fire-place with square jambs. II. *Unequal heating at different distances from the fire.* As the intensity of radiant heat is only one-fourth as great at a double distance, and so on, its effect being inversely as the square of the distance, the walls of the room are scarcely heated, and therefore reflect no heat to persons round the fire. There is usually one circular line around the fire in which persons must sit to be comfortable; and within this line they are too hot, and beyond it too cold. III. *Cold draughts* from doors and windows. IV. *Cold footbath.* The fresh entering air, being colder than the general mass already in the room, occupies the bottom of the apartment, and forms a dangerous cold-air bath for the feet of the inmates, so that they must keep their feet raised out of it by foot-stools, or wear warmer clothing. We see how anxious cats are to get out of this cold air-bath by occupying the seats of chairs, &c., instead of the carpet. V. *Bad ventilation.* The heated respired air ascends to the ceiling, and getting cool, descends, and is breathed over again; or, if the fire be not sufficiently supplied with air from the door and windows, it will come from other quarters, and bring in foul air from drains, &c. VI. *Smoke and dust.* VII. *Loss of time* in lighting the fires in the morning, and again during the day if neglected and allowed to go out. VIII. *Danger to property.* In London alone there are, on an average, about 100 fires per month. IX *Danger to the person.* Children get burnt, and the dresses of ladies, especially in these days of crinoline, often take fire by a sudden draught from the door, or coming too near the fire. X. *Expense of attendance.* It is contended that servants have more work to do in houses with open fires, than where stoves are kept. XI. *Necessity of sweeping.*

This is certainly a formidable indictment; but after the details given in the last chapter, it is not necessary to enter upon any further defence. There is no doubt that, upon some of the counts, the defendant must be found guilty; but it will be seen, in the present chapter, that the plaintiff does not come into court with clean hands, for there are many objections to the close stove, from which the open grate is entirely free. These will be stated as we proceed.

The close stove is used chiefly in those countries where fuel is scarce. One of the simplest forms is the *Dutch* stove, shown in Fig. 44. The fuel rests on the bars of a grate, near the bottom, and the air enters below the grate. The fuel is introduced by a door above the grate, which door is closed while the stove is in action, and as this is the only opening in the stove above the fuel, no air can reach the chimney, except that which has passed through the fire, thus saving the waste of warm air, which, in open fires, passes between the fire and the mantelpiece. The heating

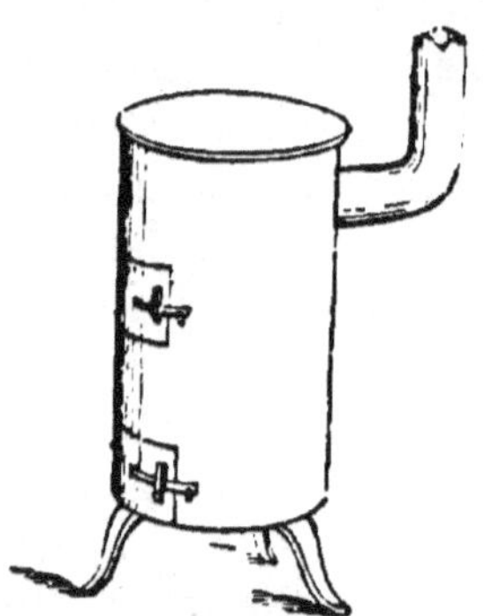

Fig. 44. The Dutch Stove.

effect of this stove is due to the whole surface of the stove and its flue, which receive the direct heat of combustion, as well as much of the heat of the products of combustion, as they escape into the chimney; and if the flue be made sufficiently long, so as to expose a large surface in the room, nearly the whole of the heat may be applied to use without draughts, or smoke, or dust. These are the good qualities of the Dutch stove; now for its bad ones. The heated iron surface acts upon the air in contact with it, so as to impair its purity and fitness for respiration. "The air," says Dr. Arnott, "acquires a burnt and often sulphurous smell, in part, no doubt, because dust, which it often carries, is burned, and in part because there is a peculiar action of the iron upon the air. It becomes very dry, too, like that of an African simoom, shrivelling everything which it touches; and it acquires probably some new electrical properties. These changes combined make it so offensive, that Englishmen, unaccustomed to it, cannot bear it. In this country, many forms have been proposed, some of them gracefully designed, with transparent talc doors, and other attractions; and they have been tried in rooms, public offices, passages, halls, &c., but have been afterwards very generally abandoned. Persons breathing the air heated by them are often affected by headaches, giddiness, stupor, loss of appetite, ophthalmia, &c. A north-east wind, which distresses many people, bringing asthmas, croups, &c., and which withers vegetation, is peculiar chiefly in being dry." This stove is much used by laundresses and others for drying, and in this application of it, the Doctor admits, it is good and economical. The ornamental varieties of it are also furnished with vases and other receptacles for water, which, by its evaporation, greatly mitigates the evils complained of; but it must be admitted that the list of objections brought against the Dutch stove forms as formidable a bill of indictment as that preferred against the open fire. Another objection, not noticed in the above quotation, arises from the overheating of the flue. It has often been known to get red-hot, and has thus led to serious conflagrations.

The *American* stove is a square close iron box, with a vessel of water upon it, to give moisture to the air. It has a plate projecting under the door, D (Fig. 45); the wood fuel is burned within it at A, and the flame passes along by B, to the chimney, C, around an inner box, which is the cooking oven of the family, opening by a door in the side of the stove. The fuel is introduced by a large door at D, in which there is a smaller door, which, as well

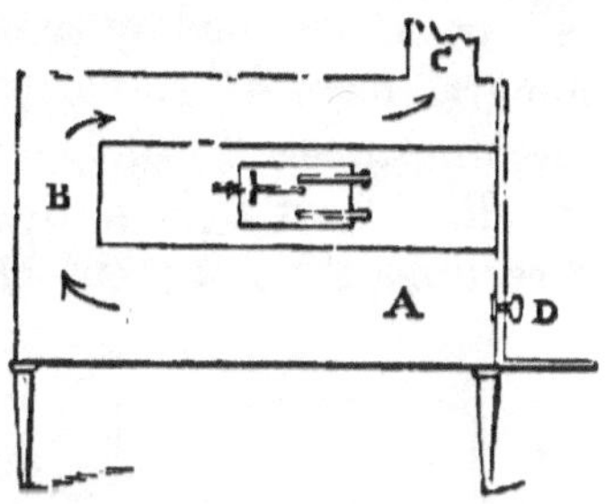

Fig. 45. The American Stove.

as the larger, is usually kept shut, because a sufficient supply of air enters by the joinings around; but in cold weather the small door is opened to increase the combustion. The stove has iron legs, about a foot in length.

In Russia, Prussia, and the North of Europe generally, the stove is a very important article of domestic furniture, in which the largest possible amount of heating effect is obtained from the smallest possible quantity of fuel. In the construction of these stoves the following points are kept in view:—

To maintain in the fire-place the high temperature necessary for the perfect combustion of the fuel, by surrounding it with such substances as are bad conductors of heat, such as fire-stone or bricks ; to have the means of regulating the quantity of air admitted to the fuel, by valves in the doors which enclose the ash-pit and fire-chamber, and by accurate fitting of the doors and valves themselves. Thirdly, to bring all the gaseous products of combustion, as they escape from the fuel, into contact with the largest possible area of slowly conducting surface, so as to maintain it at an equal temperature ; and, lastly, to make the smoke enter the chimney with the smallest velocity, or lowest temperature, that is practically consistent with the first condition. In no case should this temperature exceed 150°, nor should the metallic surface ever be raised higher than 100°, nor the stream of air issuing from it exceed 70°. In every case the combustion is regulated by limiting the supply of air, and if the heating surface be small, the fire is reduced so as to produce no more heat than can be carried off by the radiation and conduction of such heating surface.

The method in which these conditions are complied with will be understood by referring to Fig. 46, which represents a general form of stove. It may be modified according to circumstances of utility or taste, but the principle is the same in all. M I K L is a quadrangular box of any size, in the directions M I L K ; but the inside width, from front to back,

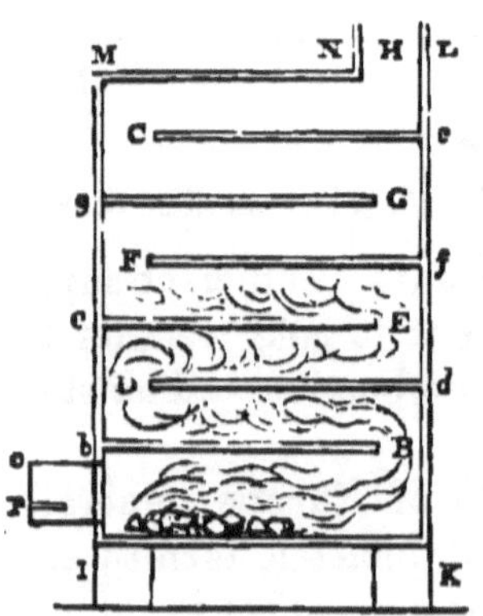

Fig. 46. The German Stove.

is generally pretty constant; it is never less than 10 inches, and seldom extending to 20 inches. The whole included space is divided by a number of partitions. The lowest chamber, B, serves for the fuel, which is placed on the bottom of the stove without any grate. The fire-place has a door, o, turning on hinges, and in this door is a small wicket, P. The roof of the fire-place extends to within a very few inches of the further end, having a narrow passage, B, for the flame. The next partition, d, is about 8 inches higher, and reaches almost to the other end, leaving a narrow passage for the flame at D. The partitions, *e f g c*, are repeated above at the distance of 8 inches, leaving passages, E F G C, at the ends alternately disposed, the last communicating with the vent in the H flue. This communication is regulated by an iron plate, or damper, N L, which can be slid across it by moving a rod, which passes out through the side. If the fuel be wood, as is generally the case, and the vent opens into the room, this passage is closed by a sort of pan, or bowl of earthenware, which is inverted over it, with its brim buried in sand, contained in a groove formed all round the hole. The whole stove is set on low pillars, so that its bottom may be a few inches from the floor of the room. It is usually placed in a corner of the apartment, which is so disposed that the chimneys can be joined in stacks, as with us. In lighting the stove, straw or wood shavings are first burnt on the hearth at its farther end, in order to warm the air in the stove and determine a current. The fuel is then laid on the hearth close by the door, and piled up and kindled, and the current, being already directed to the vent, there is no danger of smoke getting out into the room. The door, *o*, is then closed, and the wicket, P, opened, and the air supplied by this means being directed to the middle or bottom of the fuel, it is quickly kindled, and is soon burning well.

Now it will be seen, by this construction, that the flame and heated products of combustion are retained as long as possible within the body of the stove, and their heat diffused over a very extended surface, which is still further increased by making the stove narrower from front to back in its upper part. A certain breadth is necessary below, that there may be room for the bulky wood fuel; but if this breadth were preserved all the way up, much heat would be lost, because the heat, communicated to the partitions of the stove, acts with little or no useful effect, so that, by diminishing their breadth, the proportion of heating surface is increased. The whole body of the stove may, as Professor Robison remarks, be considered as a long pipe folded up, and its effect would be the greatest possible, if it really were so, that is, if each partition were split into two, and a free passage allowed between them for the air of the room.

In order that the heated surface may be as extensive as possible, the stove is not built into the wall, nor in contact with it, or with the floor. By being thus detached, both the back and bottom of the stove are sources of heat to the air of the room, and the bottom, which is the hottest part, contributes at least half the heating effect. Sometimes, however, the stove forms a part of the wall between two rooms, and serves to heat both. It is also common to have the door of the fire in the passage on the outside of the room, so that an attendant can manage it without incommoding the occupants.

The author of "A Residence on the Shores of the Baltic, 1841," refers to these stoves in the following terms :— "Within these great houses, not a breath of cold is experienced. The rooms are heated by stoves, frequently ornamental rather than otherwise; being built in tower-like shapes, story over story, of pure white porcelain, in various graceful architectural mouldings ; sometimes surmounted with classic figures of great beauty, and opening with brass doors, kept as bright as if they were of gold. In houses of less display, these stoves are merely a projection in the wall, coloured and corniced in the same style as the apartment. In adjoining rooms they are generally placed back to back, so that the same fire suffices for both. These are heated but once in the twenty-four hours by an old Caliban, whose business during the winter it is to do little else. Each stove will hold a heavy armful of billet, which blazes, snaps, and cracks most merrily ; and when the ashes have been carefully turned and raked with what is termed an *ofen gabel*, or stove fork, so that no unburnt morsel remains, the chimney aperture is closed over the glowing embers, the brass doors firmly shut, and in about six hours after this, the stove is at the hottest— indeed, it never cools."

The useful effect of this stove depends very much on retaining in the room the air already heated by it. A small open fire in the same room will actually diminish the heating effect of the stove, and even draw the warm air from adjoining apartments. In the houses of English merchants at

St. Petersburg, open fires are sometimes introduced into rooms with stoves; and the consequence is, that it is found necessary to light the stoves twice a day, and yet the houses are cooler than those of the Russians, who light them only once. To our notions, however, a cool in-door atmosphere is preferable to a nauseous stagnant one, such as the Russians and Germans are accustomed to breathe throughout the winter; and even in summer they are very averse to an open window. The temperature of the winter apartments is kept nearly always at 65°, and as every part of the room is equally warm, the inmates have no occasion to crowd round the stove as we do round the fire. " But I can testify," says Dr. Buxton, " that in German rooms there is a closeness of feeling to a person accustomed to free air, which is unpleasant, if not unwhole-some—no change of air, the windows closed as tight as can be, and the door fits as exactly as the carpenter can make it. The stove is air-tight with regard to the room, and there is nothing to occasion a current like an English open fire. The apartments of the sick almost invariably smell disagreeably. I do not, however, recollect seeing a single ventilator in Germany; but I have repeatedly seen double windows." As ventilation can only be procured at the expense of heat, the people prefer retaining the foul air to expending an extra por-tion of fuel. In the houses of the poorer classes in Russia, where the windows are single, and a number of persons occupy a small stove-heated room, a thick icy crust forms on the inside of the windows during frosty weather, arising from the condensation of the breath, perspiration, and the aqueous fumes of candles, and of the stove, &c. When a thaw comes on, this icy crust is converted into water, and a deleterious prin-ciple is disengaged, which produces effects similar to those arising from the fumes of charcoal. Persons so affected are immediately carried into the open air, and placed on the snow with very little clothing; the temples and the region of the stomach are well rubbed with snow, and cold water is poured down their throats, and the friction is continued until the livid hue of the skin disappears, and the natural colour is restored. The Chinese are wiser in this respect than the Russians, for, although their rooms may in winter be as hot and as crowded, they have two openings at the top of each window, which are never allowed to be closed, and through these ventilation is carried on.

The stove last described belongs rather to that variety called the *Swedish stove*, than to the *Russian* or *German*. In the Russian or German stove, the smoke, after rising from the fuel, recedes into the flue, and becomes cooled by contact with the walls of the circulating chambers, and the heat is by this means retained in the apartment, which would otherwise have escaped combined with the vapour. In the Swedish stove, the circumvolutions of the smoke are exposed to a vivid heat, so that every particle of soot undergoes a second combustion in the circulating channels. Some of the Swedish stoves have from four to nine channels for the circulation of the smoke; some are contrived to receive one or more boilers, and others to act as ovens; and they all greatly economise the fuel, for, according to Morveau, the quantity of wood which is consumed in twenty-three days in an open fire, with less effect, will last sixty-three days in a stove.

In erecting the ponderous German stoves it is necessary to arrange the various pieces of clay, or porcelain, so that no part should crack or give way, and thus admit the smoke or carbonic acid vapour into the room. When the parts are put together with cement, or held by iron cramps, a leakage commonly occurs at the joinings, where the different pieces of clay are differently heated, and, perhaps, were of a different baking when made; hence, by expanding unequally, and working on each other, one of them must give way. But, instead of making the joints close and using any cement, the best method is to make each upper piece stand in a groove formed in the piece below it, and then to sprinkle a little powdered chalk or clay over it, which will effectually prevent the passage of any air, and, at the same time, allow space for any expansion or contraction at the joint.

Some valuable experiments by Mr. Bull are quoted by Mr. Bernan, to show the effect of ascending and descending flues in the Russian and Swedish stoves, and of elbows or bends in the flue of the common Dutch stove. From these experiments, it appears that the same length of pipe is much more efficacious in imparting heat to a room when it has elbows than when it is straight; that a descending current may be somewhat more efficacious than an ascending one, but is about equal with a horizontal one; a horizontal pipe, with the same number of elbows, is more efficacious in imparting heat, than when placed vertically for an ascending and descending current. The cause of the increased effect is supposed to arise from the shape of the pipe forcing the heated air to make abrupt turns, in doing which it impinges against the elbows with sufficient force to invert its internal arrangement, by which a new stratum of hot air from the interior of the current is brought more frequently in contact with the sides of the pipe and particularly with the lower half of the horizontal pipe, which, from various causes, gives out very little heat to the room without the aid of elbow joints. But the advantage gained by increasing the length of pipe and number of joints has a limit very far short of that which is found to be necessary to impart all, or the greatest part, of the heat generated to the air of the room. Only five parts of heat in 100 were lost by using $13\frac{1}{2}$ feet of pipe, consisting of nine elbow joints; whereas, eight additional elbow joints, and $16\frac{1}{2}$ feet additional of straight pipe, in all $28\frac{1}{2}$ feet of pipe, were required to save these five parts, and prevent their flowing into the chimney. By diminishing the diameter of the pipe, the heating effect is increased, partly from the retardation of the current, and partly from the small pipe exposing a greater surface to the air with the same quantity of smoke than a pipe of larger diameter.

An excellent stove with a descending current was constructed by Dr. Franklin for his own use. Fig. 47 represents a vertical section, in which x is an opening in the cover, furnished with a hinge; a is a fire-chamber, in which the grating is fixed; b a space

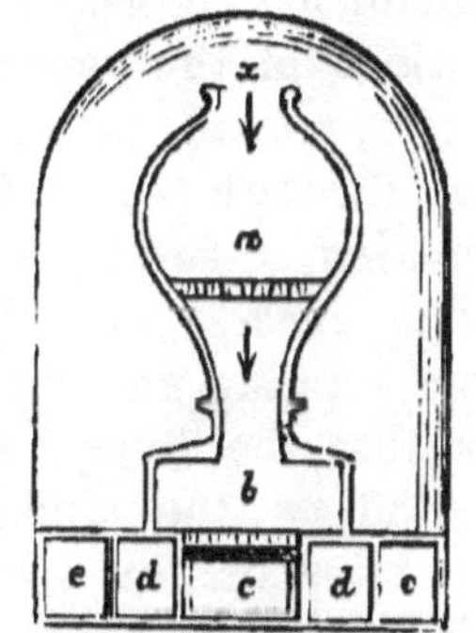

Fig. 47. Stove with Descending Flue.

containing a second grating; c the ash-pit, with a drawer to receive the ashes; $d\ e$ horizontal flues at each side of the ash-box, communicating with vertical flues which lead into the chimney. The vase and flues are contained in a niche formed by closing up the fire-place, and there is no communication between the room and the flue, except through the opening, *x*, in the lid. The fire should be first lighted at a time when there is usually a draught *up* the chimney, as already explained (page 108); but the direction of the draught had better be ascertained by holding a flame over the air-hole at the top of the vase. If the flame be drawn strongly down, the fire may be lighted by first putting in a little char-coal on the grate at *a;* then lay some small sticks on the charcoal and some paper on the sticks; set light to the paper, and shut down the lid; the air will pass down through the air-hole, and blowing the flame of the paper through the sticks, kindle them, and they, in their turn, will kindle the charcoal. The flame and hot vapour descending through the grating at *a*, passes into the chamber, *b*, and through the second grating in its bottom into the ash-pit, *c*. The hot current will then be divided—one portion turning to the left, and passing into the horizontal channels, *d e*, and entering the vertical flue, will be conducted into the chimney; the other portion will make a similar circuit on the left in the channels, *d c*, and entering another flue, will in like manner pass into the chimney. The surfaces of the vase and air-box, and the part of the horizontal channels exposed to the room, are heated by these circumvo-lutions of the vapour, and the air warmed by contact with them, spreads into the room. The larger pieces of coal that fall through the grating on the vase, are caught by the second grating, *b*, and the ashes fall through it into the ash-pit box, *c*. The success of this contrivance depends of course upon maintaining an upward steady draught in the chimney flue, so that the ash-pit drawer and a door in the chamber, *b*, to withdraw the cinders, must be made air-tight. In order to determine an upward current on lighting the fire, a small door may be made in the side of the flue, and a piece of lighted paper inserted.

Mr. Beaumont's stove also acts by a downward current. It is represented in section, in Fig. 48. The foundation, *a*, is of bricks, two courses high, and 25 inches square, with a vacant space 6½ inches wide, for the ash-hole, *b*. Upon this foundation are laid two plates of cast-iron, c, each 9 inches wide, 25 inches long, and an inch thick. The plate which covers the ash-pit draws out, and in doing so turns the ashes into the ash-pit. On these iron plates is erected a drum, with an aperture, x, for the smoke flue. This aperture, when lined with fire-bricks, is 6 inches wide, and $4\frac{1}{2}$ inches high. The drum is also lined with fire-bricks, set on edge, and is covered with a circular plate of cast-iron, s n, with a downward lip round the edge, to receive the upper edge of the drum. In the middle of the cover, n, is a hole, 7 inches in diameter, for the admission of fuel, and this is covered with a lid, moving on a pivot to regulate the admission of the air. An opening of an inch is usually sufficient for that purpose. A short rim projects from the lid,

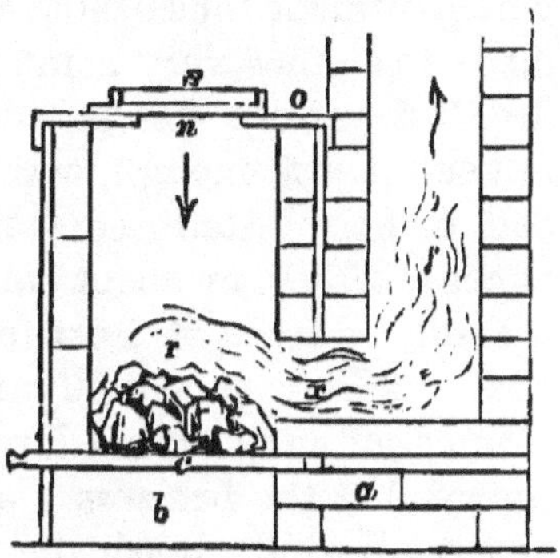

Fig. 48. Beaumont's Stove.

whereby it is converted into a shallow vessel for holding water, the evaporation of which keeps the air sufficiently moist. The fire is lighted by first throwing in a few coals, then some sticks and paper, and, lastly, some cinders or coke, with a little coal immediately over the wood, taking care to make the fuel slope away from the smoke flue. The aperture at the top is then nearly closed, and the fire is lighted. The smoke first tends to rise towards the aperture, but the heat soon determines a downward current, which sets into the smoke aperture, and carrying with it the gaseous products of combustion into the flue, f, the fire soon begins to burn brightly. At night the aperture is closed, and the fire goes out. All the fuel is consumed, the downward draught producing complete combustion; there is no soot, and nothing of the fuel remains but a red ash. The management of this stove is quite easy; all that is required being to push in the slide over the ash-pit before the fire is lighted, to let the fire burn brightly before much fuel is put on, and to keep the smoke vent, x, from being choked up, by overloading it with fuel.

Mr. Beaumont says, that although this stove thoroughly warmed the air of the office, yet the clerks constantly complained of cold feet. To remedy this, a flue was formed under the paved floor, the paving-stones forming the roof of it. The flue, which was a foot square, entered one side of the office, continued along that side, across the top, and down the other side, where it entered an upright flue in the party wall. The pavement thus heated after the Chinese fashion (page 71) made the office very comfortable. With a mere handful of fire, the warmth was so considerable, that the difficulty was to keep it low enough, without putting out the fire. An office and principal staircase were thus kept warm at an annual expense of 30s. or about 3d. a day for the cold season; whereas a similar degree of heat from another apparatus cost £18 a year. "Persons coming in from the open air have complained of our keeping large fires, and when they have been shown that the fire was a small one, burning without fierceness, and which might be contained in the crown of a hat, they have denied their belief to the fact; and insisted that the warmth which they felt must have been procured from some other source. It really does appear like magic, but the case proves the fact of one part only of the heat from the previous apparatus going to the place to be heated, and that eleven parts went up the chimney, and were wasted at the house top."

The stove shown in section, in Fig. 49, is an improvement on the Dutch stove, already noticed (page 130). The fire-chamber, a, 8 inches on each side, is enclosed by four fire-tiles, c c, 1 inch thick, placed in a cast-iron case, $\frac{3}{8}$ths of an inch thick, with a ledge to support the grate. This ledge projects $3\frac{1}{2}$ inches downwards into the ash-pit, and terminates in four short standards, or feet, placed on the sole of the stove. A space, x, of $4\frac{1}{2}$ inches, is left between this iron casing and the inner casing of the stove. Five inches above the upper edge of the tiles of the fire-box, a fire-tile, e, $1\frac{1}{2}$ inch thick, and $15\frac{1}{2}$ inches square, is fixed on brackets, so as to leave a space, r, about $1\frac{1}{4}$ inch all round, between it and the inner surface of the casing, for the hot vapour from the fuel to rise upwards. A plate of iron, or a tile, n, is fixed about 8 inches above the tile, *e*, leaving also a space, *r*, about 1¼ inch, between its edge and the casing. The roof of the stove, about 8 inches above the plate, terminates in the smoke-pipe, *d ;* the fire-door and its valve are shown at *b*, and the ash-pit door and air-valve at *s*, the upper edge of this valve being ½ an inch above the under edge of the iron casing of the smoke-chamber. The stove is enclosed in a plate-iron casing, so as to leave a space, *o*, of 1½ inch round it. This casing is open at the bottom, *m m*, and at the top, *p p*, and has two fillets projecting about ½ an inch from its surface ; no valve of any kind is attached to this outward casing, and the air circulates freely through the space, *o*, that it encloses. All the parts are accurately fitted, and no air enters the stove, except through the valves at *s* and *b*. In the speci-men described by Mr. Bernan, " the heating surface was 20½

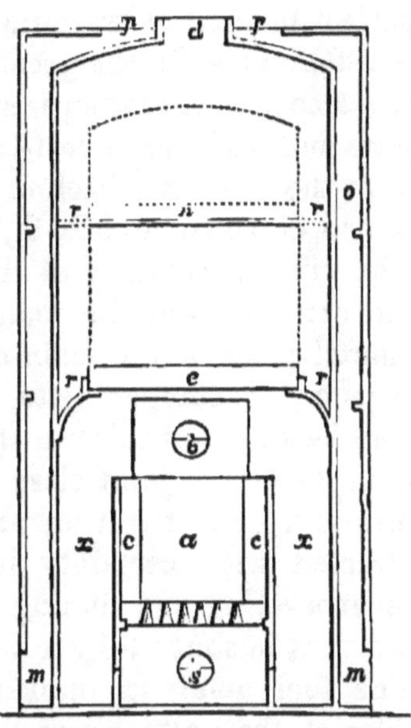

Fig. 49. Improved Dutch Stove.

square feet, and the depth of coke in the fire-chamber was generally about 5 inches; and this was found sufficient for a room containing nearly 5,600 cubic feet of space. When there is fire, the hot vapour from the fuel being prevented from rising in a stream upwards by the tile, *e*, spreads along its under surface and ascends all round the edge of the tile, through the narrow space, *r*, which brings the smoke into contact with a large surface of the iron casing, and this con-tact is prolonged until it reaches the roof, by flowing through the narrow space between the upper tile and the casing ; the whole surface of the stove thus kept in contact with the smoke, is equally heated, and the air which rises freely in the space, *o*, being brought rapidly in contact with this hot surface, is genially warmed and emitted at *p* into the room."

A combination of the stove and the grate, combining the

heating effect of the stove with the cheerful appearance and ventilating properties of the open fire, is known under the name of the *stove-grate*, or *Chapelle*; the latter name being derived from its resemblance to the chapels or oratories of the great churches. Professor Robison describes it as the most perfect method of warming an apartment. Its construction is as follows :—In the great chimney-piece is set a smaller one, of a size no larger than is sufficient for holding the fuel. The sides and back are of cast-iron, and are kept at a small distance from the sides and back of the main chimney-piece, and continued down to the hearth, so that the ash-pit is also separate. The pipe or chimney of the stove-grate is carried up behind the ornaments of the mantel-piece, until it rises above the mantel-piece of the main chimney-piece, and is fitted with a register, or damper plate, turning round a transverse axis. The best form of this register is that of an ordinary fire-place, with its axis or joint close at the front, so that when open or turned up, the burnt air and smoke, striking it obliquely, are directed with certainty into the vent without any risk of reverberating and coming out into the room. All the rest of the vent is shut up by iron plates or brickwork out of sight. The fuel being in immediate contact with the back and sides of the grate, raises them to a great heat, and they heat the air contiguous to them. This heated air cannot get up the vent, because the passages above these spaces are shut up. It therefore comes out into the room ; some of it goes into the real fire-place, and is carried up the vent, and the rest rises to the ceiling, and is diffused over the room. The heating effect of this stove-grate is remarkable. Less than a quarter of the fuel consumed in an ordinary fire-place is sufficient, and this, with the same cheerful blazing hearth, and the salutary renewal of the air. Indeed, it often requires attention to keep the room cool. The heat communicated to those parts of the apparatus which are in contact with the fuel is needlessly great, so that it has been found an improvement to line this part with thick plates of cast-iron, or with tiles of fire-clay. These, being bad conductors, moderate the heat communicated to the air. If the heat be still found too great, it may be brought under perfect management by opening passages in the vent for the spaces on each side, so that the air heated by the sides of the stove-grate may ascend directly into the flue, instead of escaping into the room. These passages may be closed by valves, or trap-doors, moved by rods concealed behind the ornaments of the fire-place.

The stove-grate is under complete control as to temperature. A cheerful fire may be ensured within five minutes, simply by hanging a plate of iron in front so as to reach down as low as the grate; and when the fire is, by its means, blown up, the plate may be taken down and sent out of the room, or set up behind the grate out of sight. If, on the other hand, the room be found inconveniently warm, the temperature may be cooled down within a quarter of an hour, by opening the side passages to any extent for the escape of the hot air. In this arrangement the ash-pit is enclosed, because the light ashes, not finding a ready passage up the chimney, are apt to escape into the room with the heated air.

Few contrivances for warming apartments have excited more attention and discussion of late years than Dr. Arnott's stove. The principle of this invention consists in allowing the fuel to burn very slowly, the admission of air for combustion being regulated by a peculiar contrivance. There are various forms and modifications of this stove, but the principle is the same in all. The stove consists of a square or cylindrical box of iron, lined with fire-clay, with a grating near the bottom for the fuel, or the fuel may be contained in a small fire-box within the stove. Sometimes the fuel is burned within a hollow cylinder of fire-clay, and then the stove is not lined with that material. There is an ash-pit below for the ashes, and the products of combustion are carried off by a vent. The chief feature of this stove is, the contrivance by which the air is admitted to the fuel. When the stove door or ash-pit door is open, the combustion is vivid; but when these are perfectly tight, as they ought to be, then the air is admitted by a regulator.

The form first tried is shown in Fig. 50, in which $a\ b\ c\ d$ represent a box of sheet iron divided by the partition, $g\ h$, into two chambers communicating freely at the top and bottom; e is the fire-box formed of iron, lined with fire-brick, and resting on a close ash-pit with a door at *b*, near which is a valved opening, by which air enters to feed the fire when the door is shut; *i* is the door of the stove by which fuel is introduced; *c* is the chimney flue. When the ash-pit door and the stove-door are shut, the quantity of air admitted by the valved opening in the ash-pit is only just sufficient to support combustion, and only a small corresponding quantity of air can pass away by the chimney. The whole box then soon becomes filled with hot air, or smoke from the fire circulating in it, and rendering it everywhere of as

Fig. 50. The Arnott Stove.

uniform temperature as if it were full of hot water. This circulation takes place, because the air in the front chamber around the fire-box, and which receives as a mixture the red-hot air issuing from the fire, is hotter, and, therefore, specifically lighter, than the air in the posterior chamber, which receives no direct heat, but is always losing heat from its sides and back; and thus, as long as the fire is burning, there must be circulation. The whole mass of air is, in fact, seen to revolve, as marked by the arrows, with great rapidity. The quantity of new air rising from within the fuel, and the like quantity escaping by the flue, *c*, are very small, compared with the revolving mass. The methods of regulating the supply of air will be noticed presently.

With this stove, Dr. Arnott, during the severe winter of 1836-7, was able to maintain in his library a uniform temperature of from 60° to 63°. The quantity of coal used (Welsh stone coal) was, for several of the colder months, 6 lbs. a day—less than a pennyworth—a smaller expense than that of the wood used in lighting an ordinary fire. The grate or fire-box, fully charged, held a supply for twenty-six hours.

Another common form of this stove is shown in Fig. 51; A B C D is the outer casing; E the fire-box over which is a dome, *k*, with a funnel, *p*, to carry off the products of combustion; *h* is the stove door; and *g* the regulator by which air is admitted. Various forms of regulators are described, a specimen of which is shown in Fig. 52. A B C is a glass tube shut at A, containing air from A to B, and mercury in the bend below B C; on the mercury at C is a float, from which proceeds an upright rod, D, kept steady by passing through a support at H. From this upright wire descends another, F G H, terminated by the plate valve, F; E is the air-tube

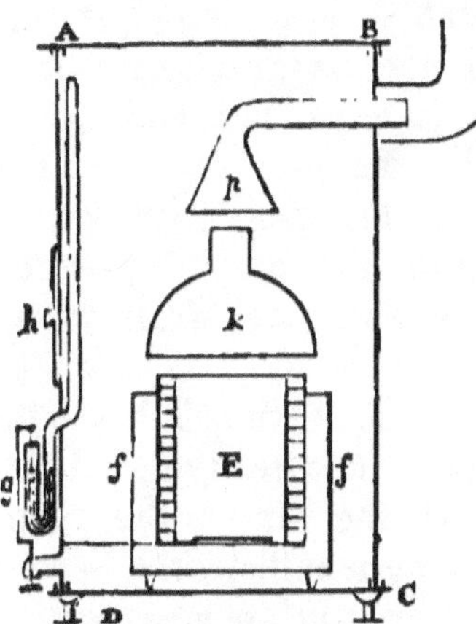

Fig. 51. The Arnott Stove.

of the stove. When the heat within is great, the air in the shut limb of the regulator at A is expanded, and forces up the mercury at C, raising the rods and plate valve, F, and thus bringing it near to or in contact with the mouth of the tube, by

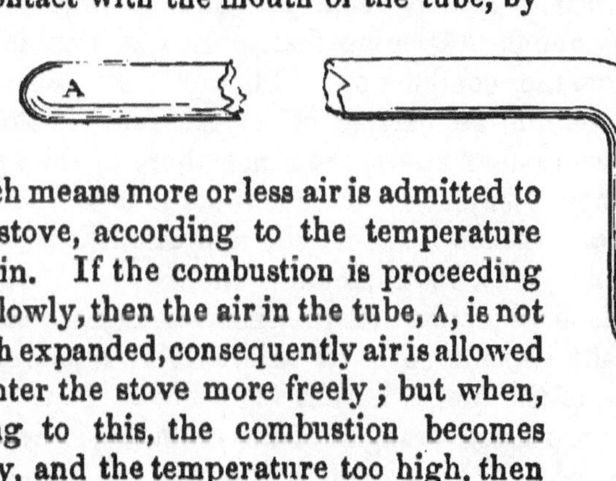

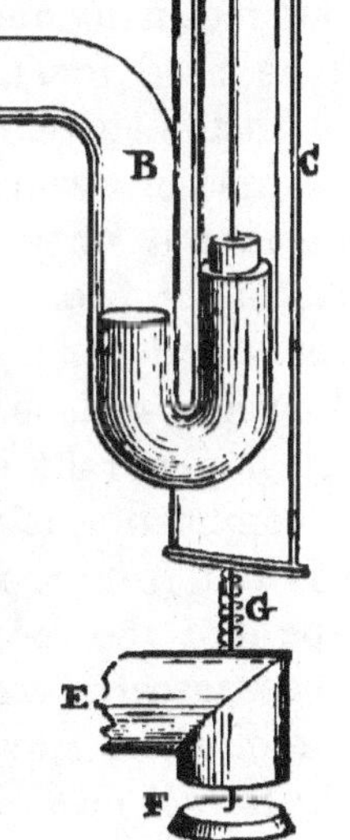

which means more or less air is admitted to the stove, according to the temperature within. If the combustion is proceeding too slowly, then the air in the tube, A, is not much expanded, consequently air is allowed to enter the stove more freely; but when, owing to this, the combustion becomes lively, and the temperature too high, then by the elevation of the plate valve, less air enters, and the temperature is moderated.

A more simple form of regulator is shown in Fig. 53; *a b c* is a bent tube shut at *a*, where it contains air, and open

Fig. 52. Regulator.

at *c*, where it is cup-shaped. The bent part at *b* is occupied by mercury; from *c* proceeds a bent tube for supplying air to the stove. When the internal heat is great, the air in *a* is expanded and forces the mercury up in *c*, and thus bringing it in contact with the mouth, prevents the entrance of air to the stove.

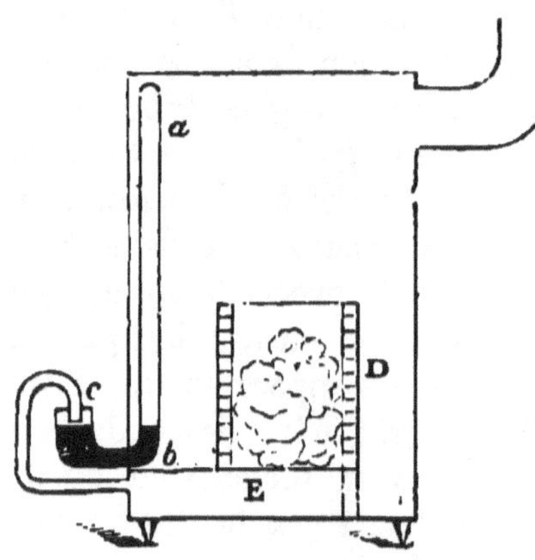

Fig. 53. Arnott's Stove.

This stove is liable to the objection already stated, viz., that the air of the room, though sufficiently heated, is nevertheless stagnant. A pound of coal requires about 150 cubic feet of air for combustion; but as a portion of the air escapes without being chemically acted on, 200 cubic feet may be allowed. Now, if a room warmed by Arnott's stove be 15 feet long, 12 feet wide, and 11 feet high, its cubic contents are 1,980 feet; and if 6 lbs. of coal per day be burnt, each pound requiring about 200 cubic feet, only 1,200 cubic feet will be used for the combustion. This quantity must pass through the stove, and be carried off by the vent, so that in the course of twenty-four hours, the atmosphere of the apartment is not once completely changed or renewed by the action of the fire. Hence it is that the apartment is so easily warmed, and hence, also, its unpleasant effect.

Another serious objection to this stove arises from that which is generally considered as its chief merit; namely, the slow combustion of the fuel, whereby carbonic oxide is generated, and, from the small draught of the chimney, is liable to escape into the room. This gas is poisonous, and its escape has been ascertained by Dr. Ure, by attaching to the ash-pit of one of these stoves a glass vessel containing a solution of subacetate of lead, which being speedily acted on by the carbonic oxide, was formed into the insoluble carbonate of lead. It is also stated that carburetted hydrogen is sometimes formed in these stoves, which, by mingling with the air, has formed an explosive mixture, and thus led to accidents.

A good application of Dr. Arnott's *close stove*, for the purpose of warming and ventilating, has been made by Mr. Charles Cowper. In the back kitchen of his house, which is but little used, he placed an Arnott's stove, and partially enclosed it in a case of sheet-iron, so as to form a kind of air-jacket, opening into which was a zinc pipe 5 inches in diameter, the other end passing through the wall into the open air. By this contrivance all the air entering at the pipe was made to spread itself over the exterior of the stove, and thus become gently warmed. The effect of this arrangement has been to make the house much more comfortable as regards temperature, and to cure the chimneys of their tendency to smoke.

Joyce's stove for burning charcoal is liable to all the objections arising from the use of this fuel in an apartment. The charcoal is prepared for this stove by reburning common charcoal in a close oven, and quenching it while hot in an alkaline solution. This is said to deprive it of its usual pungent smell in burning, but, if so, it renders it all the more dangerous, since the carbonic acid may slowly accumulate in an apartment —a bed-chamber, for example—and produce fatal consequences. The stove consists of a thin metal case, in the form of a small urn or vase. A small pipe, 2 or 3 inches long, rises through the bottom into the body of the stove, and terminates about the centre in a conical funnel closed at the top, and pierced full of holes. At the top of the stove is a valve, for the purpose of regulating the supply of air through the lower pipe, to maintain the combustion. A small portion of ignited charcoal is placed in the stove, and the remaining space filled up with charcoal not ignited; and as the supply of air is very limited, it will continue to give out heat for many hours. The whole of the charcoal is converted into carbonic acid, which escapes from the valve at the top in proportion to the quantity of air which enters at the bottom. This stove has nothing to recommend it; for the charcoal fuel is not only dangerous, but expensive. From its small size, and great calorific power, this stove excited considerable attention at the time of its introduction ; and from the statements made respecting it, the public was led to expect that some new law of combustion had been discovered, or that the old law had been suspended in its favour ; for it was gravely affirmed that the whole of the products of combustion were absorbed, or otherwise prevented from escaping from the stove, in consequence of the peculiar mode of preparing the fuel.

We come now to notice that variety of stove in which the *cockle* is introduced. This contrivance is an invention of Mr. Strutt, of Derby, and consists in making the fire-chamber of a cylindrical form, with a flat or dome-shaped head, and a pipe leading from the upper part, to carry off the smoke into the chimney. This iron fire-room, called the *cockle* from its shape, was then placed on a bed of masonry or brickwork, with a grating and ash-pit beneath, as shown in Fig. 54. At a certain distance from the cockle, *a*, is a mass of brickwork, *b b*, concentric with the cockle and its dome top, in order to allow a current of air from the passages below, or from the external atmosphere, to come in immediate contact with the whole surface of the iron chamber and pipe. This air, being thus heated and rarefied, ascends towards the head of the stove,

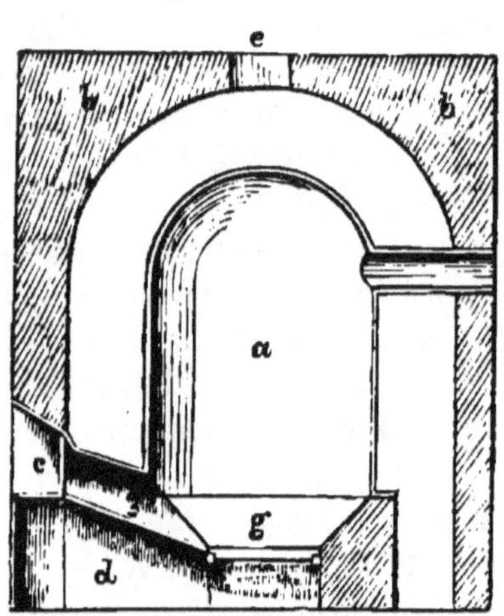

Fig. 54. The Cockle Stove.

and passes through one or more apertures, *e*, into the room required to be warmed. The fuel is supplied at the door, *c*, and passes down a sloping dead plate to the fire-bars at *g*. The ash-pit and draught-hole for the fire are shown at *d*.

In order to bring the air in contact with a greater extent of heated surface, another form is sometimes given to the cockle, by contracting its diameter, and bending the iron pipe into a serpentine form, as shown in Fig. 55. The fire-chamber is formed by placing the grating near the lower part of the conical pipe, *a*, the opening to which, for the admission of the fuel, is at *c*. Another narrow opening is made immediately in front of the fire-bars, to allow the ashes to be cleared from the bottom of the fire. The brickwork, *b*, enclosing the cockle, is in the form of a parallelogram, and the heated air escapes through *e*, and is conducted by pipes to the rooms required to be heated. The following is the working effect of a cockle of this kind, but with only one bend in the pipe, which entered the chimney lower down instead of proceeding upwards to *d*. The cockle itself was 2¼ feet wide, 6 feet high, and the sides ¾ inch thick. The brick casing was at the

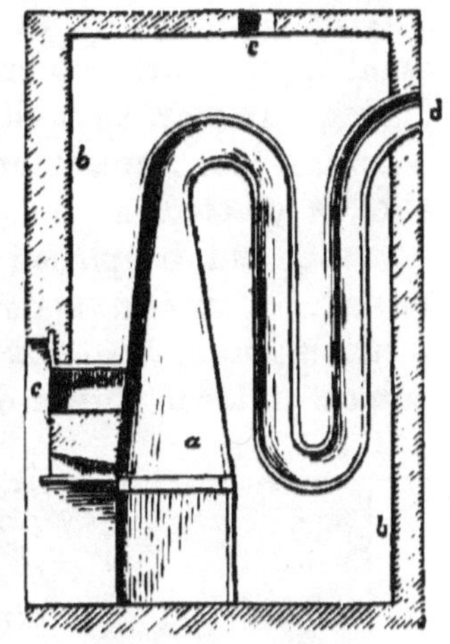

Fig. 55. Cockle Stove.

distance of 6 inches from the metal, and the descending vent within was 6 inches in diameter. The stove here described was used for warming a lecture-room 35 feet long, 27 broad, and 20 high; also a large apartment 30 feet long, 27 broad, and 18 high; besides two smaller rooms and a staircase. The fire was kindled during winter at 7 A.M., and kept burning till 4 P.M., when it was allowed to go out. The average quantity of coals consumed was rather less than half a hundredweight. The temperature of the air from the tubes varied from 120° to 180°, according to the state of the fire. The temperature of the different apartments was kept at about 60°. When first erected, the supply of air for the hot chamber was brought from without; but afterwards the air for the fuel and for the hot chamber were both taken from the apartment containing the stove, which was generally at 70°.

Mr. Strutt's residence was at Belper, and hence the cockle-stoves are often named, in honour of him, *Belper stoves*. In 1792, he warmed his large cotton factories by their means; but the cockle-stove erected by Mr. Charles Sylvester, for warming the Derby Infirmary, was long regarded as a model of its kind for a large building. In such a stove it is necessary that the area be sufficient to allow of the subterranean passage being carried out, so as to communicate with the external atmosphere at some convenient distance from the building, in order to admit a current of cool air for ventilation during summer, as well as for the supply of the stove for warming the apartments in winter. The stove should also be erected as near the area of the building as convenient, and be placed from 6 to 12 feet below the floor, in order to preserve uniformity as much as possible in the distribution of the warm air. The cockle, *a* (Fig. 56), is cubical in form, with a dome or groined arch top; it is about

Fig. 56. The Belper Stove.

3 feet in diameter, and 4 feet high, and is made of iron plates riveted together. The smoke passes off by a narrow passage at the base of the cockle through the flue, *f*. The brickwork surrounding the cockle is built with alternate openings between the bricks, as in Fig. 56, at about 8 inches distant

from the sides of the cockle. Through these apertures are inserted pipes of sheet iron, or common porcelain-ware, so as to extend within an inch of the cockle, by which means the air to be heated may be thrown near, or in immediate contact, with the surface of the cockle, if desirable. The horizontal partition, *d d*, cuts off the communication between the lower and the upper portion of the air-chamber, the arched openings in the lower half, *c c*, being the openings of the main air-flue leading from the exterior atmosphere. The fire-room and ash-pit are shown at *b b*, and the fuel is introduced by the opening at *i*.

It will be seen, from this arrangement, that the air passing from the lower flues, *c c*, through the apertures beneath the horizontal partition, and coming in immediate contact with the surface of the cockle, must find its way into the upper air-chamber, *e e*, through the numerous pipes or openings of the upper division, by which circuit its velocity will be sufficiently retarded to obtain the necessary elevation of temperature from the heated cockle. But that the air may not be burnt, it is necessary to regulate the size of the fire-chamber, so as not to heat the cockle, on an average, more than 300°. The Derby stove allows the passage of nearly 5 cubic feet of air per second, which is heated to about 130° at the instant it escapes from the upper air-chamber into the pipes leading to different parts of the building. These pipes are furnished with dampers to regulate the admission of warm air at pleasure.

If care be taken to prevent the burning of the air, this method of heating a large building appears to be wholesome and economical. It would scarcely answer on a small scale, on account of the expense of erection; nor could it be easily applied to a large building, unless constructed in the first instance, or during the erection of the edifice. The air-passages, being placed several feet below the surface of the ground, afford a convenient mode of admitting a portion of cold air to the interior of the building during summer, by means of a revolving mouth-piece, or turn-cap, placed at the opening of the air-passage, so as to receive the current of wind at the outer extremity of the passage, and thus convey it to the interior of the building.

The various objections which have been urged from time to time against this method of warming buildings, by bringing the air into contact with a surface of iron heated by fire, have led to other methods of heating the metallic surface. Thus Mr. John Sylvester, in his evidence before the House of Commons' Committee, in 1835, proposed this method of warming the New Houses of Parliament. An apparatus was to be erected beneath the house, or on the basement, constructed of cast-iron, and exposing a very large surface for the contact of the fresh air; the arrangement of the surface being such as to divide the supply of fresh air into a large number of very small streams. The under part of the metal surfaces being heated by enclosing water, or steam, the air so divided would flow in contact with such warming surfaces, and thus become heated to the temperature required. When thus heated, it would be allowed to flow under the whole area of the house, the floor of which, being perforated with a multitude of holes, would thus admit it into the body of the house. (See Part II., chap. iii.)

This brings us to the next step in the art of warming buildings; namely, by *steam*, for the details of which we refer to the next chapter.

CHAPTER III.

ON THE WARMING OF BUILDINGS BY MEANS OF STEAM AND HOT WATER.

THE method of warming buildings by steam depends on the rapid condensation of steam into water when admitted into any vessel which is not so hot as itself. At the moment of condensation, the latent heat of the steam is given out to the vessel containing it, and this diffuses the heat into the surrounding space.

The first practical application of this principle was made by James Watt, in the winter of 1784-5, who fitted up an apparatus for warming his study. The room was 18 feet long, 14 feet wide, and 8½ feet high. The apparatus consisted of a box, or heater, made of two side plates of tinned iron, about 3½ feet long by 2½ feet wide, separated about an inch by stays, and jointed round the edges by tin plate. This heater was placed on its edge, near the floor of the room. It was furnished with a cock to let out the air, and was supplied with steam by a pipe from a boiler, entering at its lower edge, and by this pipe the condensed water also returned to the boiler. The heating effect of this apparatus was not so great as was expected, in consequence, perhaps, of the bright metallic surfaces of the box not being favourable to radiation.

In 1791, Mr. Hoyle, of Halifax, took out a patent for heating by steam pipes, and his method seems to have been the foundation for subsequent attempts. The steam was at once conveyed from the boiler, by a pipe, to the highest elevation of the building required to be heated, and, from that point, by a gentle declivity, the condensed water flowed into the supply cistern of the boiler. The effect of the pipes (which were of copper) was too small, and as the apparatus was constantly getting out of order, it was pronounced a failure.

In 1793, Mr. Green took out a patent for a different method, which consisted in enclosing a hollow vessel, or worm pipe, in a boiler containing hot water or steam. The air, on its way to the room to be warmed, was made to pass through this worm, and was thus heated to an agreeable temperature. By another method, pipes from a steam boiler were enclosed in other pipes, and, in the interval between them, the air was heated on its passage to the room. This apparatus was erected in a mansion on Wimbledon Common. The encased pipe was fixed along the ceiling of the basement floor, with an inclination of 2 inches in 68 feet. The inner steam pipe was 3 inches in diameter, the outer pipe 9 inches, and both of copper. The lower end of the casing pipe was left open for the cold air to enter ; the other end was joined to a pipe 4 inches in diameter, with three horizontal elbows, that rose about 12 inches, where it opened into the first suite of rooms that were to be heated. It was supposed that the air would enter at one end in great quantity, and flow out through the small pipe at the other end into the rooms; the effect, however, was so feeble that no useful heating was produced.

About this time steam was introduced into hot-houses, not by circulating in pipes, but by being discharged into the body of the hot-house, the effect of which was to raise its temperature and moisten the air to such a degree that the plants grew rapidly and luxuriantly. It is also said to have had the effect of destroying insects.

In the winter of 1795-6, Mr. Boulton erected a steam heating apparatus in the library of his friend, Dr. Withering, "which, in point of heating, answered perfectly; but the pipes being made of copper, and soft soldered in some places, the smell of the solder was rather unpleasant to the Doctor, who was then in an infirm state of health with diseased lungs. The apparatus was, in consequence, removed to Soho, where Mr. Boulton proposed erecting it in his own house, in which he was making alterations about this time, and had it in view to heat every room in the house by steam. A boiler was put up for that purpose in one of the cellars, but some circumstance occurred to prevent his continuing the plan. The subject, however, underwent frequent discussion, and the different modes of effecting it were amply considered by Messrs. Boulton and Watt, as was known to many of their friends, no secret having been made, either of calculations of surface, or of the modes of applying them."*

About the end of the year 1799, Mr. Lee, of Manchester, under the direction of Boulton and Watt, erected a heating apparatus of cast-iron pipes, which served also as supports to the floor. This answered perfectly, and was, in point of materials and construction, the earliest of its kind. Mr. Lee afterwards had his house heated by steam, and the staircase, hall, and passages, were warmed by the apparatus shown in Fig. 57. It was placed in the underground story,

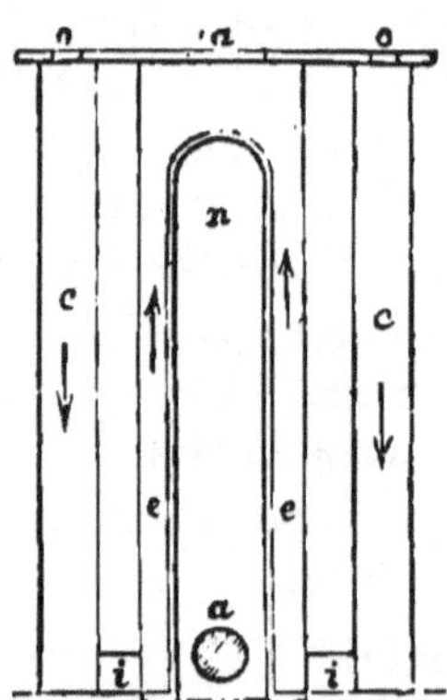
Fig. 57. Early Form of Steam Apparatus.

* "Buchanan on the Economy of Fuel, &c." 1810; 2nd edition, 1815.

and consisted of a vertical cast-iron cylinder, *a*, surrounded by a casing of brickwork, leaving a space, *e e*, of $2\frac{1}{2}$ inches all round, and having openings, *i*, below, to admit the air. This casing was surrounded, at the distance of 3 or 4 inches, by another wall, forming a sort of well, *c*. The colder and heavier air, falling to the bottom of this well, entered by the holes, *i*, into the space, *e*, where it came in contact with the cylinder, *a*, and, being heated, ascended. The entrance of the steam into the cylinder was regulated by a valve, the air being allowed to escape by a stop-cock, while the steam was entering; the condensed water escaping by a pipe not shown in the figure. The transmission of the heated air was regulated by a valve at *a*, on the top of the brickwork. This apparatus was so effective, and heated the staircase to such a degree, that after it had been in operation a short time it was necessary to suspend its action by closing the valve at *a*, or by closing the valve which admitted steam into the cylinder.

The method of heating buildings by steam has scarcely advanced since the time when Messrs. Boulton and Watt erected their apparatus for the purpose, and Mr. Buchanan wrote a practical treatise on the subject. The hot-water apparatus has, for the most part, superseded the steam apparatus, so that our details need not be very full.

In establishments where a steam-engine is in daily use, the steam pipes may be supplied from the engine boiler, its dimensions being enlarged at the rate of 1 cubic foot for every 2,000 cubic feet of space to be heated to the temperature of 70° or 80°. A boiler adapted to an engine of one-horse power is sufficient for heating 50,000 cubic feet of space. Hence an apparatus specially erected for the purpose need not be of very large size, nor is the quantity of fuel consumed great. If the fire under a small boiler be carefully managed, 14 lbs. of Newcastle coal will convert 1 cubic foot of water at 50° into 1,800 cubic feet of steam at 216°; and only 12 lbs. of coal are required to convert the same quantity of water into steam at 212°. The shape of the boiler, and the method of setting it, must also be considered, and the furnace must be arranged so as to admit no more air than is required to support the combustion. The hot air must also be kept in contact with the sides of the boiler until as much of the heat as possible be abstracted from it.   In such an arrangement, according to Dr. Arnott, nearly half of all the heat produced in the combustion is applied to use.

In estimating the extent of surface of steam pipe required to raise the rooms to the proper temperature, it is necessary to consider how the heat is expended. This is done in three ways :—1, Through the thin glass of the windows; 2, More slowly through the walls, floors, and ceiling ; and 3, In combination with the air which escapes at the joinings of the windows and doors, or through openings expressly made for the purpose of ventilation. The amount of heat lost in this way has been variously estimated by different writers, but Dr. Arnott states it thus :—That in a winter day, with the external temperature at 10° below freezing, to maintain in an ordinary apartment the agreeable and healthful temperature of 60°, there must be of surface of steam pipe, or other steam vessel heated to 200° (which is the average surface-temperature of vessels filled with steam of 212°), about 1 foot square for every 6 feet of single glass window of usual thickness; as much for every 120 feet of wall, roof, and ceiling, of ordinary material and thickness; and as much for every 6 cubic feet of hot air escaping per minute as ventilation, and replaced by cold air. A window, with the usual accuracy of fitting, allows about 8 feet of air to pass by it in a minute, and there should be for ventilation at least 3 feet of air per minute for each person in the room. According to this view, the quantity of steam pipe or vessel needed, under the temperature supposed, for a room 16 feet square by 12 feet high, with two windows, each 7 feet by 3, and with ventilation, by them or otherwise, at the rate of 16 cubic feet per minute, would be—

		Feet.
For 42 square feet of glass (requiring 1 foot for 6)		7
„ 1,238 feet of wall floor and ceiling (requiring 1 foot for 120)		$10\frac{1}{2}$
„ 16 feet per minute for ventilation (requiring 1 foot for 6)		$2\frac{2}{3}$
Total of heating surface required		20

Which is 20 feet of pipe 4 inches in diameter, or any other vessel having the same extent of surface—as a box 2 feet high, with square top and bottom of about 18 inches. It may be noticed that nearly the same quantity of heated surface would suffice for a larger room, provided the quantity of window glass and of the ventilation were not greater; for the extent of wall, owing to its slow conducting quality, produces comparatively little effect.

The same authority also supplies the following illustrations :—A heated surface, as of iron, glass, &c., at temperatures likely to be met with in rooms, if exposed to colder air, gives out heat with rapidity nearly proportioned to the excess of its temperature above that of the air around it, less than half the heat being given out by radiation, and more than half by contact of the air. Thus, if the external surface of an iron pipe heated by steam be 200°, while the air of the room to be warmed by it is at 60°, showing an excess of temperature in the pipe of 140°, such pipe will give out nearly seven times as much heat in a minute as when its temperature falls to 80°, because the excess is reduced to 20°, or one-seventh of what it was. Supposing window glass to cool at the same rate as iron plate, 1 foot of the steam pipe would give out as much heat as would be dissipated from the room into the external air by about 5 feet of window, the outer surface of which was 30° warmer than that air. But as glass both conducts and radiates heat about one-seventh slower than iron, the external surface of the glass of a window of a room heated to 60° would, in an atmosphere of 22°, be under 50°, leaving an excess of less than 30°; and about 6 feet of glass would be required to dissipate the heat given off by 1 foot of the steam pipe. In double windows, whether of two sashes or of double panes, only half an inch apart in the same sash, the loss of heat is only about one-fourth of what it is through a single window. It is also known that 1 foot of black or brown iron surface, the iron being of moderate thickness, with 140° excess of temperature, cools, in one second of time, 156 cubic inches of water, one degree. From this standard fact, and the law above given, a rough calculation may be made for any other combination of time, surface, excess, and quantity. And it is to be recollected that the quantity of heat which changes in any degree the temperature of a cubic foot of water, produces the same change on 2,850 cubic feet of atmospheric air.

The arrangement of the steam pipes has next to be considered. A common method is shown in Fig. 58, in which a
is the pipe from the boiler, rising at once to the upper story. From this pipe proceed horizontal branches, $b\,b$, to each floor. Each branch is furnished with a stop-cock at o, by which means the steam can be turned on or off at pleasure, in any one of the three stories. The water

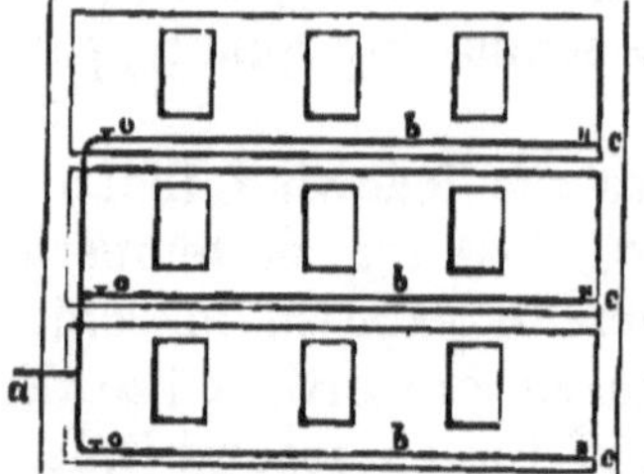

Fig. 58. Arrangement of Pipes.

arising from the condensation of the steam in each pipe, flows back into the boiler along the ascending pipe. But if it be not convenient to place the boiler below the level of the lowest floor, the condensed steam is received into a reservoir, from which it is pumped into the feeding cistern. At the extremity of each horizontal branch, c, is a stop-cock, which is opened when the steam is filling, to allow the air to blow off.

Another arrangement of the heating pipes is shown in Fig. 59. Steam from the boiler enters by the connecting pipe, a, into the heating pipe, b, placed near the floor, and this is carried, with a gentle slope, to the opposite side of the room, whence it rises into the next story, and returns along its floor to the opposite side, where it

Fig. 59. Another Arrangement.

rises to the third floor, and proceeds as before. Here, also, the condensed water flows back in a direction contrary to the current of the steam, and is removed by a siphon at a. The air-vent is fixed at the highest point of the arrangement, c.

It is necessary to prevent the condensed water from accumulating in the pipes, otherwise it would be impossible to maintain them at a uniform temperature. Moreover, this water condenses the steam so rapidly that a vacuum is formed within the boiler and pipes; and should they not be firm enough to resist the external pressure of the atmosphere, the boiler may be crushed in, and the whole system deranged. By a special arrangement, the condensed water is collected at certain parts of the system, where it continues to give out heat after the steam has ceased to flow into the pipes. In such cases stop-cocks may be employed, so arranged as to allow the water to be afterwards withdrawn from the pipes. The same cocks also serve for letting the air out of the pipes when the steam is first admitted; but when the water is returned into the boiler, the advantage of this supply of heat cannot be reserved; and in these cases a self-acting apparatus is used for taking off the water of condensation. Such a siphon is represented in Fig. 60. The pipes are so fixed that A is the lowest point of a branch pipe, so that any quantity of water that may be formed in it will flow into the siphon, A B C, at A, and escape at C, where it may be received into any vessel; for, as the water is pure distilled water, it may be useful for a variety of purposes. The water in the legs of the siphon acts as a trap to the steam in the pipe, A; hence, the length of the leg, A B, should not be less than is equivalent to the force of the steam in the pipes. When, for example, the steam is worked at the rate of 10 lbs. per square inch, the column of water should not be less than 10 feet, and even with this pressure there will be considerable oscillations unless a valve be placed at some intermediate point

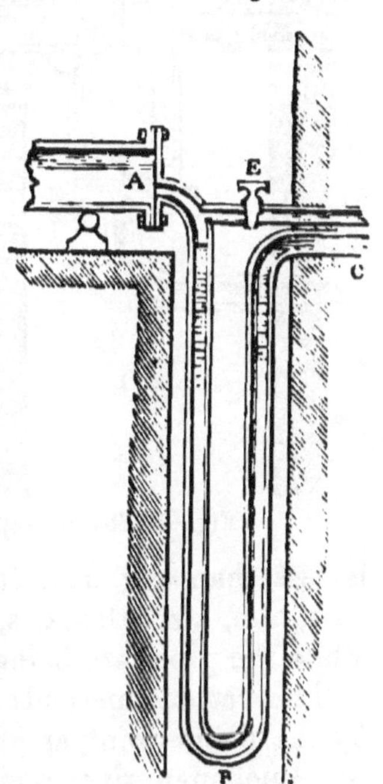

Fig. 60. Siphon.

between A and B. When the legs are both filled with water, and at rest, this valve should be open, so as to close whenever the water has a tendency to return into the pipe. The siphon should be large enough to carry off all the water of condensation, but not too large, or there would be a loss of heat in the leg, A B, from its being filled with steam, and, in all cases, the siphon should be protected from frost. In connection with the siphon, it is usual to place a cock for letting the air out of the pipe, instead of the stop-cock above referred to. Such a cock is shown at E, and it is made to range with the lower part of the pipe, because the air, being heavier than steam, will occupy only the lower portion of it.

In cases where sufficient depth cannot be afforded for a siphon, a steam trap or valve, made to open by a float ball, is employed. Tredgold's arrangement is as follows: B C (Fig. 61) is a square box attached to the end, A, of the steam pipe; D is a hollow copper cylinder, fixed to a conical valve, E. When steam is condensed, the square box will fill with water, which will float the hollow cylinder, and the water will escape and run by the pipe, F, into the drain. Whenever the quantity of water in the box is greater than is required just to float the cylinder, and when there

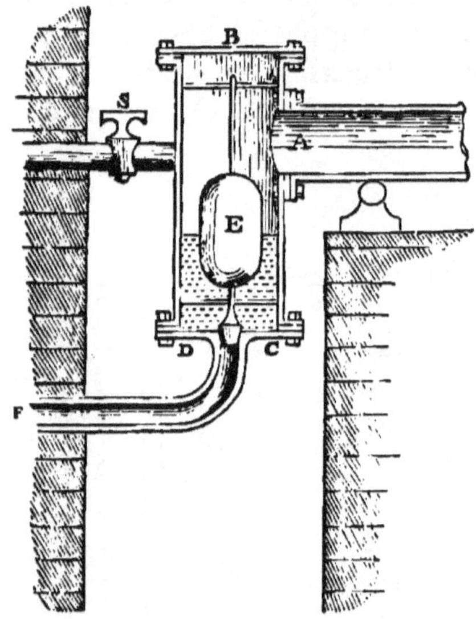

Fig. 61. Steam Trap.

is less than will float it, the valve will be closed. In this case, also, a stop-cock, s, will be necessary to let out the air while the pipes are being filled with steam.

The various methods of connecting the cast-iron pipes are by the flange joint, and the spigot and faucet, or socket joint. Mr. Buchanan gives minute directions for these, but he seems inclined to recommend the thimble joint. Care must, of course, be taken in joining the pipes to allow room for expansion. This is sometimes done in the thimble joint (Fig. 62), in which the adjoining ends of the pipes, a i, are turned true on the outside, and have a thimble, or short cylinder of wrought iron, to enclose them, leaving only a small space for the current. A piece of tin, c, or inner thimble, is interposed, and made to

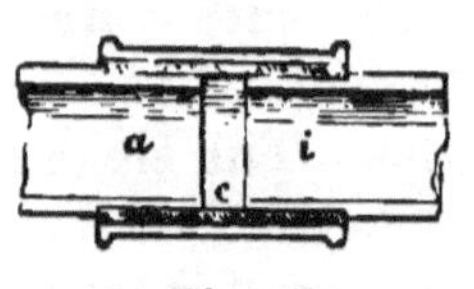

Fig. 62.

fit well to the turned parts of the pipes, which, under the influence of heat or cold, work forwards or backwards, like a piston in a cylinder. In a range of pipes 120 feet in length, there was a motion from expansion of three-quarters of an inch; but the usual allowance for the expansion of cast-iron pipes is one-eighth of an inch in 10 feet, or $\frac{1}{960}$ of their length. Cast-iron, heated from 32° to 212°, expands $\frac{1}{900}$ of its length, which is nearly one and three-eighths of an inch in 100 feet. A similar expansion joint applied to the spigot and faucet connection (Fig. 63) answered very well. Lead cannot be substituted for tin or iron cement in joints, for, by frequent heating, it becomes permanently expanded, while the iron pipes, always contracting in cooling, and the lead not participating in the contraction,

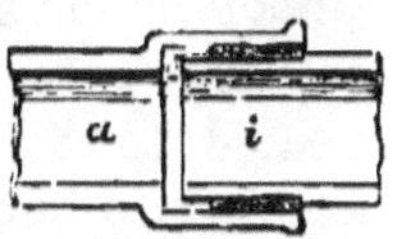

Fig. 63.

the joints soon get loose. Count Rumford introduced an expansion drum, x (Fig. 64), of thin copper, between the extremities of two pipes, $a\,i$, which, in elongating, pressed the sides of the drum inwards, and in cooling drew them outwards. The pipes should not be connected with any part of the building, but be quite independent thereof. All the horizontal branches should be supported on rollers, and nothing done to interfere with the expansion of the different parts.

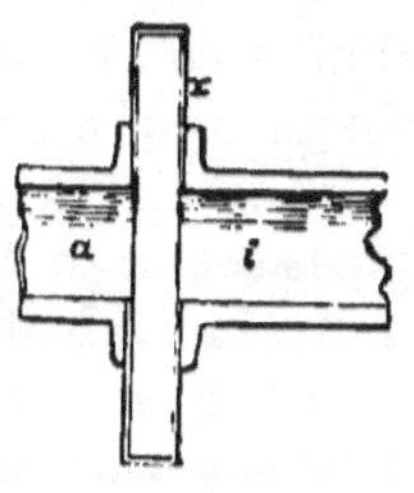

Fig. 64.

In private dwellings, where the appearance of the pipes is objectionable, they may be concealed behind perforated mouldings, or skirtings, or cornices; or the steam may be brought into ornamental vases dispersed about the room, each furnished with a small stop-cock, to allow the air to escape while the steam is entering.

The method of heating buildings by steam has been long superseded by hot-water apparatus of various kinds, which, however, may be resolved into two distinct forms or modifications, dependent on the temperature of the water. In the *first* form of apparatus the water is at or below the ordinary temperature of boiling. In this arrangement the pipes do not rise to any considerable height above the level of the boiler, so that the apparatus need not be of extraordinary strength.   One pipe rises from the top of the boiler, and traverses the places to be warmed, and returns to terminate near the bottom of the boiler.   Along this tube the heated water circulates, giving out its heat, as it proceeds.   The boiler may be open or closed.   If open, the tube, when once filled with water, acts as a siphon, having an ascending current of hot water in the shorter leg, and a descending current of cooled water in the longer leg.   If the boiler be closed, the siphon action disappears, and the boiler with its tubes become as one vessel.   In the *second* form of apparatus the water is heated to 350° and upwards, and is, therefore, constantly seeking to burst out as steam, with a force of 70 lbs. and upwards on the square inch, and can only be confined by very strong or high-pressure apparatus.   The pipe is of iron, about an inch in diameter, made very thick.   The length extends to 1,000 feet and upwards, and where much surface is required for giving out heat the pipe is coiled up like a screw.   A similar coil is also surrounded by the burning fuel, and serves the place of a boiler.

The heating of rooms by the circulation of hot water in pipes seems to have occupied the attention of a few speculative individuals long before the attempt was actually made. The first successful trial is assigned to Sir Martin Triewald, a Swede, who resided for many years at Newcastle-on-Tyne, and about the year 1716, described a method for warming a greenhouse by hot water.   The water was boiled outside the building, and then conducted by a pipe into a chamber under the plants.

But the first successful attempt, on a large scale, was made in France in 1777, by M. Bonnemain, in an apparatus for hatching chickens, for the purpose of supplying the market of Paris.   A section of this heating apparatus is shown in Fig. 65, in which *a* is the boiler, *d* a feed pipe, *o* a stop-cock, for regulating the quantity of ascending hot water, *b* the pipe by which the hot water ascends from the boiler into the heating pipes, *c c*, which traverse the hatching chamber.   These heating pipes have a gradual slope towards the boiler, to which the water returns by the pipe, *e*, carried nearly to the bottom. In this way the water, cooled by being circulated through a long series of pipes, is being constantly returned to the lowest part of the boiler, where it receives a fresh amount of heat, and being thus rendered lighter, rises up the pipe, *b*, and descends the inclined planes of the pipes, losing a portion of its heat on the way, and at the same time increasing in density; the

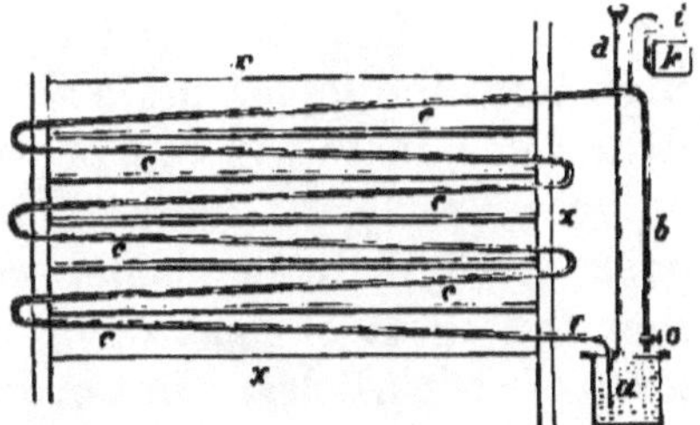

Fig. 65. Bonnemain's Arrangement.

velocity of the current depending on the difference between the temperature of the water in the boiler and that in the descending pipe. At the highest point of the apparatus is a pipe, *i*, furnished with a stop-cock, for the escape of the air which the cold water holds in solution on entering the boiler. The water that rises along with it is received into the vessel, *k*.

The arrangements of this apparatus are excellent; they have been taken as a model in many subsequent methods, although the merits of the inventor have not always been acknowledged. The plan was introduced into this country in 1816, by the Marquis de Chabannes, who was long regarded as the inventor. About the year 1822, Mr. Bacon and Mr. Atkinson introduced modifications of the apparatus, but the latter gentleman succeeded in reducing it to its most simple and practical form.

Whatever be the arrangement adopted for warming buildings by this method, two considerations must be specially attended to, namely, sufficient strength to bear the hydrostatic pressure; and freedom of motion for currents of water of varying temperatures, and consequently of varying densities. As fluids transmit their pressure equally in every direction, a column of water, rising from a strong vessel to a certain height, may be made to burst the vessel with enormous force. Thus, a tube whose sectional area is 1 inch, rising to the height of $34\frac{1}{2}$ feet from the bottom of a vessel of water, will, if the tube be also full of water, exert a bursting pressure on every square inch of the inner surface of such vessel of one atmosphere, or 15 lbs. If the sectional area of the tube be increased, the pressure remains the same, because it is distributed over a larger surface of the vessel. If a boiler be 3 feet long, 2 feet wide, and 2 feet deep, with a pipe 28 feet high from the top of the boiler, when the apparatus is filled with water, there will be a pressure on the boiler of 66,816 lbs., or very nearly 30 tons. This will show the necessity for great strength in the boiler, especially when it is considered that the effect of heat upon it is to diminish the cohesive force of its particles. But even supposing the apparatus were to burst, no danger would arise, because water, unlike steam, has but a very limited range of elasticity. The boiler just described would contain about 75 gallons of water, which, under a pressure of one atmosphere on the square inch, would be compressed about 1 cubic inch ; and if the apparatus were to burst, the expansion would only be 1 cubic inch, and the only effect of bursting would be a cracking in some part of the boiler, occasioning a leakage of the water.

The circulation of the water is brought about by the principle of convection already explained (page 32 *et seq.*) When heat is applied to a vessel containing water the principle of conduction altogether fails, for water is so imperfect a conductor of heat, that if the fire be applied at the top, the water may be made to boil there without greatly affecting the temperature below. But when the fire is applied below, the particles in contact with the bottom of the boiler, being first affected by the heat, expand, and thus becoming specifically lighter than the surrounding particles, ascend, and other particles take their place, which, in like manner becoming heated, ascend also ; and the process goes on in this way until the whole contents of the boiler have received an accession of temperature. If the process be continued long enough, the water will boil and pass off in steam ; if the boiler be closed in on all sides, so as to prevent the escape of steam, it must be of great strength or be provided with a valve to prevent an explosion. If a tube full of water rise from the top of the boiler in a vertical line to any required height, and then, by a series of gentle curves, descend, and enter near the bottom of the boiler, the process of heating is still the same. The particles of water first heated will rise, and, in doing so, distribute their heat to other particles, which will also rise; these, in their turn, will lose a portion of their heat to other particles, which rise in their turn, until at length an equilibrium is established. But as the source of heat is permanent, other particles are rapidly brought under its action, and, being heated, ascend. By continuing the process a short time the particles in the vertical tube become heated, and, by their expansion, exert a pressure on the water contained in the lateral branches; this, together with the increasing levity of the water in the boiler, establishes a current, and the water from the branches begins to set in in the direction of the boiler; the water in the lowest branch, where it enters the boiler, supplying colder and heavier particles every moment, to take the place of the warmer and lighter particles which are being urged upwards along the vertical pipe.

Now, to ascertain the force with which the water returns to the boiler, we must know the specific gravities of the two columns of water, the ascending and the descending, and the difference between them will be the effective pressure, or motive power. This can be done by ascertaining the temperature of the water in the boiler, and in the descending pipe. When the difference amounts to only a few degrees the difference in weight is very small, but quite sufficient in a well arranged apparatus to maintain a constant circulation. For example, suppose an apparatus to be at work, in which the temperature in the descending pipe is 170°, and the temperature of the water in the boiler, the height of which is 12 inches, is 178°. The difference in weight is 8·16 grains on each square inch of the section of the return pipe. If the boiler, A (Fig. 66), be 2 feet high, and the distance from the top of the upper pipe, c, to the centre of the lower pipe, d, be 18 inches, and the pipe 4 inches in dia-

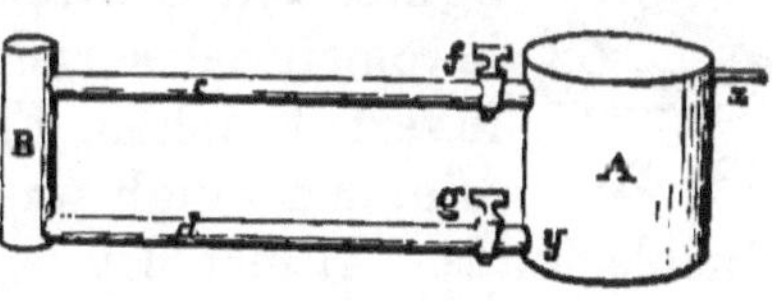

Fig. 66.

meter, the difference of pressure on the return pipe will be 153 grains, or about one-third of an ounce weight, and this will be the amount of motive power of the apparatus, whatever be the length of pipe attached to it. "If such an apparatus have 100 yards of pipe, 4 inches in diameter, and the boiler contain 30 gallons, there will be 190 gallons or 1,900 lbs. weight of water kept in continual motion by a force equal to only one-third of an ounce."*

The amount of motive power increases with the size of the pipe. The power being four times as great in a pipe of 4 inches in diameter as in one of 2 inches, as the former contains four times as much water as the latter; but, as the resistance increases equally with the power, the actual working effect is the same in pipes of all sizes. The motive power is increased by allowing the water to cool before it returns to the boiler, or by increasing the height of the ascending and descending columns of water. "By doubling the difference of temperature between the flow pipe and the return pipe, the same increase of power is obtained as by doubling the vertical height; and by tripling the difference in temperature, the same effect is produced as by tripling the vertical height." The difference in temperature may also be increased by increasing the quantity of pipe, or by diminishing its diameter,

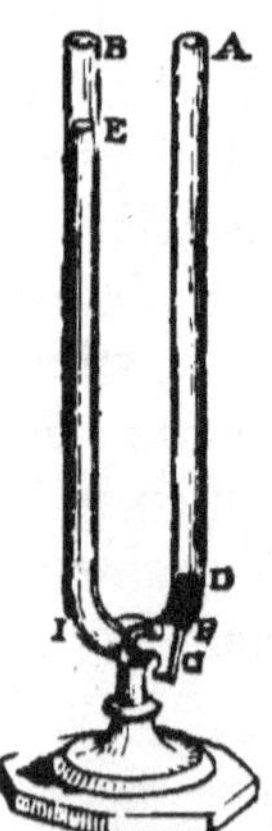

Fig. 67.

so as to expose a larger amount of surface, in proportion to the quantity of water contained in it, so as to allow it to part with more heat within a given time. But the method which must be principally depended on, when additional power is required to overcome any unusual obstruction, is to increase the height of the ascending column.

Another method of estimating the velocity of motion of the water of a hot-water apparatus is to regard the two portions of the system as the lighter and heavier fluids in the two limbs of a barometrical aëriometer. This instrument is an inverted siphon, Fig. 67, and its use is to ascertain, in a rough way, the specific gravities of immiscible fluids. If mercury be poured into one limb, A, and

* Mr. Hood, in his "Treatise on Warming Buildings by Hot Water, &c.," gives a table showing the difference in weight of two columns of water, each 1 foot high, at various temperatures. The information, together with the wood engravings contained in the next ten pages, is chiefly derived from Mr. Hood's work, a third edition of which was published in 1855.

water into the other, E, and the stop-cock at *c* be turned, so as to establish a communication between them, it will be found that an inch of mercury, F D, in one limb will balance $13\frac{1}{2}$ inches of water, I E, in the other limb; thus showing that the densities or specific gravities of the two fluids are as $13\frac{1}{2}$ to 1. If oil be used instead of mercury, it will require 10 inches of oil to balance 9 inches of water. Or if equal bulks of oil and water be poured into the limbs of the siphon, and the stop-cock be then turned, the oil will be forced upwards with a velocity equal to that which a solid body would acquire in falling by its own gravity through a space equal to the additional height which the lighter body would occupy in the siphon. Now, as the relative weights of water and oil are as 9 to 10, the oil in one limb will be forced upwards by the water with a velocity equal to that which a falling body (in this case, the water) would acquire in falling through 1 inch of space, and this velocity is equal to 138 feet per minute.

In estimating the velocity of motion of the water in a hot-water apparatus the same rule will apply. " If the average temperature be 170°, the difference between the temperature of the ascending and descending columns 8°, and the height 10 feet; when similar weights of water are placed in each column, the hottest will stand ·331 of an inch higher than the other; and this will give a velocity equal to 79·2 feet per minute. If the height be 5 feet, the difference of temperature remaining as before, the velocity will be only 55·2 feet per minute; but if the difference of temperature in this last example had been double the amount stated—that is, had the difference of temperature been 16°, and the vertical height of the pipe 5 feet—then the velocity of motion would have been 79·2 feet per minute, the same as in the first example, where the vertical height was 10 feet, and the difference of temperature 8°."

But, in all these calculations, a considerable deduction must be made for the effects of friction. In the centre of the ascending pipe the heated particles meet with the smallest amount of obstruction, and there the motion is quickest; but at and near the circumference of the pipe, the retarding effects of friction are most apparent. In the descending pipe the friction is less, for the water descends more as a whole, and is, moreover, assisted by the gravity of the mass.   In an apparatus where the length of pipe is not great, where the pipes are of large diameter, and the bends and angles few, a large deduction from the theoretical amount must still be made, to represent, with anything like accuracy, the true velocity; and Mr. Hood states that in more complex apparatus the velocity of circulation is so much reduced by friction, that it will sometimes require from 50 to 90 per cent. and upwards to be deducted from the calculated velocity, in order to obtain the true rate of circulation.

The amount of friction·not only varies according to the arrangement of the apparatus, but also according to the size of the pipes.   It is much greater in small pipes than in large ones, on account of the relatively larger amount of surface in the former; besides this, small pipes cool quicker than large ones, and this increases the velocity of the circulation, and with it the friction is also increased. When the velocity with which the water flows is the same in pipes of different sizes, the relative amount of friction is as follows :—

Diameter of the pipes . . . . $\frac{1}{2}$ in. 1 in. 2 in. 3 in. 4 in.
The amount of friction,   . . . 8,   4,   3,   1·3, 1.

So that, if the friction in a pipe of 4 inches diameter be represented by 1, the friction of a pipe 2 inches in diameter is twice as much, and a 1-inch pipe four times as much. By increasing the velocity the friction increases nearly as the square of the velocity; but as the water in a hot-water apparatus circulates with various degrees of speed in its different parts, it is not easy to calculate the amount of friction from this cause.

It will be seen, then, that when all the deductions are made, the circulation of the water is produced by a very feeble power, so that, as may be supposed, a very slight cause is sufficient to neutralise it.   Mr. Hood has known so trifling a circumstance as a thin shaving accidentally getting into a pipe effectually to prevent the circulation in an apparatus otherwise perfect in all its parts.

But the great point to be attended to is, so to dispose the pipes that the water, in its descent, may not be obstructed by differences of level, or angles in the pipes, where air may accumulate; for this, by dividing the stream, effectually prevents the circulation. For example, in an apparatus con-structed in the form repre-sented in Fig. 68, the motion through the boiler and pipe, A B, takes place by convec-tion, and through the de-scending pipe, C D, by the force of gravity, as already described. But it will be seen, that when the motion commences in the return

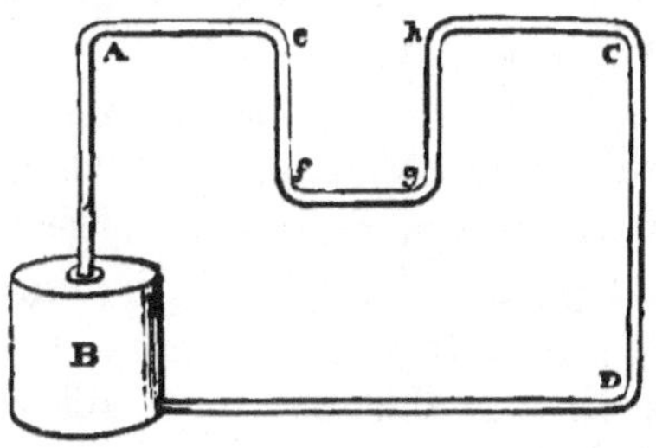

Fig. 68.

pipe, D B, in consequence of the greater pressure of C D than of A B, the water in A will be forced towards e, while the water in e f g h flows towards c. But when a very small quantity of hot water has passed from the pipe and boiler, A B, into the pipe, e f, the column of water, g h, will be heavier than the column, e f, and the current will therefore tend to move along the upper pipe towards the boiler, instead of from it. "This force, whatever its amount, must oppose that in the lower or return pipe, in consequence of the pressure of C D being greater than A B; and unless the force of motion in the descending pipe, C D, be sufficient to overcome this tendency to a retrograde motion, and leave a residual force sufficient to produce direct motion, no circulation of the water can take place."

With respect to the accumulation of air in the pipes, every part of the apparatus where an alteration of level occurs must be furnished with a vent for the air. Thus, in Fig. 68, if the air accumulate in the pipe between A and e, it is evident that a vent at c, although it would take off the air from g h and from C D, could not receive any portion of that which is con-fined between A e, or between e f; because, in that case, it must descend through the pipe, e f, before it could escape; and as air is so very much lighter than water, it cannot pos-sibly descend so as to pass an obstruction lower than the place where it is confined. The same remark applies to all cases, however large or small the descent may be, and the accidental misplacing of a pipe in the fixing, by which one end may be made a little higher than the other, will as effectually prevent the escape of air through a vent placed at the lower end, as though the deviation from the level were as many feet as it may, perhaps, be inches.

When it is required to heat a number of separate stories by the same boiler, one of two methods may be adopted. The vertical pipe from the boiler may be carried up to the highest story, and the return pipe meander through each story, until it finally terminates in the boiler. But it is obvious that in such case the top story will get the larger share of the heat, and the lower stories will be gradually less heated, on account of the cooling of the water in its passage to the boiler. The second method is to supply each story with a separate range of pipes branching out from the main pipe, and returning either together or separately into the boiler. The application of this principle, however, requires caution ; for if the branch pipes are simply inserted into the side of a vertical ascending pipe, the hot current may pass by, instead of flowing into, them. Some contrivance is therefore necessary to delay the motion of the upward current, and to cause it to turn aside at the points required. This may be done by the arrangement shown in Fig. 69, which is a variation of a figure in Mr. Hood's work. Here it will be perceived that as the water ascends from the boiler, B, it receives a check at *b*, whereby it tends to flow through the horizontal pipe at that level. The same also occurs at *c*, and by this means a nearly equal flow of hot water may be obtained. If it be required to cut off the supply of heat from one story while the others are being heated, this may be done by turning a stop-cock at *s*, by

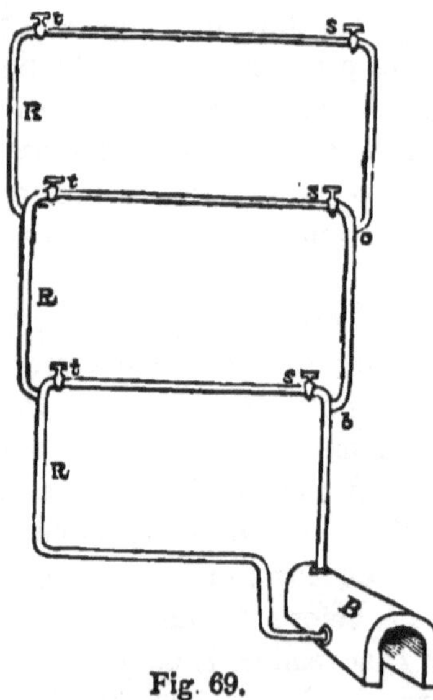

Fig. 69.

which the heated current is prevented from flowing along the particular branch so closed. But whenever a branch is closed as at *s*, it is necessary also to close the other end, *t*, of the same branch, otherwise the water in the descending return pipe, n, being warmer and lighter than that in the branch closed at *s*, will circulate therein, and thus raise the temperature of the room intended to be kept cool.

In some arrangements, the hot ascending current of the vertical main is made to discharge into an open cistern at the top, as in Fig. 70, and from the bottom of this cistern the various flow-pipes are made to branch off. By this means the expense of cocks or valves is avoided; for by driving a wooden plug into one or more of the pipes which open into the cistern, the circulation will be stopped until the apparatus is heated; but in that case water will flow back through the return pipe. This, however, may be prevented by bending a lower portion of the return pipe into the form of an inverted siphon, as shown in the figure. This will not prevent the circulation when the flow-pipe is open; but if that be closed by a plug in the cistern, the hot water will not return back through the lower pipe. Any sediment that may accumulate in the siphon may be removed, from time to time, by taking off the cap at the lower part of the bend.

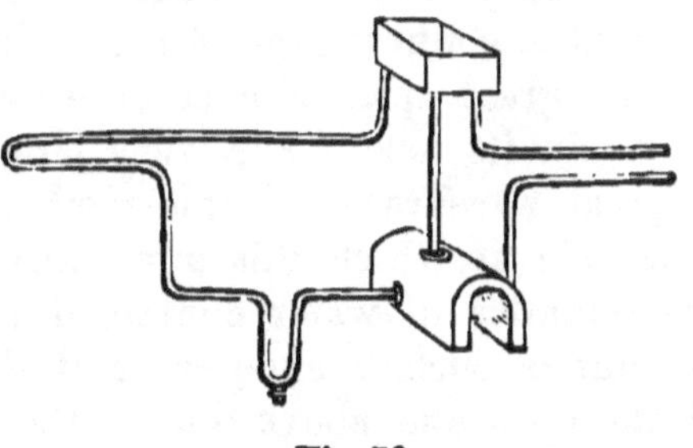

Fig. 70.

In such an arrangement as that shown in the last two figures, the vertical main pipe need not be of larger diameter than the branches, unless these extend to a very considerable distance, and then the diameter of the main pipe may be somewhat enlarged. It is not, however, desirable to increase the diameter of the main, because it is an object to economise the heat in this pipe, and there are circumstances in which a small main loses less heat than a large one, as, for example, in the arrangement shown in Fig. 70. If one main pipe, 8 inches in diameter, supply four branches in a given time, it is evident that, by reducing the main to 4 inches in diameter, the water must travel four times faster through the smaller pipe to perform the same amount of work; and, under such circumstances, the water will lose only half as much heat in passing through the small main as it would do in ascending the larger one, for the loss of heat sustained by the water is directly as the time and the surface conjointly.

Hence, in warming by the same boiler two rooms separated from each other by a considerable distance, the pipe connecting the two rooms may be of smaller diameter than the pipes used for diffusing the heat. Thus, a pipe of 1 inch diameter may be used to connect pipes 4 inches in diameter.

The great specific heat of water, whereby it is enabled to retain its heat for a very long time (see page 47), is a great advantage of this method of warming buildings. The rate at which this apparatus cools depends chiefly on the quantity of water contained in it with respect to the amount of surface exposed, and the excess of temperature of the apparatus above that of the surrounding air; but for temperatures below the boiling point, this last circumstance need only be taken into account in estimating the velocity with which this apparatus cools. Now, the variation in the rate of cooling for bodies of all shapes is inversely as the mass divided by the superficies. In cylindrical pipes, the inverse number of the mass divided by the superficies is exactly equal to the inverse of the diameters; so that, supposing the temperature to be the same in all—

In pipes of . . . . 1 2 3 4 inches diameter,
the ratio of cooling will be . . 4 2 1·3, 1.

That is, a pipe of 1 inch in diameter will cool four times as quickly as a pipe of 4 inches in diameter, and so on. These ratios multiplied by the excess of heat in the pipes above that of the surrounding air will give the relative rates of cooling for different temperatures below 212°; but if the temperatures be the same in all, the simple ratios given above will show their relative rate of cooling, without multiplying by the temperatures.

These calculations supply practical rules for estimating the size of the pipes under different circumstances. If the heat be required to be kept up long after the fire is extinguished, large pipes should be used; if, on the contrary, the heat is not wanted after the fire is put out, then small ones will answer the purpose. Pipes of larger diameter than 4 inches should never be used, because they require a very long time to be heated to the proper temperature. Pipes of 4 inches in diameter are well adapted for hot-houses, green-houses, and conservatories. Pipes of 2 or 3 inches may be used for warming churches, factories, and dwelling-houses. Such pipes retain their heat for a sufficient length of time, and they can be more quickly and more intensely heated than larger pipes, so that, on this account, a smaller quantity of pipe will often suffice.

With respect to the quantity of pipe required for warming a building of ascertained size, it is necessary to bear in mind the rate at which a given quantity of hot water in an iron pipe will impart its heat to the surrounding air. Now, it has been shown by Mr. Hood, that the water contained in an iron pipe 4 inches in diameter internally, and $4\frac{1}{2}$ inches externally, loses ·851 of a degree of heat per minute when the excess of its temperature is 125° above that of the surrounding air; and as 1 cubic foot of water in losing 1° of its heat will raise the temperature of 2,990 cubic feet of air the like extent of 1°, so 1 foot length of 4-inch pipe will heat 222 cubic feet of air 1° per minute, when the difference between the temperature of the pipe and the air is 125°.

There is also to be taken into account the loss of heat per minute arising from the cooling power of glass, ventilation, radiation, cracks in doors and windows, and other causes. An allowance of from $3\frac{1}{2}$ to 5 cubic feet of air ought to be made per minute for each person in the room, so that, for the purposes of respiration, this quantity will have to be discharged, and an equal supply of air brought in to be warmed.

According to Mr. Hood's experiments one square foot of glass will cool 1·279 cubic feet of air as many degrees per minute as the internal temperature of the room exceeds the temperature of the external air. If the difference between them be 30°, the 1·279 cubic feet of air will be cooled 30° by each square foot of glass, that is, as much heat as is equal to this will be given off by each square foot of glass.

From these and other calculations, for which we must refer to Mr. Hood's able work, the following corollary is drawn :— "The quantity of air to be warmed per minute in habitable rooms and in public buildings, must be from $3\frac{1}{2}$ to 5 cubic feet for each person the room contains, and $1\frac{1}{4}$ cubic feet for each square foot of glass. For conservatories, forcing-houses, and other buildings of this description, the quantity of air to be warmed per minute must be $1\frac{1}{4}$ cubic feet for each square foot of glass which the building contains. When the quantity of air to be heated per minute has been thus ascertained, the quantity of pipe that will be necessary to heat the building may be found by the following rule :—Multiply 125 (the excess of temperature of the pipe above that of the surrounding air) by the difference between the temperature at which the room is purposed to be kept, when at its maximum, and the temperature of the external air; and divide this product by the difference between the temperature of the pipes and the proposed temperature of the room; then, the quotient thus obtained, when multiplied by the number of cubic feet of air to be warmed per minute, and this product divided by 222 (the number of cubic feet of air raised $1°$ per minute by 1 foot of 4-inch pipe) will give the number of feet in length of pipe 4 inches diameter, which will produce the desired effect."

When 3-inch pipes are used, the quantity of pipe required to produce the same effect will, of course, be different. To obtain it, the number of feet of 4-inch pipe obtained by the above rule must be multiplied by $1\cdot33$. If 2-inch pipe be used, the quantity of 4-inch pipe must be multiplied by 2.

To determine the quantity of pipe required to maintain a constant temperature of $75°$ in a hot-house, let it be supposed that the external air occasionally falls as low as $10°$, and calculate from this temperature. The amount of heat to be supplied by the pipes is obviously that which is expended by the glass, the cooling power of which is exactly proportioned to the difference between the internal and the external temperature, the actual cubical contents of the house making no difference in the result. If such a house have

800 square feet of glass, it can easily be calculated, from the preceding data, that this quantity will cool down 1,000 cubic feet of air per minute from 75° to 10°, which will require 292 feet of 4-inch pipe. If the maximum temperature of the pipe be 200°, and the water be at 40° before lighting the fire, the maximum temperature will be attained in about four hours and a half; with 3-inch pipe in about three hours and a quarter; and with 2-inch pipe in about two hours and a quarter—depending, however, upon the structure of the furnace and the quantity of coal consumed. If the external temperature be higher than 10°, the effect will be produced in a proportionally shorter time.

In churches and large public rooms, with an average number of doors and windows, and moderate ventilation, a more simple rule will apply for ascertaining the quantity of pipe required. Where a number of persons are assembled, a large amount of heat is generated by respiration, so that a very moderate artificial temperature is sufficient to prevent the sensation of cold. In such a case the air does not require to be heated above 55° or 58°, and the rule is to take the cubical measurement of the space to be heated, and dividing this by 200, the quotient will be the number of feet of 4-inch pipe required.

The efficiency of any form of hot-water apparatus will, of course, greatly depend on the boiler, which ought to be so constructed as to expose the largest amount of surface to the fire in the smallest space ; to absorb the heat from the fuel, so that as little as possible may escape up the chimney; to allow free circulation of the water throughout its entire extent, and not be liable to get out of order by constant use. A variety of boilers are figured in Mr. Hood's work, and their respective merits considered on scientific grounds. One of these boilers is shown in Fig. 71. It is of cast-iron, and the part exposed to the fire is covered with a series of ribs 2 inches deep, and about one-fourth or three-eighths of an inch thick, radiating

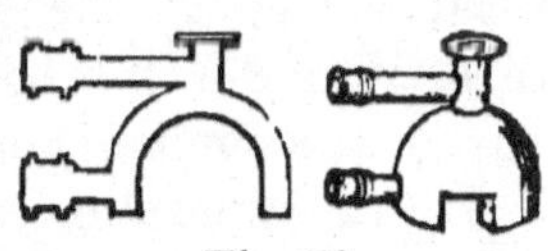

Fig. 71.

from the crown of the arch at an average distance of 2 inches from each other. These ribs greatly increase the surface exposed to the fire, exactly where the effect is greatest; for, being immediately over the burning fuel, it receives the whole of the heat radiated by the fire. The form of this boiler being hemispherical, will also expose the largest amount of surface within a given area. The boiler shown in Fig. 69, being of wrought-iron, and, therefore, thinner than cast-iron, absorbs the greatest amount of heat from the fuel.

With respect to the size of the boiler, it has been shown by experiment that 4 square feet of surface in an iron boiler will evaporate 1 cubic foot of water per hour when exposed to the direct action of a tolerably strong fire. The same extent of heating surface which will evaporate 1 cubic foot of water per hour from the temperature of 52°, will be sufficient to supply the requisite amount of heat to 232 feet of 4-inch pipe, the temperature of which is required to be kept 140° above the surrounding air; or 1 square foot of boiler surface exposed to the direct action of the fire, or 3 square feet of flue surface, will supply the necessary heat to about 58 superficial feet of pipe, or, in round numbers, 1 foot of boiler to 50 feet of pipe. But as this is the maximum effect, a somewhat larger allowance ought in general to be made. If the difference of temperature be 120° instead of 140°, the same surface of boiler will supply the requisite amount of heat to one-sixth more pipe, and if the difference be only 100°, the same boiler will supply above one-third more pipe than the quantity stated.

With respect to the furnace, the rate of combustion of the fuel will depend chiefly on the size of the furnace-bars, provided the furnace door be double and fit tightly. The ash-pit should also be provided with a door to exclude the excess of air when the fire is required to burn slowly. A dumb-plate should also be provided, to cause the combustion to be most active at the hinder part of the furnace instead of directly under the boiler. The fuel will thus be gradually coked, the smoke consumed, and the fuel economised.

In an apparatus containing 600 feet of 4-inch pipe, the area of the furnace-bars should be 300 square inches, so that 14 inches in width and 22 inches in length will give the amount of surface required. To obtain the greatest heat in the shortest time, the area of the bars should be proportionally increased, so that a larger fire may be obtained. The fire ought at all times to be kept thin and bright, and to obtain a good effect from the fuel, 1 lb. weight of coal ought to raise 39 lbs. of water from 32° to 212°.*

The best kind of pipes for hot-water apparatus are those with socket-joints, flange-joints having long been out of use for this purpose. Where the socket-joints are well made, there is no fear of leakage, for the pipes themselves will yield before the joints will give way, or before the faucet end of one pipe can be drawn out of the socket of the other. The joints must be well caulked with spun yarn, and filled up with iron cement, or with a cement made of quicklime and linseed oil.

Soft or rain-water ought always to be used in the hot-water apparatus, because if hard-water be used, its salts will form a sediment, or crust, in the boiler, and interfere with its action. But as there is very little evaporation from this kind of apparatus, the boiler will not require cleaning out for years, if a moderate degree of attention be bestowed on the water employed.

When the apparatus is not in use, care must be taken to prevent the water from freezing in the pipes, or the sudden expansive force of the water in freezing may crack them. If the apparatus is not likely to be used for some time during winter, it is better to empty the pipes than incur the risk of freezing. It has been proposed to fill the pipes with oil instead of water, and as the boiling point of oil is nearly three times higher than that of water, it was thought that a temperature of 400° might be safely given to the pipes. It was found, however, that the oil at high temperatures became thick and viscid, and at length changed into a gelatinous mass, completely stopping all circulation in the pipes.

In the forms of apparatus to which the preceding details refer, the temperature of the water never rises to the ordinary

---

* In the Cornish engines 65½, and even 85 lbs. of water have been raised from 32° to 212°, by the combustion of 1 lb. of coal. This is a far more favourable result than has been produced with any other boilers or qualities of coal than those employed in the experiment.

boiling point (212°); but we have now to notice a method in which the temperature of the water is often beyond 300°; this is the high-pressure method contrived by Mr. Perkins.* In its simplest form, the apparatus consists of a continuous or endless pipe, closed in all parts, and filled with water. There is no boiler to this apparatus, its place being supplied by coiling up a portion of the pipe (generally one-sixth of the whole length) and arranging this in the furnace. The remaining five-sixths of the pipe are heated by the circulation of the hot water, which flows from the top of the coil, and cooling in its progress through the building, returns to the bottom of the coil to be re-heated. The diameter of the pipe is 1 inch externally, and half an inch internally, and is formed of wrought iron. The coil in the furnace being entirely surrounded by the fire, the water is quickly heated, and becoming also filled with innumerable bubbles of steam, these impart a great specific levity to the ascending current. At the upper part of the pipe, the steam bubbles condense into water, and uniting with the column in the return pipe, which is comparatively cool, the descent is rapid in proportion to the expansion of the water in the ascending column, or, in other words, according to the relative specific gravities of the two columns of water.

As the expansive force of water is almost irresistible, in consequence of its extremely limited elasticity, it is necessary in the high-pressure apparatus to make some provision for the expansion of the water when heated. The necessity for this will appear from the fact, that water heated from 39·45° (the point of greatest condensation) to 212°, expands about $\frac{1}{23}$ part of its bulk; and the force exerted on the pipes by this expansion would be equal to 14,121 lbs. on the square inch. The method adopted is, to connect a large pipe, called the expansion pipe, $2\frac{1}{2}$ inches diameter, with some part of the apparatus, either horizontally or vertically. It should be placed at the highest point of the apparatus; and at the

* One authority on this subject is Mr. Richardson's "Treatise on the Warming and Ventilation of Buildings, showing the advantages of the Improved System of Heated Water Circulation, &c." Second Edition. London, 1839.

bottom of the expansion pipe is inserted the filling pipe, through which the apparatus is filled. While the apparatus is being filled with water, the expansion tube is left open at the top; water is then poured in through the filling tube, and as it rises in the pipes drives out the air before it. When the pipes are full, the filling pipe and the expansion tube are carefully closed with screw plugs. It is important to expel all the air from the pipes, and this is done, in the first instance, by pumping the water repeatedly through them. The expansion pipe is, of course, left empty, as its use is to allow the water in the pipes to expand on being heated, and thus prevent the danger of bursting. From 15 to 20 per cent. of expansion space is usually allowed in practice.

The furnace is generally so arranged in the building required to be heated, as to allow the tube proceeding from the top of the coil, to be carried straight up at once to the highest level at which the water has to circulate; here the expansion tube is situated, and from this point two or more descending columns can be formed, which, after circulating through

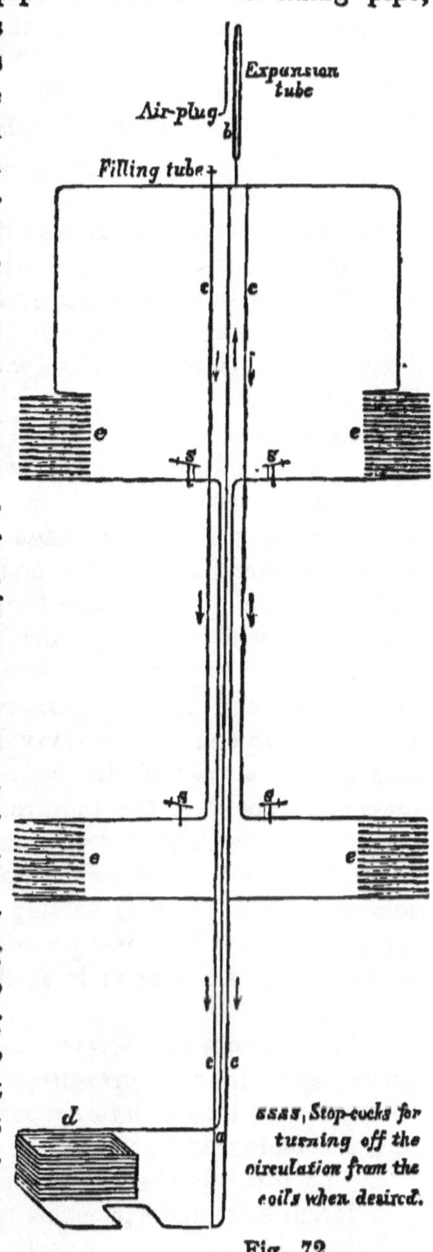

Fig. 72.

different and distant parts of the building, unite at length in one pipe, just before entering the bottom of the coil in the furnace.

The whole arrangement will be better understood by referring to Fig. 72, in which *a* is the ascending column ; *b* the expansion tube ; *c* the descending columns; and *d* the coil in the furnace.

The heat is communicated to the air of the rooms from the external surface of the pipes, which are coiled up as at *e e*, and placed within pedestals, ranged about the room with open trellis work in front, or they may be sunk in stone floors, placed behind skirtings, or in the fire-places of each floor, the flues being stopped, or arranged in any other convenient manner.

In consequence of the great internal pressure which these tubes have to sustain, considerable care is required in their manufacture.   They are made of the best wrought iron, rolled into sheets a quarter of an inch thick, and of the proper width.   The edges are then brought nearly together in the whole length of the iron, which is generally about 12 feet. In this state it is placed in a furnace and heated to a welding heat.   One end is then grasped by an instrument firmly attached to an endless chain, revolving by steam power, and a man applies a pair of circular nippers, which, when closed, press the tube into the required size, and which he holds firmly while the tube is drawn through them by the engine. The edges are thus brought into perfect contact, and are so completely welded, after passing two or three times through the nippers, that a conical piece of iron driven into the end of the tube will not open it at the joint sooner than at any other part.

When the tubes are screwed together at each end, they are proved by hydrostatic pressure, with a force equal to 3,000 lbs. on the square inch of internal surface.   In this state they are sent to London, and such is the purity and ductility of the iron, that the tubes can be easily bent, while cold, into coils of different sizes and shapes, as required.

When the tubes are properly arranged and fixed in the building, the whole apparatus is filled with water by a force pump, and subjected to considerable pressure before lighting the fire. In this way faulty pipes or leaky joints are detected.

The tubes are joined by placing the ends within a socket, forming a right and left hand screw, the edge of one tube having been flattened, and the other sharpened; they are then screwed so tightly together, that the sharpened edge of one pipe is indented in the flattened surface of the other. Another method of connecting the pipes is by a cone joint. A double cone of iron is inserted into the ends

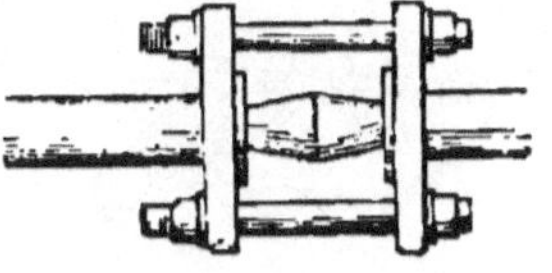

Fig. 73.

of the pipes to be joined, and is made tight by two screw bolts, as shown in Fig. 73. This joint is quickly made, and is very strong.

The furnace varies in form and dimensions according to circumstances; but a very common arrangement is shown in

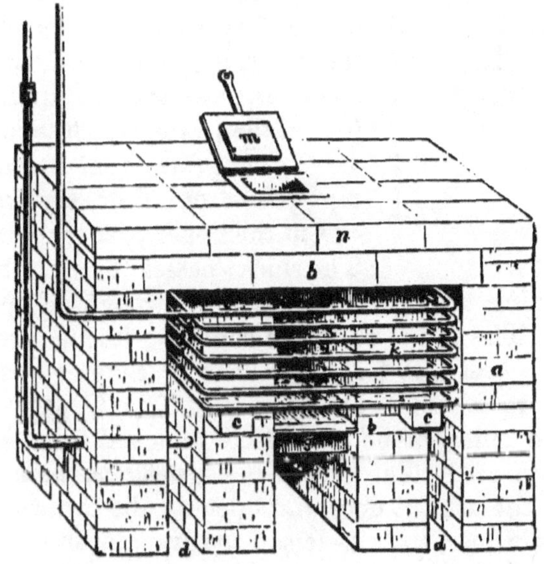

Fig. 74. The Furnace.

Fig. 74. The size is about $3\frac{1}{2}$ feet square, increasing to 6 feet, according to the extent of pipe connected with it. The fire occupies a small space in the centre, raised about 1 foot from the ground, and the fuel is supplied through the hopper door, *m*, at the top. The outer casing, *a*, is of common brickwork ; *b b* are Welsh fire-lumps ; *c c* are fire-bricks, supporting the coil, *k*; *d d* are reservoirs for the dust and soot, which would otherwise clog the coil; *g* bearing-bars for the grate ; *h* is the grate; the fire-door is double, and

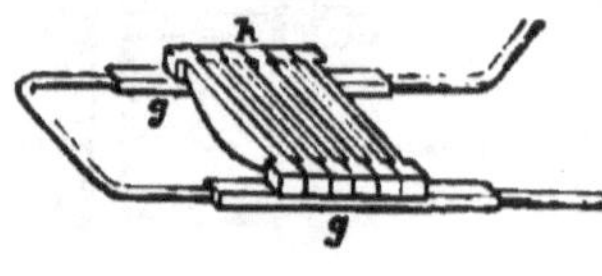

Fig. 75.

there are also doors to the ash-pit and dust reservoirs. Fig. 75 shows the descending tube entering the fire-chamber, and passing through the bearing bars, *g g*, of the grate, *h*. Fig. 76 is a section of the back well or reservoir, *d d*, formed so as to support the coil, and to cause the soot and dust to fall to the bottom.

In this arrangement of the furnace, the ignited coal is surrounded on three sides by a thickness of 9-inch fire-brick, or Welsh lumps ; the hopper door is also placed in one of

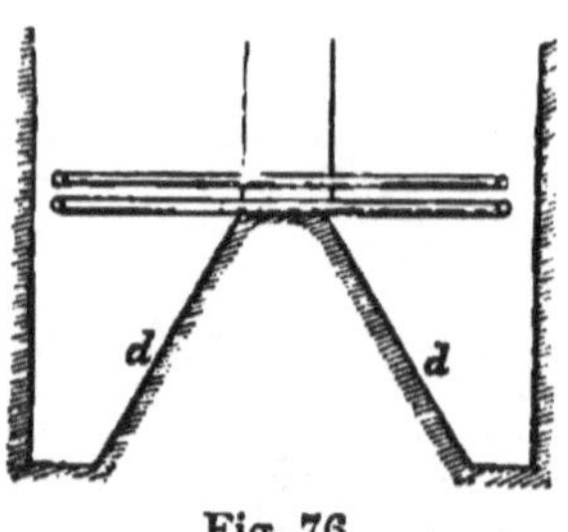

Fig. 76.

these lumps ; the coil is contained in a chamber round the fire-brick, $4\frac{1}{2}$ inches wide ; the pipe enters this chamber, passing through the bearing bars of the grate, which tends to preserve the grate from burning ; the pipe passes out from the top of the coil, at the upper part of the chamber. The smoke passes through the chamber containing the pipes, and escapes through an opening at the back. The coil is in actual contact with the fire only in front. The best fuel for this furnace is coke or Welsh hard coal, such as is not liable to clog. The furnace may be placed in a cellar, or be completely removed from the building to be warmed. The heat of the furnace can be moderated by closing the ash-pit door and opening the furnace door, or the reservoir door, so as to lessen the draught and admit cold air to the coil.

In the apparatus erected at the British Museum for warming the print-room and the bird-room, the furnace is in a vault in the basement story, and the pipes, entering a flue, are carried up about 40 feet to two pedestals, one in each room ; one containing 360 feet of pipe, and the other 400 feet. About

140 feet of pipe are employed in the flow and return pipes in the flue, and 150 feet are coiled up in the furnace. In this way, 1,050 feet of pipe are employed: the apparatus is very powerful, and supplies the requisite amount of heat. The print-room is about 40 feet long, by 30 feet wide, and the ceiling contains large sky-lights. The temperature of 65° can easily be maintained in this room during winter. The fire is lighted at 6 A.M., and is allowed to burn briskly till sufficient heat is produced in the rooms, when the damper in the flue is partially closed. A slow fire is thus maintained; at 11 A.M. a fresh supply of fuel is added, and this supports the fire till 4 P.M., when all the fires at the Museum are extinguished.*

The above details will suffice to show the nature and application of this apparatus. For its adaptation to houses and public buildings, under a greater variety of circumstances, we must refer to Mr. Richardson's work. We fully agree with him, that in any building where this apparatus is intended to be erected, it ought not to be introduced as an after-thought. " It should be remembered, that as its complete success, and its economical character, depend, in a great measure, upon due consideration of its benefits being given at the commencement of a building, so it ought, in future, to engage the primary consideration of the architect and builder."

It is, however, of great importance to ascertain whether this apparatus is perfectly safe, for even a doubt on the subject must be fatal to its general introduction. The average temperature of the pipes is stated to be generally about 350°; but a very material difference in temperature, amounting sometimes to 200° or 300°, is said to occur in different parts of the apparatus, in consequence of the great resistance which the water meets with in the numerous bends and angles of this small pipe. The temperature of the coil will, of course, give the working effect of the apparatus, but the temperature of any part of the pipe will furnish data for estimating its

* Mr. Hood states, on the contrary, that, owing to the smallness of the pipes in the high-pressure apparatus, the coil cools so rapidly when the fire slackens in intensity, that the heat of the building is materially affected by the least alteration in the force of the fire, instead of maintaining that permanence of temperature which is so peculiarly the characteristic of the hot-water apparatus with large pipes.

safety ; for whatever is the temperature, and, consequently, the pressure in the coil, must be the pressure on any other part of the apparatus; for by the law of equal pressures of fluids, an increased pressure at one part will generate an equally increased pressure at every other part of the system.

A very elegant method of ascertaining the temperature of a heated surface of iron or steel consists in filing it bright, and then noting the colour of the thin film of oxide which forms thereon.* Mr. Hood states, that in some apparatus, if that part of the pipe which is immediately above the furnace be filed bright, the iron will become of a straw colour, showing a temperature of about 450°. In other instances it will become purple = about 530°, and in some cases of a full blue colour = 560. Now, as there is always steam in some part of the apparatus, the pressure can be calculated from the temperature, and a temperature of 450° = a pressure of 420 lbs. on the square inch; 530° = 900 lbs.; and 560° = 1,150 lbs. per square inch.

Although these pipes are proved, at a pressure of nearly 3,000 lbs. per square inch, and the force required to break a wrought-iron pipe of 1 inch external, and half an inch internal diameter, requires 8,822 lbs. per square inch on the internal diameter, yet these calculations are taken for the cold metal. By exposing iron to long-continued heat, it loses its fibrous texture, and acquires a crystalline character, whereby its tenacity and cohesive strength are greatly weakened.

In order to make this apparatus safe, Mr. Hood suggests that, instead of hermetically sealing the expansion pipe, it should be furnished with a valve, so contrived as to press with a weight of 135 lbs. on the square inch. This would prevent the temperature from rising above 350° in any part. The pressure would then be nine atmospheres, which is a limit

		Degrees Fahr.
* Steel becomes a very faint yellow	. . . . . .	at 430
„	pale straw colour	„ 450
„	full yellow	„ 470
„	brown	„ 490
„	brown, with purple spots . . .	„ 510
„	purple	„ 530
„	blue	„ 550
„	full blue	„ 560
„	dark blue, verging on black . .	„ 600

more than sufficient for any working apparatus where safety is of importance.

But, supposing the apparatus were to burst in any part, the effects would by no means resemble those which accompany the explosion of a steam boiler. One of the pipes would probably crack, and the water, under high pressure, escaping in a jet, a portion of it would be instantly converted into steam, while that which remained as water would sink to 212°. This would have the effect of scalding water under ordinary circumstances, but the high pressure steam would not scald, because its capacity for latent heat is greatly increased by its rapid expansion, on being suddenly liberated, so that, instead of imparting heat, it abstracts heat from surrounding objects. The only real danger that would be likely to ensue would be from the jet of hot water, and this must, in any case, be of trifling amount.

CHAPTER IV.

FURTHER DETAILS ON WARMING BY MEANS OF THE OPEN FIRE-PLACE.

THE first edition of this work, published in 1850, describes the various methods of warming buildings by means of the open fire-place, the close stove, hot-air apparatus, steam and hot water, and examples of each method, were given to illustrate the principles involved in the various methods. Similar details are given in this new edition, although in some cases they are expressed a little more fully. We reserve for the present chapter a notice of the Report of the Commissioners appointed by the House of Commons to inquire into the best practical method of warming and ventilating dwelling-houses.* There is no new principle involved

* The commissioners were Messrs. Fairbairn, Glaisher, Wheatstone and Playfair; J. S. Campbell was secretary. The commission was appointed in May, 1856. The report, which was made to the General Board of Health, was ordered to be printed 25th of August, 1857. It was not signed by Dr. Playfair, on account of his appointment as Professor of Chemistry in the University of Edinburgh preventing him from attending to the work of the commission.

in this Report; but as it is quite impossible that such men as the commissioners should touch any subject without throwing new light upon it, we have felt it to be our duty to state briefly a few of their results respecting the warming of dwellings by means of the open fire-place, this being the only method that it was deemed desirable to inquire into, seeing that the habits of the people are not likely to adapt themselves to any other so long as coal is abundant.

The first point that attracted the attention of the commissioners was the imperfect mode in which coal is burnt in an ordinary fire-place, the result being a large amount of smoke and soot, which taints the air, clogs the organs of respiration, soils our furniture, and shortens the duration of daylight by arresting a portion of the sun's rays. This expensive nuisance may be got rid of by methods more or less simple of constructing the grate and feeding the fire. In 1785 James Watt took out a patent for the prevention of smoke in furnaces, the principle of which was to supply the fire from above, downwards, by means of a reservoir of fuel in contact with the ignited mass. Combustion was supported by a strong lateral current of air passing through the fire into a flue on the other side, aided by a slight downward current through or beside the fuel, which descends by its own weight as the fire consumes. A separate fire is maintained near the entrance to the flue through which the smoke of the first fire passed and was effectually consumed.

These principles have been applied by various patentees for improvements in the structure of the open fire-place, as in Cutler's contrivance, described at p. 115. A year after Cutler's patent (1816), Deakin attached a metal box containing coal for one day's consumption to the back part of the fire-place, and as fuel was required it was drawn forward into the grate by means of a screw, and in this way, by supplying the coal horizontally, the smoke was nearly all consumed. In the same year Hawkins patented a feeding shovel for supplying coal to the fire at the bottom. The shovel had a cover so as to form a sort of box or pan, and in the handle was a sliding rod connected with a piston, by pressing which the coals were thrust into the fire. In 1825 Atkins supplied ccals from the back, the bottom of the fuel chamber being made to slope at a sharp angle towards an opening at the back of the grate. In 1846 Tillett patented an arrangement of Cutler's feeding apparatus, by which time Dr. Arnott had perfected his smokeless fire-place, p. 116, which, although not patented, has been made the subject of subsequent patents. In Jeake's patent, in 1854, the front of the fuel box and the bars of the grate are made in one, and move together in a sliding frame, the object being to bring the fire down upon the fuel below instead of the fuel being raised upwards. In this way the fire, by being gradually lowered, admits air to the fuel, which is thus gradually consumed, and the fire-grate, which may be of average height in the morning, exhibits only a low fire in the evening, when the supply in the fuel box is exhausted. In 1854, also, Rawe forced the coals in small supplies into the lower part of the fire through a fuel pipe which connects the bottom grating of the fire-place with a side reservoir of fuel, the poker being used as a lever for introducing a fresh supply.* In 1854 a patent was taken out by Bachhoffner for getting rid of the smoke of one fire by passing it through the incandescent coke or anthracite of an upper or supplementary fire; or instead of having two separate kinds of fuel, the coals in the lower grate, when sufficiently coked, may be lifted with a shovel into the upper grate, and fresh coals added below. Leighton, in 1856, surrounded the sides and back of a fire-grate with a fuel chamber, the fuel being brought forward by the poker as required. A bright clear fire is thus produced from the coal undergoing a process of distillation previous to its application, the coal of one day becoming the coke of the next. In Hoole's patent a double circular register is introduced, consisting of two plates arranged above each other, the spaces of

* I have adopted a method which, rude and imperfect as it is, has some advantages in economising fuel, burning much of the smoke, and getting rid of the nuisance of a smoky room in windy weather. The grate of my study has a false bottom, and my plan is to shovel the coals into the unoccupied space between it and the real bottom. The volatile products thus distil into the fire above and are consumed. The live cinders may be transferred from time to time to the top, or cinders of the previous day's kitchen fire be added, and fresh coals put in below. In this way the fire gives out more heat, requires less attention, and consumes the greater part of the smoke.

the one opposing the solid parts of the other. One of the frames is made movable, so that the openings may be diminished or closed by means of a screw in front of the fire-place. In Owen's patent nearly all the parts of the fire-place which come into immediate contact with the fire are cast in one piece, including also the hearth-place, for the purpose of obtaining heat from the radiation from, and the conduction of, metal surfaces. In this, as in the former patent, double grates are introduced between the fire and the fuel box below, for the advantage of an under-current of air; but this plan requires the removal of the double grating when it is required to wind up fresh fuel.

A second class of smoke-consuming fire-places is based upon Franklin's fire cage (described at p. 99, Fig. 29). The commissioners think that, although good in principle, the form of these rotatory grates differs from the ordinary fire-grates sufficiently to create a prejudice against their general adoption. Moreover, much heat is lost which might be obtained by conduction, the grate being in a measure isolated and turning on an axis by means of a lever or small winch between the cheeks of the fire-place. There is no doubt, however, as to the smoke-consuming capabilities of the arrangement, especially as the skeleton cylinder admits of being separated into compartments by means of a longitudinal dividing plate, so that the fuel may be thrown into the cylinder at the back of this dividing plate, when, by turning the frame, the fresh fuel may be driven under that which is already incandescent.

A third class of inventions is for the prevention of smoke by means of a downward current. We have already given examples of this kind. (See p. 87, Fig. 19; p. 137, Fig. 47; and p. 139, Fig. 48.) The downward current is intended to consume or rather to prevent the formation of smoke; but it is suggested in the Report that the chief difficulty "must have consisted in obtaining the due supply of atmospheric air in quantities equivalent to the amount of gas generated in the fire, a difficulty not inconsiderable when the coals are supplied as ordinarily put on by hand from time to time, and in irregular quantities." There are two patents, one by Williamson, in 1855, and the other by Marsh, in 1856, the principle being to have a flue at the back of the fire-grate communicating above with the chimney. The fire is lighted in the usual way, and when an upward current is established in the chimney, access to it is closed by a damper, while a valve in the flue being opened, the products of combustion pass down into the flue and so into the chimney; after this the fire is fed with coals in the usual way.

Another class of contrivances for consuming smoke generated in an open fire-place is by means of hot-air chambers above. Thus Olding, in 1854, constructed a triangular chamber, the vertical side being formed by the back of the fire-place, and the other two sides by registers, one inclining from an aperture in the chimney downwards, and the other, from about the same spot, upwards. The three sides of the triangle are slightly separated, so that the smoke, heated air, &c., pass into the chamber where the smoke is consumed, while the gaseous products escape into the chimney. Arrangements of this kind are not very satisfactory, since it is more desirable to produce perfect combustion without visible waste products, than to seek to get rid of these products by an after process.

Another form of fire-grate for preventing or mitigating the quantity of smoke is by deflecting hot air downwards, and by directing cold air into and through the fire. Thus Stevens, in 1853, placed a deflecting plate at the back of the grate, shelving down towards the fire, for deflecting over it a current of warm air, supplied to it by side flues and through passages underneath and about the grate. The air so heated is distributed over the fire downwards, and assists in the combustion of the smoke. Leslie's fire-grate is situated very near the floor of the room. It communicates directly with the external air by two pipes an inch in diameter on either side of the fire-grate in front. We have already seen (p. 84) that this method, which we believe to be quite sound, was contrived by Sir John Winter in 1658, and forms a prominent feature in Gauger's fire-places (p. 88).

Variations in the form or construction of the register is the subject of numerous patents. We have already seen in Count

Rumford's contrivances (p. 112), and in much earlier inventions (p. 84, *note*), how important the register is in preserving the warmth of the room by preventing the hot air from ascending freely into the chimney, and if arranged so as to admit of regulation, of diminishing the maximum draft to the required minimum. Edwards, in 1804, closed the top of the stove-grate with two inclined metal plates forming a kind of pointed roof, but leaving a narrow aperture for the passage of the smoke. Slate, in 1850, inclined the register plates, contrary to the usual method, from the front to the back of the chimney, that its action might be increased by inner cheeks to the fire-place, to be drawn forward from the sides for an increased draught. A good form of register is that attached to Arnott's smokeless fire-place (Fig. 33), a similar form to which was made the subject of a patent in 1854, affording one out of innumerable arguments for an entire change in our patent law system. In 1855, Vasnier patented a register plate, extending from the back to the front, containing an opening, supported by racks at any desired elevation.

In connection with the use of the register may be mentioned contrivances for economising and utilising the heat by returning warm air into the apartment. This idea has been so abundantly illustrated in the case of Gauger's fire-places and Franklin's Pennsylvanian fire-place (p. 97, Fig. 28), as hardly to require further illustration. (See also Lloyd's arrangement, p. 125, Figs. 37, 38.) Under this head may be mentioned the fire-grate proposed by Professor Hosking in 1851, by which the fire of a room should fulfil the conditions required for ventilation. The commissioners object to this method of making one contrivance do the work of two, on the ground that the apartment will be inadequately warmed. In Hosking's arrangement " the fire-grate is set so as to allow a space between itself and the brickwork setting, and is closed at the top by an iron plate, open only for the register flap or valve over the fire itself." External air is admitted to the closed chambers by a pipe in communication with the outer air, and is directed, in any way most convenient, under the hearth in front, and so to and under the hearth at the back, in which sufficient holes are made to allow of the air entering by the tube or channel to rise into the chamber about the fire-box or grate. Openings of any desirable form may be made through the cheeks of the grate into the air chambers at the level of the hearth. " An upright metal plate set up behind the openings in the cheeks of the grate, but clear of them, bends the current of warm air in its passage through the inlet holes, and thus compels the fire to allow what is not necessary to it to pass into the room ; and if the opening over the fire to the flue be reduced to the real want of the fire, there will remain a considerable supply of tempered air, waiting only an inducement to enter, for the use of the inmates of the apartment. An opening directly from the room into the flue upon which the fire is acting at a high level in the apartment will afford this inducement, by allowing the draught in the flue to act upon the heated and spent air under the ceiling,* and to draw it off, thus inducing a flow of the fresh and tempered air from about the body of the grate into the room."

A description of a cottager's stove, which seems to be well arranged, is given at p. 127, Figs. 42, 43. A smoke-consuming stove has been contrived by Edwards for the working classes, and is adapted for cooking, &c., as in the cottager's stove. It is said to consume only 14 lbs. of coal in from twelve to fourteen hours, at a cost of about twopence. The grate has a fire-clay brick back and sides. It can be easily fixed. There is no ash-pit, and the cost is 20s., exclusive of fixing. Fire-clay lumps are used in the sides and back of a grate by Pierce, with an air chamber around them communicating with the outer air, which, being gently warmed, is let into the room. Valves are placed for regulating the supply of air.

Grates have been also contrived for economising fuel and heat by combining reflection from solid surfaces with conduction and radiation. Such grates are usually costly, require a considerable area for their accommodation, and much cleaning and attention to preserve the polish · unimpaired. They are mostly adapted for large rooms, and have a bright, cheerful appearance from the divergent and inclined metal surfaces reflecting the brilliancy and warmth of the fire.

As early as 1795 a patent was taken out for a removable

* On this subject see, however, the experiments described at p. 210.

reflector, and in 1805 polished metal reflectors were placed on each side of the fire-place, to be turned at any angle, to reflect the heat of the fire into the room. In 1816 the fire-grate was enclosed in a hollow metal globe opening in front of the grate. In 1852 the hearth, cheeks, and faces of the grate were made of polished steel. In the same year there was a patent, No. 552, for a hearth of radiating metal bars in a double set, made slightly convex. In the same year, No. 1,015, the lower part of the fire-place is filled with a metal apron of open work to increase heat by radiation. Jobson's method has already been mentioned (p. 126). In the same year a grate was formed with a metallic surface extending from the bars (which were vertical and inclining inwards) into the room, and so, becoming heated, radiated around. In Mr. Sylvester's invention " the hearth is formed of a framework of hollow radiating metal bars, diverging and fan-like in arrangement, upon the furthest end of which the burning fuel is supported. The air for combustion passes through the hollow bars to the fire, which also derives a supply in front in the usual way. The ends of the bars on which the fuel rests become intensely hot. The remaining portion or hearth from conduction becomes likewise heated, and radiates its warmth around. The fire, being situated upon the hearth, allows the greatest possible length of surface to the cheeks or sides of the stove, which are of polished metal, and contribute greatly to the amount of heat afforded by radiation. The smoke escapes through the apertures of a kind of louvre at the back, and the ashes pass between the bars into a receptacle beneath."

The commissioners also examined a number of open fire-grate stoves. They refer to one under the date 1781, which bears some resemblance to the stove-grate or *chapelle* described at p. 142 ; but furnished with a double back or air chamber, into which air is conducted from some external source, and passing upwards in a tortuous direction, becomes tempered, and is permitted to pass out into the apartment through apertures in the side of the air chamber. This invention is referred to in the Report as being "of interest, as combining at a very early period sound principles of construction, and seeming to be the original of its class ;" whereas it is only one of the numerous variations of Gauger's invention and Franklin's Pennsylvanian stove. Indeed, from the description, it would seem to be identical with Gauger's figure, which we have copied (p. 92, Fig. 24). In Sharp's patent, in 1781, says the report, "the air chamber is fitted with three rows of horizontal shelves: the centre row open to the sides; the two side rows, one on each side, open to the centre; the air, therefore, which enters from below, is compelled to follow a zig-zag or tortuous direction until it passes out at the apertures in the side. The intention is to delay the air in its passage up through the chamber, and bring it in contact with a series of heated surfaces, from which to derive an increase of heat." A somewhat similar arrangement was patented in 1855, and again, in 1856, in Witler's patent, one of the advantages of which is, that the interior of the metal facing and the back of the grate are lined with fire-bricks; but this is no new contrivance, for it will be seen by reference to page 142 that the parts of the chapelle in contact with the fuel were improved by being lined with tiles of fire-clay.

A fire-grate in use at the London Hospital has its back composed of fire-bricks, behind which is an iron lining, and behind the lining a chamber communicating with the outer air, by which means a supply of warm and pure air is distributed within the ward in which the fire-place is situated.

Various minor arrangements are noted, such as the method of clearing the grate of its contents before lighting, in order to avoid dust. Indeed, the usual method of raking out the fire has often struck me as being about as sensible as brushing a nailed-down carpet, so as to transfer all its dust from the floor to the furniture. To prevent the clouds of dust from the fire-grate, the grate has been made to turn upon a pivot, and discharge its contents over a chamber at the back covered with a sloping grating, through which the dust and ashes pass while the cinders roll back into the grate. The chamber communicates with an ash-drawer beneath. The grate has also been made movable, so that it may be carried out of the room to be cleaned and made ready for lighting, but in this way much of the heat from conduction is lost. A movable tray of net-work or perforated metal has been placed between the bottom of the fire-grate and the level of the hearth. A series of inclined metal bars is placed between the grate and the separator, movable on pivots, to be turned at any angle to reflect back the heat. Many contrivances have also been made for concealing and removing the waste fuel and ashes below. In 1795 a space below the fire-grate is enclosed for the reception of the ashes, which could thus be carried away by pulling out a drawer in front. A receptacle has also been formed within the hearth, covered with a movable metal plate of open work, through which the ashes fall. The grate has also been placed on a hollow basement of metal, or stone, or marble, within which is the ash-drawer. In this arrangement a fender is not wanted, as is the case where a radiating hearth-plate is used, the cinders falling to a lower level between the spaces of the bars; an ash-drawer may also be placed below the bar. A movable tray or sifter of wire-work has also been fitted inside a shallow ash-pan. On the movable tray a series of thin metal strips were arranged similar to louvre boards to serve as heat reflectors and to hide the cinders. These metal strips may be brought close together to prevent the escape of dust while sifting the ashes into the pan; the cinders may then be returned to the fire, and the apparatus re-arranged without much trouble.

Every one must have felt the inconvenience of the common method of putting out a fire by taking off the fuel with the tongs or shovel. As long ago as 1805 there was a patent for a metal case for putting over the fire and extinguishing it without dust or waste of fuel, or by a vertical screen pulled down from above or drawn forward from the sides. This patent curfew was revived in 1854, a movable shutter being made to draw down and exclude the air; but that it should be made the subject of a patent is remarkable. The movable shutter, when made to act the part either of an extinguisher or blower, embodies an ingenious idea more worthy of a patent. Thus Sherringham, in 1853, had a blower in front of the fire-place to regulate the draught according to the height at which it was adjusted above the fire, or when raised in front of the grate to form a protection against accidental fires, or in conjunction with a second screen when brought in contact the fire soon becomes extinguished, and when partly separated maintains a slow combustion.

The subject of fire-guards deserves attention. The portable wire-work guard, which is always either in or out of the way, is troublesome ; but if made to form part of the fire-place, as was done in 1802, we get a useful contrivance. Two circular pieces of wire-work, one on each side of the fire-place, were made to draw out and to meet in front, so as to enclose the fire within an efficient and easily removable screen.

The Commission were not able to bestow much attention on close stoves, but they insist on the objection in their action in drying the air to an uncomfortable or even injurious degree, while they have little or none of the action of an open fire-place in promoting the ventilation of an apartment. With respect to the moisture of the air, it is stated to be " absolutely necessary that water be present in the air to the amount of little less than 3 grains at $50°$, to 4 grains nearly at $60°$, and to more than 5 grains at $70°$, in every cubic foot of air. The wet and dry bulb thermometer furnishes a measure of the amount of water present in the air, and the above amounts will be present when the wet bulb thermometer reads about $45°$, $54°$, and $63°$ respectively, and the simultaneous readings of the dry bulb thermometer are $50°$, $60°$, and $70°$ respectively. It is, therefore, evident that the dry and wet bulb thermometer should be attendant on the use of the stove as applied to apartments. The instrument is simple in its construction, inexpensive, and involves no difficulty in its management." We shall return to this subject when we come to speak of the conditions required for efficient ventilation (see p. 207).

The objection to metal stoves that they burn the air has been endeavoured to be met by substituting pottery-ware for metal. A stove of this kind by Rammell, patented in 1854, for burning anthracite, has a downward draught passing through the fire into the hollow stone below containing the ash-pit, from which the exit flue passes into the chimney. The mass of fire-bricks which surrounds the ash-pit and forms the base or stand, is traversed by numerous air passages, through which air rises, is heated, and passes into the apartment. The danger with stoves that stand away from the fire-place and burn with a downward draught, is, that some of the products of combustion may be constantly welling into the apartment, to the prejudice of its occcupants.

The commissioners insist upon the necessity of keeping the floor of the room at a comparatively high temperature, in order that the feet may not be constantly in a cold air bath, such as must necessarily be the case in our present chance arrangements for supplying air to the fire; and they find naturally that the floor of that room was the warmest in which an air channel was led from the outer air to supply the fire with oxygen, and the temperature of that room was the most equable throughout. The commissioners also recommend that the chimney flue should not be more than 9 inches in diameter at the widest part, nor be situated in the outer wall, so as to become chilled by contact with the external air. They suggest that every flue should be provided with a closing apparatus; that the aperture for the escape of the smoke should be placed at the back of the fire to increase the intensity of combustion and promote the radiation of heat; that firebrick linings to the grate should be in general use as well as reflecting surfaces, to direct and increase the amount of radiant heat into the room; that sunk ash-pits and concealed ash-pans be used to prevent the escape of dust; that the fire should not be on a level with the floor; that, as a rule, the fire-grate is best situated which may be seen from the greatest number of points in the room; that a good frontage of fire surface should be exposed, without, however, requiring any corresponding increase in the depth of the grate from back to front; that those arrangements be used which prevent the formation of smoke; that the fire-grate be studied with a view to produce a better and more economical consumption of fuel, and the more equable distribution of heat, but not as a contrivance for the ventilation of rooms—the Commission being of opinion that so long as the fire-grate is studied with a view to this two-fold application, it will not succeed well in the performance of either.

We cannot conclude this part of our subject without describing the fire-grate recommended by the Commission appointed for Improving the Sanitary Condition of Barracks and Hospitals. There is nothing new in its construction, but it appears to be made up from a judicious selection of the best features of old inventions already described. The grate is placed as much forward in the room as possible; the part in which the fire is contained is of fire-brick; the bottom being partly solid checks the consumption of fuel. A supply of air is admitted from behind the grate, and is thrown on the top of the fire to assist in preventing the smoke; the sides are splayed so as to throw the heat by radiation as much as possible into the room; the opening into the chimney has no register; there is a chamber behind the grate into which air is brought from the outer air and warmed by the large heating surface of the back of the grate, increased by flanges, and after being heated to from 56° to 70° Fahr., the air passes into the room by a shaft cut out of the wall which terminates in a louvred opening placed out of reach, or a shaft of sheet iron may be fixed to the wall to serve the same purpose (see p. 224, Fig. 92). In the accompanying figures the fire-lump lining of the grate is shown by the shaded portion; the back lump has grooves in it terminating in holes just at the bottom of the splay, which form air channels for admitting air at the back over the fire. The hearth is made of a plate of cast-iron. The grates are of three sizes, according to the cubic contents of the room. A grate with a fire opening of 1 foot 3 inches is for a room of not more than 3,600 cubic feet of contents; a grate with 1 foot 5 inches of opening is for rooms between 3,600 and 7,800 cubic feet; a grate with 1 foot 9 inches opening is for rooms up to 12,000 cubic feet; above which capacity two grates will be required. Fig. 77 shows the ordinary fire-place, with the method of setting the stove and forming the air chamber. The contrivance for admitting the external air into this chamber will depend on circumstances. If the fire-place be built in an external wall the openings for fresh air may be made in the back, but if in an internal wall the channel from the outside may be either between the flooring of the room and the ceiling joists of the room below, or in the spaces between the joists, or by a tube or hollow beam carried below the ceiling of the room below.   These horizontal ducts should contain 1 square inch of sectional area for every 100 cubic feet of room space ; the grating covering the opening to the outer air should not be larger in total area than the flue, so that the clear area through the grating would be only half that of the flue.   If the shaft is of great length the sectional area should be rather more, but if communicating directly with the outer air the sectional area should be rather less than that recommended.   Care should be taken to draw the supply of air from a point where there are no nuisances, such as gully heads, gutters, &c., and that it be taken as high above the ground as possible.   From the air chamber at the back of the fire-place the air is conducted into the room by a shaft (see Fig. 92), and through a louvred opening placed near the ceiling ; the clear area through the louvre being made much larger than the area of the shaft, the louvre being bevelled upwards so as to cause the air to impinge against the ceiling, to prevent a cold draught being felt when the fire is not lighted.

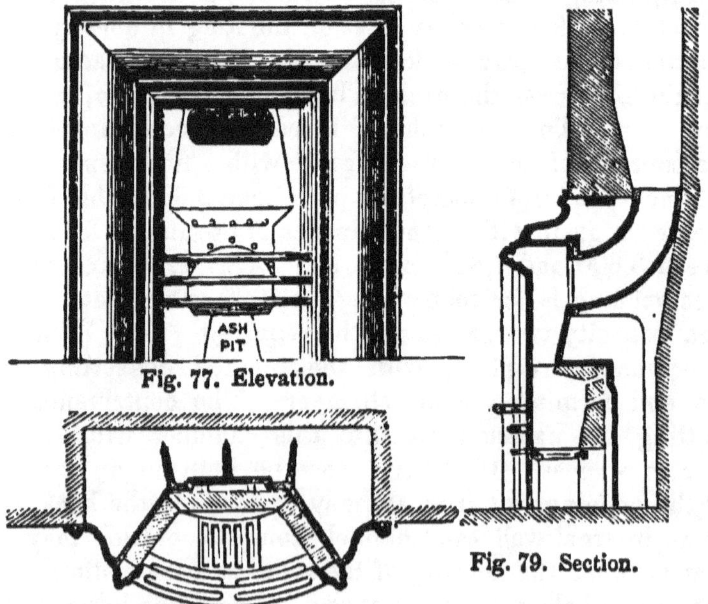

Fig. 77. Elevation.

Fig. 79. Section.

Fig. 78. Plan.

Remodelled Fire-grate.

PART II.

CHAPTER I.

REAUMUR remarks, "Ce que la Nature apprend est reçu de bonne heure," and as Nature is the best, as well as the earliest teacher, the first example in the history of ventilation may be taken from the lower animals; and it would seem that a more difficult, or, apparently, more hopeless problem, does not exist in our rooms and crowded assemblies, our mines and ships, than in the case about to be proposed.

Imagine a dome-shaped building, perfectly air-tight, except through a small hole at the bottom, capable of containing thirty or forty thousand animals, full of life and activity— every portion of the enclosed space that can be spared being filled with curious machinery—the problem is, how to warm and ventilate such a space, so as to maintain a proper temperature, and yet to give to every individual within it a proper supply of air.

Now, this is the condition of a common bee-hive, and if, with all our machines, and contrivances, and scientific resources, the combined operation of warming and ventilating a room be difficult or unsatisfactory, how infinitely more so must be that of a small bee-hive, crowded with bees, the greater part of the interior filled up with combs of waxen cells, and only one small opening for the ingress and egress of the inhabitants, or for the escape of foul air and the entrance of fresh.

In a common hive, there is absolutely no other door or window, or opening, than this small entrance hole; for, on taking possession of a new hive, the bees stop up all the cracks and chinks with a resinous substance named *propolis*, for the purpose of keeping out insect depredators; and the proprietor, with the same object, generally plasters the hive to the stool, and, in order to keep off the rain, covers it with a heavy straw cap, or turns a large pan over it.

It must not be supposed that, because the vitality of insects is greater than that of warm-blooded animals, bees are not affected by the same agencies which affect us, for they are so, and in a similar manner : they fall down apparently dead if confined in a close vessel; they perish in gases which destroy us; they perspire and faint with too much heat; and are frozen to death by exposure to too much cold.

Huber introduced some bees into the receiver of an air-pump. They bore a considerable rarefaction of the air without any apparent injury; on carrying it further they fell down motionless, but revived on exposure to the air. In another experiment, three glass vessels, of the capacity of sixteen fluid ounces, were taken; 250 worker bees were introduced into one, the same number into another, and 150 males into the third. The first and the third were shut close, and the second was only partially closed. In a quarter of an hour, the workers in the close vessel became uneasy; they breathed with difficulty, perspired copiously, and licked the moisture from the sides of the vessel. In another quarter of an hour, they fell down apparently dead. They revived, however, on exposure to the air. The males were affected more fatally, for none survived; but the bees in the vessel which admitted air did not suffer. On examining the air in the two close vessels, the oxygen was found to have disappeared, and to have been replaced by carbonic acid; other bees introduced into it perished immediately. On adding a small portion of oxygen gas to it other bees lived in it; but they became insensible instantly on being plunged into carbonic acid, but revived on exposure to the air; they perished in nitrogen and hydrogen gases. Similar experiments, performed with the eggs, the larvæ, and the nymphs of bees, proved the conversion of oxygen into carbonic acid in all three states. The larvæ consumed more oxygen than the eggs, and less than the nymphs. Eggs put into foul air lost their vitality. Larvæ resisted the pernicious influence of carbonic acid better than the perfect insect would have done, but the nymphs died almost instantly therein.

These, and many other analogous experiments, prove that the respiration of bees has a similar vitiating effect upon a confined atmosphere, as the respiration of larger animals, and that bees require constant supplies of fresh air in the same manner as other living creatures. They also require their dwelling to be kept moderately cool. When from any circumstance, such as exposure to the sun, over-crowding, or the excitement produced by fear, anger, or preparation for swarming, the temperature of the hive is greatly raised, the bees evidently suffer. They often perspire so copiously as to be drenched with moisture; and on fine summer nights thousands o f them may be seen hanging out in festoons and clusters for the purpose of relieving the crowded state of the hive.

On inquiring into the method adopted by the bees for renewing the air of the hive, Huber was struck by the constant appearance of a number of the workers arranged on each side of the entrance hole, a little within the hive, incessantly engaged in vibrating their wings. In order to see what effect a similar fanning would produce on the air of a glass receiver containing a lighted taper, M. Senebier advised him to construct a little artificial ventilator, consisting of eighteen tin vanes. This was put into a box, on the top of which was adapted a large cylindrical vessel of the capacity of upwards of 3,000 cubic inches. A lighted taper, contained in this vessel, was extinguished in eight minutes; but on restoring the air and setting the ventilator in motion the taper burnt brilliantly, and continued to do so as long as the vanes were kept moving. On holding small pieces of paper, suspended by threads, before the aperture, the existence of two currents of air became evident; there was a current of hot air rushing out, and at the same time a current of cold air passing in. On holding little bits of paper or cotton near the hole of the hive a similar effect was produced; they were impelled towards the entrance by the in-going current, and when

they encountered the out-going current they were repelled
with equal rapidity.*

These two currents are established in the hive by the fanning motion of the bees' wings. The worker bees perform
the office of ventilators, and the number at one time varies
from eight or ten to twenty or thirty, according to the state
of the hive and the heat of the weather. I have frequently
watched their proceedings with interest. They station themselves in files, just within the entrance of the hive, with their
heads towards the entrance, while another and a larger party
stand a considerable way within the hive, with their heads
also towards the entrance. They plant their feet as firmly as
possible on the floor of the hive, stretching forward the first
pair of legs, extending the second pair to the right and left,
while the third, being placed near together, are kept perpendicular to the abdomen, so as to give that part a considerable
elevation, then uniting the two wings of each side by means
of the small marginal hooks with which they are provided, so
as to make them present as large a surface as possible to the
air, they vibrate them with such rapidity that they become
almost invisible. The two sets of ventilators, standing with
their heads opposed to each other, thus produce a complete
circulation of the air of the hive, and keep down the temperature to that point which is fitted to the nature of the animal.
When a higher temperature is required at one particular
spot, as, for example, on the combs containing the young
brood, the nurse bees place themselves over the cells, and by
increasing the rapidity of their respirations, produce a large
amount of animal heat just where it is wanted. The carbonic
acid and other products of respiration are got rid of by
ventilation.

The laborious task of ventilating the hive is seldom or never
intermitted in the common form of hive, either by day or by
night, during summer. There are separate gangs of venti-

* I have repeated this experiment more than once. The bees are evidently
annoyed by it, and a bee will seize hold of the little bit of paper, fly away
with it for a few feet, and then drop it. This was done several times before
the bee became aware of the thread that suspended it. The bee then traced
the thread to my hand, and proceeded to attack me, when I yielded to the
brave little fellow, and ceased to annoy the hive.

lators, each gang being on duty for about half an hour. In winter, when the bees are quiet, and their respiration only just sufficient to maintain vitality, the ventilating process is not carried on ; but by gently tapping on the hive, its inmates wake up, increase the number of their respirations, and consequently the temperature of the hive, to such a degree, that the air becomes intolerably hot and vitiated. To remedy this a number of worker bees go to the entrance of the hive, and begin to ventilate the interior as laboriously as in summer, although the open air be too cold for them to venture out.

Bearing in mind the details given in the Introduction, and the conclusion arrived at (p. 10) that the animal frame is a true apparatus for combustion, we can understand how bees regulate the temperature of their hive : when greater heat is wanted they increase the rapidity of their respirations, or, in other words, they burn more carbon ; but they get rid of the products of combustion, and also prevent the heat from accumulating by the process of ventilation. Bees in general maintain a temperature of 10° or 15° above that of the external air ; but at certain periods this temperature is greatly increased. Mr. Newport observed in the month of June, when the atmosphere was at 56° or 58°, that the temperature of the hive was 96° or 98°. This high temperature arose from the nurse bees incubating on the combs, and voluntarily increasing their heat by means of increased respiration. In winter, on the contrary, when only just sufficient heat is required to maintain vitality, less carbon is burnt, and the temperature of the hive is accordingly low. In one observation by Mr. Newport at 7.15 a.m., on the 2nd January, 1836, when there was a clear intense frost, and the thermometer in the open air stood a little above 17°, a thermometer permanently fixed in the hive marked a temperature of 30°, or two degrees below the freezing point. The bees were roused by tapping on the hive, and in the course of sixteen minutes the thermometer rose to 70°, or 53° above the temperature of the external air. On another occasion, when the temperature of the hive had to be raised to about 70°, the external air being at 40°, the bees soon cooled it down to 57° by their mode of

ventilation, and kept it at that point as long as the hive continued to be excited.

By this process of ventilation also bees get rid of noxious
odours in the hive. Huber found that on introducing into
the hive some penetrating vapour disagreeable to the bees,
they always increased the amount of ventilation until they
got rid of it. Humble-bees adopt the same method of dis-
pelling pernicious odours; but it is remarkable that neither
their males, nor those of domestic bees, seem capable of using
their wings as ventilators. "Ventilation is, therefore," says
Huber, "one of the industrial operations peculiar to the
workers. The Author of Nature, in assigning a dwelling to
those insects where the air can hardly penetrate, bestows the
means of averting the fatal effects which might result from the
vitiation of their atmosphere. Perhaps the bee is the only
creature entrusted with so important a function, and which
indicates such delicacy in its organisation."

The circumstances under which our rooms are placed, are
more favourable to ventilation than the bee-hive. Whether
the ventilation be left to chance, or whether any special
apparatus be erected for the purpose, the foul air must be got
rid of, and fresh air, adapted to the purposes of respiration,
admitted in sufficient quantity, that is, at the rate of about
15 or 20 cubic feet per minute for each individual in the
room.* We have seen in the Introduction that it is by the
amount of impurity introduced into the air by respiration and
combustion, and not by the diminution of oxygen, that air is
to be judged of as to its healthy or unhealthy condition. We
have seen also (p. 13) that the quantity of carbonic acid
expired by human beings varies with the age, sex, state of
body, and sleeping or waking condition of the individual.
The average quantity may be taken at 537·5 grains per head
per hour corresponding to 1,029·5 cubic inches, at 32° and
30 inches pressure. The highest average for an adult man
per hour is 1,208 cubic inches. Wax, tallow, and oil produce in burning about 200 per cent. of their weight of carbonic acid, or by burning 2 lbs. of stearine in 1,800 cubic

---

* It is remarkable how this number fluctuates in the writings of different
authorities, as will be seen further on (see p. 214).

feet of air, the quantity of carbonic acid would amount to four per cent. of the total volume, producing air as impure as if it had passed through the lungs. There is also another source of impurity arising from the imperfect combustion of our lamps and candles. Perfect combustion produces from the carbon of the illuminating material and the oxygen of the air, carbonic acid, consisting of 1 equivalent of carbon and 2 equivalents of oxygen. Imperfect combustion produces carbonic oxide = 1 eq. of oxygen + 1 eq. of carbon. Carbonic acid is a heavy gas at ordinary temperatures, and will not support combustion or respiration, nor will it burn itself. Carbonic oxide is a comparatively light gas, and will not support combustion or respiration, but is itself inflammable, burning with a lambent blueish flame, as may be sometimes seen on the surface of smouldering coals in our grates. Both carbonic acid and carbonic oxide are poisonous, but the latter is more so than the former; one per cent. of carbonic oxide in the air being fatal to life, while from four to five per cent. of carbonic acid will allow respiration to be carried on, though with difficulty; and even with much larger proportions of carbonic acid the air may be breathed for a short time.

Taking it for granted that the carbonic acid and carbonic oxide generated by the burning fuel in the grate are got rid of by the chimney shaft, and that there are no poisonous gases from sewers, &c., the question is, first, what amount of carbonic acid in the air of the room is injurious. The average amount of carbonic acid in the open air is only 4 parts in 10,000; it is, of course, much larger than this in the open air of cities and densely crowded districts, and probably larger still in every room and enclosed space where people are collected and lights are burning. No system of ventilation will probably ever succeed in making the air of a room as healthy as the outer air, where Nature disposes of the waste products of respiration and combustion in the manner already alluded to (p. 11), in building up vegetation : the rain and waters of the earth also absorb much of the carbonic acid and sulphurous acid which contaminate the air, in consequence of the great solubility of those gases. Writers are not agreed as to the minimum proportion of carbonic acid in the air that is injurious; some say 1 per cent.; others only ½ per cent., but either proportion is greatly in excess of the 4 parts in 10,000, which we find in the air of a healthy country district. Chemists judge of the deterioration of the air by the amount of the carbonic acid detected in it (see p. 15 *ante*); they have no means of estimating the animal effluvia, referred to by Dr. Faraday (p. 20 *ante*); but it may be taken for granted that the air of any room or hall, or public building, that affects our senses unpleasantly, must be unhealthy.*

A good system of ventilation must reduce the proportion of carbonic acid in the air as much as possible without producing other inconveniences, such as draughts to the head, cold baths for the feet, or any considerable lowering of temperature. On the contrary, it must not only produce pure air from without, but must also maintain that air at an equable mean temperature by one or other of the methods described in Part I. A good system of ventilation, moreover, must adjust the proper equilibrium between the air and the dissolved aqueous vapour, since there is no doubt that one of the sources of mischief in a badly ventilated room arises from the presence of too large or too small a quantity of moisture.

When air contains as much vapour as it can hold at a given temperature it is said to be *saturated*. The average amount of aqueous vapour contained in the open air in this country

* Professor Roscoe has determined the amount of the carbonic acid in the air of various localities, as shown in the following table:—

Localities.	CO_2 in 1,000 vols. of air.	Cubic capacity of enclosed space.	No. of persons.	No. of cub. ft. per head per minute.	Aq. vap. Saturating quantity = 100.
	vols.	cubic ft.		cubic ft.	
Open air	0·37	—	—	—	65·5
Wellington barracks	1·242	7,920	16	13·3	66·2
Do.	1·189	7,920	16	13·0	59·5
Do.	1·418	7,920	20	—	65·0
Large school-room .	2·371	22,140	164	6	75·0
School-room . . .	3·100	4,640	67	4	74·0
Crowded theatre—					
1. Air from gallery	3·212	—	—	—	} 47·0
2. Pit	2·637	—	—	—	

throughout the year is about 82 per cent. of the total amount that it can hold. Hence it has been concluded that the aqueous vapour of rooms, &c., artificially heated, should not vary greatly from this amount. In the warming and ventilating arrangement of the House of Lords, Mr. Goldsworthy Gurney found that an agreeable atmosphere as regards moisture is obtained when the difference between the wet and dry bulb thermometers, at a working temperature of 64°, is more than 3° and less than 9°. This corresponds to an amount of aqueous vapour varying from 82 to 55 per cent. on the saturating quantity.

Now the quantity of water exhaled by a man per hour is about 309 grains. The quantity of air at 60°, half saturated with aqueous vapour, required to take up this 309 grains so as to become three-fourths saturated, is about 280 cubic feet. Hence, in order to effect the proper equilibrium between the air and the dissolved aqueous vapour, about 221 cubic feet of air must be given to each individual per hour. This, of course, refers to the watery vapours only. When this " exceeds 80 per cent. of the total possible quantity, the necessary evaporation and diffusion from the lungs and the pores of the skin is checked ; and when the aqueous vapour is 50 per cent. the exchange proceeds too rapidly, and unpleasant sensations of dryness are experienced."*

The sources from which a supply of fresh air finds its way into an apartment may be *accidental* or *special, natural* or *artificial.* All openings not intended for the purpose of ventilation, such as chimneys, doors, windows, &c., may be considered as accidental or natural, and we have no precise information as to the amount of ventilation derived from such sources ; that is, how much fresh air enters, and spent air issues, from our windows, doors, and chimneys under given circumstances. It appears, from some remarkable experiments made by Professor Roscoe (on the suggestion of a German chemist), that a certain amount of gaseous diffusion takes place through brick and mortar walls. A quantity of carbonic acid was evolved in a room of 2,560 cubic feet capacity ; there was no fire in the grate, the flue was closed, and the

* Roscoe. Report on the Chemical Relations of Ventilation. May, 1857.

four doors and two windows were shut. The carbonic acid contained in the enclosed air was determined at consecutive half-hours : at the end of the first half-hour it had diminished from 0·7 to 0·3 per cent. of the total volume of air, although all direct ventilation was checked. After this the amount of carbonic acid remained constant, possibly from the continued respiration of two persons in the room. The exchange of carbonic acid through closed windows, doors, and walls, appears from this experiment to be very great. In order to form some idea of the amount of gaseous diffusion which takes place through brick and mortar walls, Roscoe determined the quantity of carbonic acid which diffuses through a common brick. For this purpose a brick was cemented with pitch into the end of a box, 3 feet long, 9 inches broad, and $4\frac{1}{2}$ inches deep. The interior of the box was lined with pitch, and carbonic acid was led into the box through two tubes cemented into the sides. After the box had stood for some minutes, to allow the gas to diffuse equally throughout the space, a sample of the contained air was collected, after which a similar sample was taken every hour, and the quantity of carbonic acid in each determined. In order to exclude error arising from any possible leakage in the box, a second series of analyses was made in the same way, except that the whole of the brick was covered by a layer of pitch, whereby the leakage of the box was determined. The result of the experiment was that when the enclosed space contained 16 per cent. of carbonic acid, more than 2 per cent. escaped in two hours. Another experiment with a piece of dried mortar of the size of the brick, and with hydrogen instead of carbonic acid, showed that a still greater exchange took place than was found with the brick. Hence, " the beneficial action of our brick and plaster walls is, therefore, not merely confined to taking up or giving moisture to the air, for they are eminently hygroscopic ; but a diffusive interchange goes on within the pores of the brick and mortar ; so that our walls become, to a certain extent, an aid to ventilation. The well-known unhealthiness of iron or new and damp houses may probably be, to some extent, thus accounted for."*

* A curious illustration of the porous condition of the plaster ceilings of

It has been commonly supposed that the heated carbonic acid formed by respiration, and by the combustion of lamps and candles, ascends and forms an atmosphere of impure air in the upper part of rooms not artificially ventilated at the top; so that persons breathing the air above the level of the chimney opening were breathing a more unhealthy air than those below such level. It is found, however, that the known laws of expansion of gases by heat, and of the diffusion of gases, are sufficient to equalise the amount of carbonic acid throughout the enclosed space. Roscoe's experiments have shown that there is no accumulation of impure air in any particular part of the room, as was proved by examining specimens of air taken simultaneously above and below the level of the chimney opening in a room not artificially ventilated. This remark, however, does not apply to the air in various parts of crowded and heated public buildings, as may be seen by reference to the table at p. 206 *note*, where the air collected from the gallery of a crowded fashionable theatre was found to contain much more carbonic acid than a similar specimen of air from the pit. In such case the carbonic acid was caught as it were while being generated, and in a locality where it mingled its own proportion with that of the current ascending from the cooler pit, where the proportion was already much in excess.

This mingling of the various layers of air in a room was well made out in some experiments by Mr. Campbell, an account of which is included in the Report already referred to. He adopted the obvious method already described in Part I., p. 124, of filling a small balloon with a light gas, and weighting it until it was nearly of the same density as the air in the stillest part of the room. When placed opposite to and near the fire, F, Fig. 80, the balloon expanded, ascended, and moved steadily along the ceiling from the fire-place towards one or other of the windows, w, when it descended to the floor,

rooms may sometimes be noticed in old houses, where the form of heavy beams of wood or rafters is made out by the darker colour of the ceiling immediately below them. The diffusion of the gases through the plaster probably drags the dust with them, but on the plaster immediately below the beam, the dust would settle and accumulate by adhesion, and thus account for the darker colour.

moved towards the fire-place, and again ascended. If any one moved about the room, or if there were a draught from a door or window, or other slight disturbing cause, the direction of the balloon was somewhat altered. As the motion of the balloon indicates the motion of the air, it follows that air near the fire must be continually ascending, and "as it can neither escape nor accumulate at the ceiling, it must flow from the place where it ascends, that is, from above the fire-place towards the windows and walls, where it contracts and becomes heavier, falls by its own weight, and is forced downwards by fresh quantities of heated air, ex-

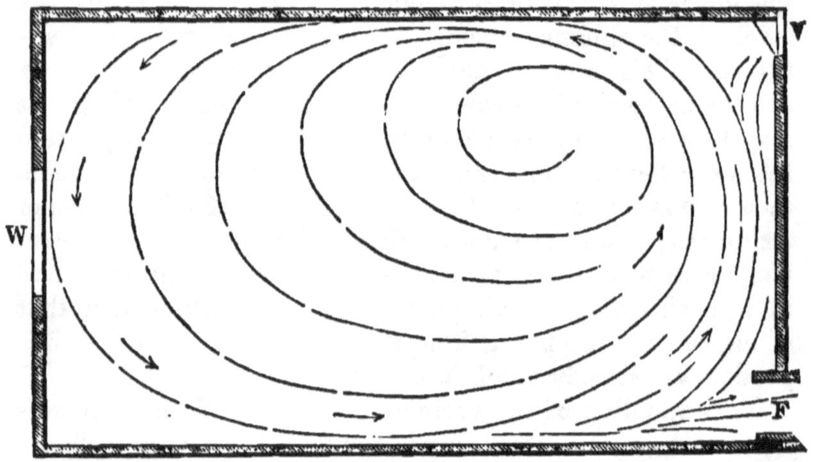

Fig. 80. Air currents in a room warmed by an open fire.

panding and following in the same tract. In like manner, because air cannot accumulate on the floor, the descending currents at the windows, and those originating there from the coldness of the glass, must give rise to currents moving towards the fire-place near the floor, in the direction in which the balloon actually moved; and, further, any person in the room must cause movements in the air, such as were shown by the movements of the balloon. If, then, the air of a room be circulating thus rapidly, foul air cannot accumulate in any great excess at any part of it, but, on the contrary, different qualities of air must be speedily mixed."

Filaments of floss silk about 6 inches long, teased out and made very fine, were fastened to the ceiling (as in Fig. 81), and also to pens attached to a pole reaching from the floor to ceiling, while others were fastened to the mantelpiece. Where the air was stagnant the ends of the vanes pointed downwards, where it was descending they pointed downwards and moved about; where the air was moving horizontally the filaments were bent in the same direction, and

Fig. 81. Vanes attached to ceiling.

were more or less bent, according to the force of the moving power at different points. In ascending air the vanes pointed upwards. Here, too, it was evident that the air was rising at the mantelpiece and flowing rapidly along the ceiling in lines radiating from a point above the fire. It was further remarkable " that the ventilator in the chimney was not drawing air from the ceiling so as to interfere with the direction of vanes passing close to and above it, which pointed directly away from it." (See v., Fig. 80.)

The force of the current, the existence of which was thus ascertained, was measured by an anemometer (Fig. 82) formed by a piece of cardboard, C, of known dimensions,

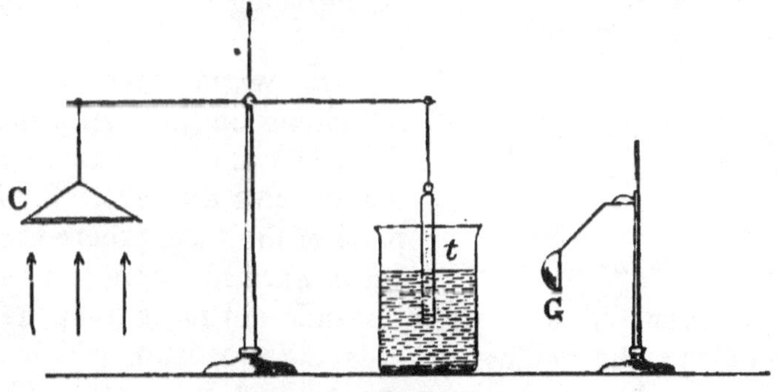

Fig. 82. Anemometer.

suspended to one arm of the beam of a balance, and placed at the edge of the mantelpiece in the ascending current. The graduated stem of a broken thermometer, *t*, was suspended to the other end of the beam, and was placed in a glass vessel containing water ; weights were placed on the cardboard till the zero point of the graduated stem was level with the surface of the water. The degrees were read with the assistance of a magnifier, G, and the number of degrees moved indicated the force acting on the card. The value of each degree was found by adding weights to the card. In this way it was ascertained that the force of the upward current at the mantelpiece was considerable, and that it varied in strength. It was strongest in the centre, but extended to both sides of the mantelpiece ; this upward current had a force of from 15 to $4\frac{1}{2}$ grains to the square foot; the force diminished as the fire got low ; but the same action went on even when the fire was extinguished.

The currents were made visible by means of a fuming apparatus consisting of a sponge filled with muriatic acid suspended over a small basin of ammonia. This is a better contrivance than smoke, which, when warm, moves independently of the general current in the room. The fumes showed the same currents as before, and also an eddy above the mantelpiece (Fig. 83) falling along the wall for about 2 feet.

Fig. 83. Eddy over Fire-place.

" On warm days, when the sun shines on the carpet through the windows, and no fire is lighted, the currents are reversed. Those parts of the room where the carpet is warmed by the sun become the warmest. The air there ascends and flows from the windows along the ceiling towards the ventilator, which works freely, opening and shutting at short intervals. The air then enters the room by the chimney and escapes by the doors."

But when the fire is lighted the whole air of the room is in rapid circulation, much more so than when there is no fire, and the experiments seem to show "that an open chimney with a fire lighted will serve to remove foul air from dwelling-rooms, without any special opening communicating with the chimney from the upper part of the room." If this be true the chimney valve, which has been so much advocated and so much used, is of little or no use.

The quantity of air that escapes from the room up the chimney is very large, and Mr. Campbell's experiments show that when seated by the side of a comfortable fire, currents of air are constantly streaming over the surface of our bodies. No wonder that colds and rheumatic affections are so common in every household, under the usual arrangements of the fire-place, and that a cold will often run through the whole family at the end of autumn when fires are begun for the winter. An anemometer placed in the chimney of a room in which the fire was lighted showed an escape of air from the room of 1,004 cubic feet per minute. In another room where there was no fire, but while the chimney was yet warm, the instrument was held in the chimney about 6 inches down, and it appears that 125 cubic feet per minute were escaping from a room whose cubic contents were 10,159 feet, so that in about an hour and a quarter the quantity of air which escaped from the room was equal to its cubic contents. Dr. Roscoe has shown that the different qualities of air in a room were equally mixed, and Mr. Campbell's experiments tended to confirm his conclusions, and he thinks that no special ventilation beyond that of the chimney is required, so long as the chimney is warm, provided means be taken to admit the outer air freely, and to warm it before entering "to save fuel," as it is said, but we should also add, to prevent cold draughts to the persons of the occupants, especially to the feet.

No efficient system of ventilation can be devised until it is agreed how much fresh air per minute is required to be supplied to each individual for the purposes of healthy respiration. That is, the quantity must be settled as regards the building or room required to be ventilated, since the quantity to each individual must vary according as the enclosed space is occupied day and night, as in hospitals, prisons, &c.; or only during a portion of the day, as in schools, counting-houses, workshops, public assemblies, &c. In the one case the sources of vitiation of the air are permanent and continuous, and may acquire a dangerous degree of power, as in the wards of fever or other hospitals, in which case the ventilation should be energetic; whereas in the second case, where the number of inmates is liable to fluctuation, where people are constantly going in and out, and doors are being frequently opened and shut, a more moderate system of ventilation may suffice. Writers have not generally admitted that the quantity of air required by each person may vary according to circumstances, and each writer framing his own estimate from the cases investigated by him, gives a result which may bear no kind of relation to the quantity determined on by another observer on altogether different data. Thus Peclet concludes, on experimental grounds, that a man requires 5 cubic feet of air per minute, Vierordt gives only $2\frac{1}{2}$ cubic feet, Reid 10 and Arnott 20 cubic feet. Roscoe also concludes, from his examination of the air of soldiers' sleeping-rooms, that 20 cubic feet of air per minute per man are required to remove completely the products of respiration and animal putrescent effluvia.

There are, however, other conditions which must regulate the supply of air, such as whether the individuals are healthy or sick, young or old, asleep or awake, active or inactive. General Morin, in his recent work on ventilation,* has given the result of his inquiries into this as well other parts of the subject, and has contrasted the experience of other writers with his own. He quotes Peclet as one who has studied the subject sufficiently to pronounce an authoritative opinion. According to that writer, in a school dormitory where there was a ventilation of 3·53 cubic feet per minute† for each bed, there was a faint disagreeable odour, and he admits that this amount should be a minimum of ventilation when the air of the room is mixed with that of ventilation, and there is no par-

* " Études sur la Ventilation." 2 vols., 8vo. Paris, 1863.
† Morin's unit is the cubic metre per head per *hour;* but in all cases I have reduced this to the cubic foot per *minute.*

ticular cause of unhealthiness; but when the ventilation takes place from below upwards, through numerous orifices in the floor, a supply of from 4·12 to 6·47 cubic feet per head per minute renders the air sufficiently pure. This last calculation refers to the ventilation of the Chamber of Deputies, where the sitting lasted some hours only, and where the discharge of air sometimes amounted to 10·58 cubic feet per head per minute. In this hall, capable of containing a thousand persons, the air was vitiated in half an hour when there was no ventilation; so that each individual vitiated at least 4·7 cubic feet of air per minute, notwithstanding the frequent opening of the doors and the escape of air by openings above.

In 1843 a Commission, presided over by M. Arago, concluded from its examination of a prison that the ventilation ought to be raised as high as 5·88 cubic feet per head per minute. This had long been the amount demanded by sanatory officers for hospitals; but in 1852, when the warming and ventilation of the Hospital Lariboisière was rearranged, a continued ventilation of warm air in winter and of cold air in summer was demanded in the proportion of 11·77 cubic feet per head per minute in the wards, and of half that quantity in the room where the patients took their exercise. A case is mentioned of a ward occupied by wounded men, in which 35·31 cubic feet of air per minute per bed was scarcely sufficient to keep the air sweet. Morin found that in the lecture-room of the *Conservatoire des Arts*, a ventilation of 8·8 cubic feet per minute per auditor was hardly sufficient in winter, when the temperature would occasionally rise to 71·6 Fahr., so that a ventilation of from 14·71 to 17·65 cubic feet per minute per head came to be considered as a minimum. In the meeting-room of the Academy of Sciences it was found that the removal of from 16·47 to 17·06 cubic feet of air per head per minute was sometimes insufficient to keep the air pure, while the ventilating arrangements gave rise to distressing currents of air when only a few orifices of supply were provided. It has also been found, from numerous observations in the Hospital Lariboisière, that the removal of from 35·31 to 41·19 cubic feet of air per minute per bed did not always prevent the wards from having a disagreeable odour, and it was even recommended to raise the amount to 58·85 cubic feet. At the military hospital of Vincennes the ventilation has been as much as 70·62 cubic feet per minute. This proved to be inconvenient, and the medical officer required that the quantity of air evacuated should be reduced to 17·65 cubic feet per head per minute. This was tried for three months, and found to be insufficient, especially in the fever wards. The ventilation was then readjusted to the rate of about 35·31 cubic feet per minute per bed.

Of course where gas is burning an allowance must be made for each burner, which not only vitiates the air but raises the temperature. The result of numerous experiments in the theatres of Paris has shown that a supply of 17·65 cubic feet per minute to each spectator will be sufficient. Care must, however, be taken to raise the temperature of the incoming air to about the normal temperature of the enclosed space, and to distribute it in such a way as to prevent the currents from being felt: means must also be provided for increasing or diminishing the ventilation at will within certain limits. Hence, too, the necessity of intelligent supervision, for it often happens that the most costly arrangements if left to themselves will go wrong, while if regulated and controlled they will perform their part admirably. Hence in every public establishment a skilled superintendent should have the charge of the warming and ventilating arrangements.*

General Morin considers that 20 cubic feet per head per minute is not sufficient ventilation in the sleeping-rooms of

---

* In the Report on Barracks the commissioners relate a case in point. In a hospital which was ventilated by one of the most perfect apparatus they had anywhere seen, and which professed to supply between 4,000 and 5,000 cubic feet of air per bed per hour, the atmosphere of the wards was found to be stagnant and foul. On pointing this out, an inquiry was instituted, when it appeared that one of the valves of the supply pipe had been tampered with, apparently for the purpose of saving fuel by diminishing the quantity of warm air supplied to the sick. In some prison cells, the commissioners did not find the air by any means so fresh as it ought to have been, and in some instances, where the ventilation was dependent on a fire, or upon gas-lights, no one had taken the trouble to light them, so that the ventilating force had ceased to act, and the cells or rooms were virtually unventilated. In two of the theatres of Paris, where an elaborate system of ventilation had been constructed at the expense of the city, and which depended on keeping up two fires which acted as the ventilating force, the fires soon ceased to be lighted, and the uncomfortable condition of the crowded interior was actually attributed to the failure of the method adopted for ventilating.

barracks, and he proposes to raise it to 23·54 cubic feet, with means for increasing the volume under certain circumstances, which he thinks might be done by connecting the ventilating apparatus with the heating apparatus of the kitchen.

Experiments made in the stables of the Omnibus Company at Paris showed that a renewal of the air amounting to from 94·16 to 111·81 cubic feet per minute per horse was about sufficient to keep the air fresh, and at the proper temperature and hygrometric state.

In all the above results, it was found that when ventilation was energetic, the vitiated air, compared with the fresh air sent in below, had an increase of volume in the proportion of 3 to 2. The vitiated air, as already noticed in the experiments of Leblanc (p. 14, *ante*), is in a state of putrescence most dangerous to inhale. General Morin's assistants have been exposed to considerable danger from this source, one of them having been struck down in a state of asphyxia, and another made very ill. This will give some idea of the kind of poison we are liable to breathe in crowded rooms and assemblies where no special arrangements are made for ventilation.

The art of ventilation, in its simplest form, consists in letting out the foul air of an apartment or other enclosed space, and bringing in fresh air in such quantity as not to prove disagreeable or injurious to the occupants. Some writers divide the subject of artificial ventilation into two branches, which they call the *plenum* method and the *vacuum* method. By the first, air is forced by mechanical contrivances into the interior of a building, and the vitiated air is allowed to escape by openings contrived for the purpose ; or, to speak more accurately, the force or impetus of the incoming air ought slightly to compress the air of the room, and assist the efflux of the vitiated air. By the second method the vitiated air is drawn out of the building by means of mechanical contrivances, or by the agency of heat artificially excited, or simply by its own levity, and the fresh air thus finds an entrance through channels adapted for the purpose.

There can be no doubt that the introduction of mechanical apparatus, such as bellows, fans, pumps, &c., either for driving in fresh air, or for extracting foul, is objectionable, not only from the liability to get out of order, but also from the superintendence required. That method must be considered as the best, for private houses at least, which is self-acting ; while for public buildings the self-acting method should still be adopted, subject, however, to a certain amount of control on the part of a competent officer. The self-acting principle must depend on that which regulates the draught of our smoke flues and the chimneys of our lamps, namely, that a given volume of air expands and becomes lighter when heated ; 1,000 cubic feet of air at 32° becoming 1366·5 cubic feet at 212°. Moreover, a cubic foot of air at 30° weighs 569·2 grains, while it weighs 557·8 grains at 40°, 546·8 grains at 50°, 536·3 grains at 60°, and 526·2 grains at 70°, the pressure as indicated by the barometer being constant. Hence it will be seen that a cubic foot of air at 40° is 11·4 grains less in weight than at 30°, and this difference in weight for each successive 10° becomes less, until between 60° and 70° it is 10·1 grains.

We have seen in the Introduction that the ascending and descending currents in air and water depend on these differences in temperature, the warmer fluid ascending, and the colder and heavier descending. Ventilation of rooms and buildings, and the warming of buildings by hot water, depend on this principle. The greater the difference in temperature, the greater will be the difference in weight, and the more rapidly will the current flow. But these heated ascending currents readily part with their heat on contact with cold surfaces, such as windows and outer walls, and ascending currents became quickly converted into descending ones.

Air being thus liable, from its excessive mobility consequent on the small size and independent action of its particles, to be acted on by heat, to expand and to contract, to obey, as it were, the beck and call of every calorific agent near or distant, is liable to expend its moving force in whirls and rotations, or to waste its travelling energy in the friction of its molecules on each other, or on other substances. In every circulation of air these whirls are inevitable, but our arrangements should be such as to favour them as little as possible. Thus in our waste air channels we should avoid change of direction, obstructions, and roughnesses, or anything that leads to inequality in the currents of air themselves. When air escapes, and still more when propelled, through gratings where the openings are of the same dimensions as the closed spaces, the air becomes obstructed and reflected in passing, and forms whirls and eddies when passed (see Fig. 84), so that its *vis viva* becomes quickly

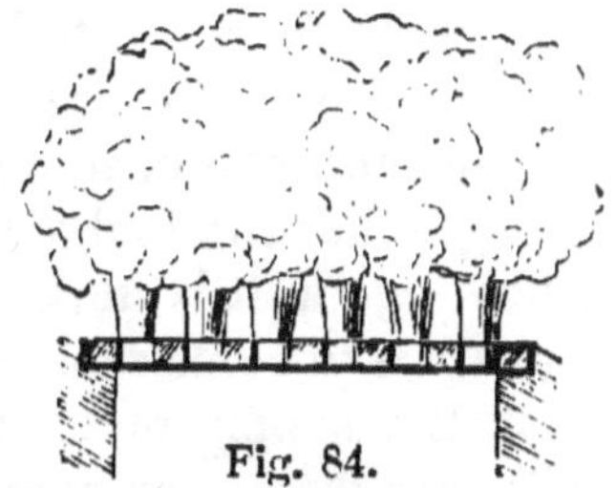

Fig. 84.
Air passing through a grating.

expended. Even when air is propelled by machinery along a channel into a room or other wider space, it readily wastes itself in these whirls, as shown in Fig. 85. When, on the contrary, air passes from a colder into a warmer space along a tube of good size, the particles move in lines which converge towards the opening of the pipe in various directions, and with no very great rapidity (see Fig. 86). In this way there is a sort of draught or suction in the direction required, with little or no eddy, while by

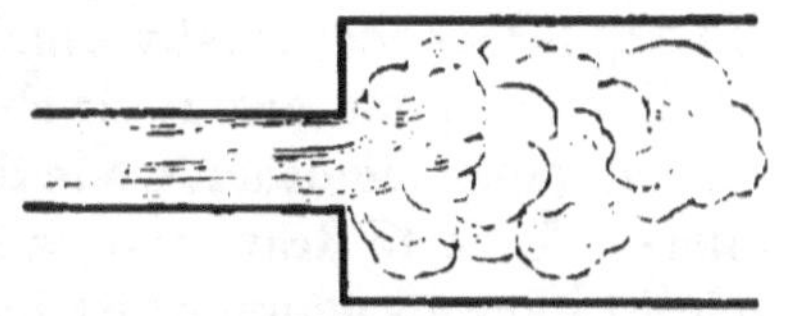

Fig. 85. Air propelled from smaller into larger channel.

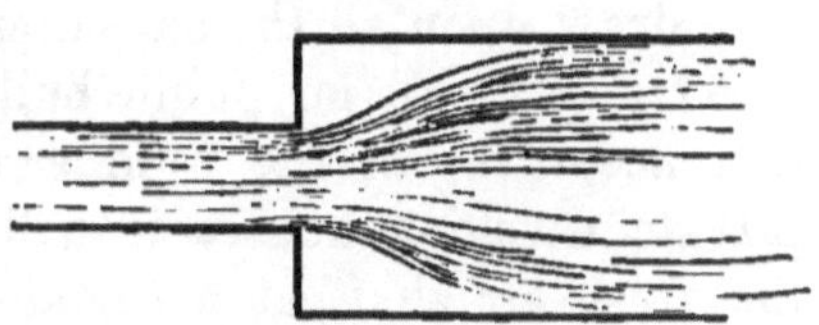

Fig. 86. Air passing from a colder into a warmer space.

multiplying these supply-pipes, the velocity can be diminished, the supply increased, and the persons present supplied with fresh air without being annoyed by draughts.

But the grand point is to get rid of the foul air, for if this be done, the fresh will flow in without much difficulty, since in every room or enclosed space occupied by a warm-blooded animal, to say nothing of fires, lamps, and candles, the air is less dense than that outside. *Get rid of the bad air* is the maxim of every sound ventilator, and Morin wisely insists upon this addition, *Get rid of it at the very spot where it is generated.* As, for example, in the ward of a hospital, the infected air should be removed, not by one or two foul-air shafts, however capacious, for in such case the foul air may creep from bed to bed, and do its deadly work before it finds its way to the air shaft, but every bed should have its own special ventilator communicating with the large central ventilator, so that the foul air is got rid of as soon as engendered. Then, again, it is important to determine the spot where the foul air is to be discharged. The discharge pipe must not be near the supply-pipe, or the foul air will become mingled with the fresh, nor near the heating apparatus for a similar reason. All these arrangements, which are comparatively easy in planning the building, if the architect will only condescend to study them, become difficult when the building is already finished, and the ventilator has to supplement the architect.

The different channels by which the foul air is collected should open into one general foul-air shaft, and be so arranged as not to draw upon each other, while the collecting shaft should have sufficient force to draw upon all the feeders. It must not be liable to have its action upset by wind outside, or the opening of doors and windows inside ; that is, means must be provided, either by a fire in the discharge shaft, or by a fan, to enable it to draw upon all the subsidiary shafts in the building.

Arrangements for public buildings should admit of regulation according as the number of inmates fluctuates ; and in private dwelling-houses it will always be easy to contract the fresh-air shaft at a certain point within certain limits. Knowing the temperatures inside and outside, however little the former exceeds the latter, it will nearly always be possible, by a proper adjustment of the orifices of the fresh-air pipe, to bring in such a volume of air as may be required without any further care, and without having to look after any mechanical contrivances, such as fans, &c.

The question as to what part of the room the fresh air is to be admitted is not so easily answered. There is no doubt that if the fresh air has been heated to 100° or 120° or upwards, it must enter at a higher level than the lungs of the persons present, or it will produce great personal discomfort. Its levity will cause it to rise and temper the cold air of the room before it feels the influence of the outgoing current. Currents of hot air entering the room near the ground are almost as intolerable as currents of cold air in a similar position. The former produce unpleasant sensations about the chest, head, and eyes, and the latter act as a cold bath to the feet and legs. In theatres and other places where the air enters by numerous orifices in the floor with a velocity of 1 foot or $1\frac{1}{2}$ foot per minute (sufficient to bend the flame of a candle 45°), persons exposed to it are liable to contract rheumatic affections in the reins and lower extremities. Moreover, air admitted through the floor, whether cold or warm, is apt to raise the fine dust of the floor so as to irritate the lungs. In fact, the French engineers are agreed that the fresh air, whether hot or cold, must not be introduced at the level of the floor.

The question as to what point or points of the room to introduce the fresh air, is further complicated by the fact that our winter arrangements for warming and ventilation do not always suit the ventilating requirements of summer. Ventilation, in fact, is more difficult in summer than in winter, as the incoming air, being more heavy, is liable to subside and pass out without being diffused. Morin recommends that in summer openings communicating with the outer air should be made in or about the cornice, so as to bring in the air in the form of a thin sheet, or in numerous threads, so as to spread over the ceiling, and gradually sink to ventilating openings placed at a lower level, where it would escape and drag with it the vitiated air, whether light or heavy. We have already in the Introduction stated some objections to this method; but we are bound to admit that in the case of an efficient method of ventilation, our opinion may well be reconsidered, seeing what grave objections belong to the method of admitting cold air at the level of the floor, and where, moreover, the ventilating openings, if under the control of the inmates, are almost sure to be closed or stopped up. In a very able report of the Commissioners for Improving the Sanatory Condition of Barracks and Hospitals,* the question was carefully considered as to

---

* The Commissioners were Messrs. Sutherland, Burrell, and Galton. The Report is dated April, 1861. Reprinted 1863.

where the inlets for fresh air should be placed. On tracing the course of the air currents produced by inlets near the ceiling, such as those caused by drawing the window-sash a little way down, it was found that the air thus admitted soon ceased to exist as a distinct current, for at a very short distance from the inlet it mingled with the general mass of the air and disappeared. Considering also, from the experiments already noticed, that the air in a closed room with a fire revolved in spheroids (as shown in Fig. 80, page 210), and that an open fire-place thus tends to preserve the air of the room in an average state of purity and temperature—considering, too, that every room was to be provided with a capacious foul-air shaft—it was determined to place all inlets of air close to the ceiling. The form adopted was that of iron or perforated air bricks of different sectional areas, according to the number of men the room was intended to contain, allowing 1 square inch of opening for every 60 cubic feet of contents of the room; but 1 square inch to every 120 cubic feet of the room was deemed sufficient if air from without were warmed by passing round the fire-grate by one of the methods already described in Part I. Two or more such inlets were recommended, one on each of the opposite sides of the room, but not opposed to each other; and to prevent draughts, each inlet was covered by a wooden cornice several times its length, sloping upwards to the ceiling at an angle of 45°, the upper side formed of perforated zinc, with holes from one-eighth to one-sixth of an inch in diameter; while still further

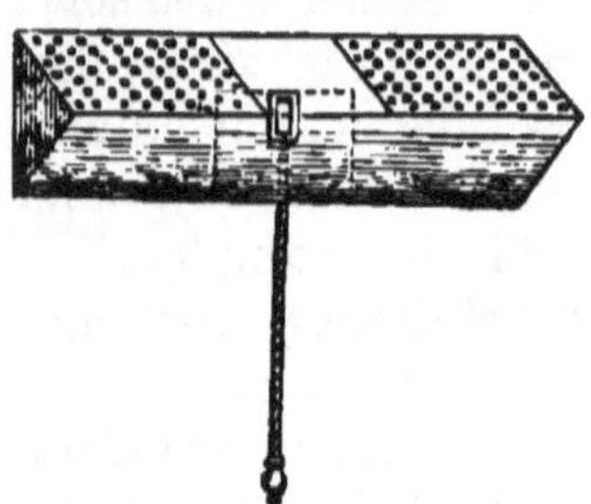

Fig. 87. Perforated Zinc Cornice.

to break up the force of the current, the front of the cornice opposite the inlet was of wood. The area of perforated zinc, through which the air passed into the room, was from three to six times the area of the inlet from the outer air. Fig. 87 shows the ventilating cornice over the inlet, with the front of diagonal ends of wood, and the upper surface of perforated zinc, except opposite the inlet, where it is of wood. In a new building these inlets would be made in the thickness of the walls by means of air bricks at intervals, as required ; each one on the inside to be faced and fitted with iron or slate louvres 1½ inches apart, sloped upwards toward the ceiling, and capable of being closed at pleasure. Jennings' air bricks, Fig. 88, may be used, or Sherringham's ventilators, to be afterwards described. Fig. 89 shows the inlet in section. It is a perforated zinc cover within the room, and a valve v, and cord working on pivots for closing the inlet.   The valve is weighted at its upper edge, so that it will fall down to the position shown by the dotted line, and leave the inlet open when not purposely raised and held by the cord. The valve, which may be of zinc or galvanised iron, should fit very loosely, so as to leave, when closed, at least from half an inch to an inch between it and the sides and bottom of the inlet holes. o is a grating for preventing birds from building in the opening ; e w the external wall, and c the ceiling of the room.

For the discharge of foul air, the Commissioners recommend shafts made of three-quarter inch deal, very smooth inside (Fig. 90), or

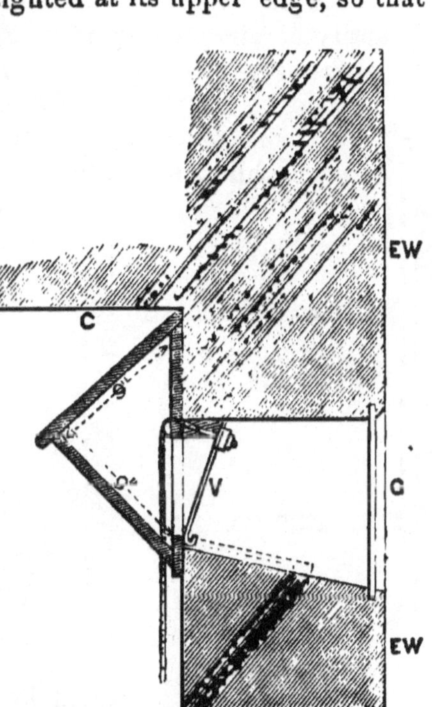

Fig. 88. Jennings' Air Brick.

Fig. 89. Ventilating Opening.

glazed pipes built into the wall at an angle of the room as far as possible from the inlet openings. The sectional area

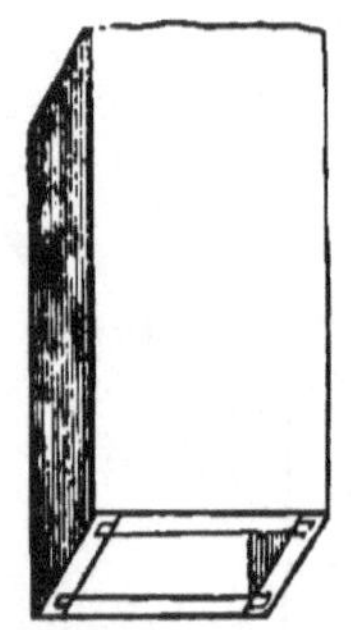

of each shaft depends on the cubic contents of the room; such as 1 inch to every 50 cubic feet of room space on the top floor, 1 inch to every 55 cubic feet for the next floor, and 1 inch for every 60 cubic feet of space for the lower floors. When the windows were opened, it was found that there was very little upward draught in these shafts, for in such cases the temperature of the room was very nearly the same as that of the outer air ; but when the windows were closed and the rooms were occupied, the current up the

Fig. 90. Portion of Foul-Air Shaft.

shaft was energetic. In rooms in the Wellington Barracks, for example, with a cubic capacity of 7,920 cubic feet, a quantity of air equal to from 8,000 to 9,000 cubic feet per hour passes up the shaft. Each shaft, therefore, removed from the rooms about 600 cubic feet per man per hour, the rooms being occupied by thirteen men each, while the chimneys removed a similar quantity per man. The foul-air shafts are carried from one angle of the ceiling to 3 or 4 feet above

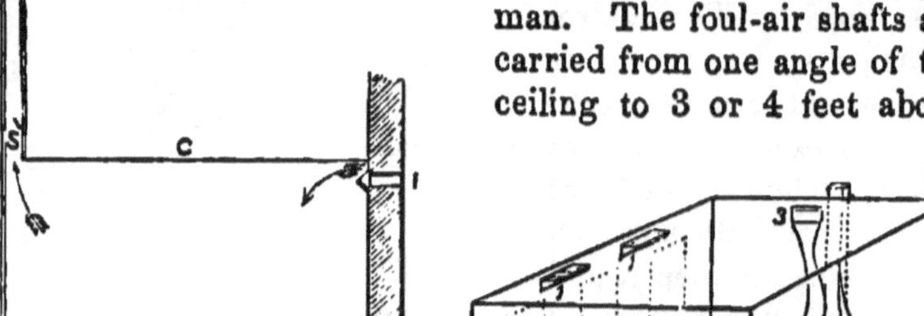

Fig. 91. Shaft and Inlets.

Fig. 92. Arrangements for Warming and Ventilating.

the room, and are protected by louvres to prevent the rain beating down. Fig. 91 will show the relative position and arrangements of the shafts, s s‘, and inlets, ɪ ɪ (c being the ceiling of each room); while Fig. 92 shows the entire

arrangement for ventilating and warming a barrack-room;
1 1 are the cold air inlets; 2 is an inlet for air from the
outside to be warmed in a space behind the fire-grate (see
Fig. 79, p. 198), and it will be seen that this air, after having
been warmed, passes up an air-flue in the walls, and is
admitted into the room through the louvre, 3, placed a little
under the ceiling. The outlet foul-air shaft is shown at 4, but
this should be placed as far as possible from the fire-place.

In practise it was found necessary, to prevent the annoyance
produced by occasional down draughts in windy weather, to
make the entrance to the foul-air shaft at the level of the
ceiling in the form of an inverted louvre, as in Fig. 93.
Morin, who has studied these arrangements, and approves
of them in principle, but has adopted some variations in
detail, quite admits the necessity of getting rid of the old
plan of introducing fresh air at the level of the floor. His
inlets he would form in the outer wall at the level of the
floor, but would make debouche into the room at the level

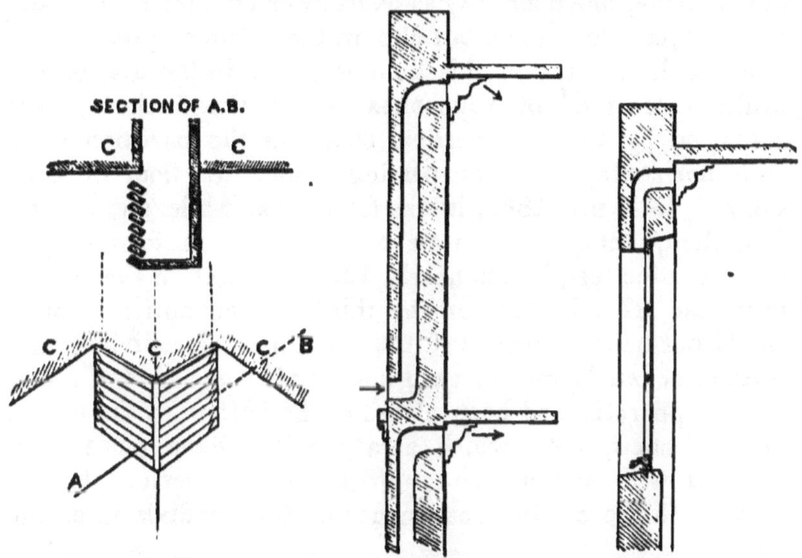

Fig. 93.　　　　Fig. 94.　　　　Fig. 95.
Air-shaft Louvre.　Ventilating Openings.　Ventilating Opening.

of the ceiling through a perforated cornice, as shown in
Fig. 94; or he would arrange them in the plate bands of the
window, so as to be out of sight, as shown in Fig. 95. It is

necessary, however, not only to distribute the ventilating openings so as to prevent draughts, but also to make them of larger proportions or in greater number than has hitherto been supposed necessary. There should also be a decided difference between the temperature inside compared with that outside; and as the velocity of the inflowing air is proportional to the square root of this difference of temperature, experience shows that the velocity of the inflowing air is often less than that of the air in the foul-air shaft. There must be a certain proportion between the sizes of the fresh-air channels and foul-air shafts. The sections of these channels must be made in the inverse ratio of the velocity which the differences in temperature require, but subject to variation with the seasons. It is, however, fully admitted that in a building of several stories, each story must have its own fresh-air shaft, or if there be one common to the building, it must be divided in the direction of its length, so as to form separate and independent channels. Unless this be done, one floor may so overpower another as to draw, not only its own supply, but also on that of its neighbour. A remarkable instance of this kind is given in the case of the Military Hospital of Vincennes, where the fresh air was conveyed by means of vertical shafts in the partition walls with horizontal branches passing under the floor of each story. In April, 1860, it was found that while on the first floor the quantity of fresh air per bed per minute was equal to 8·24 cubic feet, it was nearly 129 cubic feet on the second floor, and 97 cubic feet on the third. Such an irregularity would not have happened if the shaft had been divided into distinct channels, one for each floor, or if some kind of registering apparatus had been placed at the bottom in the mouth of each shaft, both which arrangements have since been adopted with success, although there has been a loss of velocity in the air in consequence of the subdivision of the shaft.

General Morin approves of the method, where it can be adopted, of establishing mixing chambers for mingling the cold air and the warm in proper proportions, both as to temperature and moisture, before admitting it into the rooms which are to be ventilated. This method, originally adopted in the ventilation of the Houses of Parliament, as will be described further on, has been used with success in some of the public buildings in Paris. With respect to the temperature to which the air should be raised, the varying feelings of individuals cannot be taken into account. In rooms warmed by means of an open fire, the ventilation proceeds more rapidly in proportion as the fire is brisk; and under such circumstances a higher temperature can be maintained without inconvenience than in rooms warmed by hot air from some distant part of the building; but even in such case, if ventilation is active, a higher temperature may be maintained than when it is sluggish. Morin gives from 68° to 71·8° Fahr. as the temperature which will, under most circumstances, be found to be the most agreeable to maintain.

Where cold air and air artificially heated are brought into the same apartment, they should be thoroughly mixed, for which purpose they are made to flow along the supply pipe in a direction parallel to each other, the pipe being divided by a wooden or other diaphragm for the purpose. The hot air must occupy the lower division of the pipe, so that, when they mix, the warmer and lighter air will rise up into the colder, and the common current will have a mean temperature, which can be varied according to circumstances.

A good deal has been written about the advantages of obtaining a supply of fresh air for ventilation from a height of 50 or 100 feet. Dr. Reid adopted this method, and it has also been applied to the new buildings at Guy's Hospital, London, where a hollow shaft has been erected to the height of 95 feet, down which the air rushes, and is warmed by hot-water apparatus below. One argument for this plan is, that the air thus taken from a height is fresher and cooler than at a lower elevation. This is a mistake, especially at night; for it was discovered by Mr. Six, as long ago as the year 1783, that it is often considerably warmer 200 feet from the ground than on the ground itself. Prevost and Pictet made similar observations.*　Becquerel has also

* In a volume of this series, published in 1863, entitled " Experimental

recently communicated to the Academy of Sciences at Paris the fact that, under a clear sky by night, and also sometimes by day, the temperature of the air increases in ascending, within certain limits; that from the surface of the ground to the height of about 52·5 feet the temperature is sensibly uniform, winter and summer, the tendency, however, being rather to increase in ascending within these limits; and it would be necessary to rise to the height of between 400 and 500 feet in order to get a reduction of 1° C. Experiments tried at the *Conservatoire des Arts et Métiers* at Paris showed that outside the window of the second floor, 51·6 feet from the ground, the air was rather higher in temperature than that outside the first-floor window, 27 feet from the ground.

If, then, we cannot claim an advantage for air taken from an elevation, on account of its superior coolness, there can be no doubt as to its advantage on account of its superior purity, since it is not so likely to be contaminated with the emanations from sewers, and numerous offensive waste products on the surface. It is nearly always objectionable to have the source of supply in cellars and other places low down in the building; but as it is often necessary to have the hot water coils or other heating apparatus in this position, it may be difficult to avoid this. But, in many cases, it may be possible to have a channel, if only of canvas, communicating with the outer air.

In the method of what may be called spontaneous ventilation, where an opening is made for the escape of the hot vitiated air, sufficient attention is not bestowed on the form of the ceiling; and where a chimney valve is introduced, it is nearly always too low down. Suppose the room to be turned upside down, and filled with water, the question is, Where ought we to place an opening that would most effectually drain off the contents? Certainly not where the chimney valve is usually placed, for that would leave several inches of stagnant water. If level with the ceiling, most of the water would escape by the chimney valve; but if the ceiling were flat, as it usually is, there would still be shallow

Essays," the above facts are more fully stated, p. 113, in connection with the history of the modern theory of dew.

pools of stagnant water that could only be got rid of by evaporation. When we want to pour water into a bottle in the shortest possible time, a funnel is used; and its shape is admirably adapted to its purpose. So also, when we carry a light on a journey, we use a lantern, which is a perfect example of a well ventilated portable lighthouse. Our ceilings ought to be constructed on similar principles for draining off hot vitiated air. They should not be flat, nor should the foul-air passages be on a lower level; but the ceilings should be dome-shaped, coved, arched, groined, or of the form of a truncated pyramid, as shown in Fig. 96, so as

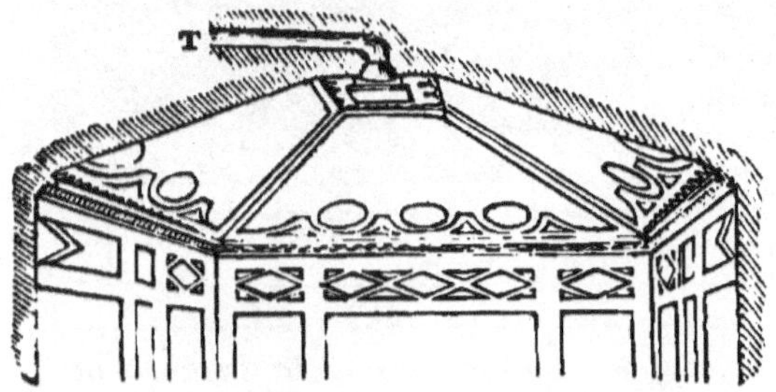

Fig. 96. Best form of ventilating Ceiling.

to rise in the centre; and at the centre, or most elevated point, the ventilating tube, T, should be placed. When curved lines are not used, ceilings of this form ought always to be adopted; they are not much more expensive than flat ones; they have a better effect, and are vastly superior as far as ventilation is concerned, supposing an opening be made in the central or highest point for the escape of the vitiated air.

In some of the old buildings which still excite the admiration of persons of cultivated taste, by the beauty of their arrangements and architectural details, we sometimes meet with special provision for ventilation, arranged on the truest principles. Thus, in the " Hall of Baths " in the Alhambra, at Granada, the roof is perforated with ventilating openings, and is not only of the best possible form for the purpose of ventilation, but the openings themselves are of the best possible shape, being wider at the lower extremity than at the upper; and in order that these openings may present the least possible amount of friction to the outgoing air, they are provided with short tubes of baked earth, covered with a green vitreous glazing. This beautiful roof is shown in Fig. 97, and two of the elegant ventilating tubes are shown separately on a larger scale in Fig. 98.

Fig. 97   Roof of the Bath in the Alhambra.

Tredgold, who has many sound and some unsound views on the subject of ventilation,* saw the necessity of attending to the form of the ceiling, and of placing the ventilating opening in the highest point. He gives some sensible directions for the ventilation of a church, which, of course apply equally to any other public building, and, to a certain extent, to private houses. He advises that the spaces for the admission of cold air be abundantly large, and divided as much as possible ; but he commits the common mistake of placing them in or near the floor (see Fig. 100), so that the air may not have to descend upon any one. By making the openings large, and covering them on the inside with rather close wire-work (sixty-four apertures to the square inch), he imagines that most of the current may be prevented ; and that it may

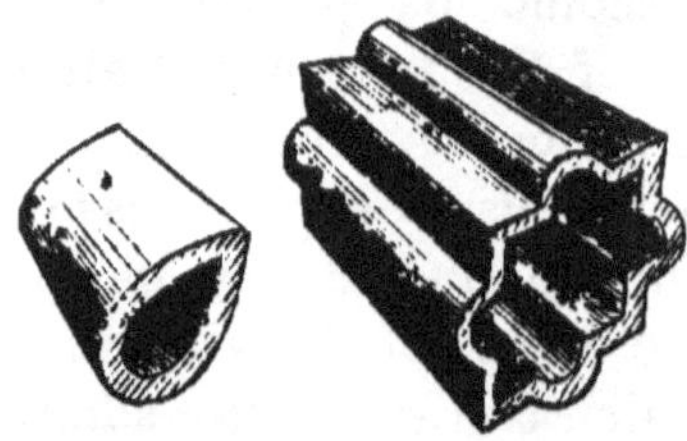

Fig. 98.   Ventilating Tubes.

* "Warming and Ventilating." Second edition. London, 1836.

be still further prevented by bringing tubes under the paving to admit fresh air into the central parts of the church. He says nothing about cold feet, although he advises that these openings be provided with shutters, so as to close them when desirable, forgetting that, with such an arrangement, the shutters would probably never be opened. Provision should be made for the escape of the warm air at different parts of the ceiling through air-trunks furnished with registers. The form of the. mouth of the vent tube is a circular aperture, with a balanced circular register plate, P (Fig. 99), to close it. This plate should be larger than the aperture, in order that the air may be drawn into a horizontal current, for the purpose of taking away the portion of air next the ceiling. If the tube were left without a plate, the air immediately under it would press forward up the tube, and very little of the worst air which collects at the ceiling would escape. As it is not always possible to conduct the vent tube at once in a vertical line from the highest point of the ceiling, there is no objection to giving it a horizontal direction for some distance. In Fig. 99,

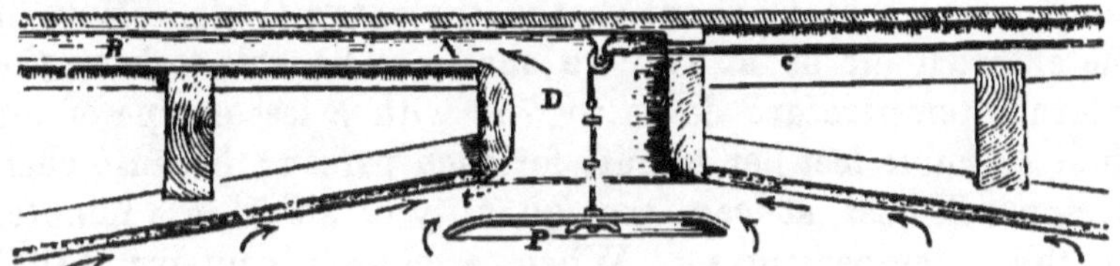

Fig. 99. Form of Ceiling, Register and Vent Tube.

the vent tube, A B, is horizontal, and is conducted between the timbers of a floor. This figure also shows how the timbers may be disposed, so that there may be a rise in the centre without loss of space.* c is a cord passing over a pulley, D, for raising or lowering the register plate, P. This plate is balanced by a weight attached to the lower part

---

* In Tredgold's figure, the timbers on each side of the ventilating opening D, are made to dip, as shown in the dotted line at *t* (Fig. 99). This ought always, if possible, to be avoided, as it prevents the free passage of the air; and even such a slight impediment as this might cause a stratum of air near the ceiling to cool and descend before it had time to escape up the opening.

of the cord, which passes down nearly to the floor of the room, where it is secured by a hook.

Where the vent tubes can be carried up vertically from the ceiling to the top of the building, it is better to do so (as in Fig. 91), because the friction of the hot ascending current is thereby diminished. If the vent be made through the ceiling of a church into the space in the roof, and from this space an air tube be taken up within the steeple or bell-turret, an effectual ventilation may be obtained without adding outlets to the roof. Where external appearance is less regarded, a common louvre-boarded top, for an outlet from the roof, will answer. All side and end windows should be kept closed; for if the apertures at the ceiling be of the proper size, and due provision be made for supplying fresh air, these open windows, as already explained, will diminish, not increase, the amount of ventilation. The reason has been already stated why ventilation is difficult to maintain in warm weather. Of course it becomes especially so in very calm warm weather. Mr. Tredgold gives a case of this kind:—Suppose we wish to provide ventilation sufficient to prevent the internal air from being of a higher temperature than 5° above that of the external air. Now, if the external air be at 70°, we shall not be able to keep the internal temperature down to 75° with a less escape of air than $2\frac{1}{2}$ cubic feet per minute for each person ; because each person will heat, at least, that quantity of air 5° in a minute, at these temperatures. When a church contains 1,000 persons, and the height from the floor to the top of the tube is 49 feet, the sum of the apertures that will allow 2,500 cubic feet of air per minute to escape, when the excess of temperature is 5°, must be equal to 12 square feet. If the height be only 36 feet, the size of the aperture must be 14 square feet nearly. When the ceiling is level, this area should be divided among five or more ventilators, disposed in different parts of the ceiling; but in a vaulted or arched roof, three are recommended to be placed in the highest part of the ceiling, as at D, in Fig. 99.

It is also recommended, that the openings for admitting cold air be about double the area of those at the ceiling.

The air should not be taken from very near the ground, nor from a confined place. In designing and constructing a new building, flues might be made for the special purpose of supplying the interior with fresh air. Each flue might open in the cornice, pass down between the piers, and under the flooring of the church or other building, and terminate in apertures which would be covered with gratings. By disposing some of these flues on each side of the church, they would act with the wind in any direction. These exterior openings should, however, be covered with a grating, to

Fig. 100. A method of Ventilating a Church.

prevent birds from building in them, and thus stopping them up. The accompanying sketch (Fig. 100), from a design by Mr. Garbett, will show at a glance the arrangements required for the proper ventilation of a church; but before the desirable objects of properly warming and ventilating churches and other public buildings are fully attained, it will be necessary for architects to combine a profound knowledge of their art, with a good acquaintance with chemical and physical science.

CHAPTER II.

ON VENTILATION BY MEANS OF MECHANICAL CONTRIVANCES.

VENTILATION may be assisted by *mechanical* contrivances, or by the introduction of *heat,* so as to produce currents in a particular direction, or it may be *spontaneous;* that is, certain self-acting arrangements may enter into the structure of the room or house, and not be liable to derangement from the carelessness or neglect of attendants. Of these three methods, the first requires personal attendance, such as the arranging or winding up of apparatus, thus requiring punctuality and thought, and hence liable to be neglected. The second method also requires the lighting of fires or of gas-burners, thus entailing trouble and expense—sufficient inducements to lead to the neglect of the ventilating force. M. Morin, as already noticed (p. 216, *note*), has given a long account (not meant to be amusing, though it is eminently so), of the failure of two elaborate schemes of ventilation as applied to two of the theatres at Paris, from the parsimony of the managers, the idleness of the attendants, as also the prejudice of the performers. The freshness produced by pure air was mistaken for chilliness, and the *prima donna* actually complained of cold at a time when the thermometer marked a temperature of 70° and upwards. The third method of ventilation must, then, be the best, in the sense that automatic machines are nearly always better than human machines for doing mere drudgery, or that periodical kind of work which does not interest the workman in its performance. If we can make our ventilation so far self-acting as to depend only upon kindling the gas that gives us light, or the fire that gives us warmth, it will be successful, if well arranged.

But first we have to describe some of the mechanical contrivances for ventilation, and these we shall chiefly repeat from the first edition of this work. We may remark, however, that when the ventilating fan is used in factories, and is set going by the same lever that shifts the strap from the loose to the fast pulley of the machinery, it can hardly be called *mechanical* in the sense above intended. It is rather *self-acting*, inasmuch as it is independent of the care of the attendants.

One of the simplest mechanical contrivances for ventilation is the *wind-sail* used on board ship. It consists of a sail spread out to the wind: from the lower part proceeds a cylinder of canvas distended by hoops, which may be carried down through the hatches, to any deck or hold where fresh air is required. Its action depends on the force of the wind, and the mode of arranging it. It is of no use in calm weather, when ventilation is often most needed; and it is equally unavailable in stormy weather, when the hatches are battened down, and the men crowded below. Indeed, unless some contrivance could be made for getting rid of the vitiated air by other openings, the supply of fresh air by the wind-sail must always be partial and defective.

The *hand-fan* has been used from time immemorial, especially in warm climates, where it is often made of an enormous size, and being wielded by an attendant with the dexterity equi red by long practice, its effect is powerful in giving motion to the air, and producing the sensation of coolness, by bringing a larger supply to the person, and abstracting the heat by its motion. The *punkah*, as commonly used in India, is nothing more than a gigantic fan, suspended in the centre of the apartment, above a bed or table. Attached to one side is a line, which passes out of the apartment through the wall to an attendant on the outside, who gives motion to the large extended surface within, and thus prevents the air from stagnating. Some years ago, a steam-engine was sent from England to move the punkahs in the palace of the Nabob of Oude. A machine, called the *zephyr*, has been proposed by Mr. Dobson, for giving motion to the air of a room. Two sails, or punkahs, crossing each other at right angles, were mounted on a frame, and a rotatory motion was given thereto, by suspending it from a case containing a mechanism like that of a bottle-jack. This case was suspended by lines passing over pulleys in the ceiling, and balanced by weights, so that the sails could be made to play at any elevation. In all these contrivances motion is given to the air, but the rooms containing them are not ventilated thereby; the vitiated air is whirled and whisked about, but not driven out, and its place supplied by fresh air.

This objection does not apply to the *fanning-wheel*, or *blower*, now so commonly used for ventilating factories and other places where a steam-engine is constantly at work to supply the required moving power. The fanner was invented by Dr. Desaguliers in 1734. Its object was stated to be for "changing the air of the room of sick people in a little time, either by drawing out the foul air, or forcing in fresh air, or doing both successively, without opening doors or windows." This, it was supposed, would be of very great use in all hospitals and prisons, and would also serve to convey air into a distant room, "nay, to perfume it occasionally." The wheel, as first invented, was 7 feet in diameter, and 1 foot wide, and had twelve radii or partitions (Fig. 101), approaching

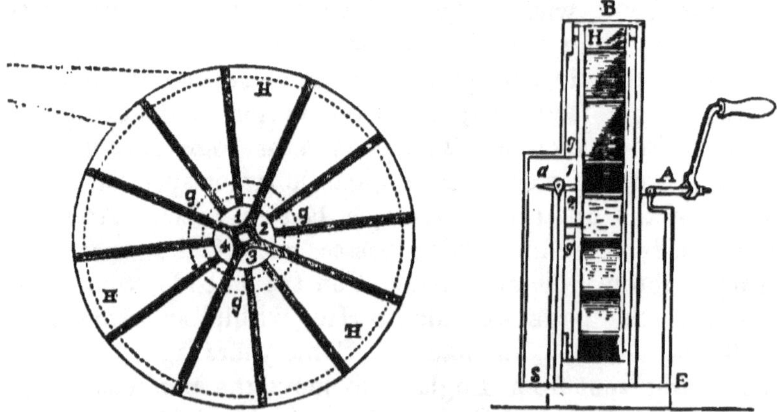

Fig. 101. Desaguliers' Fanning Wheel.   Fig. 102. End View, with Case.

within 9 inches of the axis, leaving a circular opening 18 inches in diameter, marked 1, 2, 3, 4, in Fig. 101. This

wheel was enclosed in a concentric case (Fig. 102), furnished
with a blowing-pipe, B, on the upper part, and a suction pipe,
s, communicating at *a* with the central opening in the wheel,
which was turned by a handle attached to the axis, A, which
passed through the case and rested on a standard, E.   The
fanner was made so as to revolve easily, but as closely to the
concentric casing as possible, without any communication with
the air, except through the suction and blowing-pipes.   To
ensure this, a ring of blanketing was fixed within the case,
g g, and a similar ring at H H, so that the edges of the vanes
being in contact therewith, the air would have no other

escape than by the blowing-pipe,
B, Fig. 103. By the revolution of
the wheel, the air within the case
was rapidly impelled by centrifugal force to the circumference,
where it was condensed, whirled
round, and forced out, in a powerful current, through the opening
of the blowing-pipe, B, while
the partial vacuum thus formed

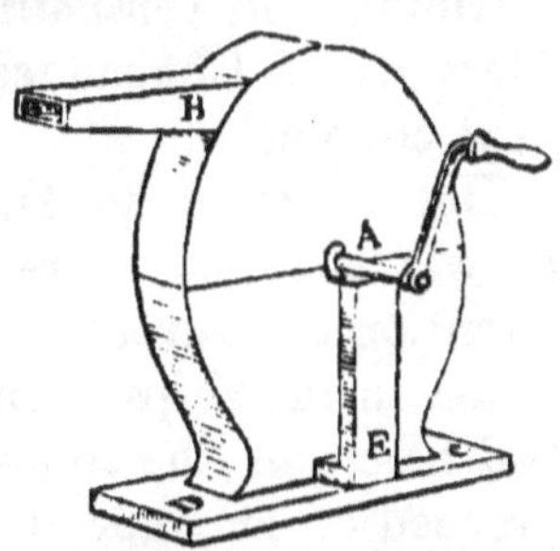

Fig. 103. Fanning Wheel.

set a current of air in motion towards the centre, which
current entering at s, and passing up into *a* (Fig. 102),
was distributed between the vanes, and, driven to the circumference, passed out in a powerful continuous blast at B.
The suction-pipe, s, could be made to communicate with the
external air by means of a pipe, or with a space containing
heated air, and the blowing-pipe could be connected with
a room, which could thus be filled with cool fresh air, or with
warmed air, the quantity being regulated by the speed of
the wheel. If foul air had to be drawn out, the suction-pipe
was connected with the space containing it, and the blowing-
pipe with the external air.

In the year 1736, a wheel of this description was erected
over the ceiling of the House of Commons, for the purpose
of drawing out the vitiated air, in the manner just described,
a man being kept constantly at work during the sitting of
the House, to turn the wheel. It was stated that this wheel
was " able to suck out the foul air, or throw in fresh, or do

both at once, according as the Speaker is pleased to command it, whose order the ventilator waits to receive every day of the session." This apparatus continued to be used for ventilating the House until the year 1791, when the chief clerk of the House, Mr. Holland, proposed its removal from the room over his own private apartments, to the centre of the roof immediately over the House, as being a more advantageous position. This was accordingly done, and continued in operation until 1817, when a similar contrivance was recommended for the ventilation of the House of Lords. It was not, however, erected, for in 1820 the whole business of warming and ventilating both Houses was entrusted to the Marquis of Chabannes, whose plan will be noticed in the next chapter.

But to return to Dr. Desaguliers. About the time when he was engaged in ventilating the House of Commons, the attention of Government was directed to the want of ventilation in the ships of the Royal Navy, in consequence of the bad health of the troops that were embarked at Spithead, to proceed on an expedition against the Spaniards. Numbers were relanded and sent to the hospital, and the ships are said to have "stunk to such a degree that they infected one another." "The Lords of the Admiralty applied to Dr. Desaguliers, to show them the model of his centrifugal wheel and air-pipes; and after the exhibition, some of them went to see the operation of the wheel fixed over the House of Commons. Sir Jacob Ackworth, the Surveyor of the Navy, attended them, and seemed to approve of the machine as much as they did; and the Doctor was ordered to make a blowing-wheel, with its pipes, to be tried on board the *Kinsale* at Woolwich, but less than that at the House of Commons, that it might not take up too much room in the ship." Accordingly, the Doctor attended with a small wheel, but Sir Jacob did not condescend to be present. The machine was said to answer admirably. A quantity of pitch and other substances was burnt in the carpenter's room, and the smoke arising therefrom was drawn above deck by a few turns of the wheel. On reversing the valves, air was forced between decks with great energy. Every one present was delighted with the action of this ventilator, and Sir Jacob, hearing of its success, appointed another day for a repetition of the experiment, but requested the Doctor not to attend himself, but to send his carpenter with the apparatus. The particulars of this trial are amusingly told in a letter from the carpenter, Kembel Whattley, to Dr. Desaguliers. —" When Sir Jacob came on board, he was very complaisant to me, and asked me if I was the person that was appointed by Dr. Desaguliers to attend him in order to try the experiment of the air machine, and I told him I was. Then said he to the men, 'hoist the wind-sails;' and the wind-sails were hoisted. 'Now,' says he to me, 'we have cut two scuttle-holes at each end of the ship, and you shall see what the wind-sails will do. It is our old way when at sea ;' and while they were hoisting the sails, I went down under deck to put the engine in order. But I had not been there long, before I was called for. So when I came up, it was to see that the wind-sails that were put down would blow out a candle at one of the scuttle-holes. 'Now,' said he, 'I would have you work the engine, and see whether that will throw out so much air as our wind-sails you see do.' 'Lord! sir,' said I, 'that, I imagine, was not the intent of the thing; it was to draw out the foul air from any part of the ship that there were tubes to convey it from. It is impossible that a thing which is but 3 inches by 5, should throw in as much air as a thing 2 feet 6 inches diameter.' So we talked awhile, and at last he told me that he could not stay, but that he had thought so before, and that he was sorry that the machine would not do. 'Pray, sir,' said I, 'let there be a great smoke made in the carpenter's store-room, and see whether the engine or your wind-sails will destroy it first.' Then he told me that he could not possibly stay ; 'but that gentleman there,' said he, pointing to a pretty lusty man that was present, 'shall be with you, and he and you may try the machine as you please ; and I shall think the same of it, from his report, as if I were present.' So, sir, it was then left to the gentleman and me to try it; and I burned pitch in the carpenter's store-room, and made a great smoke, and ordered the engine to be worked, and drew it out in less than five minutes' time. Then I turned the valves, and brought in fresh air ; and, as I thought, it gave the gentleman entire satisfaction ; but, however, we made as great a smoke as before, and put down the wind-sails, and then the smoke was driven into several parts of the ship—and that not in half the time that your engine did it ; and then it went out above deck. Sir Jacob told me afterwards that he was sorry that it succeeded no better, but he thought it might be a very pretty thing in a house. Sir Jacob desires his humble service to you."

Dr. Desaguliers complains justly, that " not one of the Lords of the Admiralty, who talked of having many of the ventilators made for the preservation of the health of the persons then going to Jamaica, condescended to witness one experiment ; and Sir Jacob, who condemned the thing, would not once be present to observe its operation. But thus ended my scheme, which, I hoped, would have been of great benefit to the public."

The great objection to this plan for ventilating ships, is the necessity of employing men to turn the wheel. The dangers arising from defective ventilation are not of that obvious character which, in many other cases, lead men at once to seek out and apply the remedy. The aerial poison is invisible, and, although chemists and educated persons, who study its nature, are aware of its insidious action in inducing disease and undermining the health, it is difficult to persuade the multitude, whether of subordinates or of persons in authority, that pure air is as necessary to health and vigour of body, as food, and sleep, and cleanliness. On board a ship every one has his regular routine duties, the use of which are obvious to those who command as well as to those who perform them, and they are accordingly performed with cheerfulness. But to give the common sailor, in addition to his other duties, the task of turning a wheel for the purpose of pumping out air from between decks, is not likely to be of obvious utility, either to him, or to many of his commanding officers. No system of ventilating apparatus is ever likely to be adapted to the conditions of a ship, unless it resembles the excellent system of lightning conductors, invented by Sir W. Snow

Harris; it must be always in its place, ready for use, under all possible circumstances, whether wanted or not. Before Harris's conductors were introduced, every ship was furnished with a set of movable conductors, packed up in a box, to be taken out and applied when wanted. Now, the taking out and erecting of these conductors was an extra duty, a special service, and was seldom or never performed. A thunderstorm comes on, the ship had not been struck in other storms, why should it be struck in this? and, accordingly, the conductors are left to slumber in the hold. So with any form of ventilating apparatus that gives extra trouble to officers or men; the ship's company have never been suffocated for want of air—why should they now? Hence all these new-fangled contrivances are dismissed with scorn.

Very differently circumstanced is the ventilating fan when made a permanent fixture in a factory, and the wheel is connected with the force which sets in motion the various machines of the establishment. The ventilator then fulfils all the conditions required. It is always in its place, gives no trouble, does its duty efficiently, and requires no superintendence. In speaking of the ventilation of factories, Dr. Ure remarks, that the engineers of Manchester do not, like those of the metropolis, trust for a sufficient supply of fresh air into any crowded hall, to currents physically created in the atmosphere by the difference of temperature excited by chimney draughts; but the factory plan is to extract the foul air in measurable volumes, by mechanical means of the simplest and most unfailing kind, especially by eccentric fans, made to revolve with the rapidity of nearly 100 feet per second; and thereby to ensure a constant renewal of the atmosphere in any range of apartments, however large or closely crowded they may be. The effect of one of Fairbairn and Lillie's four-guinea fans upon a large factory is truly admirable. It not only sweetens the interior space immediately, but renders the ingress of bad odours from without impossible. In a weaving mill near Manchester, where the ventilation was bad, the proprietor caused a fan apparatus to be mounted. The consequence soon became apparent in a curious manner. The work-people complained that the ventilator had increased

their appetite, and therefore entitled them to a corresponding increase of wages.

When such a fan, placed at one end of an apartment about
200 feet long, is in full action, it throws the air so powerfully
out of it, as to create a draught at the other end of the room,
capable of keeping a weighted door 6 inches ajar. When
connected in the attics with a horizontal pipe, into which
vertical tunnels from each room are inserted, it draws out
the air so rapidly from them, as to cause a breeze from every
part of the adjoining floors, thus producing an excess of
ventilation in the apartments. The simple and cheap contrivance of perforated cast-iron boxes, placed on every story
in communication with the fan, is the method now in use. A
side and a front view of the fan are given in Figs. 104, 105,
such as have been used of late years for ventilating factories,
for removing through tunnels the dust disengaged in cleaning
fibrous materials, such as cotton, hemp, &c., for blowing air
into forge fires, and many other similar purposes. It consists

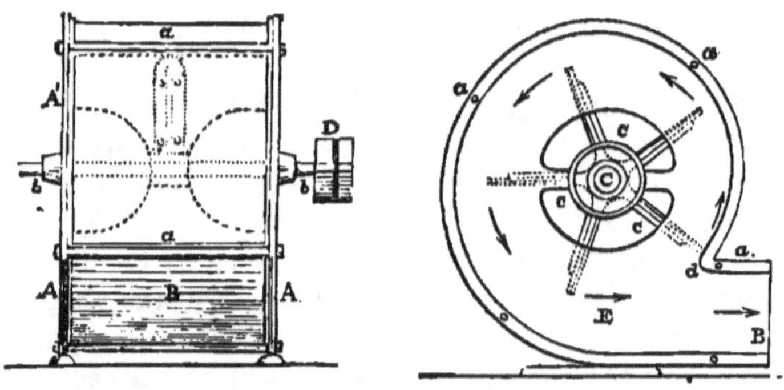

Fig. 104. Side.   Ventilating Fan.   Fig. 105. Front.

of two cast-iron end plates, A A, with a central circular opening, $c\ c\ c$, from the circumference of which the outline of
each plate enlarges spirally, the point nearest the centre
being near d, and that furthest off being under E. This
pair of parallel plates is connected by bolts, $a\ a\ a$, a mantle of
sheet iron being previously inserted into grooves cast in the
edges of the end plates, so as to enclose a cavity with an
elongated outlet at B, to which a pipe is attached for carrying
off the air in any direction. Within this cavity a shaft, c,

revolves in bearings, *b b*, placed centrally in the frame-plates, A A. On this shaft a boss is wedged fast, bearing five flat arms, *c c c*, to which are riveted five flat plates or wires, of the shapes shown between *a* and *a*, in Fig. 104, having a semi-circular piece cut out of them on each side, about the size of the end opening. On one side of the shaft, c, beyond the box-bearing, the fast and loose pulleys, D, are fitted for receiving the driving band, and for turning the wings in the direction shown by the arrow. Thus the air is driven before them out of the end orifice, B, while it enters by the side openings at *c c c*. By the centrifugal force of the revolving wings, the air is condensed towards their extremities, and makes its escape from the pressure through the orifice B, while it is continually drawn in at the sides by its tendency to restore the equilibrium. The fans are sometimes constructed so as to have their mantles concentric with their central shafts, as in Dr. Desaguliers' fan. The improved fan (shown in Fig. 105), is called the *eccentric*. The air which escapes through the outlet B has undergone compression during its whole progress through the spiral space with the revolving wings, and is equal in density to that compressed at their extremities by the centrifugal force. The fan, therefore, discharges considerably more air than that with a chamber concentric with its wings (as in Fig. 101), because in the concentric fan there is considerable loss of power, on account of a large quantity of air being carried round by the leaves of the fan, instead of passing out through the discharge pipe at the circumference; but in the eccentric fan, each wing or leaf, in passing the point *d*, acts as a valve to cut off the entrance of the uncondensed air, which would cause an eddy, and retard the proper current by the inertia of its particles. When the fan is required to draw air out of a series of independent rooms, it has its circular side openings, *c c c*, enclosed within caps, which are connected with pipes communicating with such rooms. Slide or throstle valves may be placed in the exhausting, as well as the condensing pipes, for regulating the distribution of the rarefying or blowing power.*

* "Philosophy of Manufactures." London, 1835.

The fan produces its greatest effect when the extreme points of its leaves move through about 80 feet per second. The mean velocity of that portion of the vanes by which the air is discharged, is about seven-eighths of the velocity of the extremities ; but owing to the inertia of the air, there will be a loss in the velocity of the issuing current which will increase with the increased speed of the vanes ; so that, in general, the current will be discharged with a velocity equal to about three-fourths of the velocity of the extremities. This velocity measured in feet per second, multiplied by the area of the discharge pipe in square feet, will give the number of cubic feet of air discharged per second. If the effective velocity of the vanes be 70 feet per second, and the sectional area of the discharge tube be three square feet, then $70 \times 3 = 210$ cubic feet of air discharged per second, or 12,600 cubic feet per minute. As a cubic foot of air weighs 527 grains, there will be about 13 cubic feet of air to a pound ; therefore $\dfrac{210 \times 60}{13} = 969$ lbs. weight of air set in motion per minute, with a velocity of 70 feet per second. The height from which a heavy body must fall in order to acquire a velocity of 70 feet per second is 76.5 feet, which, multiplied by the number of pounds weight moved per minute, will give the power necessary to discharge this quantity of air at the stated velocity ; and this product divided by 33,000 (the number of pounds weight that one horse will raise one foot high per minute), will give the amount of steam power required. Therefore $\dfrac{76.5 \times 969}{33,000} = 2.24$, or nearly $2\frac{1}{4}$ horses' power will be required to discharge the given quantity of air at the velocity stated.*

The Reform Club-house in London is ventilated by a fan capable of throwing 11,000 cubic feet of air per minute into a subterranean tunnel under the basement story. The condensed steam from the small engine that works the fan, supplies three cast-iron chests with the heat required for warming the building. At the General Post-Office, London, a fan is also used as the ventilating force for a scheme of

* Ure, " Philosophical Transactions." Hood, " Warming and Ventilation."

ventilation contrived by Mr. E. A. Cowper. Air is introduced into the large rooms, kitchens, &c., by means of a main trunk communicating with the open air at the top of the building, while at the bottom of the main is a large fan driven by steam power, which forces air through the main at the rate of about 30 feet per second. The air on entering the main is filtered by means of three screens of wire gauze with different sized apertures placed vertically, with pockets beneath for the reception of solid matter. Some idea may be formed of the amount of solid impurities in the air of London, from the fact that the meshes get choked in the course of a few days, and require to be cleaned with a brush, while in the course of ten days dirt accumulates in the pockets to the depth of an inch. Three degrees of fineness are used for the wire gauze, the coarsest containing 12 meshes to the linear inch, the medium size 16 meshes, and the finest 20 meshes. From the main shaft are branch mains proceeding to each room, and in each room are branches connected with them by a certain fixed size of aperture, or by valves, so as to supply a certain definite quantity of air in a given time to the room. The air is diffused from the branches by means of holes $\frac{3}{4}$ inch in diameter. These perforated branches ramify under all the tables, and are placed wherever they are required. •In the large room, which is 90 feet long by 50 feet wide, and where 200 people are often assembled, the relief afforded by this arrangement was very remarkable. It may, perhaps, be supposed that the air streaming into a building from these perforated trunks may produce the unpleasant effect of a draught from every aperture; but Mr. Cowper finds that when the air enters the main at no greater velocity than $2\frac{1}{2}$ feet per second, no draught is felt. This velocity is reduced to about $1\frac{1}{2}$ foot per second in the branches, and so little is this felt, that the men cannot tell when the fan is at rest or in motion, except in the former case by the deterioration of the air, which does not happen in the latter. Mr. Cowper's three conditions for successful ventilation are—1st, Let the air enter with small velocity; 2ndly, Be sure that it does enter, or in other words, employ a ventilating force such as a fan ; and 3rdly, Give plenty of area, so that enough air may enter at the small velocity mentioned. In a large building the air in the main should be kept under a slight pressure, such as that of $\frac{2}{10}$ths of an inch of water. The foul air is got rid of by suitable openings, and the products of combustion from the gas are removed by placing a funnel over each gas flame ; the funnel has an opening of 5 inches at the mouth, and is connected with a $1\frac{1}{2}$ inch pipe discharging into a chimney, or into the outer air. The distance between the top of the lamp glass and the bottom of the funnel should be about $1\frac{1}{2}$ inch, so as not to point th flame. It is an advantage to keep the pipe hot (but not so hot as to melt the solder), in order that the water produced by the combustion of the gas may be kept in the state of vapour. Galvanised iron answers well as the material for these pipes, which, of course, improve the air of the room by acting as a ventilating force.

The Archimedean screw has been proposed as a substitute for the fan in the ventilation of buildings ; but it appears to be in every respect an inferior machine. The merit has been claimed for it of being entirely self-acting, requiring no power to set it in motion, except the ascensive force of the vitiated air itself, which, acting on the threads or spirals of the screw, causes it to revolve, and so effects the discharge. It is evident, however, that unless driven by power, the Archimedean screw can have no effect, except to retard the ascent of the current of air, just as the small screws, or smoke-jacks, which spin so merrily in kitchen-windows and in bakers' shops, are driven by the air, and do not, of course, assist in the ventilation : they may do some service in dispersing the air so as to prevent it from pouring in in a torrent, but this effect may be produced by means of perforated zinc, wire gauze, &c. In one of the hospitals at Paris, air is propelled by an Archimedean screw worked by a steam-engine, with, it is said, less loss of force than by the fan-blowers, and by an ingenious provision the pitch of the screw is made to adapt itself to the velocity of the engine, an arrangement by which the air current is maintained at a uniform strength.

Pumps and bellows have also had their share of attention as instruments of ventilation. At the time when Dr. Desaguliers was endeavouring to get his ventilating fans introduced into the navy, Dr. Hales came forward with a rival scheme, which he termed the "ship's lungs," and he was applied to by Government to fix his apparatus on board the *Captain*, a seventy gun ship, by way of experiment. A double ventilator of this kind is shown in Fig. 106. It consisted of two outer cases, B D Q C, each 10 feet long, 4¼ feet wide, and 13 inches deep inside. The midriff or valve, z (Fig. 107), was framed of wood, and fixed at one end to each case by iron hinges, and a slip of leather was nailed over the

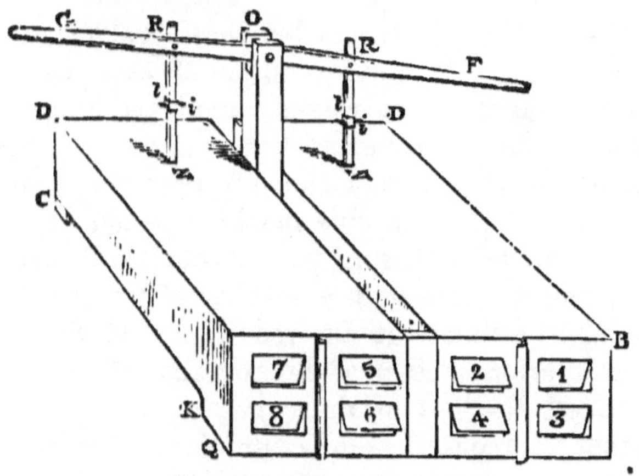

Fig. 106. Hales's Ventilator.

whole length of the joint, to make it air-tight. This valve moved easily up and down, as near the surface of each case as possible. Iron rods, R R, were fixed about 6 inches from the movable end of the midriff at N, and were furnished with joints made like two links in a chain, to allow them to preserve a perpendicular position in the motion caused by the rising and falling of the midriffs. The upper ends of these rods were attached to a lever, G F, 12 feet long, moving on a pivot at o, and capable of being worked by two men. The valves marked 1 to 8, each 22 inches long, 6 inches deep, and suspended by copper hinges, were an inch broader and longer than the openings; and their borders, as well as the corresponding borders of the valve openings, were lined with list or woollen cloth, to deaden their noise when falling. A box with a large aperture covered the emission valves, from which the air was conveyed by a pipe into the part of the ship that was to be ventilated. Thus it will be seen that the construction of this machine closely resembles that of the common bellows. The air enters by those valves which are hinged to open inwards, and is emitted at each rise and fall of the midriff, through the valves which are hung so as to open outwards into the covering-box, whence it is conveyed through a tube to the parts of the ship requiring ventilation.

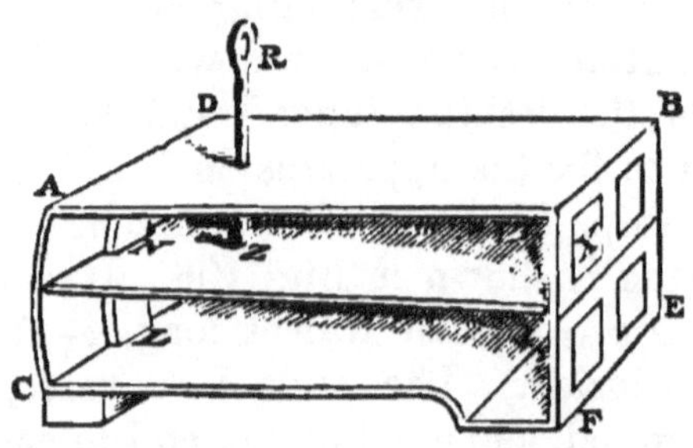

Fig. 107. Ventilator opened, showing the Valve.

Dr. Hales calculated that his machine would expel a tun of air at each stroke, or 6 tuns per minute; and that the air issued from the aperture with a velocity of twenty-five miles an hour. This estimate is far too high, and the machine itself is far inferior to that of his amiable rival, Dr. Desaguliers; indeed, the use of the rotatory fan at the present day, and the total practical oblivion of the "ship's lungs," is a sufficient commentary on the respective merits of the two inventions.

In the experiment in the *Captain*, Sir Jacob Ackworth condescended to be present, and appears to have behaved to Dr. Hales with civility. It is very probable that on this occasion, the objection urged against this machine was, that it was not self-acting, but required too constant attention of the seamen to be of any use, for the Doctor, in his treatise, endeavours to combat such objections in the following terms :—" As to the labour and difficulty of working these ventilators, how frivolous and groundless it is when the matter is rightly considered; for as they are chiefly wanted where there is a great number of men, so the labour of it, equally divided among them, is very inconsiderable; for if two men can hold to work them for a quarter of an hour, four men, by changing hands—*spell* and *spell*, as they term it —may well work for an hour. And suppose there be 500 or 480 men in a ship, and every one takes his share of the work, then, once in five days, it will come to every man's turn to work at it for half an hour. And suppose there be in a transport or *Guinea* slave ship 200 men, as there is often about that number, then it will come to every man's turn to work the ventilators for half an hour once in forty-eight hours ; but here, as the ventilators will be less than the above described ventilators, so will the labour of working them be also less. This, supposing it necessary to do it incessantly night and day, which need not be in a man-of-war when the port-holes can be opened, and there is any degree of wind ; which, suppose it be half the time of the crew's being on ship-board, then it will come to each man's turn but once in ten days. This calculation is made on a supposition that every individual takes his turn at the ventilator ; but let us allow an abatement of one-fifth for officers, sick, &c., then will the work be no more than half an hour to each man in eight days. But suppose it were to be incessant, can half an hour in five days be thought so hard and great a degree of labour as to render the working of the ventilators an impracticable thing ? Is not the benefit proposed thereby, viz., the saving yearly of the lives of thousands, a sufficient reward for so small a pittance of labour ? Shall it be said of the brave and undaunted sailor, that rather than pull his hand out of his bosom, and work for an hour once in ten days, he will choose to lie down and suffer his brave manly spirit to be suffocated in a frowsy stench—a stench that has destroyed the lives of millions of the stoutest and bravest, for the lamp of life is sooner thereby quenched than many are aware of."*

* The title of this book is curious, and it promises more than the machines described in it were calculated to perform. It is as follows :—" A description of Ventilators, whereby great quantities of fresh air may with ease be conveyed into Mines, Gaols, Hospitals, Workhouses, and Ships, in exchange for their noxious air. An account also of their great usefulness in many other respects ; as in preserving all sorts of grain dry and sweet, and free from being destroyed by weevils both in granaries and ships, and in preserving many other sorts of goods ; as also in drying corn, malt, hops, gunpowder, &c., and for many other useful purposes. Which was read before the Royal

All this argument is perfectly sound, and it must be admitted, that each sailor ought to "work for an hour once in ten days," in order to keep the ship well ventilated. It must also be admitted, that under the old system of lightning conductors, the approach of every storm ought to have been a sufficient warning to cause the erection of these safe-guards, in case the ship should be struck. There are many things in life which men ought to do, and much learned and scientific eloquence is repeatedly urged in favour of their doing them ; but as indolence, indifference, and ignorance are not easily moved to exertion, the benefit must, if possible, be conferred without occasioning thought, trouble, or exertion to those who are to share in its advantages.

Such a contrivance was introduced into English vessels of war at the very time when the respective merits of Dr. Desaguliers and Dr. Hales's schemes were being discussed. This was Mr. Sutton's air tubes, which will be noticed in the next chapter. These were perfectly successful; but as the plan was made the subject of a patent, and some objection had been made to the paying for the use of it on board each ship, the scheme seems to have died with the inventor, for we find the complaints of the defective ventilation of ships to be as numerous as ever, and no further improvement appears to have been made until about the year 1785, when wooden pipes about 9 inches square were introduced (for which brass tubes were afterwards substituted), running from between decks along the side of the ship, and opening into the air over the gunwale of the forecastle.* The importance of this contrivance will be seen, when it is considered that in frigates the sleeping-places of the men are excluded from direct communication with the external air; and that a number of men crowded together in hammocks for hours together in a small, dark, confined space, must be highly injurious to health. Attempts had been made to remedy

Society in May, 1741. By Stephen Hales, D.D., F.R.S., Rector of Farringdon, Hampshire, and Minister of Teddington, Middlesex. London, 1743."

* This contrivance was first pointed out by Dr. Gilbert Blane, in his work "On the Diseases Incident to Seamen" (London, 1785), and the idea was suggested to him from a similar contrivance in *La Nymphe*, a French frigate.

this by small scuttles cut in the sides; but this was frequently objected to as weakening or endangering the ship.

Among mechanical contrivances may be mentioned Dr. Arnott's *Ventilating Gasometer*, worked by water power. A cylinder or gasometer is made to move up and down in a circular trough of water, contained with itself in a case, furnished with valves, through which air is alternately admitted and discharged during each ascent and descent of the gasometer, in a manner similar to that of the blowing-machine of an iron blast-furnace. The cylinder is suspended from one end of the beam, and a balance weight at the other end. Connected with the beam is a small piston, working in a barrel, beneath which water is admitted by a pipe, connected with a tank of water 60 feet above. The pressure of this column, acting under the piston, sets the beam in motion, and raises the ventilating cylinder to its highest position. A cock or valve, acted on by a rod from the beam, then shuts off the column of water, and at the same time opens a way for the escape of the water in the small barrel. The ventilating cylinder, which is heavier than its counterpoise, being thus free to move, descends by its own weight; the water-cock is then opened by a touch from the rod, and the piston again rises, and produces another oscillation of the beam. The cylinder contains about 125 cubic feet of air, and as this moves up and down eight times per minute, it will supply a building with 2,000 feet of fresh air in that time. In cold weather the air may be warmed by the self-regulating stove with water-leaves.*

* Dr. Arnott's stove, described p. 144, &c., has been furnished by its inventor with a *water-jacket*, forming what is called a *water-stove*. This jacket forms an external case or lining to the stove, and is filled with water, which is heated by the fire within; thus not only is the surface of the stove a source of heat, but it may distribute its heat to other tubes or vessels filled with water, and the heating surface may be indefinitely increased by connecting the pipes with very thin flat boxes of sheet copper filled with water, and set up side by side about half an inch apart, in any convenient place, like so many thin portfolios or books of maps. If the pipes are properly arranged, there will be a circulation of water between these *water-leaves*, as they are called, and the water-clad stove.

CHAPTER III.

ON THE VENTILATION OF BUILDINGS, SHIPS, MINES, &c., BY
MEANS OF ARTIFICIAL HEAT.

AMONG the special contrivances for producing ventilation, combustion occupies a prominent part. By applying heat to the air in the upper part of the ventilating tube, the air of the place requiring ventilation is drawn upwards with increased rapidity, and fresh air rushes in with a proportional increase of rapidity to supply its place. This method of producing artificial ventilation seems to have been first described by Rodolphus Agricola, in the sixteenth century. In his book, *De re Metallica*, he speaks of the method of drawing the foul air out of a mine, by suspending a large fire in the middle of the shaft—a method which has been practised in mines ever since his time. This method does not appear to have been adopted in the ventilation of crowded rooms, until the year 1723, when Dr. Desaguliers was requested to endeavour to improve the arrangements made some years before by Sir Christopher Wren, for the ventilation of the House of Commons. Wren's plan was as follows :—A large square hole was made in the ceiling at each corner of the House, and over each hole, in the above room, was erected a hollow, truncated pyramid, 6 or 8 feet high, constructed so as to be closed at pleasure. The vitiated air of the House escaped by these holes when the temperature was sufficient for the purpose ; but it often happened that the colder and denser air of the upper room not only stopped the ascending current, but poured down in cataracts upon the members below. This defective arrangement was remedied by Dr. Desaguliers in an ingenious manner. He constructed a closet at each end of the upper room between the pyramids, and conducted a trunk from the pyramids to the square iron cavities that surrounded a fire-grate in each closet. When, therefore, the fires were lighted in these grates, air ascended from the

House, through the heated cavities, into the closets, and was
thence discharged up the chimneys. This arrangement is
represented in Fig. 108, in which *c c* are the pyramids at one
extremity of the room, opening from the ceilings of the

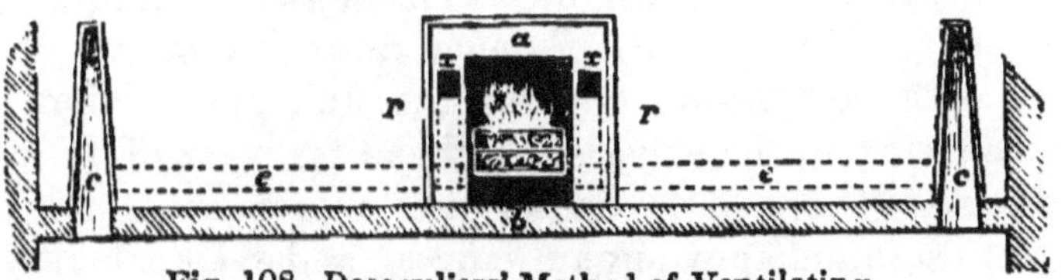

Fig. 108. Desaguliers' Method of Ventilating.

House; *e e*, two pipes leading from them to the fire-grate,
a b. The heat of the fire, rarefying the air in the iron
cavities, *x x*, a current would be produced in *e e*, and the
air from the pyramids would flow out at *x x* into the closets,
and thence into the chimney.

The principle of this arrangement is perfectly sound, and
there is no doubt that it would have answered the purpose
required, if it had had fair play. The cause of its failure
is curious.   Mrs. Smith, the housekeeper of the House of
Commons, feeling herself aggrieved at being disturbed in
the possession of " her rooms," discovered an easy method of
persuading the honourable members that the philosopher's
plan had failed. She carried her point, " by not having the
fires lighted until the House had sat some time, and was very
hot; for then the air in the closets that had not been heated
went down into the House, to an air rarer and less resisting,
whereby the House became hotter instead of being cooled.
But when the fire had been lighted before the meeting of
the members, the air went up from the House into the closets
and out of their chimneys, and continued to do so the whole
day, keeping the House very cool." The failure of this plan
led to the introduction of the rotatory fan already noticed
(p. 237).*

* " Sir George Beaumont and some other members observing that the
design of cooling the House was frustrated, asked me, in 1736," says the
Doctor, " if I could not find out some contrivance to draw the hot and foul
air out of the House by means of some person that should entirely depend
upon me, which I promised to do, and effected—calling the wheel a *centrifugal* or *blowing wheel,* and the man that turned it a *ventilator.*" As the

About the time of the controversy between Dr. Desaguliers and Dr. Hales, respecting the merits of their machines for ventilating ships, as described in the last chapter, a new rival appeared, with a contrivance which far exceeded either of theirs, in point of practical utility, from the circumstance of its being self-acting. Mr. Samuel Sutton, a brewer, being moved with compassion towards the unhappy soldiers who were suffering in the ships at Spithead for want of fresh air, felt himself "obliged to do all that was possible for their relief in these unhappy circumstances," and even submitted to all sorts of slights and humiliations rather than forego his laudable desire to benefit mankind in general, and the navy in particular, by the introduction of his apparatus. Without at all desiring to call in question the humane motive of Mr. Sutton, it must still be confessed, that in the introduction of his apparatus, he had a keen eye to his own interest. Not that this is objectionable in any inventor, for there can be no

name of Desaguliers has been mentioned several times in these pages, a slight notice of him may be interesting. He was born at Rochelle in March, 1683. His father was a French Protestant refugee, who sought refuge in England after the revocation of the Edict of Nantes. He was sent to Christ Church, Oxford, and in 1702, when only nineteen, gave lectures on experimental philosophy at Hart Hall. He married in 1712, settled in London, and had the merit of first introducing to the public lectures on natural philosophy. The novelty of the method, the earnestness of the teacher, and the beauty of the 'experiments, attracted fashionable and even royal audiences. In 1714 Desaguliers was elected a Fellow of the Royal Society, and between that date and the year 1743 he contributed to its *Transactions*. He also published volumes of lectures, &c., on natural philosophy, and translations of S'Gravesande's "Perspective" and Nieuwentyt's "Religious Philosopher," &c. The spirited engravings representing feats of mechanical strength in Brewster's work on Natural Magic are from some admirable etchings in Desaguliers' lectures. The Duke of Chandos made Desaguliers his chaplain, and presented him with the living of Edgware. He also became chaplain to the Prince of Wales. But, in spite of this apparent prosperity, there is a tradition, based on some lines by the poet Cawthorn, that he died in great poverty.

> "Here poor, neglected Desaguliers fell!
> How he who taught two gracious kings to view
> All Boyle ennobled, and all Bacon knew,
> Died in a cell, without a friend to save,
> Without a guinea, and without a grave!"

Desaguliers certainly did remove to lodgings over the Piazza in Covent Garden, where he continued to give lectures, and it is very possible that he shared the fate of inventors, and became involved in debt. At any rate, his sons did not inherit his poverty; for we find that one of them was a colonel in the Royal Artillery, and a great favourite of George III. He died in 1775.

doubt that a benefit conferred by a man upon his country, is deserving of reward ; but the mixed motive is objectionable— urging the invention forward on the plea of humanity, and, at the same time, asking for a large pecuniary reward. When Dr. Franklin and Count Rumford advocated the general introduction of their inventions, on the ground of humanity, the motive was pure and honourable, for they took out no patent and hinted at no reward, seeking only to be useful to their fellow-creatures.

Mr. Sutton's invention is, however, meritorious, and in his curious and amusing narrative,* we read a minute account of its origin and progress. It originated in the following circumstance. In a room which had three fire-places, the windows and doors were made to fit as tightly as possible, so as to exclude the external air. Having made a large fire in two of the fire-places, it was found, naturally enough, that the wind came down the chimney of the third fire-place with such force as to blow out a candle. This suggested the idea of ventilating the different parts of a ship; for as a fire is always kept burning on board, it was supposed that a pipe or cavity opening from any part of the ship to the fire, would draw the air along it to feed the fire, thus occasioning a fresh supply to the part of the ship whence the air was subtracted. This idea being once conceived, Sutton sought every oppor- tunity of consulting naval men on the subject of the ventila- tion of a ship. On one occasion, he says, " being at a coffee- house near the Admiralty, I placed myself nigh some gentle- men of the navy, and inquired of them, as I had before of others, as to the usefulness of the forementioned change of air, who all, to a man, acknowledged that it would be of the utmost service, and upon their unanimous approbation of it, I told them that I could procure such a change of air ; upon which one of the company went to another table, and the rest followed him ; and I heard him tell the others that he

* "An Historical Account of a New Method for extracting the Foul Air out of Ships, &c." By Samuel Sutton. London, 1745. A second edition was published in 1749, containing two favourable accounts of the invention, read before the Royal Society by Dr. Mead and Mr. Watson, and a Discourse on the Scurvy, by Dr. Mead, who thought that that fatal disease would be greatly mitigated by the introduction of Sutton's apparatus on board ships.

heartily pitied me as being really mad, and out of my senses."
Sutton had solicited an interview with the Lords of the
Admiralty, which was granted, and he received a letter of
introduction to Sir Jacob Ackworth. On presenting it, a
meeting was appointed five days afterwards at seven in the
morning. The brewer was punctual, but the knight kept
him waiting the whole day, and it was not till the evening
that he condescended to exchange a few words with him :—
"Sir, I suppose you intend to throw air into the wells of
ships?" "No; I propose to draw it out by means of fire."
"Do you know how far you are to draw it out?" "Not 6
inches; for if I can extract it never so small a distance, the
incumbent air will press forward, of course, and cause a constant change." Sutton then expressed a hope that a time
might be appointed for a trial of his scheme, but the knight
replied that no experiment should be made, if he could hinder
it. This unmannerly treatment did not daunt the brewer.
He petitioned the Lords of the Admiralty, and obtained an
order to make an experiment in a ship of war at Woolwich.
Whereupon he proceeded to erect his apparatus, and had
completed it, except the soldering of two pipes, when a
messenger from the builder of His Majesty's yard appeared,
and ordered the workmen ashore. In spite of all remon-
strances, the work was suspended, and next day the apparatus
was taken down, and the holes were plugged up. Under
these discouraging circumstances, Sutton introduced himself
to Dr. Mead, the king's physician, who at once encouraged
the scheme, and succeeded in getting Martin Folkes, the
President of the Royal Society, to favour it. Under this
powerful patronage, the Admiralty were induced to order a
trial to be made of the apparatus on board any of His Majesty's
ships in the river. Accordingly, Sutton fixed upon the hulk
at Deptford, but he had great difficulty in getting his orders
executed: the workmen of the King's Yard "were busily
employed in trying the usefulness of another machine, in-
dustriously set on foot to supplant mine." "The excessive
shyness and caution of the gentlemen of the yard led me to
conclude that my scheme at last would be set aside, in spite
of all the steps I could take to prevent it; and I was con-

firmed in this opinion when I found the pipes were made of wood between 5 and 6 inches wide, in such an unworkman-like manner, that to render them tight, I was forced to get size and paper from Deptford to put over the joints ; and that, moreover, many hands were employed in erecting wind-sails, in order to show that they could thereby procure as much air as my scheme would afford." But, at length, in September, 1741, the trial was made before some of the Lords of the Admiralty, the Commissioners of the Navy, Dr. Mead, Martin Folkes, Esq., and several other members of the Royal Society. Sir Jacob Ackworth welcomed this distinguished company, by remarking, " I am sorry that you are come to see the trial of such a foolish experiment, that I tried myself yesterday, and it would not shake a candle." Sutton ventured to reply that the apparatus would be in good humour that day, and that the end of every one of the pipes would blow out a candle. The experiment was accordingly made, and although Sutton complains that the tarpaulins which he had placed over the hatches had been removed, the success was complete, and his friends were satisfied.* The result of this trial was, that in November following, Sutton was sent by the Lords of the Admiralty to Portsmouth to fit up his apparatus in the *Norwich* man-of-war. Sir Charles Wager gave him a letter to the Commissioner at Portsmouth, in which he sensibly remarks, " this contrivance is approved by much wiser men than I am in such things, and, therefore, I desire you would let Mr. Sutton have all the encouragement and assistance you can give him." He also requests that Sutton may " meet with no obstruction or discouragement from anybody that may think themselves wiser." After this, as may be supposed, Sutton had nothing to complain of in the Portsmouth dockyard.

Sutton now thought it high time to ask for a " suitable reward for his useful invention, and reasonable satisfaction for his trouble, loss of time to the neglect of his other affairs,

* Mr. Watson reported to the Royal Society that Sutton's machine brought up air " from the bread-room, orlop, and well of the ship at the same time, in such quantity, that large lighted candles being put to the end of the tubes, the flame was immediately sucked out as fast as applied, though the end of one of the tubes was above 20 yards distant from the fire."

and expenses in the execution of the same." He plied the Admiralty with petitions, but received no answer until the 11th June, 1743, when he was furnished with an extract from a letter from the captain of the *Norwich*, containing his report as to the working of the apparatus on a voyage to the Coast of Guinea, the West Indies, and back. The captain's report is as follows :—"As to the air-pipes which were put on board of me, I was obliged to stop up two of them, by reason the fire came down between decks—the other, to the well, was kept open ; but the ship making water enough to keep her sweet, I was not able to judge of their use, having been so healthy as to bury only two men all the time I was on the coast." The healthy state of the crew during such a voyage was, at the period to which we now refer, something so extraordinary, that the captain's report, which was intended to condemn the scheme, is really a high eulogium on it, seeing that one of the pipes was allowed to remain open during the whole voyage.

At length the Admiralty made their report, in which they stated that the apparatus " does not, in all respects, come up to the expectation, and that the use thereof is dangerous and liable to accidents by fire; yet as the said Mr. Sutton has employed a great deal of pains and time about the said invention for the benefit of the navy, and had encouragement from their Lordships to do so, and their Lordships, being desirous to give encouragement to persons who shall turn their thoughts to any inventions that may tend to the advantage of the navy," directed him to be rewarded with the sum of *one hundred* pounds ! Of course Mr. Sutton was very much disappointed, and very angry. He attributes his failure to the undue preference given to Dr. Hales's ventilators.

Mr. Sutton received the hundred pounds " on account," and did not cease to urge the merits of his invention upon the Admiralty, until he got an order to have his apparatus fitted to several ships. He then looked out eagerly for the reports of their respective commanders, and was fortunate in getting a favourable return from Admiral Boscawen, dated Table Bay, 9th April, 1748, in which he says, " I cannot help thinking the air-pipes fixed in the men-of-war have been of great service, by purifying the air between decks, and thereby preventing the scurvy." After this, the career of Sutton was crowned with success, which he modestly attributes to "the wisdom and zeal of the present Right Honourable the Lords of the Admiralty, and the Right Honourable and Honourable the principal officers and Commissioners of His Majesty's Navy, who, having taken the whole affair into their serious consideration, were so thoroughly satisfied of the great advantage that must accrue to the nation from the faithful execution of my scheme, that they have contracted with me for fixing my engine on board His Majesty's ships, whether laid up or in commission." As Sutton makes no further complaint, we must suppose he was satisfied with the pecuniary part of the arrangement. As to his zeal for the good of his country, which he talks so much about, he took care that no one but himself should derive pecuniary benefit from the plan, by securing his invention by a patent.* This, however, at length proved more fatal to the scheme than the powerful opposition of Sir Jacob Ackworth, and the cool indifference of the Lords of the Admiralty. Sutton charged £30 for each ship of the Royal Navy, or of the East India Company, into which the apparatus was proposed to be introduced; and as this was thought too much for a benefit which many persons in authority were disposed to question, the scheme was abandoned in a year or two, and, after the death of Sutton, all trace of its existence seems to have been eradicated from the minds of ship-builders and seamen, and Sir Jacob was left in undisturbed possession of his favourite wind-sails.

Mr. Watson's paper, which was read before the Royal Society, contains a very good account of Sutton's invention. He describes the copper used for boiling the ship's provisions, and the method of fixing it, with two openings below, divided by an iron grate. The first opening, having an iron

---

* The application of the machine, as stated in the patent, is for removing noxious air from "mines and caverns in the earth, dungeons, prisons, and all infected places." It may also be used in "hot-houses and walls, which will greatly warm the earth for the speedy production of its fruits, and also in granaries, for the preservation of corn and grain."

door, is for the fire, the other for the ashes. In ordinary cases, the combustion of the fire is supported by air drawn through the ash-pit; but, on board ship, as both the fire hole and the ash-pit hole are furnished with doors to prevent the escape of fire, the air must be supplied by some other means. Accordingly, one or more holes, *r s*, Fig. 109,* are made through the brickwork in the side of the ash-pit, *u*, and tubes of lead or copper are fitted closely therein, and

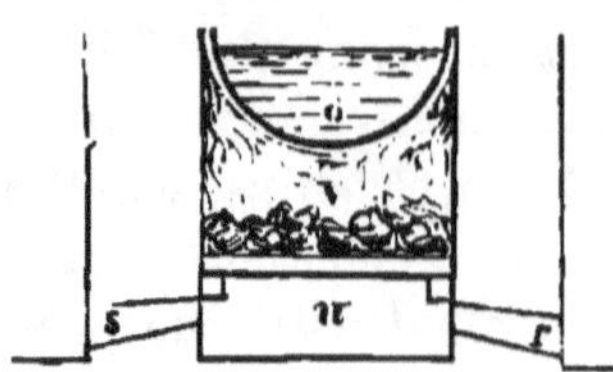

Fig. 109. Ash-pit and Tubes.

conducted from thence into the well, and other parts of the ship; thus drawing off therefrom the foul air, and, sending it through the fire, v, it escapes up the chimney. At the same time, a supply of fresh air rushes in at openings about the ship, to occupy the place of the bad air. This circulation of air not only goes on while the fire is burning, but so long as the fire-place, copper, or brickwork remain warm, as was observed on board the hulk at Deptford, when the draught of air through the tube lasted about twelve hours after the fire was taken away. "This being considered, as the dressing the provisions for a number of people will take up some hours every day, the warmth of the brickwork and flues will continue a draught of air from one day to the next, Mr. Sutton proposes thus to circulate the air by the same and no greater expense of fire, than is customarily used for the necessities of the ship." The larger the ship, the greater the number of men on board, and the larger the quantity of provisions, so that more time and fuel will be required in preparing them, and the more perfect will be the ventilation. The size and number of the tubes is of little consequence, for the larger the tubes, and the greater their number, the less the velocity of the air, and *vice versâ*. Mr. Watson notices, as an essential condition of the perfect action of the tubes, that both the fire door and the ash-pit door be kept closed. In large ships

---

* In the plan, Fig. 110, B is the ash-pit, B B the copper pipes opening into it, C the oven, D a vent-hole, and K K the pipes, continued to any part of the ship.

there is not only a copper but also a fire-grate, L (Fig. 110),
like that used in kitchens. Behind this grate, copper tubes,
F F, were also fixed and carried through the brickwork, so
that one extremity thereof projected about a foot into the
chimney, G, and the other
end opened into the hold,
or any other part of the
ship; so that the air rushed
along this tube into the
draught of hot air in the
chimney. To obviate the
objection to the space occupied by these tubes on board
ship, it is advised that only
one tube, of a convenient
size, be attached to the side
of the ash-pit, and, as soon
as it passes through the main
deck, to give it the form
which occupies least room ;
and from this main tube,
branches might ramify to
different parts of the ship,
these branches being carried
between the beams which
support the deck, till they
meet the sides of the ship,
where they could be con-
ducted also between the
beams into the places in-
tended.

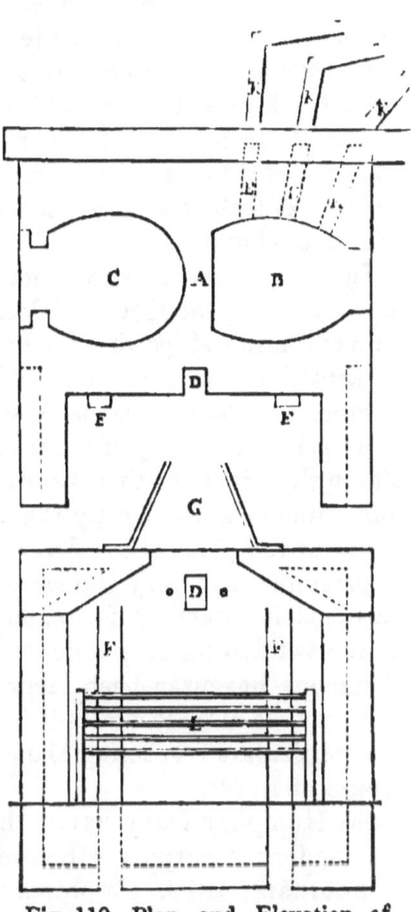
Fig. 110. Plan and Elevation of
Sutton's Method.

How admirably adapted
is this plan to the ventila-
lation of steamers. A large central trunk might be made
to feed the furnace, and into this trunk smaller branches from
every cabin and sleeping berth might discharge their foul
air, and thus maintain every part of the vessel in a state of
perfect salubrity. That Sutton's plan has not been entirely
forgotten, is evident from its having been applied in order to

get rid of the offensive effluvia arising from the coppers of soap-boilers, tallow-melters, and others, which often become a nuisance to a whole neighbourhood. The copper is set in the usual manner, and the furnace and ash-pit furnished with doors, so as to admit of being perfectly closed ; the lid of the boiler is made to fit very tight, and a pipe rising from it is carried into a channel which opens into the ash-pit; the fœtid matters rising from the boiler are in this way made to pass through the fire into the smoke-flue. This plan is said to have answered perfectly, so that a factory, which was formerly most offensive, became entirely free from offensive odours.

In the two schemes thus detailed, that of Dr. Desaguliers, for ventilating the House of Commons, and that of Mr. Sutton, for ventilating ships, &c., we have the principle of ventilating by artificial heat carried out with perfect success. A large number of plans have been subsequently contrived on the same principle, many of them made subjects of patents ; and, although it is more than probable that the respective inventors not only did not copy them from, but had never heard of either of the plans above described, yet, as they are identical in principle, and very similar in detail, it is not necessary to particularise them. A few examples, however, may be noticed of the ventilating of public buildings, and as the House of Commons has often been made the subject of experiment in this way, as already noticed, it may be interesting to state a few particulars respecting the warming and ventilation of the House of Lords.

Sir Humphry Davy having been requested to devise some scheme for the purpose, submitted to the Lords Commissioners, in February, 1810, his proposals ; and in September, 1811, in a letter to the Earl of Liverpool, he thus briefly recapitulates the heads of his plan :—" To convey fresh air into the House, I propose flues of single brick connected with the flues for sending hot air through the vaults under the floor, and I propose that this fresh air should be admitted by numerous apertures in the floor of the House, and supplied to the flues by pipes of copper or plate iron from the free atmosphere. The air in this case will be always fresh, and, by regulating

the fire, may be more or less heated, according as the temperature of the room is low or high.

" To carry off the foul air, I propose two chimneys, or tubes
made of copper, placed above the ventilators, and connected
with wrought iron tubes, which can be heated by a small fire,
if a great draught is necessary, as in cases when the House
is full.

" Should this plan be adopted, there would be no necessity
for opening windows; the foul air would be carried off from
above; warm air, or cold air, whichever is necessary, may be
supplied from below, and there would not be, as now, any
stagnation of air."

The plan accompanying this letter, of which the above is
an extract, is shown in Fig. 111. v is one of the ventilating
apertures in the ceiling of the
House, covered with a chimney
of copper, c; this is continued
by an iron tube, i, which passes
through a small furnace, F. c'
is another copper tube connected with the iron one. The
upper end of this tube was only
1 foot in diameter; it opened
into a cowl on the roof. The
furnace, F, was contained in a
fire-proof house, erected for
the purpose on the roof.

This plan does not seem to
have been very successful; for
Mr. Adam Lee, in his Report
to the Lords' Committee in
June, 1813, states, that on very
crowded nights it was impossible, by means of the present
ventilators, to draw off the

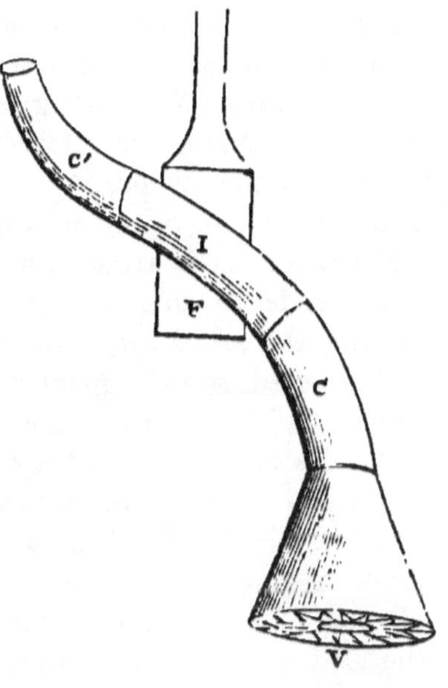

Fig. 111. Sir H. Davy's Method of
Ventilating.

heated air; the temperature in the House frequently rose to
80°, and would have been higher if the windows had not been
open.   Instead of the ventilation pipe, 1 foot in diameter, it
was proposed to erect enlarged pipes of 3 feet diameter, fur-

nished with registers to close them, to prevent cold air from blowing into the House when the ventilation was not wanted. These pipes were to be conveyed in an oblique direction to the fire-proof house, and to be capped at the top with a cowl-head. The fire to the ventilator was considered unnecessary, and even objectionable, on account of smoke getting into the House down the ventilator. " I have, at various times, taken an opportunity," says Mr. Lee, " of going on the top of the House, and have put my head over the ventilation pipe when the fire was at full heat, and have not perceived the hot air coming from the House. I have likewise tried, at other times, without fire, and have found a very strong current of hot air from the body of the House."*

Mr. Lee's plan for ventilation was tried and failed. There is no doubt, that after abolishing the furnace, and introducing wide tubes, a down current was as likely to be admitted into the House, as an ascending current out of it; and the contriver, who thought himself a wiser man than Sir Humphry Davy, has afforded a sufficient satire on his own improvements by proposing to place rotatory wheels in his wide tubes, in order to make them discharge the air the right way. It is satisfactory to learn that their lordships did not accede to this proposal. They consulted Mr. James Wyatt, the architect, who made some changes in the House, and erected some apparatus. This perished in the fire, in 1834, which led to the destruction of both Houses.

In the following year, a Select Committee of the Commons examined a number of witnesses, consisting chiefly of scientific and practical men, with a view to discover the best, or, at least, a good method of warming and ventilating the new Houses of Parliament about to be erected. In their report, the Committee advised that some plan should be systemati-cally adopted before the commencement of the new buildings, from a conviction that whatever plan should afterwards be selected, " provision should be made for its adoption, in the first instance, by the architect, so as not only to ensure its

---

* In this Report it was also stated that the flues were arranged horizontally round the chamber of the House, 100 feet in length and upwards, and that the smoke remained in them for a considerable time, sometimes producing a strong smell of sulphur in the House itself.

success, but to prevent needless expense and inconvenience ;" and that, for this purpose, "the whole space immediately below the two Houses, as well as that between the ceiling and the roof, be prepared and altogether reserved for such arrangements as may be necessary for the object in view." The plans proposed by Dr. Reid were favourably noticed, and it was recommended that some, if not all, of his alterations should be submitted to the test of actual experiment, " as the only means of ascertaining with accuracy the soundness of the principles laid down in the evidence, and their useful application to the future Houses of Parliament."

The temporary building for the House of Commons having been found very defective, in respect both of warmth and ventilation, this building was placed at the disposal of Dr. Reid. It had been warmed by the ordinary warm water system ; the large flat tablets through which the water circulated were placed in a room under the House, and occupied a surface of about 9 feet square ; they were 4 feet high.

Dr. Reid's arrangements were as follows :—Two or three feet beneath the floor of the House, a second floor was formed, containing about twenty apertures, each about 18 inches square. Beneath the second or lower floor was a long passage, A, Figs. 112, 113 ; opening into this were two others of an equal width, B and C ; in the passage, B, was placed the warm water pedestal. Large folding-doors were placed before the entrances, and within these passages ; the temperature of the house above depended on the relative adjustment with each other of these folding-doors. Fresh air, either warm or cold, according to the season, could be produced, and exchanged from warm to cold, or the contrary, as the variable external temperature of the day or hour required. This will be understood by referring to the section (Fig. 112) and the plan (Fig. 113). The fresh air entered from Old Palace Yard, through the perforated wall, D. If the folding-doors 1 and 2 were opened, and all the rest closed, the air would enter the passage A, passing through the pedestals placed in B, and warm air only would be supplied to the House above. If air moderately warmed were required, the doors 3 and 4 were opened in addition to 1 and 2, and two currents, one cold and the other

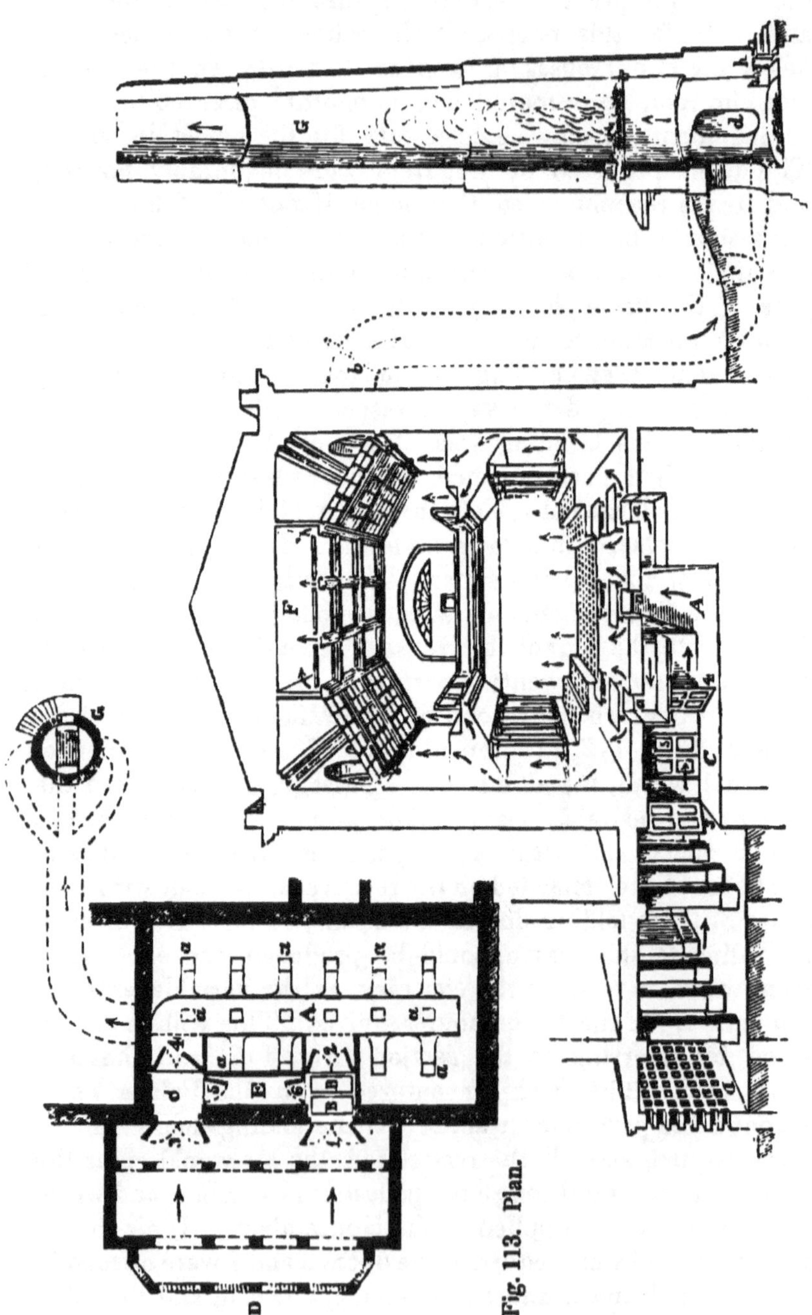

Fig. 112. Section of temporary House of Commons, showing the Ventilating Apparatus.

Fig. 113. Plan.

warm, were then produced, which met and blended together in the passage A, and then ascended. If air of the external temperature only were required, the doors 3 and 4 were alone opened. If required to be only moderately warmed, 3 and 4 were opened, 1 half-opened, 2 closed ; the small folding-doors, 5 and 6, were then opened, and a slight current of warm air passed through the small passage, E, and mixed with the cold current entering at C. The folding-doors in this passage could likewise be opened when 3 and 4 were closed, and a current of warm air would then be conveyed to one end of the passage A.

The air, whether warm or cool, ascended through the apertures $a\ a\ a$, into the space beneath the real floor of the House. Immediately over these openings were large platforms, supported by short feet, the effect of which was to disperse the great body of air admitted. The air then entered through openings made in the actual floor of the House, these openings being exceedingly small, very close together, and about 300,000 in number. They were about one-sixth of an inch in diameter on the surface of the floor, but expanded downwards, to prevent their being stopped with dirt or dust. The sides of the House under the galleries were battened or brought forward 5 or 6 inches, and in the space thus formed between the framing and the wall, the air ascended and passed out through the floors of the members' galleries, perforated for the purpose in the same manner. The floor of the House and galleries was covered with a thick horse-hair matting, with large meshes, to allow the air to ascend through them.

The force which set this great body of air in motion was the ventilating shaft, G, in which a powerful upward current was generated by means of a large fire, as will presently be explained.

In summer, when the air transmitted into the House was required to be cool, various contrivances could be resorted to in the chamber immediately behind the perforated wall, D. The air might be made to pass into the chamber, A, over wet surfaces, and be cooled by evaporation, or ice might be suspended in netting between the piers in the chamber.

A new ceiling was also constructed a few feet below the

former one, for the purpose of favouring the transmission of sound. This ceiling was divided into three portions, the central portion being horizontal from one end to the other ; the other two compartments inclined so as to make an angle of 30° with the floor of the House. These two inclined portions were glazed, but the centre was panelled, so as to assist in the ventilation of the House. An inclination was also given to the ceiling beneath the members' galleries, corresponding exactly with the inclination of the lateral compartments in the newly constructed ceiling above.

The ventilation of the House was accomplished in the following manner :—Each panel of the centre compartment of the ceiling was raised by blocks several inches above their styles, thus admitting the air of the House into the space, F, between the two ceilings. The rapid removal of this vitiated air, and the consequent rushing in of fresh air from below, was effected by the large shaft, G, erected in Cotton Garden, at a distance of about 20 feet from the eastern wall of the building. About 10 feet from the surface of the ground was a very large coke or coal fire, which produced a powerful current up the shaft. Now the space, F, between the two ceilings of the House, opened at the north end into a large square shaft, which was continued downwards, and opened underground into the circular shaft, G. The consequence of this arrangement was, that when the current of hot ascending air was produced in the circular shaft, there was a downward draught through the square shaft, thereby rapidly withdrawing the air from within the House, and causing the fresh air to rush into it from openings in Old Palace Yard. A damper at b, in the square shaft, regulated the draught in the shaft, G ; and consequently, as it was more or less opened, the supply of air to the House could be regulated according to the number of members present.

The height of the ventilating turret above the ground was 110 feet : it was 12 feet in diameter at the base, and about 8 feet at the summit.

The system thus described was in operation for some years, and might, we think, be pronounced one of the most extensive, and, upon the whole, most successful experiments in the warming and ventilation of a building that has been

made in this country. The arrangements showed considerable skill, and displayed a good knowledge of the subject.
That they were not completely successful need not excite
surprise when it is considered that the plans of some of
the most eminent scientific men have been partial failures.
That Dr. Reid should have failed in doing what he proposed
to do in the case of every building which he took in hand is
no wonder, when it is considered that each building presents
its own peculiar set of difficulties, and that the facilities are
either very few or absent altogether; for, as Dr. Birkbeck
remarked, in his evidence before the Committee, " Heating
and ventilation, especially the latter, seldom enter into the
mind of the builder when he projects his building; he begins
as if he did not know that ventilation could be necessary ; he
trusts to the doors and to the windows, to neither of which
belongs the business of ventilation. The doors admit the
occupants to the chambers; the windows the light ; and
apertures ought to be introduced to admit air for ventilation
as regularly as the other openings." Or, as Dr. Faraday
remarked in another place, " the builder makes the doors
and the windows to fit as tightly as possible, and then the
poor chemist is called in to provide fresh air." Under such
circumstances, the poor chemist can only do his best. The
laws of nature will not accommodate themselves to him ; he
can only apply them as far as they admit of application in a
building where everything seems to have been arranged for
the express purpose of defeating their operation. And even
when the best arrangements are made which the circumstances
will admit of, their efficient working requires the constant
superintendence of a man of intelligence, instead of an ordinary stoker or porter; for if the room, or court, or hall, or
church, or whatever it may be, be very crowded, the ventilation must be promoted as much as possible, and the warming
restrained. If, on the contrary, the building contain only a
few persons, and the external temperature be low, the warming
must be increased, and the ventilation diminished. To meet
all the circumstances of the case, for summer and for winter,
for night and for day, without any assistance from the architect who designed the building, and your arrangements

constantly exposed to defeat by careless attendants leaving doors open, or by people constantly coming in or going out —to do all this to the satisfaction of every one, is a task which few scientific men would undertake. It was the fashion to cry down Dr. Reid, and to call him by all sorts of ugly names : this is very easy, as is every kind of criticism which consists in mere abuse and fault finding ; but, although we are no partisans of Dr. Reid, we venture to state our opinion, that in the case of the temporary House of Commons, where all the arrangements were left in his own hands, he succeeded in the proposed object of removing the vitiated air, and keeping up a constant supply of warm or cool air to fill its place. The following extract from a parliamentary document contains, in few words, both the praise and the censure of this system, and with this we take leave of the subject :—

" A strong current of prepared air is now admitted, immediately under the entire surface of the floor, which is pierced with many thousand holes : after passing through these apertures, the air is again distributed into many millions of other holes, by means of a hair-cloth carpet, through which it is drawn up towards the ceiling, where admirable arrangements have been made by Dr. Reid for discharging it through apertures in the edges of the panels ; and thus the foul air is carried rapidly along a tunnel to feed the great furnace which creates this current of ventilation. It is obvious that the air so drawn up through the hair-cloth carpet must be charged with particles of ground dust or mud from the members' feet ; and that (so impregnated) it must be inhaled by those within its reach. I heard many members complain that it rests upon their faces, and enters their eyes and nostrils and mouths ; and, from woeful experience, some members know that it can find its way to their lungs."*

When Dr. Reid's system came to be revised, and Mr. Goldsworthy Gurney was appointed to superintend the arrangements for warming and ventilating the Palace of Westminster, some of the details introduced by Dr. Reid in the temporary House of Commons were retained. The fresh air is taken from the courts of the palace, filtered through

* Sir F. Trench to Viscount Duncannon. Par. Pap. No. 204, Sess. 1838.

screens, and, during winter, warmed by being passed over iron boxes or batteries filled with steam. During summer these batteries are covered with wet cloths, and a number of spray jets, formed by causing jets of water to play against small discs of metal, which spread the water into filmy sheets, cool down the entering air by evaporation, and charge it with the requisite amount of moisture. These batteries and spray jets are arranged in mixing chambers, situated immediately under the floors of either House, and the air thus prepared streams into the House through the perforated floor, formed of iron grating, the floor of the raised benches being also perforated. The perforations are covered with a porous horse-hair cloth or matting, which prevents the upward currents from being felt. The force which sets these currents in motion is an enormous coke fire, maintained in one case in one of the buttresses of the Victoria Tower, which is made hollow for the purpose, and in the other case in a chimney-shaft of considerable dimensions. These fires are connected, by means of closed passages, with the ceilings of the two Houses, through the raised panels of which the vitiated air escapes on its way to maintain the combustion of the coke fires, after the manner shown in Fig. 112, p. 266. In the lower part of the palace is a series of steam boilers, both for high and for low pressure steam, from which proceeds an immense assemblage of pipes to every part of this vast structure, which serve either as sources of heat or ventilating forces. The condensed water of these pipes is returned to the boilers.

During the unusually warm weather of the summer of the year 1858, the Thames was in a constant state of putrefactive fermentation, in consequence of the use to which it was so unwisely applied, namely, that of a common sewer to a city which covers upwards of 150 square miles. The Palace of Westminster, situated on the banks of this pestiferous stream, notwithstanding its elaborate arrangements for ventilation, had its supplies of air more than usually contaminated. Mr. Gurney found that the air entering the House of Peers and the House of Commons through the proper ventilating channels could be purified from the river effluvia by means of the spray jets, while the air entering by open windows in the libraries and committee rooms looking towards the river could be purified by causing it to filter through canvas, moistened with a weak solution of chloride of zinc and chloride of lime, fixed to all the windows. In the month of June, however, the river became so unusually offensive that Mr. Gurney was compelled to report that he could no longer be answerable for the health of the two Houses. Accordingly various other plans were proposed for purifying the air, among which was one by Mr. Charles Cowper, based on Dr. Stenhouse's experiments on the disinfecting powers of charcoal. It had been known from the time of Saussure that freshly burnt box-wood charcoal exerted a remarkable absorptive power on gases, taking up 90 times its own bulk of ammoniacal gas, 85 of hydrochloric acid gas, 65 of sulphurous acid, 55 of sulphuretted hydrogen, 35 of carbonic acid, 9·4 of carbonic oxide, 9·2 of oxygen, 7·2 of nitrogen, and only 1·7 of hydrogen, an order almost identical with that of the solubility of the same gases in water. The remarkable action of finely divided charcoal on putrescible matter had also been known : animal matter in a high putrefactive state ceases to be offensive when covered with a layer of charcoal : it continues to decay, but it emits no fœtid odour ; the carbon which it evolves is dissipated as carbonic acid, while the hydrogen remains in the form of water, and the nitrogen as nitric acid. The action of the charcoal has been shown by Dr. Stenhouse to consist in a rapid process of oxidation, dependent on its power of condensing oxygen. So efficient and rapid is the action of the charcoal that Dr. Stenhouse proposed to employ a respirator filled with charcoal as a covering to the mouth and nostrils in an infected atmosphere, and to use trays or screens filled with powdered wood charcoal in dissecting rooms, in the wards of hospitals, in water-closets, and in places where putrescent animal matter is present. In all such cases the disinfecting powers of charcoal have been very apparent. Mr. Cowper proposed to have the air for supplying the Houses of Parliament drawn through a large chamber or room filled with sticks of charcoal free from dust, and, as a further precaution, to draw the air out of the base of the Clock Tower, keeping all windows and doors shut, so that all the air must enter at the belfry, about 200 feet or more above the ground.*

In theatres and similar places, where a large central chandelier is used for the purposes of illumination, advantage may be taken thereof as a powerful ventilating agent. This was done many years ago by the Marquis of Chabannes, who was engaged to warm and ventilate Covent Garden Theatre ; and his arrangements will be understood by referring to Fig. 114, in which *a* is the chandelier; *d*, a pipe of wrought iron for the purpose of carrying off the heat and the products of combustion ; *e*, a wooden case, into which air flows at *o* and *s* from the ceiling ; *m m*, pipes which conduct the vitiated air from other parts of the house. In one of the galleries was placed a furnace, the combustion of which was supported by the vitiated air from several tiers of boxes. A similar furnace was placed over the stage, and the gas chandelier ventilated the centre. The vitiated air from all parts of the house was discharged above the roof, through three trunks, each terminating in a cowl, *u*. The air admitted into the theatre to replace that which was carried off by this powerful ventilating apparatus† was warmed by means of a furnace, called a *calorifère*, placed at every entrance and staircase which communicated with the external air. The

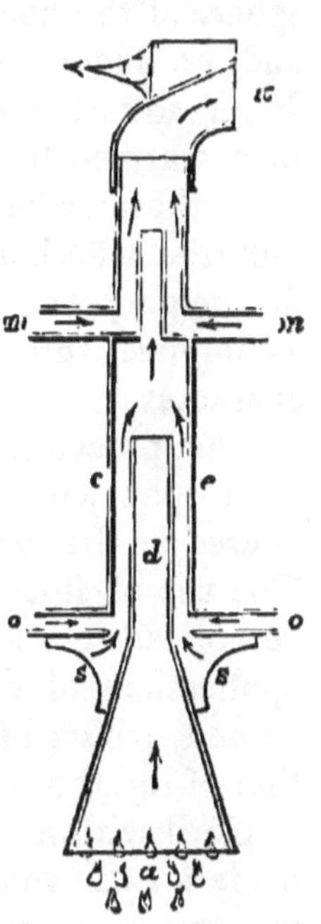

Fig. 114. Chabannes' Method.

* During the summer of 1859, the Thames being also in an offensive condition, it was placed under the medical care of Professor Miller, of King's College, London. The offensive condition of the river increased with the temperature, which in July frequently reached 74° or 75, when the mud left exposed to the action of the sun putrefied and produced a sickening stench, and also acted as a ferment on the putrescible, but not previously putrid matter in the body of the river. The remedy applied was to pour into the sewers large quantities of lime, chloride of lime, and carbolic acid, the deodorising effects of which were very apparent during the hot weather, and were probably the means of preventing much sickness in the metropolis.

† The *sun-lights* which are now so common in public buildings act as very energetic ventilators. They are placed high up in an excellent situation, and must be very efficient, provided suitable means are arranged in the roof for discharging the foul air.

stage, and the parts behind the curtain, were warmed by steam cylinders placed below the stage. Calorifers were also placed at every other point whence a draught of cold air was likely to issue. The effect of all these arrangements was, upon the whole, satisfactory; and it is certain that this theatre was better warmed and ventilated than any other in London. Complaints, of course, were made. The atmosphere of the house was said to have a dry and stifling effect; and, no doubt, in cold weather, the air must have been dry; for, if admitted at and below the freezing temperature, and then warmed to 65° before it was inhaled, it would feel dry. But those who complained most loudly probably never inquired whether pure dry air at 65° is not far better fitted for the purposes of respiration than the vitiated air of crowded assemblies, the moisture of which is of the most offensive character.

The preceding details will sufficiently illustrate the principle upon which ventilation is conducted when fire or flame is used as the force to.give motion to the ventilating current. The use of hot water, steam, &c., as ventilating agents, will be noticed in another chapter. There are one or two special applications of ventilation, in which flame and fire are concerned, which belong to this chapter; these are the ventilation of lighthouses and of mines.

Until within the last seven or eight years, no provision was made for the ventilation of lighthouses, a neglect or oversight the more extraordinary when it is considered that the efficiency of a lighthouse depends on the brilliancy of the light exhibited, and this, in its turn, depends on the perfection of the combustion. If no means be taken to carry off the products of combustion, they must accumulate within the lantern, and greatly interfere with the usefulness of the light, as well as injure the health of the attendants.

Let us consider for a moment what a lighthouse is, and what are the nature and amount of the products of combustion generated within it. A lighthouse may be defined as a small room raised to the top of a tower sufficiently strong to resist the action of the waves and wind, as in the Eddystone, and the wind in all cases; to bear all the beating and pelting of the storm, and yet to be only walled with glass. Within this transparent room or lantern, a brilliant light or many brilliant lights must be kept constantly burning during sixteen hours on a winter's night, and during eight hours in summer. According to one arrangement, a large and very powerful lamp is fixed in the centre of the lantern, and this burns or consumes from 12 to 14 pints of oil in one hour. According to another arrangement, twenty or thirty small Argand lamps, each with a polished reflector behind it, are mounted on a revolving frame, and these consume from 15 to 20 pints of oil in one hour.

Now, as oil in every 100 parts contains 78 parts of carbon, 11·5 parts of hydrogen, and 10·5 of oxygen, it will be seen that the products of combustion must chiefly consist of water and carbonic acid. Now there is enough hydrogen in 1 lb. of oil to produce rather more than 1 lb. of water; because 1 part of hydrogen combines with 8 parts of the oxygen of the air to produce 9 parts of water.

The 78 parts of carbon in 1 lb. of oil will, in like manner, produce $2\frac{86}{100}$ lbs. of carbonic acid; that is, the carbon will deprive the air of nearly 3 lbs. weight of its oxygen, thus spoiling $13\frac{1}{4}$ lbs., or $172\frac{1}{2}$ cubic feet of air, by depriving it of its oxygen.

Such being the products of combustion of 1 lb. of oil, it is easy to ascertain the products of the combustion of $19\frac{6}{10}$ pints of oil, the quantity consumed per hour in the Tynemouth lighthouse. The most obvious inconvenience arises from the water, of which not less than 20 fluid pints are produced per hour; for that is the given quantity, if the vapour, as it is given off, were condensed. Now the lantern itself, in cold weather, affords a powerful means of condensation, especially when a cold frosty wind is blowing upon it. In such case, the vapour is not only condensed into water, but the water is frozen, and the plate-glass of the lantern is often covered with a crust of ice, varying from a quarter to half an inch in thickness. If this ice were perfectly pure and transparent, it would dim and distort the light; but the vapour of water from the oil carries with it minute particles of carbon or soot, which condense with the water, and become entangled with the ice, thereby producing a further opacity. The carbonic acid is chiefly injurious to the attendants. The men at the Eddystone lighthouse told me, some years ago, that during the long nights of winter, they had great difficulty of breathing in the lantern, and that the "foul air" descended into the sleeping apartment below, and produced great inconvenience. They also complained of the enormous amount of labour which they had every morning in cleaning the glass panes of the lantern, and the difficulty of getting rid of the ice. It was sometimes even dangerous to scrape it off, from the risk of fracturing the glass.

The attention of the Trinity Board had long been directed to the removal of these evils, and about the year 1842 they requested Dr. Faraday to turn his attention to the subject. He did so, and after visiting various lighthouses, and making himself master of all the facts of the case, he devised a remedy as simple and complete as could be desired. The results of his investigation were given by him to the members of the Royal Institution, in a lecture, on Friday evening, the 7th of April, 1843, which I had the privilege of attending.

In those lighthouses containing a single lamp in the centre of the lantern, the remedy consisted in lengthening the chimney of the lamp, or rather in placing over the glass chimney a tube of sheet iron, and carrying it through the roof of the lantern into the open air, the upper extremity of this tube being defended from the weather by a cover of some kind. In the other arrangement a central chimney was also constructed, and over the glass chimney of each lamp was placed one extremity of a small tube, and this tube was curved in such a way, that the other extremity opened into the central chimney. These tubes, one for each of the twenty or thirty lamps, were supported by the frame which carried the lamps and their reflectors, and as the frame revolved, the ends of the tubes described each a small circle within the central chimney without touching it. In this way the small tubes carried off all the products of combustion, without interfering with the reflectors. The result in both cases was perfect: the central chimney over the large lamp carried off all the products of combustion; and the short tubes over the lamps in the revolving lights also discharged the products of combustion into the central chimney, and this conveyed them to the outer air. The consequence was, that the interior of the lantern was always dry and healthy, and the windows remained perfectly bright. This system, as Dr. Faraday well remarked, may be called an adaptation of *sewerage* to the atmosphere. Aërial sewers are employed to carry off the refuse of the spoiled air, instead of allowing it to accumulate in the house or apartment.

The success which attended this simple and beautiful application of ventilating chimneys, suggested to Dr. Faraday its introduction into dwelling-houses, for the purpose of completely and effectually discharging into the external air the products of the combustion of gas-lamps. He was, moreover, incited to this in consequence of an application from the Managing Board of the Athenæum Club, who found that in the library of that institution, the bindings of many of the books, especially of those on the upper shelves, were very much corroded, an effect which was attributed to the products of combustion arising from the gas-lamps with which the library was lighted. Now 1 lb. of ordinary London gas produces, during combustion, as much as $2\frac{3}{4}$ lbs. of water, rather more than $2\frac{1}{2}$ lbs. of carbonic acid, and takes from the atmosphere $2\frac{1}{4}$ lbs. of oxygen; thus spoiling $19\frac{1}{3}$ lbs. of air, or 251 cubic feet. But in addition to these products, sulphurous acid is also sometimes produced, owing to the presence of certain sulphurous compounds, which are not wholly removed in the process of purification. This sulphurous acid, in contact with the air, becomes converted into sulphuric acid, which attacks walls, furniture, books, &c. Dr. Faraday collected some of the watery products of combustion from the gas-burners at the Athenæum, and found it to contain sulphuric acid; the ventilating tubes placed over the flame were corroded by the acid water in the places where it condensed, and formed a solid sulphate within the tube, of iron or of copper, according to the metal used. But Dr. Faraday did not attribute the corrosion of the books entirely to this source, but partly also to the heat, and partly to certain substances used by the leather dresser.

It is common to see in shop windows large glass bells suspended over the glass chimneys of gas-burners. These are, of course, of no use in carrying off the products of combustion, but merely serve to prevent the flame from blackening the ceiling. But if a pipe from the top of each lamp be led out into the open air, or into the chimney of the room, not only are the products of combustion carried away, but the gas-burners themselves often become powerful and efficient ventilators to the whole apartment, instead of being, as before, a powerful source of vitiation. The inconvenience to be guarded against is the condensation of water in the pipe, for at a short distance from the gas-flame, the watery product of combustion becoming cooled, condenses into water before it reaches the extremity of the ventilating tube; and if the tube ascends all the way from the burner, the water will even flow back and extinguish the flame, or otherwise annoy the persons in the room.

But as the appearance of these ascending ventilating tubes in a room is rather unsightly, Dr. Faraday got rid of them altogether by making the hot air from each burner descend instead of ascending. This he accomplished by furnishing each burner with two concentric glass chimneys of unequal height, the lower one being the interior. The exterior or higher of the two chimneys is covered with a plate of mica, so as to prevent the draught from ascending higher than the top of this chimney. The descending current is established by applying heat to the bend of a ventilating tube, fixed at the bottom of the two chimneys, and turning upwards among the ornaments of the chandelier. When this current is fully established, the gas is lighted, and the mica plate placed over the outer chimney. Each Argand burner is supplied with air in the ordinary way through the centre, and the products of combustion are carried from the top of the inner chimney, down through the space between that and the exterior chimney, then along the descending ventilating tubes up into a central vertical shaft, which serves also to suspend the chandelier and to enclose the gas-pipes; the products of combustion are then received into a box above, and from this proceeds a pipe into the open air. A globe of ground glass, open only at the bottom, is placed over each lamp, and has an elegant though unusual appearance. It is said that the two glass chimneys produce more perfect combustion, and, consequently, a greater amount of light, than with an ordinary Argand burner with only one chimney. The flame is certainly larger, and of a redder colour than the ordinary gas flame.

Many years ago Tredgold recommended a siphon for withdrawing the foul air from the interior of apartments. "If an inverted siphon," he says, "be placed with one leg in the chimney, so near to the fire that the air in that leg will be warmer than the air in the other leg, motion will take place; for the air will ascend in the warm leg and go up the chimney, and a descending current in the cool leg will take the air from the room. To render the application of this principle successful, the mouth of the tube should be at the ceiling of the apartment; the lowest part of the curve should be, as much as convenient, below the point where the heat is applied; and the aperture through which the air flows into the chimney should be formed so that the soot may not fall down the tube; also, the mouth should have a register to close it, or regulate the ventilation."

The ventilation of a coal-mine is regulated on the principle of descending and ascending draughts. The reader is aware that those enormous deposits of coal which form so large and important a portion of the mineral wealth of Great Britain, are called *coal-fields*, in which the coal, situated at various depths from the surface, is separated into a number of distinct layers or strata, of various thicknesses, by means of layers or strata of slaty clay, called *shale*, and coarse hard sandstone, called *grit*, forming altogether what are called the *coal-measures*; or in other words, beds of sandstone, shale, clay, and coal, lie one above another, in repeated alternations, to a great depth. The strata of coal, however, technically called *seams*, are very thin, compared with the other associated beds. Though extending under large tracts of country, they are often only a few inches thick, and never more than 6 or 8 feet, except one seam in Staffordshire, which is 30 feet. But the interposed strata of grit and shale often exceed

700 feet in aggregate thickness.   Under this series is the mountain limestone, forming various calcareous strata of variable thickness, sometimes exceeding 900 feet. This limestone rests on a bed of old red sandstone, varying in thickness from 200 to 2,000 feet.   The term *coal-formation* sometimes includes these two great series of strata, although, in general, the coal-measures lie above them, the lowest coal-seam commonly resting immediately on the mountain limestone.

The various deposits which form the coal-measures do not occur in regular horizontal unbroken planes.   When first deposited, they were doubtless in this condition, but at various times, this horizontal position has been disturbed by some upheaving force from below, whereby the coal-measures have, in many districts, been made to assume the shape of a huge trough or basin, rising on all sides from a central point, the sides of the basin being composed of sandstone or limestone, and the middle filled up by strata superior to the coal-measures, such as magnesian limestone and new red sandstone.   Now it follows from this arrangement that the edge or boundary line of each stratum must appear at the surface somewhat like the concentric layers of an onion cut in two.   This " coming to the day," or appearance of the coal at the surface of the ground, is called the *basset* or *outcrop*, and serves to determine the outer form or side of the basin. But the internal upheaving force (whatever it may have been) which converted the horizontal strata into basin-shaped arrangements, seems, at the same time, to have produced certain fissures or fractures, often nearly vertical, and stretching through the whole mass.   These rents are called *dykes*, because they divide the seams or bands of coal into *fields*, and some of them are so considerable as to find a place in geological maps.

In order to ascertain where the deposit of coal is most advantageous for working, boring is resorted to, and when the spot is determined, a cylindrical or elliptical shaft, from 10 to 15 feet in diameter, is sunk. The depth may vary from 25 fathoms (150 feet) to 300 fathoms (1,800 feet) before the seam intended to be worked is reached.   When this is done, the sinking of the shaft is discontinued, and a broad straight passage, called a *bord* or *mother-gate*, is driven from it into the seam of coal in opposite directions. This bord is 12 or 14 feet broad, and of the whole height of the seam, so as to expose the rock above, which is now called the *roof*, and also the stratum below, which forms the *thill* or floor. It is also necessary to drive a passage, called the *drip-head*, *dip-head*, or *main level*, for collecting the water of the mine. From this level gallery, numerous other galleries are driven towards the rise of the strata, till they reach either the outcrop of the seam, or the dip-head gallery of an adjoining colliery. The direction of the bords is arranged so as to follow the natural cleavage of the coal, which forms their sides, and, consequently, is not always at right angles with the dip-head. When a bord has been excavated some distance, narrow passages, called *headways*, are driven from it at regular intervals on both sides, and exactly at right angles, if the natural cleavage of the coal be cubical, as it generally is; and when these have been driven eight or ten yards, they are made to communicate with other bords, which are opened parallel to the first, and on each side of it. In this way, the bed of coal is entirely laid open, and intersected by broad parallel passages about 8 yards apart, communicating with each other by narrower passages or headways, which cross them at right angles, and also traverse the whole extent of the mine, breaking up the seam into immense square or rectangular pillars, which are left standing between the two. In this state, a coal-mine has been aptly compared to a regularly built town, the bords being the principal streets, the headways the narrower streets which cross them, while the pillars of coal form the masses or blocks of buildings.

As these pillars of coal form frequently as much as three-fourths, and never less than one-third of the whole seam, many methods have been contrived for removing them without danger. The best method of working is that called *panel-work*, by which the mine is divided into districts or panels, separated from each other by walls of coal 40 or 50 yards thick. The coal is extracted from each in succession, beginning usually with the one most distant from the shaft. Large pillars of coal are first left between the bords to support the roof; the pillars themselves are then removed, the roof being supported in the meantime by wooden props, and the place where these props replace a pillar is called a *jud*. In time, the jud is removed, and then the unsupported roof of the mine falls in. The heap of ruins thus occasioned by the successive drawing of continuous juds, is called a *goaf*. Corresponding with this heap of rocky fragments, and produced by it, is a cavity in the mine like an inverted basin, including a thin belt of air, which surrounds and partly permeates the goaf. This has been the source of dangerous accidents, as will be noticed hereafter.

Fig. 115 is the plan of one story of such a mine, in which the panels, *a a a a*, are not entirely laid open by galleries;

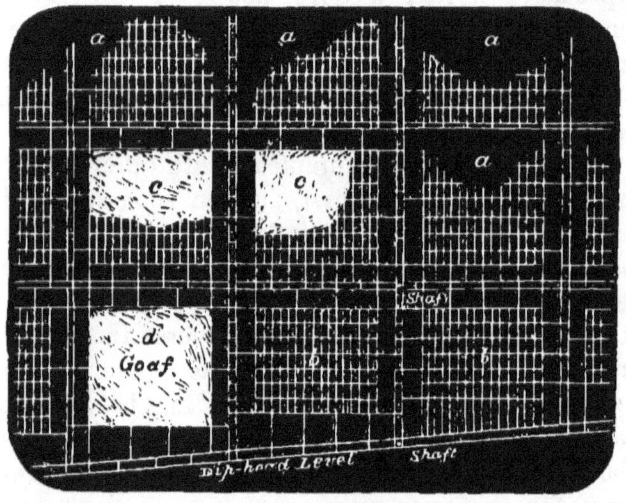

Fig. 115. Panel-work.

b b are laid open, but no pillars as yet removed; in *c c*, the pillars are being extracted, and the roof is falling in, its ruins forming a *goaf;* the panel, *d*, is entirely worked out and abandoned.

When the prospects of the mine appear to be favourable, another shaft is, in some cases, sunk at some distance from the first, and when a communication has been established between them, one is made the *downcast,* and the other *upcast;* that is, the air is conducted from the downcast shaft through all the bords and workings, which it is made to traverse in succession by means of *stoppings* or doors in various places, to obstruct its passage and give a proper direction to the current in passing to the upcast shaft. The force which sets this ventilating current in motion, is a large fire kept constantly burning in some part of the upcast shaft. The supplies of fresh air passing into a mine must, of course, vary considerably. In the Wallsend Colliery, they vary from 2,000 to 3,000, and occasionally 3,800 cubic feet per minute. In some of the large workings, the air has to traverse many miles of gallery before it reaches the upcast shaft, and is frequently twelve hours in doing so, moving at the ordinary rate of 2 or $2\frac{1}{2}$ feet per second. Many coal-mines are worked without this second shaft, its place being supplied by dividing the single shaft into two distinct portions, by means of an air-tight partition called a *brattice*, one division being downcast, and the other upcast. The larger shafts (those 15 feet in diameter) are sometimes divided into three parts, one of which is used for raising the coal to the surface, another for working the pumps for the drainage of the mine, and a third for ventilation, for bringing up the air that has passed through the workings.

The necessity for perfect ventilation in a coal-mine is more urgent than in other mines, on account of the escape from the coal of large quantities of carburetted hydrogen gas (called *fire-damp* by the miners), which, mingling with the air of the mine in certain proportions, forms a mixture which explodes on contact with flame. This gas is very much lighter than common air, mingles readily with it, and when poured out into the workings, moves along with the ventilating current in the direction of the upcast shaft. The quantity of gas thus poured out is very considerable, but subject to great variation, some seams being more *fiery*, or full of gas, than others; and, in working these fiery seams, it is not uncommon for a jet of inflammable gas to issue from every hole made for the gunpowder used in blasting. But, in addition to this constant supply, there is danger of sudden discharges from cavities in the coal, laid open by the hewer's pick-axe. The gas issues from these cavities with considerable noise, and forms what is termed a *blower*. These blowers are sometimes so constant in their action, that the gas is collected and conveyed by a tube into the upcast shaft, continuing for months or years to pour out hundreds or thousands of hogsheads of fire-damp per minute. When thus provided for, the blowers are not necessarily a source of danger; but when one of the reservoirs containing the pent-up gas of centuries, and consequently under an enormous pressure, is suddenly broken open, the gas is set free in torrents, and mingling with the air of the mine, forms an explosive mixture which the first spark or naked flame may ignite, and thus cause a fearful destruction both of life and property. Nor is the explosion itself always the thing to be dreaded most; for the ignition of the fire-damp kindles the coal-dust, which always exists in great quantities in the passages, and, in a moment, causes the mine to glow like a furnace. This conflagration is necessarily succeeded by vast volumes of carbonic acid, or *choke-damp*, as it is emphatically called, from its suffocating character, and this destroys those whom the explosion had spared.

It was to guard against accidents of this character that Sir Humphry Davy invented his safety lamp, a beautiful and simple contrivance, consisting merely of a common oil-lamp, the flame of which is completely enclosed within a cylinder of wire gauze, a substance which will not admit of the passage of flame; so that, although the lamp be introduced into an explosive mixture, the flame will not pass through the gauze to ignite it. Of course the efficacy of the lamp depends on the soundness of the wire gauze; for if this be broken and injured, the flame is not protected; or if the lamp be moved swiftly through an explosive atmosphere, the flame may be blown against, and even through, the meshes of the gauze, and, in either case, might lead to an explosion. When the lamp burns in an atmosphere highly charged with fire-damp, the gas gets within the meshes, and burns with a blue flame, which heats the wire gauze to redness. Even this state of the lamp will not produce an explosion, but of course it was never intended that the workman should go on working with the lamp in this condition. The blue flame within the lamp ought always to be a caution to him to retire, until the mine be rendered safe by ventilation. From too great reliance, in all cases, on the Davy lamp, from neglect, and from various other causes, this lamp has disappointed the expectations of those most interested in its use; and experienced men now look for safety rather to improved methods of ventilation, than to contrivances for lighting the mines. The general plan of ventilation now in common use will be understood from the following details, in addition to those already given.

When a seam is begun to be worked, there is, of course, only one available shaft for ventilation, and this is divided into two portions, as at *a b* (Fig. 116), for the ascending and descending currents; and as it is not safe for the men to be ever more than a few yards in advance of the course of the

Fig. 116. Mode of Ventilating Passages.

current, they begin working the seam with two parallel bords, connected at intervals by cross passages, which are successively stopped by wooden partitions, *c c c*, leaving no communication except through the one last opened, or that which is farthest from the shaft. Temporary partitions are also placed at *e e*, to direct the current to the very spots where the men are at work, as at *w w*. When the workings are more advanced, the direction of the current through every part, by *stoppings* or partitions, becomes a matter of no small complexity, as will be seen by the plan (Fig. 117), where the arrows represent the course of the air from the downcast shaft, *a*, through all the galleries to the upcast shaft, *b*. It will be seen that in most places the current is divided between the parallel bords; this is called *double coursing;* and its advantage is, that if any part of the mine is more fiery or dangerous than the rest, the current can there be confined to one course, and thus have its velocity doubled; while in the parts containing least gas, the same current can be allowed to expand into three passages, which is called *treble coursing*. The double stoppings in Fig. 117 represent those in which doors of communication are required. These are made in pairs, in order that a person may pass through them, as a barge through a canal lock, without allowing the main bodies of air to communicate. To ensure this, they are sometimes

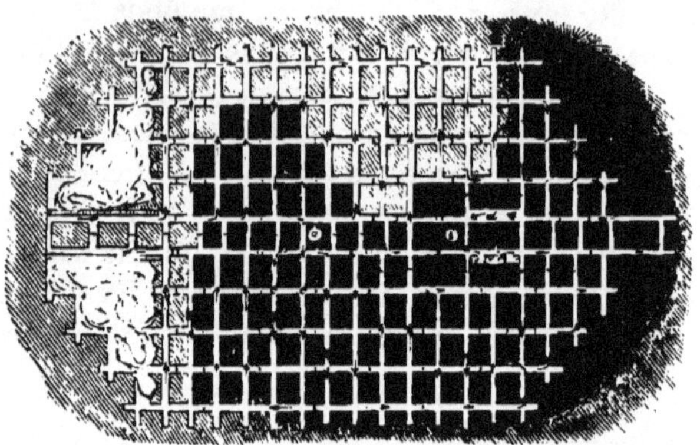

Fig. 117. Plan, with Ventilating Arrangements.

made even treble, and a boy is placed in charge of each pair or set of three, whose duty it is to prevent them from being all opened at once.

As it is not safe to allow the foul air from the more fiery parts of the mine to come in contact with the fire at the bottom of the upcast shaft, which sets the whole ventilating current in motion, it is usual to divide the air as it enters the mine by the shaft, *a*, Fig. 117, into two distinct currents, one of which proceeds through the passages, *e e*, into the safe parts of the mine only, while the other, *c c*, circulates through the fiery parts represented by the lighter shade, including the goafs, or old abandoned workings, which are always the most dangerous receptacles of gas. The purer current alone is allowed to pass through the furnace, *f*, before entering the upcast shaft, *b*. The other current is conducted through

Fig. 118. Dumb Furnace.

d, and enters the shaft at a higher level by a tunnel cut obliquely through the roof of the seam, as in Fig. 118, where *s* represents the upcast shaft, *b* the impure current, and *a* the pure current, feeding the furnace, which, when thus constructed, is termed a *dumb* furnace.

The goafs, or abandoned workings, are sometimes of vast extent, and are known to occupy from 13 to 97 acres of ground. They may be compared to enormous inverted bowls or basins, in which the inflammable gas from various parts of the mine accumulates, and, from its lightness, occupies, at first, the upper part of the goaf: as it increases in quantity, or even as the atmospheric pressure diminishes, it may suddenly fill the goaf, and issue from its lowest edge as from the edge of an inverted bowl, and, mingling with the air of the mine, form an explosive mixture, thus giving rise to many sad accidents. Such appears to have been the origin of the explosion in Haswell Colliery, Durham, in September, 1844, by which ninety-five persons perished. Dr. Faraday, who, in conjunction with Sir Charles Lyell, visited the mine after the accident, with a view to devise some remedy against the recurrence of similar accidents, recommended that the goaf itself be ventilated. He thought it would not be desirable to attempt this by driving the contents of the goaf through any parts of the mine which are occupied by human beings ; but that the goaf cavity might be exhausted of noxious air by means of a pipe, rising as high as possible, from 4 to 8 or 10 feet into it, and communicating at its other extremity with the upcast shaft. Dr. Faraday expressed himself as being disheartened at the apparent hopelessness of finding out any good general remedy for these explosions, which were not simply the effects arising from the mixture of gases, but from the combustion of the coal-dust and coal-gas produced by the first explosion. In the fatal case at Haswell, the place where the accident originated had been ascertained, and the progress of the fire could be traced on the scorched beams and props of the galleries, and by the deposits of coke made from the coal-dust which the explosion raised. To this circumstance the great force of the explosion was due, and not to the first escape of gas. A similar explosion had been known to take place in a cotton-wadding manufactory, the whole atmosphere of the place being fired by means of the particles of cotton in it. Of all the workmen killed in the Haswell accident, perhaps not one was really burnt to death, but suffocated by the choke-damp. In one part of the workings, the explosion had produced sharp vibrations, like the firing of gunpowder; and in another, the burning went on slowly, like a common fire. But, although two panels were blown into one, and solid stoppings of brickwork thrown down, there was no indication of accident in the shaft. If the stoppings had not been blown down, and the supply of air had continued, the mine would have taken fire, and the men been burnt instead of choked. Every part of the Haswell Colliery had been examined, accompanied by the mine-viewer, and recommendations had been received from the best-informed men on the spot; and they were convinced that the conditions under which such accidents happen were so variable, that no general practical rule could be obtained. Far more information, however, was required. The plan of splitting the air courses was good, as far as the power of the upcast shaft admitted; but if carried too far, it would produce stagnant points, which could not be prevented by any arrangement consistently with the ever-moving condition of the works. The abolition of the use of gunpowder and lighted candles would, in some cases, double the price of coals. But the great source of danger was the mental condition of the miners. With regard to the present race, this was so hopeless that nothing could be done for them. Although smoking was strictly forbidden, they had been known to contrive to light their pipes in dangerous workings, even from the Davy lamp; and Dr. Faraday had himself, on one occasion, sat down with an open candle, to watch the preparations for blasting, and, when he inquired for the gunpowder, he was told he was sitting on it. Dr. Faraday expressed his opinion of the safety of the Davy lamp when properly used, and of its being a complete and practical contrivance, to which he would willingly trust his own life, as he had already done on many occasions.

Fans are now getting into use for the ventilation of coal-pits. A large fan, worked by a steam-engine, is placed over a short shaft communicating with the upcast shaft by a lateral channel; and a double trap-door, forming a kind of rough valve, is placed over the mouth of the upcast shaft, and kept closed except when the corves are passing.

CHAPTER IV.

ON SPONTANEOUS VENTILATION.

THE necessity of placing ventilating arrangements as far as possible beyond the direction and control of the inmates of the house or room to be ventilated has been sufficiently insisted on. Ventilation, like respiration, should be an unconscious act, so to speak, producing inconvenience only when it is interfered with or interrupted. Arrangements for it should form an adequate proportion of the structure of the building, so as to admit fresh air and discharge the foul with as much regularity as the windows admit the light and the chimney-shaft discharges the smoke.

One of the earliest mechanical contrivances for ventilation

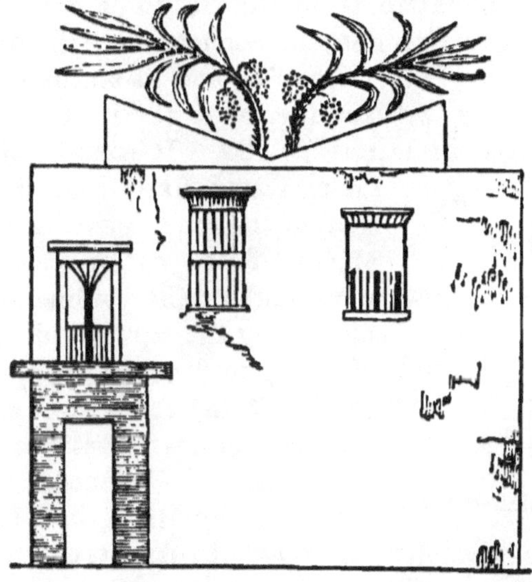

Fig. 119. Wind Conductor of Egypt.

is the *mulguf*, or wind conductor of the ancient Egyptians, and still in use in modern Egypt. It was erected at the top of the house, as in Fig. 119, and consisted of a frame covered or enclosed on all sides, except at the mouths, which were open in the direction of the prevailing winds. The roof of the mulguf sloped down from each open end to the centre, where a partition divided it, and deflected the wind down into the apartments below. Mr. Wilkinson, in his work on Egypt, gives a view of part of Cairo, showing the mulgufs on the houses of the modern Egyptians. The ancient mulgufs were double, as shown in the figure, but the modern ones are single, and the opening is in the direction of the prevailing north-west wind. They consist of strong framework, to which several planks of wood are nailed, according to the breadth and length proposed; and if required of cheaper materials, reeds or mats, covered with stucco, are used instead of planks.

This contrivance acts on a similar principle to the *wind-sail* noticed in a former chapter; but, being fixed in position, it acts spontaneously or independently of the inmates of the house.

The chimney-valve is another of those spontaneous contrivances that contribute to the health of a room. It was devised by Dr. Franklin, in connection with his Pennsylvanian fire-place (Fig. 28, p. 97), and its merits are described in the inventor's own language at page 98. It is represented in its simplest form in Fig. 120. It consists of an oblong metal frame fixed into the chimney-shaft of the room near the ceiling. The object of the contrivance is to take advantage of the ventilating force furnished by the upward draught of the chimney to draw off the upper strata of the air of the room through the frame into the flue, whilst it prevents down-draughts. A balanced metal valve was fitted by Dr. Arnott (whence this

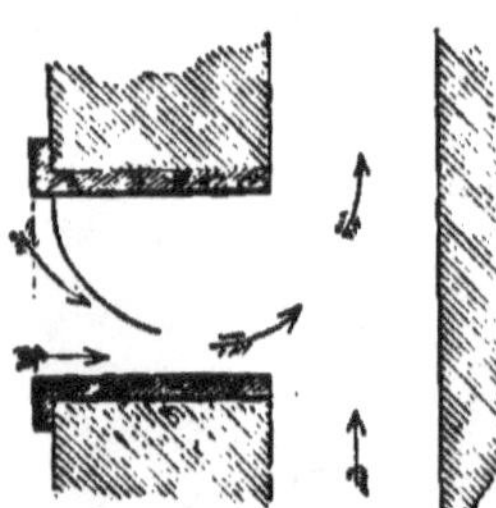

Fig. 120. Chimney-valve.

contrivance is usually known as "the Arnott chimney-valve"), or a light flap of silk may be supported behind a perforated metal plate placed in the frame opening into the room.*   It

* The metal valve or silk flap is apt to make a noise in falling, which may be prevented by attaching a slice of cork to the metal plate, or by having a valve of thin cork or some similar material.

is remarked in the Barracks' Commission Report that this valve, like every other, requires certain conditions for its action. If the throat of the chimney be very wide, the quantity of air and smoke which pass up the shaft from below will be more than the chimney at its narrowest part, where the ventilator is placed, can accommodate, and the smoke will consequently pass through the valve into the room. Hence it is necessary in fitting this valve to contract the throat of the chimney, so as to leave a balance in the draught, to be supplied by air passing through the valve ; but as the amount of this balance or the number of cubic feet of air which can pass through this valve into the chimney per hour is very limited, this form of ventilator is not adapted for a room likely to be crowded. I can speak from experience of its use in a room occupied daily by four or five persons, with four candles burning every night. There is always a strong draught through the valve into the chimney, the smell of dinner quickly passes away, and the room always feels fresh and pleasant. I have not made any special experiments on the action of this valve beyond holding a piece of lighted paper near it, when the flame is drawn in, but after the considerable doubt that has been thrown by Mr. Campbell's experiments (see p. 210, Fig. 80), as to whether the valve is really of any use at all, it would be rash, without further experiments conducted under varied conditions, to recommend strongly or to condemn the chimney-valve. The Barracks' Commissioners recommend it as a very simple and economical ventilator for non-commissioned officers' rooms.

A contrivance known as Sherringham's ventilator, Fig. 121, consists of an iron air-brick, or box, inserted close to the ceiling of the room, and communicating directly with the outer air. To prevent the air from coming in by stray currents, there is placed at the mouth of the opening, within the room, a valve hinged at its lower side, and opening towards the ceiling, so that the inflowing current required to supply the chimney draught is thrown up

Fig. 121. Sherringham's Ventilator.

towards the ceiling, and more or less diffused among the general mass of air in the room. This ventilator may, under certain conditions, act as an outlet; but when the room is closed, and there is a fire in the grate, it must act as an inlet for fresh air. As such—that is, as an inlet—it is well placed and well arranged, and is adapted to a room that is not likely to be crowded. A ventilator similar in principle has been introduced into the upper panes of window frames.

There are three ventilators which seem to have been suggested to the inventors by the experiment described at page 165 of the first edition of this work, and which we now repeat in this place. The late Professor Daniell, of King's College, was in the habit of showing this experiment in his lectures, and the following figure has been copied from the apparatus in the college museum. The arrangement was introduced into the former edition of this work for showing the necessity of avoiding bends and angles in ventilating-tubes, since they increase the friction and deprive the heated column of some of its ascensional force by cooling ; also, where several vent-tubes are employed, they should all be of the same vertical height, or the highest vent will prevent the efficient action of the lower ones, so that there may actually be a smaller discharge through two tubes than through one only. So also, when several openings are made above the level of the floor of a room, the highest may be the only one capable of acting as an abduction-tube, the other lower openings often serving as induction-tubes, discharging cold air into the room, and, in doing so, lowering the temperature of the hot vitiated air, and preventing its escape; thus not only causing the bad air to be breathed over again, but filling the room with unpleasant draughts. But if the highest abduction-tube be too small to carry off the requisite quantity of hot air, the tube next below it in elevation at any part of the room will act as an abduction-tube.

If the lower openings for the admission of cool fresh air be too small in proportion to those for the escape of the hot air, a current of cold air will descend through one part of the hot-air tube, and the hot air will ascend through another part of the same tube, an effect which we have already seen (p. 201) takes place in the ventilation of a bee-hive. This effect may also be shown by a very pleasing experiment. Place a lighted taper in a flat dish (Fig. 122), and cover it with a glass receiver, furnished with a long glass chimney placed immediately over the flame. If the bottom of the receiver does not come into very close contact with the dish, enough air will enter to support combustion, and the draught or current of hot air will escape up the chimney, and the taper will continue to burn for any length of time. If we now shift the receiver a little on one side, so that the flame may not be immediately under the chimney, the products of combustion will impinge upon the glass, and, cooling down and mingling with the air of the receiver, will contaminate it so much, that the taper immediately begins to burn dimly, and is soon extinguished. On bringing the chimney over the flame, it will speedily improve in appearance; the smoke and other products of combustion will be rapidly discharged, and the receiver will become bright and transparent as before. But suppose we cut off all communication with the external air from below by pouring a little water into the dish, so as to cover the mouth of the receiver, we shall then have the case of a room which is provided with a vent tube near the ceiling, but has no provision for admitting fresh air from any lower openings; in such case, the fresh air will seek to enter by the ventilating tube. If this be large enough, the outgoing hot air and the incoming cool air will divide the tube into two parts. But if, as in the experiment before us, the ventilating tube or chimney be too narrow, the hot and cold currents will interfere with each other; the tendency of the hot air to rise and of the cold air to descend will prevent the escape of the one and the entrance of the other, and the taper will soon be extinguished for want of fresh air. But if the chimney be divided into two portions by a flat strip of tin-plate passed down it, as in Fig. 122, and the taper be lighted and placed in its former position, it will continue to burn for any length of time; for, by this arrangement, the two currents of hot and cold air are prevented from interfering with each other; the hot air will pass up one channel and escape, and the cold air will descend the other channel to feed the flame.   By holding a piece of smoking paper or the glowing wick of a taper on one side of the chimney, the smoke will be drawn down, thereby indicating the descending current of cool air; while, on the other side, the smoke will be driven up by the ascending current of heated air.

Fig. 122. Ascending and Descending Currents.

In the same manner these counter currents may be frequently noticed in churches and other crowded places, where due provision is seldom made for the entrance of fresh air and the escape of the foul.   It is usual in summer to mitigate the effects of the hot vitiated atmosphere by throwing open the windows.   A portion of the foul air, it is true, escapes by these channels, but a counter current immediately sets in through each of them, exposing the persons near them to the dangerous effects of draught, and also cooling the foul air which is seeking to escape, and sending it down to be breathed over again.

The three ventilators based on the principle of the foregoing experiment profess to combine an outlet for the foul air and an inlet for the fresh in the same contrivance. They were examined by the Barracks' Commissioners, who state, that under certain fixed conditions all three ventilators effect both objects; but if these conditions be varied, any one of them may become wholly outlets or wholly inlets. The conditions essential to their operation are, that the room to which they are applied be closed (as the receiver is with a water lute in Fig. 122), and then, if a number of persons be crowded into the room with the fireplace, doors, and windows shut, and if a ventilating tube be carried from the ceiling of the room above the roof of the building, there will be an irregular effort at an interchange between the air of the room and the outside air; irregular counter-currents will be established, and the room will be badly ventilated, if at all.   If now the tube be divided longitudinally from top to bottom by means of a thin partition, the currents will be quite distinct, as in the experiment, Fig. 122, a current of air will descend into the room continuously on one side of the partition, and the current of foul air will ascend from the room continuously on the other side of the partition.   One half of the tube supplies fresh air to the inlets of the room, and the other half removes the foul air, so that if the size of the tube be properly adjusted the air of the room is kept sweet.

Watson's ventilator (Fig. 123) is the simplest arrangement, which consists of a square tube with a division in the centre, without any contrivance for diffusing the descending current. Mackinnell's ventilator (Fig. 124) consists of two tubes, one within the other, with a space between them.   The inner tube is the longer, and projects above the outer at its upper end; the inner tube also projects a little below the outer

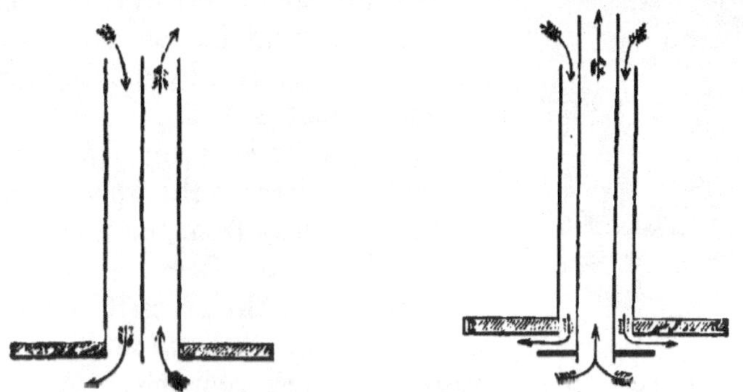

Fig. 123. Watson's Ventilator.   Fig. 124. Mackinnell's Ventilator.

tube in the ceiling to give support to a flange projecting parallel to the ceiling and concealing the opening of the outer tube.   It is stated that the greater length of the inner tube determines the upward current which takes place in it, so as to become the foul-air shaft; the efficiency of this tube, however, must depend, not upon its length but upon its temperature, and that is kept down by the outer tube, which acts as the fresh air inlet, and the descending current striking

against the flange is thrown out in the plane of the ceiling,
and so diffused. Without having had an opportunity of
examining this contrivance, I should have thought the arrangement would have been better if the hot vitiated air had
been allowed to flow along the ceiling, and make its escape
by the opening in its own plane, instead of cooling the hot
air by allowing a colder and denser stratum to pour in upon
it. The opening for the escape of hot vitiated air should be
at the highest point, as in the examples furnished by a
lantern or street gas-lamp.

The third contrivance on this principle is Muir's ventilator
(Fig. 125). It consists of a square tube divided into four
parts, A A, B B, by means of partitions
which are carried above the top of the
tube, and the box is completed outside
and above the roof by louvre boards, as
in the figure. The object of the divisions and louvres is to procure not only
the upward and downward currents of
the ordinary kind, but to take advantage
of light winds, which by striking through
the louvres at any angle will cause a
stream of air to be projected down into
the room, and assist the upward current
on the side away from the wind.

The Barracks' Commissioners state
more than once the necessity for a closed
room in order that these three ventilators may work properly. As soon as
a door or window is opened they become upcast shafts, and cease to supply
air. Also, if there be a fire-place in
the room with a strong fire in it, and
the doors and windows be closed, they
become downcast shafts, and the fire
will supply itself from them.

Fig. 125. Muir's Venti-
lator.

In certain cases they may be ap-
plicable, as in single rooms standing apart, such as churches,
chapels, schools, libraries, &c., warmed by stoves, and where

the doors are kept shut for hours at a time; in stables also, of a certain construction, they may be useful. These ventilators are recommended for ventilating the holds of sloops and hospital ships.

In the second edition of this work, published in 1858, it is stated, p. 285, that cases may occur where the principle of introducing fresh air at the same level at which the foul air is allowed to escape, may be adopted for want of a better. Mr. E. A. Cowper communicated to me his plan, which seems one of the least objectionable on this principle. He places a perforated box along each side of the room, with a pipe carried up some feet on the outside. The room being supposed to be close in other respects, and warmed by the occupants, or by means of steam-pipes or otherwise, a current of air sets in down one pipe into the room, while another current passes out of the room up the other pipe. The wind blowing on one side of the building, or the sun shining on it, sets the current in motion, and when once it is started there is a column of external cold air in one pipe, and of warm air from the room in the other pipe. The action is then the same as if the cold air pipe were removed, and the air had direct access to the perforated trunk with which it was connected, while the hot air pipe acts as an aërial sewer for draining off the foul air. Thus, as long as the room is warmer than the external air, ventilation will continue, but it may be in either direction, according as it is first started. The pipes or chimneys may both be on the same side of the building, so as to prevent the current from being accelerated by a high wind acting on one pipe, and as the equilibrium is unstable, the current is sure to commence. This apparatus will not, of course, be of any use unless the air in the room is warmer than the external air. Dr. Arnott also mentions a case in which he got rid of foul air and introduced fresh air at the same level: this was in the dormitory of the Field Lane Ragged School. Six tubes, formed of plank of about a foot square, opened from the ceiling into two ventilating shafts by horizontal branches. Three tubes connected with one branch were for the escape of the ascending hot foul breath and exhalations, while the other three were for the admission of fresh air, which it was supposed would " subside gently, and spread among the sleepers." It was observed that ventilation did not begin immediately on the entrance of the crowd, but by arranging a gas-lamp so as to discharge its burnt air into the ascending shaft, the interchange of currents immediately commenced.

One of the objections to ventilating openings is, that they occasionally bring down cataracts of cold air instead of allowing the escape of the foul air. Dr. Arnott remedies this by covering the ventilating opening with wire gauze, and stretching over this a curtain of light cloth, called a *curtain valve*, so that the air may pass from within outwards by pushing forward the light curtain; but the air cannot pass in the opposite direction, since the attempt to do so would press the curtain against the gauze and close the passage Some of the courts of law at Westminster were ventilated by taking out some of the side windows from the lantern in the roof and stretching a netting over the opening. On the outside, across the netting, were placed a number of strips of canvas about 4 or 6 inches deep, fixed by the upper edge. When the warm air of the court sought an exit it lifted these curtain valves and breathed out, but if a cold wind attempted to enter, it shut the valves down on the netting, and thus excluded it.

CHAPTER V.

ON HOT WATER AND STEAM AS A VENTILATING FORCE, AND ON THE COMBINED METHODS OF WARMING AND VENTILATING.

Some of the methods described in the last chapter for ventilating a building include also arrangements for warming it. Although it is customary to associate the two processes, they are really distinct, each requiring special provisions. It has been seen that the Houses of Parliament have frequently been made the subject of experiments in the art of warming and ventilation. That the experiments have not always succeeded has been already shown, and the reason, probably, is to be found in their novelty. The members of either House whose province it has been to order the erection of the various descriptions of apparatus, cannot fairly be charged with the failure, since it is reasonable to suppose that if a tried and approved method had existed, it would have been ordered; and the reports published on the subject do not diclose any method which may be pronounced perfect.

The centrifugal wheel of Dr. Desaguliers continued to be used for ventilating the House of Commons until the year 1820, when the Marquis of Chabannes was allowed to undertake the warming and ventilation of the House. He proposed to erect a small furnace over the ceiling, the combustion of which was to be supported entirely by the vitiated air of the House; but this plan being objected to, he caused a large case or trunk to be constructed over the body of the House, below the roof, into which ventilating tubes were conducted from different parts of the House; four of these tubes opened from under the galleries, to prevent the stagnation of the impure air in those parts, and six openings in the ceiling led into the main trunks, and were each continued in separate trunks to the top, so that the draught from every part was equal. Sixteen steam cylinders were placed within the main trunk, and the heat thereby produced was intended to rarefy the air in the ventilating tubes so powerfully, as to cause its quick ascent and escape through a large cowl of 4 feet diameter outside the building.

The House was warmed by means of twelve steam cylinders ranged under the seats of the House, and the external air was brought to these cylinders by a large air trunk, from which there was a separate branch to each cylinder.

In these arrangements, there was no deficiency either of heating or of ventilating power. On the contrary, the heating surface seems to have been in excess, and was not under perfect command. At any rate, the atmosphere of the House was declared to be uncomfortable, and, after a few years, another system was tried.

The use of hot water as a means of ventilation was introduced by Mr. Deacon, in 1813. The air was drawn from an underground tunnel or cellar by means of a fan, which forced it into the rooms through small iron or earthenware tubes placed in boiling water. The vitiated air was conducted into a tube or channel at the ceiling, and conveyed above the roof, where it was practicable to do so. Iron plates were also sometimes used instead of pipes. They were placed parallel to each other, with a space of about $1\frac{1}{2}$ inch between them. These plates were surrounded by boiling water, and the air rose in the space between them. When cold was desirable the pipes or plates were immersed in cold or artificially cooled water, and the air thus cooled was thrown into the room by the fanner. If the room was of large size, the fan had to be turned by a man; this is, of course, objectionable, because human machines are not always to be depended on, and they are, for such purposes as turning a wheel, expensive. Smaller fans were kept in motion by the elasticity of a spring, or the fall of a weight. Mr. Deacon's apparatus was fixed in some public buildings, but does not seem to have made any permanent impression on the public mind.

Among the plans submitted to the Committee of the House of Commons, in 1835, for warming the Houses of Parliament, that of Mr. Sylvester appears to have great merit. It was not a mere theoretical plan, for it had been tried, although on a smaller scale than that now proposed, in the lunatic asylum for Kent. The general principle of this plan is to introduce the fresh air slowly, and in any required quantity, by means of an underground channel, $a\,b$ (Fig. 126), about 9 feet square and 100 yards in length, which forms a communication with the atmosphere and the basement floor of the building; the outer extremity of the channel being furnished with a cowl, arranged so as always to have its mouth to the wind. The fresh air flowing along this long tunnel would receive in winter an accession of about 15° of heat, and in summer it would be cooled to a similar extent. It would then pass into a cockle similar to that of the Belper stove (Fig. 56, p. 150), where it would be heated to within 5° of the temperature required in the House. From this cockle, it would spread into the space, $d\,d$, under the floor, and then rise through a large number of small holes drilled in it, into the body of the House. The vitiated air would then be carried off through a number of openings, *i i*, in the ceiling, arranged so as to be opened or closed at pleasure, by means of a contrivance communicating through *x* to the basement. The vitiated air, after passing through these openings, would flow into the cavity, *n*, below the roof, and thence be discharged into the open air by the turn-cap, *o*,

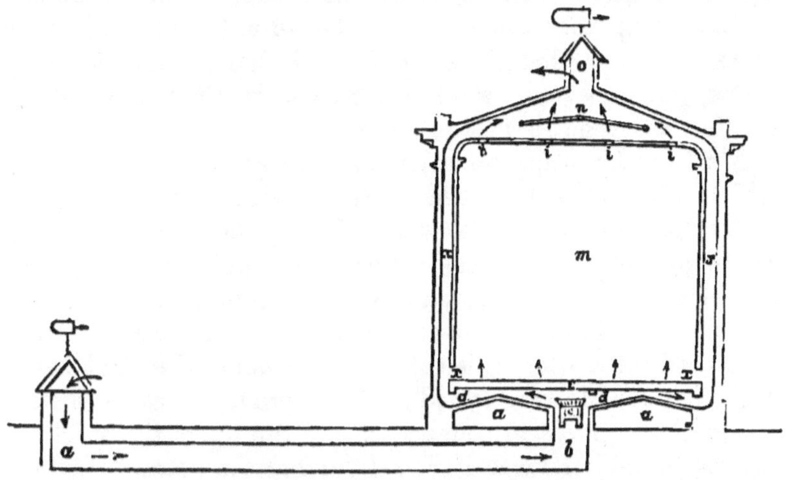

Fig. 126. Sylvester's Method.

formed so as to have its mouth always turned from the wind. To ensure the required velocity and direction of the ventilating current, a series of pipes, *n*, filled with steam or hot water, were to be placed in the cavity of the roof. When it was required to raise the temperature of the House higher than usual, the amount of ventilation was to be diminished by closing the apertures in the ceiling, and allowing the vitiated air to escape through channels, *x x*, in the walls. The velocity at which it was proposed to set the air in motion through the channel, for supplying the fresh and discharging the vitiated air, was 4 feet per second; but it was to flow into the House at the rate of only half a foot per second, thereby producing a current which would scarcely move the flame of a candle. The area of the apertures distributed throughout the floor would be about 665 feet; and including the House, the staircases, and corridors, &c., it was calculated that there would be 200,000 cubic feet of air changed six times per hour.   When asked whether he proposed to make any arrangements for securing the purity or cleanliness of the fresh air to be introduced, Mr. Sylvester replied, that it would be extremely desirable to have a communication with some large inclosure for the fresh air, such as a large building like Westminster Hall, between the House of Commons and the outer air, that the air might be admitted into this large inclosure, and allowed to settle and deposit its blacks or smuts, just as water, before being used, is allowed to deposit its mud and sand in a large cistern.

Most of the plans for warming and ventilating buildings, which have been described in these pages, are on a large and comprehensive scale, adapted to public buildings, and requiring not only a considerable expenditure of money, but also of space, for their erection and effective action.   By distributing the heated air over the whole of the under surface of a perforated floor, it is thereby distributed throughout the space required to be warmed; and by providing some powerful ventilating force in connection with the top of the building, also perforated, the warm or cool current can be made to pass through the building with any required velocity.   But it is obvious that such extensive arrangements are not adapted to a small building or a private house.   In such cases, different arrangements must be made, and these are not always successful.   If, for example, the air be heated by stoves, and instead of being sent into the room through a perforated floor, it is admitted in small currents at an elevated temperature, it ascends rapidly to the ceiling, and expends the greater portion of its heat on that surface, while the lower part of the room remains cold, because airs of very different temperatures do not readily mingle together.*   On this account Mr. Perkins recommends that the tubes used in ventilation be placed at or near the floor, by which means the warm air is forced to descend and mingle more intimately with the colder air in the room; and the warm air having

---

* A method of mixing cold air with air artificially heated, is described at p. 227.

thus parted with its heat, is itself drawn off. When hot water or steam pipes are used, the air can only be moderately warmed; and as the ascensional force in such case is not great, the ventilating openings can be placed at any des ired point.

This plan of placing the ventilating openings near the floor is liable to many objections. It gets rid entirely of the spontaneous method of ventilation, so that should the ventilating force not be wanted, as in summer, or be neglected or suffered to decline, there is no ventilation at all. This has been proved in several arrangements for ventilating barracks, hospitals, theatres, &c., in France and elsewhere, as already noticed. Place the ventilating openings at a low elevation and the occupants of the space to be ventilated are at the. mercy of a man who may neglect to throw a shovel-full of coals on the fire, or, indeed, may neglect to light the fire at all. A coil of pipe, it is true, takes a good while to cool, and possesses many advantages provided the force be kept up; but the argument ought not to be admitted on the score of economy, that as the ventilating power can only be obtained at the expense of the heating power, much of the heat used to warm the room must be lost if the ventilating openings be placed in the ceiling; and that if the temperature be moderate, the products of combustion and respiration may be cooled, and thus deprived of their ascensional force before they have time to escape by the ventilator. Such arguments as these may lead to dangerous practice.

In the warming of a building by Mr. Perkins's system of 1-inch tubes, the ventilating force is a coil of such pipes, and he proposes to place the ventilating openings either singly near the floor, or in conjunction with a second opening at the ceiling. " In the ventilation and warming of a private dwelling, I would begin, first," says Mr. Richardson, " with the staircase. This we ought to consider the principal artery of the house; and if this were well warmed by a current of warm fresh air flowing into it, and a constant change effected by a ventilating outlet, warmed, so as to ensure its effective operation, great part of the business would be effected, as the staircase would supply all rooms not in use with warm air in a sufficient degree, and would gradually ventilate the whole building, rendering it unnecessary to have further ventilation, except in the principal living and sleeping rooms of the family." But every room in the house might be ventilated, by placing two or more spare columns of tubing in flues concealed within the thickness of the wall. It will be seen, by reference to Fig. 72, p. 179,* that where the flue passes in its course through two or more stories of small rooms, it is proposed to make an opening about 6 inches square from each room into the flue, and this, it is said, if provided with a proper outlet at the top, would effectually ventilate every room. This statement, however, is very loose, since no reference is made to the cubical contents of each room, nor to the number of occupants. The flue should, of course, be vertical, and enclose the expansion tube at the top, where it should terminate in a tin funnel provided with a turn-cap, to prevent downward currents of air. Soon after the fire was lighted in the furnace below, all these openings into the flues would become so many artificial fire-places, drawing from the room a constant current of cooler air into the flue, which, being warmed to a very high temperature by the great quantity of pipe within it, the current of warm air would rapidly ascend into the open air above, thus affording all the advantages of constant ventilation. In summer, when the warming effects of this system are seldom wanted, the circulation may be turned off from all the rooms by the stop-cocks, and the effects of the hot pipes be confined within the flues. The ventilation would then be carried on as usual, and no additional warmth be experienced from the action of the pipes. The advantages of this arrangement for our changeable climate are obvious, for on a cold day in summer, the stop-cocks being opened, the circulation would proceed through the coils in the rooms, and thus raise the temperature as desired.

Thus it will be seen, that by having a flue of the whole height of the building for the reception of the hot water tubes, the vitiated air can be drawn out of the room at any

---

* This system is described at p. 162, as being still in operation at the British Museum. This is not so, larger pipes having been lately introduced.

point. By means of the lower opening, the temperature of the room is equalised, and the effects of currents of unequally mixed air removed or mitigated; while the upper opening carries off the effluvia of the room. The openings should all be furnished with slides, so that they may be contracted or enlarged at pleasure.

In large public rooms, the size of the ventilating openings ought to be accurately determined by the architect. They ought to be large enough to allow every person in a crowded room to have a proper supply of air for healthy respiration. In a less crowded state of the room, the openings may be diminished by means of slides. By increasing the temperature in the flues, their ventilating power is, of course, increased, and this may be done by arranging a coil within the flue at each opening.

In connection with this system of warming and ventilating may be mentioned a method which seems to be full of objections; namely, that by which the fresh warmed air is admitted into the room by openings near the ceiling, and the vitiated air drawn out through openings near the floor. Argument in favour of this plan is based on the idea that, with upward ventilation, a great part of the vitiated atmosphere of crowded rooms is liable, by the slightest check or condensation, to be thrown down and mixed with the air which is already partly unfitted for the purposes of respiration. But let the ventilating current descend, it is said, and we have a bright atmosphere of pure air, which, as it becomes contaminated by respiration, is drawn downwards and discharged. It is scarcely necessary to point out that the vitiated air from the lungs, having a temperature of 98°, naturally rises through the air of the room, which is of the temperature of 60° or under, and, if forced downwards by any means, must be breathed over again by the occupants of the room before it can be discharged at the level of their legs and feet in opposition to the laws of gravity. It is difficult to see how such an objection is to be answered, unless the velocity of the outgoing current be so considerable as to amount to a strong wind; and it is, or ought to be, the object of all ventilation to prevent the motion either of the incoming or outgoing current from being felt. This plan of ventilation by descent has been put into operation at the Model Prison, at Pentonville, where the solitary system of discipline is enforced, thus giving rise to the necessity of having a separate cell for each prisoner. In each cell the windows are fixtures, and the doors are effectually closed, so that the only mode of introducing the requisite supply of fresh, and of abstracting the vitiated air, must be by artificial means. The objection to applying ordinary modes of ventilation, by opening windows or by similar means, is the facility such openings give to the transmission of sound.

The method by which this descending ventilating current is produced is compared by Major Jebb* to the ventilation of a coal-pit, in which, as already explained, the fresh air entering the down-cast shaft, passes through the numerous galleries and workings of the mine, and escapes by the up-cast shaft, the ventilating force consisting of a large fire in the up-cast shaft. In applying such a system to the ventilation of a prison, the objects proposed to be attained were— 1st, The regular supply of a sufficient quantity of fresh air, and, when necessary, of warmed air, into each cell, without subjecting the occupant to any inconvenience from the draught. 2nd, The withdrawal of a like quantity of vitiated air. 3rd, That no additional facilities of communication between prisoners in adjoining cells should be afforded by the means made use of, and, therefore, that the transmission of sound be carefully guarded against. The reader who wishes to inspect all the details of the arrangements by which these objects are carried out, is referred to Major Jebb's paper, and the copious series of engravings by which it is illustrated; but a general idea of this method may be conveyed by the following remarks, to any one who has studied the various methods of warming and ventilating as described in this little volume.

In the basement story is a case or boiler, with a proportion

---

* "On modern Prisons: their Construction and Ventilation." By J. Jebb, Major Royal Engineers, Surveyor-General of Prisons. With ten plates, 4to. Published separately from "Papers on subjects connected with the duties of the Corps of Royal Engineers." Vol. VII. London, 1844.

of pipes adapted to the circulation of hot water, and in connection therewith is a large cold air flue open to the outer air, for supplying air to be warmed in passing over the boiler and pipes. This air then passes right and left along a horizontal flue, under the floor of the corridor of the prison; and from this flue a communication is established by small lateral flues with each cell, both on the lower and two upper floors, each small flue terminating in a grating under the arched ceiling of each cell. "The object of making the point of entry at the top of the cell instead of at the bottom, and diffusing it through a grating on an extended surface, is, that no unpleasant draught may be experienced by the occupier of the cell—which, in a confined situation, would be the case, were it brought in at the level of the floor—and that he may not have any inducement to frustrate the intention of ventilation, by stopping it up." A corresponding quantity of foul air is extracted by means of a grating placed close to the floor of each cell, diagonally opposite the opening by which the fresh air is introduced. This grating covers a flue which passes up the outer wall, and communicates with a main foul air flue placed in the roof, and terminating in a ventilating shaft rising above the top of the building. By this arrangement the total lengths of each pair of flues respectively used for introducing fresh air into the cells, and extracting foul air from them, are rendered nearly equal on all the stories. This promotes uniformity of action; and the advantage due to the ascending system, and to difference both of temperature and altitude, is also secured. "Another provision of some importance should be adverted to. Fresh air should be taken into the main flues, communicating with all the cells in the respective wings or divisions, from the side which happens to be exposed to the wind. The force or pressure produced by a very moderate breeze, combined with the other arrangements and circumstances which are favourable for ventilation, will generally cause a sufficient current to pass through the cells without any fire being lighted in the extracting shaft for ensuring it. The operation of the system will, by these means, at all times be improved, and a considerable saving of fuel will be effected." The same flues are used for ventilating the cells both in winter and in summer; the only difference between the arrangements of the two seasons being, that during the summer, when air is introduced into the cells at its natural temperature, a fire is lighted when necessary in the ventilating shaft; during winter, when the temperature of the air must be raised, a fire is lighted in the heating apparatus below, the smoke and disposable heat from which, being discharged into the shaft, answer the same purpose.

It has been shown by experiment, in the Pentonville Prison, 1st, That from 30 to 45 cubic feet of pure fresh air is made to pass into every cell in a minute, and that this abundant ventilation goes on with great regularity. 2nd, That this current of ventilation, and a temperature of from 52° to 60°, can be uniformly maintained in the cells during the coldest weather, at an expense of less than one farthing per cell for twenty-four hours; and the summer ventilation, by means of a fire lighted in the extracting shaft, has been kept up at less than half the expense.

We come now to notice an application of steam to the purposes of ventilation, which is, in all respects, peculiar. It was remarked, many years ago, by Dr. Thomas Young, that whenever any elastic fluid is forced from a jet with a very small velocity, the stream proceeded for many inches without any observable dilatation, and then diverged at a considerable angle into a cone, and at the point of divergency there was an audible and even a visible vibration. When the pressure is increased, the apex of the cone approaches nearer to the orifice of the tube, but no degree of pressure seems materially to alter its ultimate divergency. The distance of the apex from the orifice is not proportional to the diameter of the current; it appears rather to be the greater the smaller the current, and is much better defined in a small current than in a large one. Popular illustrations of this curious fact may be seen every day. A puff of smoke from a factory chimney, on being first shot out, may often be seen to assume the form of a ring, the diameter of which does not greatly exceed that of the chimney, but as it ascends in a still atmosphere, it gradually increases in size. In the firing of ordnance on a calm day, these rings may be seen on a grand scale, and still more perfectly if the mouth of the cannon be greased, and no shot used. The same phenomena may also be observed, on a small scale, in the smoke of tobacco projected from the mouth of a skilful smoker. The rotating clouds of smoke from the chimney of a steam-boat have also a tendency to form these conical rings, but from its abundance, and the motion of the vessel, the form is not very defined. But the rings of smoke produced by the combustion of bubbles of phosphuretted hydrogen, show the structure and motion of these rings very admirably. These hollow rings are seen to revolve on the axis of the cylinder from which they are projected, and gradually expand on rising into the air: each of these enlarging rings may be viewed as a magnified element of the cone issuing from the jet in Dr. Young's experiment.

It was further observed by Dr. Young that the stream of air projected from an orifice drew into its current light bodies near it, which were free to move. This lateral communication of motion in a fluid stream was noticed in water by Venturi. This attractive force seems to arise " from the relative situation of the particles of the fluid in the line of the current with respect to that of the particles in the contiguous strata, which, whatever may be the supposed order of the single particles with respect to each other, must naturally lead to a communication of motion nearly in a parallel direction, and this may properly be termed friction. The lateral pressure which urges the flame of a candle towards the stream of air from a blow-pipe, is probably exactly similar to that pressure which causes the inflection of a current of air near an obstacle. Mark the dimple which a slender stream of air makes on the surface of water ; bring a convex body into contact with the side of the stream, and the place of the dimple will immediately show that the current is inflected towards the body; and if the body be at liberty to move in every direction, it will be urged towards the current in the same manner as, in Venturi's experiment, a fluid was forced up a tube inserted into the side of a pipe through which water was flowing. A similar interposition of an obstacle in the course of the wind is probably often the cause of smoky chimneys."

If, instead of the jet of air used in these experiments, we employ a jet of steam, produced under a pressure of 32 lbs. to the square inch, the attractive power is very considerable. The steam, as it escapes from the boiler, forms a cone, as in Dr. Young's experiments, and the quantity of air set in motion is equal to 217 times the bulk of the cone of steam. The force with which the particles of air surrounding this cone are drawn towards it was illustrated by Dr. Faraday in a lecture at the Royal Institution, in various striking experiments. Hollow balls of 1 and 2 inches diameter were drawn into the cone, and sustained floating in the line of its axis even when, by an arrangement of the apparatus, the axis was thrown 35° out of the perpendicular. An upright glass tube, 18 inches long and 1 inch diameter, having one extremity plunged in water and the other drawn into a capillary jet, was immediately exhausted of its contained air, the water being drawn up from the end of the tube, when the capillary jet was placed within the indraught of air occasioned by the cone of steam. By surrounding this cone of steam with a cylindrical jacket, the effects were still more remarkable in increasing the draught power of the jet. The air within the jacket is expelled, and a partial vacuum produced, whereby the air rushes in to supply the vacant space, sweeping before it, in its current, any light bodies, such as paper shavings, hollow balls, &c., and projecting them with considerable force from the top of the jacket.* In the arrangement proposed by Mr. Barry for ventilating the House of

---

* It was shown, many years ago, by Clement Desormes, that when steam, under high pressure, is allowed to escape from an orifice pierced in a plate, or the flat side of a boiler, and a flat disc is brought close to this plate, the disc is powerfully attracted to the plate. In this case, the elastic force of the steam issuing from the jet, and which tends to separate the plate and disc, diminishes rapidly in its course from the centre to the edges of the disc ; at the same time, the radial currents, by their indraught, bring the two plates together with a power which is so much greater than the former, that the two surfaces adhere.

This experiment may be shown in a popular manner by the following contrivance :—Cut a couple of cards each into a disc of about 2 inches in diameter, and perforate one of them at the centre, and fix it on the top of a tube, such as the barrel of a common quill; then give the other card a slight

Lords, this jacket formed the ventilating shaft, and its value will be seen from the following sketch of the general arrangements proposed for warming and ventilating the House, as gathered from a lecture by Dr. Faraday at the Royal Institution, on the 26th March, 1847.

Mr. Barry's plan has been applied to the royal antechamber, the House of Peers, and the public lobby. It consists, first, in causing a current of air of regulated temperature to pass beneath the impervious floor of these apartments, and afterwards to rise to a chamber at the top of the building, from whence it is diffused in great abundance, but imperceptibly, throughout the three apartments; and secondly, in drawing off the vitiated air, and discharging it with great rapidity into the atmosphere. To accomplish these objects, methods have been contrived for—1st, Warming the building through an impervious floor, as in the case of a Roman bath. 2nd, Effecting a system of currents. 3rd, Providing means for causing 10,000 cubic feet of air per minute to proceed on a prescribed course and regulated velocity. 1st, As to the mode of warming: a steam cockle, supplied from one of Lord Dundonald's boilers, is traversed by a quantity of air tubes firmly fastened into it. The air which passes through these tubes is the source of warmth. This apparatus, with its furnace, is placed beneath the public lobby, and the current of warm air passes beneath its impervious floor, then beneath that of the House of Peers, and, lastly, beneath the floor of the royal antechamber beyond. With warmth, the air acquires a certain degree of motive power in the rising parts of the passages, which carries it onward till it reaches the reservoir chambers at the summit of the building; from thence it is made to pass down into the apartments by their walls, and so distributed, without draught, to be breathed by the inmates of these rooms. This gradual diffusion of the

bend, and place it over the first, with the convexity upwards, so that the orifice of the tube may be directly under and almost in contact with the upper card; hold the two cards horizontally, and blow through the tube, it will be found impossible to blow off the upper card.

The attractive force of the blast of air may also be shown by placing the upper card upon the table with its concave surface upwards: then bring the other card immediately over it, and blow through the tube; the card will start up from the table and adhere to the other, so long as the blast is sustained.

air is accomplished by, 2nd, A system of currents, which are caused by subjecting the air to inequalities of temperature. Descending by the walls of the building, it is cooled by the windows, &c., and thus its velocity downwards is increased. Arriving at the level at which it is at once heated and deteriorated by respiration, combustion, &c., the air again rises in the centre of the room, and passes through the ceiling into a foul air chamber, which is in connection with a chimney. Through this chimney the air is driven by a steam jet, which, as already stated, will set in motion 217 times its own bulk of air.   It was shown by Dr. Faraday, in this lecture, how the steam cockle employed to give warmth in winter, might, by filling it with water from the Artesian well, become a source of coolness in summer. The advantages of Mr. Barry's method of ventilation are thus summed up : 1st, The prevention of local draughts. 2nd, The prevention of the stains and disfigurements resulting from such draughts. 3rd, The avoidance of all movement and dispersion of the dirt and dust of the House by currents occasioned in it, which currents, if existing, would tend to render the air impure. 4th, The avoidance of all sudden changes of temperature. Finally, it was noticed that all parts of the House were fire-proof, and that this scheme of ventilation was under a disadvantage, as it had to be adapted to buildings which were not planned with reference to it.

Objections have been made to the vacuum principle of ventilation, on the ground that the air within the room or building thus ventilated is rarer than that without, and that air, even slightly rarefied, occasions languor and uneasiness to persons who are not in robust health, whereas the opposite condition, or condensed air, has a bracing effect both on the body and on the mind. Schemes have been proposed at different times for making air-tight rooms, in which air was to be pumped in or out, according to any degree of pressure adapted to the wants and feelings of the occupants. Thus Dr. Henshaw, in 1664, acting upon one of Mr. Boyle's speculations, proposed such a room " by which any person may receive the benefit of a removal to another climate, at any season of the year, without removal from his own house, or neglecting any employment whatever." This air-tight room was to be occupied two or three hours in the morning in chronical cases ; but in acute diseases the patient might remain in it during the whole course of the disease, as in intermittent fevers, in which case the air was to be rarefied in the cold fit, and condensed in the hot fit. We are not aware whether these fanciful speculations were ever put in practice, but the idea was revived some years ago by Mr. Vallance, who proposed to construct air-tight rooms, with an aperture in the ceiling for pumping in the air, and a peculiarly constructed door for admitting the occupants in and out. The doorway was 6 feet high and 6 feet wide, and was fitted with a cylinder of wood, closed at both ends, and placed upright. In the side was an opening 4 feet wide, and on the opposite side a similar opening. In the centre of this cylinder was a perpendicular revolving shaft, with four leaves crossing at right angles, fitting the cylinder as closely as its revolving motion permitted, and yet preventing the escape or the air at the edges. When a person entered the room, he placed himself between two leaves, like a turnstile, and in this way interfered as little as possible with the enclosed air. A pipe was fixed to the aperture in the ceiling and carried through the roof, where it was inserted a few inches into a cistern of water. Air was injected into the room by means of machinery. When the weather was warm, the injected air was cooled by being passed through pipes surrounded by cold water ; and if heated air were required, the pipes were surrounded by hot water. As the fresh air was pumped in, as much vitiated air was forced out at the pipe in the ceiling, and it escaped through the water in the cistern, which thus ingeniously regulated the pressure of the air in the apartment. When a room is thus filled with condensed air, its expansive force is exerted so that every crevice about it becomes a channel to let air out instead of into it, and thus draughts are effectually prevented.*

From some experiments on this subject by Dr. Junot, it is stated that " when a person is placed in condensed air, he breathes with increased facility; he feels as if the capacity of

* Vallance, "Observations on Ventilation," as quoted by Mr. Bernan.

his lungs were enlarged; his respirations become deeper and less frequent; he experiences in the course of a short time an agreeable glow in his chest, as if the pulmonary cells were becoming dilated with an elastic spirit, while the whole frame receives at each inspiration a fresh vital impulse. The functions of the brain get excited, the imagination becomes vivid, and the ideas flow with a delightful facility; digestion becomes more active, as after gentle exercise in the air, because the secreting organs participate immediately in the increased energy of the arterial system, and there is, therefore, no thirst."

Dr. Ure, in advocating the *plenum* method of ventilation,* gives an example of the effects of condensed air upon some workmen engaged in sinking a shaft to a great depth through the bed of the river Loire, near Languin. In this district the seams of coal lie under a stratum of quicksand, from 20 to 22 yards thick, and they had been found inaccessible by all the modes of mining previously attempted. M. Triger, an able engineer, constructed a shaft encased with strong tubing, formed of a series of large sheet-iron cylinders riveted together. At the top of this cylinder was an air-tight antechamber, into which air was condensed by forcing-pumps with sufficient force to repel the water from the bottom of the cylinder, and thus enable the workmen to excavate the gravel and stones to a great depth. The compartment at the top had a man-hole in its cover, and another in its floor. After the men had entered they shut the door over their heads, and then turned the stop-cock of a pipe in connection with the condensed air in the under-shaft. An equilibrium of pressure was soon established in the antechamber by the influx of the dense air from below, whereby the man-hole in the floor could be readily opened to allow the men to descend. Here they worked in air maintained at a pressure of three atmospheres (or 45 lbs. on the square inch) by the incessant action of leathern valved pumps, driven by a steam-engine. While the dense air thus expelled the waters of the quicksand out of the shaft, it infused such energy into the miners, that they could easily excavate double the work

* Supplement to the " Dictionary of Arts, Manufactures, and Mines."

which they could do in the open air. Upon many of them the effects were painful, especially upon the ears and eyes, but before long they became quite reconciled to the bracing atmosphere. Old asthmatic men became effective workmen ; deaf persons recovered their hearing ; while others were sensible to the slightest whisper.* Much annoyance was at first experienced from the rapid combustion of the candles, but this was obviated by the substitution of flax for cotton in the wicks. The above arrangement is now common in engineering, as, for example, instead of the old method of coffer-dams for the piers of bridges.

In ventilating a building on the plenum method, Dr. Ure recommends that the air be thrown in by means of a fan situated in the basement story,† and instances the method adopted at the Reform Club House (already noticed, p. 244), where there is a large fan revolving rapidly in a cylindrical case, capable of throwing 11,000 cubic feet of air per minute into a spacious subterranean tunnel under the basement story. This fan is driven by a steam-engine of five-horse power. The steam of condensation of the engine supplies three cast-iron chests with the requisite heat for warming the whole of the building. Each of these chests is a cube of 3 feet externally, and is distributed internally into seven parallel cast-iron cases, each about 3 inches wide, which are separated by parallel alternate spaces of the same width, for the passage of the air transversely as it is impelled by the

---

* Many years ago, Mr. Roebuck and another person allowed themselves to be shut up in a cavity excavated in a rock, which served as a reservoir of air for equalising the blast of the bellows in an iron foundry on the banks of the river Devon, near Alloa, in Scotland. As much as 9,300 cubic feet of air were injected per minute, under a pressure of 5 inches of mercury. It was found that sound was greatly magnified, "as we perceived when we talked to each other, or struck anything : particularly the noise of the air escaping at the blow-pipe, or waste valve, was very loud, and seemed to return back to us." There was, however, no wind to disturb the flame of a candle, neither was it blown out when it was placed in the eduction pipe of 16 inches diameter, through which the air passed into the furnace.

† As powerful blasts of air are not required for the purposes of ventilation, a rapid movement of the fan is not necessary. Fans making 2,000 revolutions per minute are exceedingly disagreeable from the noise and vibration occasioned by them. Quantity of air, not velocity, is the object, and for this purpose, fans of 10 or 12 feet diameter, moving slowly, are to be preferred

fan. Dr. Ure describes this arrangement as judicious, economising fuel, because the steam of condensation which in a Watts's engine would be absorbed and carried off by the air-pump, is here turned to good account, in warming the air of ventilation during the winter months. "Two hundredweight of fuel suffice for working this steam-engine during twelve hours. It pumps water for household purposes, raises the coals to the several apartments on the upper floors, and drives the fan ventilator. The air, in flowing rapidly through the series of cells placed alternately between the steam-cases, cannot be scorched as it is generally with air-stoves, but it is heated only to the genial temperature of from 75° to 85° Fahr., and it thence enters a common chamber of brickwork in the basement story, from which it is let off into a series of distinct flues, governed by dialed valves or registers, whereby it is conducted in regulated quantities to the several apartments of the building." In the top story of the building is a large furnace, the draught of which is intended to draw off the air after it has served the purposes of warming and ventilation in the rooms below. Messrs. Easton and Amos are the contrivers of this system.

The arrangements in Sir John Robinson's house at Edinburgh have often been referred to as a sanitary model, the system of ventilation being so perfect that "while the mass of air in the rooms and passages is constantly undergoing renewal by the escape of the vitiated air above and the admission of large supplies of fresh air from below, no currents are perceived in the apartments, which even when crowded with company and amply lighted preserve a remarkable freshness of atmosphere." The sectional area of the cold air passages is about 14 square feet, and they are left open in the coldest weather, provided there is not much wind. The air passages are formed of cylindrical flues of earthenware, 9 inches in diameter, built into the gables, close to the smoke-flues. The lower ends of the ventilating flues open into spaces between the ceilings of the respective rooms and the floors above ; and one or more exit air-flues is provided for each room. The hot, vitiated air passes up through the ceilings by a continuous opening of about 1½ inch in width, behind one of the fillets of the

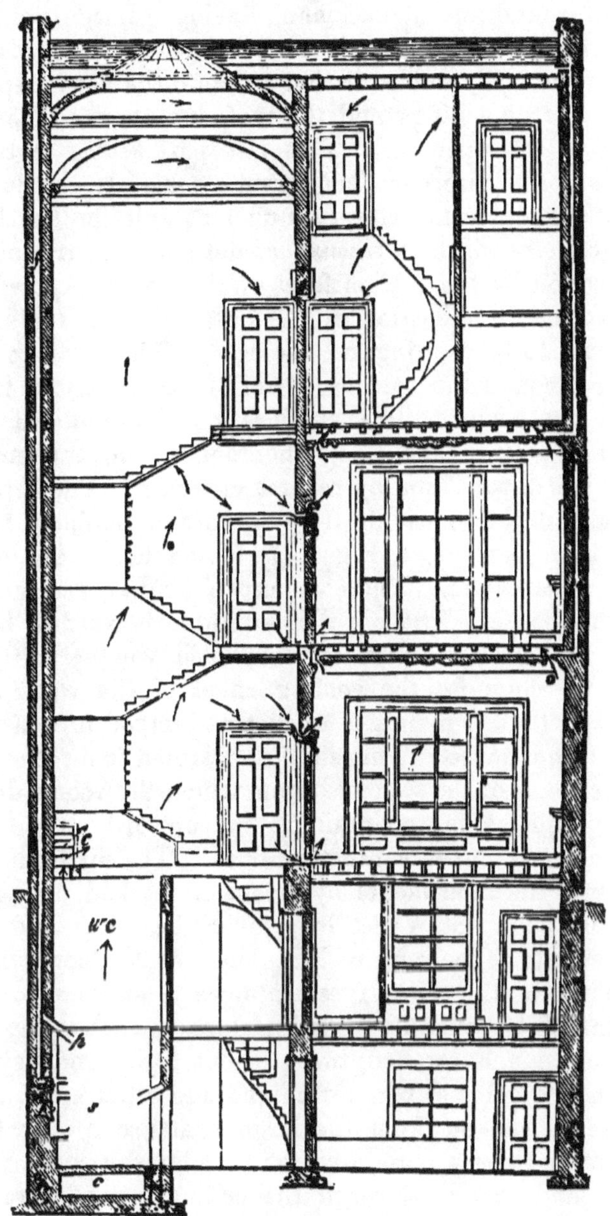

Fig. 127. Warming and Ventilating Arrangements in Sir John Robinson's House.

cornice, all round the rooms, and, having passed into the space between the ceiling and the floor above, it ascends by the flues in the wall, and is discharged into the vacant space between the attic ceilings and the roof, and thence through the slates to the open air. This last part seems to be a defect in an otherwise excellent arrangement. If the joints of the slated roof do not afford a sufficient exit for the hot, vitiated air, there will be a resistance, and consequent cooling or condensation by the cold surfaces of the slates, exposed as they are to the direct action of the outer air. A turret or louvre seems to be wanting on the roof. The passage for the hot air through the cornice is not visible from the floor of any of the rooms. The air flues terminate above the ceilings of the attics, and *below* the roof, to prevent smoke being carried down them by reverse currents. The supply of fresh air to the house is from a garden behind; it is conveyed by a passage, c, Fig. 127, which has a sectional area of 8 square feet. There is also a similar passage in front of the house. The air thus admitted is warmed by a cockle to from 64° to 70°. In very cold weather, 70° is preferred, to allow for the cooling effect of the walls and windows, and thus to maintain a constant temperature of 60° throughout the house. The air thus warmed is discharged into the well, *w c*, of the staircase, from which the rooms draw the supply required for maintaining the upward currents in the chimneys and in the ventilating flues. The air from the well gets into the apartments by means of masked passages, 4 or 5 inches wide and 4 feet long, over the doors, and by openings about 1 inch in width under each door. The sectional areas of these passages are more than equal to the areas of the chimney and ventilating flues, so that as the air within is not much rarefied, there is but little tendency in the outer air to enter at window chinks and other apertures. The course of the air from the large aperture c over the stove, through the staircase, over and under the doors, into the rooms, and thence through the ceilings, and upwards by the escape-flues, is shown by the direction of the arrows: the quantity of escape is regulated by means of throttle-valves at the mouth of each escape-flue, by which the rate of the ventilating current can be increased or diminished. The kitchen is ventilated in a similar manner. One flue proceeds from the ceiling over the fire-place, and another from over the gas cooking-stoves. The first flue is built in the gable close to the smoke-flue, and the second passes upwards by the back of the cistern and pipes of a water-closet, thus protecting them from the action of frost. p is the pipe conveying the smoke from the fire which heats the cockle into the smoke-flue, $f f$. At d is a damper for regulating the draught of this fire.

In the above arrangement, the cockle-stove was used as the source of heat. There are many cases in which the Arnott stove may be used as a means of warming and ventilating, when placed in one of the lowest rooms of the house, and used as a source of heat to the air supplied to the house from without, as in the following ingenious application of it by my late friend Mr. Charles Cowper. In a letter to me a few years ago he says :—

"I tried an experiment this winter, and derived considerable advantage from it, for the water in the jugs in the top rooms of my house did not once freeze, notwithstanding the intense cold. My house consists of four floors of two rooms each, with a wash-house outside at the back. The back kitchen is but little used, so I put one of the smallest Arnott stoves, 14 inches square, in it, applying a sheet-iron plate to close up the chimney of the kitchen range. This heated the staircase a little way, but the heat

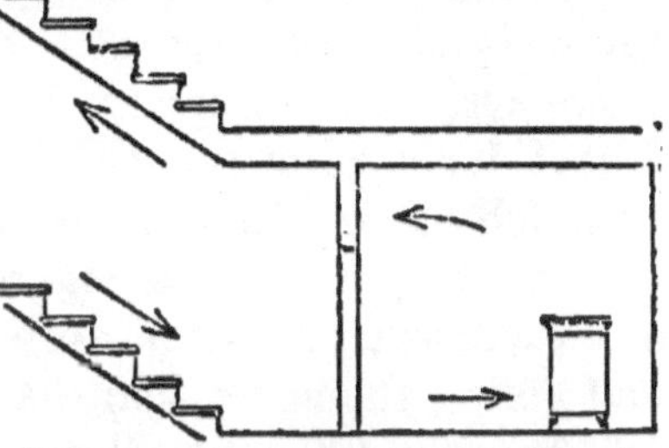

Fig. 128. Method of Warming and Ventilating.

could only get up by means of an upward current under the flight of stairs, and a downward current on the stairs, as shown in Fig. 128. I found that in all states of the wind there was a strong inward current of air at a door opening into the outer air from the back kitchen. There were also inward currents of air even at the top windows of the house. I believe this is the case in nine houses out of

ten, although the house being warmer than the outside, the
air ought to enter at bottom, and escape at top. This shows
that there is no proper entrance provided for the air, and
consequently it is no wonder that we have smoky chimneys.
I therefore had a zinc pipe, 5 inches diameter, A, Fig. 129

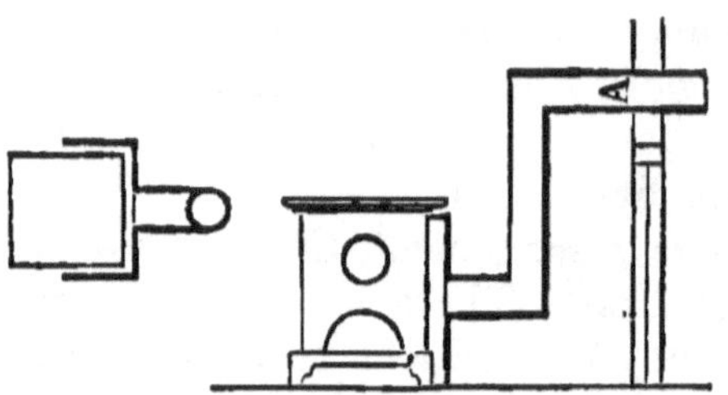

Fig. 129. Arrangement of an Arnott Stove.

brought through the wall, and directed against the side of
the stove, to which I fitted a piece of sheet-iron, so that all
the air entering at the pipe might be forced to spread itself
over the exterior of the stove. I have a damper in the pipe,
but it is left full open when the stove is in use. I have thus
a 5-inch column of air always pouring into the house, and
heated to a comfortable temperature by the stove. This has
much diminished the tendency of the fires to smoke, although
there is still sometimes a down draught in the unused
chimneys. The chimneys in regular use never smoke now.
I consider it quite successful as far as it goes; but it would
be much better with a larger stove and a larger pipe. I had
nothing to guide me as regards the size of the pipe, except
a few experiments by opening the back door $\frac{1}{8}$, $\frac{1}{4}$, and $\frac{1}{2}$ inch,
and noting the effect, and the area of passage thus produced.
In the coldest weather the pipe admitted about as much air
as the stove could take the chill off. If I were going to do
it again, I should make the case to surround as much of the
stove as possible, and make the pipe A much larger, say 10
inches, or with a larger stove 12 inches. I think it is the
right principle to have a large free opening for air at the
bottom of the house. This would stop the cold draughts in
at windows, and prevent down draughts in flues and smoky
chimneys. The air thus entering must have the chill taken

off it, say raised to 50° or 60°; and there should be apertures from the staircase (which is the air main) into the different rooms, that is, if the leakage round the doors is not enough. Perhaps the best plan would be, holes through the top of the door (as in Fig. 130), with a shield to throw the air up if desired. If a room be supplied with air at 50°, a very small fire in the room would serve for comfort, and for carrying off the foul air. It might perhaps be thought that the warm air would all go up to the top of the house, but I find that the staircase is very considerably cooler at the upper part, and gets gradually warmer and warmer in descending from the top to the bottom. I have no doubt that a larger entrance-pipe for the air would send the heat up higher, but I have no fear of too much heat going to the top. With my

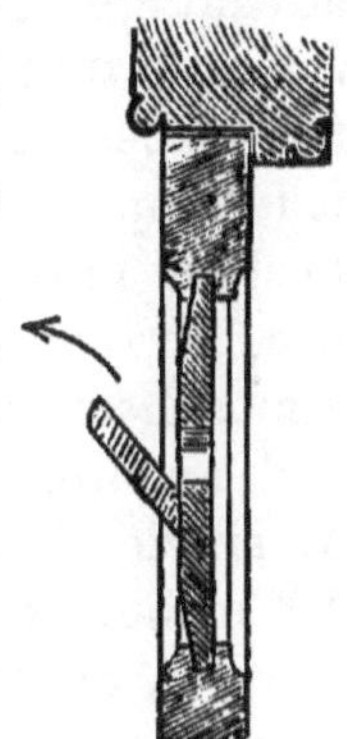

Fig. 130.

5-inch pipe, I have still both ascending and descending currents on the staircase, and I think this will always be the case.

"I had a good deal of trouble at first by the products of combustion from the stove coming back into the room round the iron plate, which was not built in. I found that this was owing to the flue of a copper in the washhouse entering the same chimney near the bottom, so that the air blew through the copper flues, and down the chimney into the room. I made a wooden stopper covered with canvas, to fit the front of the copper furnace, which effectually cured this defect."

A combined method of warming and ventilating was recommended in the Report on the Warming and Ventilation of Dwellings, to which reference has been already made. The difficulty of applying a good system of ventilation to all descriptions of dwelling-houses is admitted, and especially to old houses, where the flues and other constructions are not adapted for its introduction; but much might be done in every dwelling if the supply of air for the fire were separated from that required for ventilation. In new buildings the necessary contrivances, flues, channels, &c., could easily be introduced, and a good system of warming and ventilating be at once adopted. Thus, for example, in the section shown in the accompanying steel engraving, an attempt is made to keep the air of the room and that which passes through the fire separate; and thus, while securing the advantages, to get rid of the defects of chimney ventilation. Suppose that in such a house there are eight rooms with the fire-places arranged back to back against the partition wall; it is proposed in this case to convey all the products of combustion into a single vertical flue, $b\,b$, while to supply the fire, air ducts or channels, $f\,f$, leading from the external atmosphere, are introduced beneath the flooring in each room, and opening to the fire at the hearthstone. The chimney or single flue would probably not require to be more than 10 inches in diameter, and might be made of clay-pipes vitrified or glazed inside. Immediately above the fire-place in each room, the smoke-flue, $b\,b$, would have a descending branch flue to fit into the throat above the fire-grate, and this part would be constructed so as to be air-tight in relation to the surrounding air chambers. On this plan the products of combustion from all the fires of the house are collected into one flue with the kitchen fires at the bottom, so as to ensure more or less heat passing up the chimney at all times of the year. Around the smoke-flue, b, it is proposed to leave an open annular space, $a\,a$, passing up the whole length of the chimney, from the top of the kitchen flue to the full height of the shaft at $h\,h$, Fig. 1. This might be made of an octagonal form, as shown in plan, Fig. 2. This chamber would become the means of relieving the rooms of their vitiated air, the heated smoke-flue causing a constant current to rise through it, carrying along with it the injurious products of each room by the apertures, $c\,c\,c$, and passing off above by the apertures, $h\,h$, beneath the chimney cornice. "Thus, the fire being supplied with air by a sufficiently capacious air duct, the constant loss of heat and draughts from windows and doors are obviated, while at the same time the air of the room is kept pure by the passing away, at all times during the day and evening, of those portions least fitted for respiration, and without the possibility of the passage of smoke through the apertures intended for ventilation." Should one smoke-flue be liable to counter-draughts descending from the fires on one side to those of the other, two smoke-flues might be fixed in the air chamber, as at *k k*, Fig. 3; or the single flue might be divided by a partition as at *n n*, Fig. 4; either of which plans would prevent ascending currents from one room descending into another room. It is clearly seen that this system would not only diminish the quantity of smoke from the fires, but would retain the air surrounding the smoke-flue at all times in a rarefied state, ensuring a constant current of fresh air passing through the different rooms, and requiring no other fire except that of the kitchen to be lighted. The perfectly straight vertical flue would admit of great facility in brushing and cleaning, and by extending the tube or tubes downwards, a dust-hole, *g*, Fig. 1, might be formed under the kitchen fire, from which the soot could be removed as it accumulated, at convenient intervals. A perfectly close and tight damper should also be fixed in the throat of each fire that communicates with the vertical smoke-flue, so as effectually to shut off any particular room from the smoke-flue during the summer months when fires are not used.

A great saving of fuel would be produced by double panes of glass in small rooms, and double sashes in large rooms, with a stratum of 5 or 6 inches of air between the two sashes. In rooms where the glazing surface is large, double sashes are more needed than in smaller rooms. Double windows would also greatly diminish the effect of street noises.

The Commissioners found that the use of gas for heating purposes, in places remote from the coal districts, was too expensive, but many attempts have been made to ventilate the rooms of an ordinary dwelling-house in which gas is used for illuminating, by means of the heat thereof. The following plan is by Mr. R. Brown, of Manchester. Through an opening in the ceiling is passed a wide tube, one end of which conveys the foul air to the outside of the house, and the other projects a little below the level of the ceiling. The gas-pipe enters on one side, and is bent so as to hang perpendicularly in the centre of the tube, and carries an annular burner at the lower extremity. The burner is surrounded by a glass chimney, which is supported at its top on a metal cone-piece, and secured to the lower extremity of the tube by screws. The whole of this arrangement is surrounded by a hemispherical glass shade, the mouth of which is uppermost, and its upper edge is a few inches below the level of the ceiling. The shade is attached at its upper edge by screws to a metal ring, and is hinged to a second ring fixed to the ventilating tube by radial arms. This outer shade can be lowered by means of a cord, for the purpose of lighting or cleaning. A highly polished metal reflector is also added to increase the effect of the light. The air of the apartment passes off in the strong draught occasioned by the burner, and a fresh supply of air is admitted at the lower part of the room.

In the ventilation of public buildings which are open chiefly by night, such as theatres, concert rooms, lecture halls, &c., the means adopted for lighting usually form a powerful ventilating force. A direct experiment was made by M. Morin, to show how far the gas used for lighting the room might not only remove the vitiated air, but be the means of introducing a proportional quantity of fresh air. For this purpose the window frame was removed from the window of a large dining-room, and the space was filled up with a zinc box, $a\,b\,c\,d$ (Fig. 131), divided by vertical partitions, $e\,g$, into three compartments; the middle compartment had an opening, t, near the bottom, by which the air was drawn out of the room, and near the top on the further or exterior side was an opening, $l\,l$, for the discharge of the vitiated air. About midway in this compartment were a dozen jets of gas, before which was placed a curved glass pane, $m\,m$, through which the dining-room was illuminated. Thus a ventilating force was established by means of the gas jets in this central

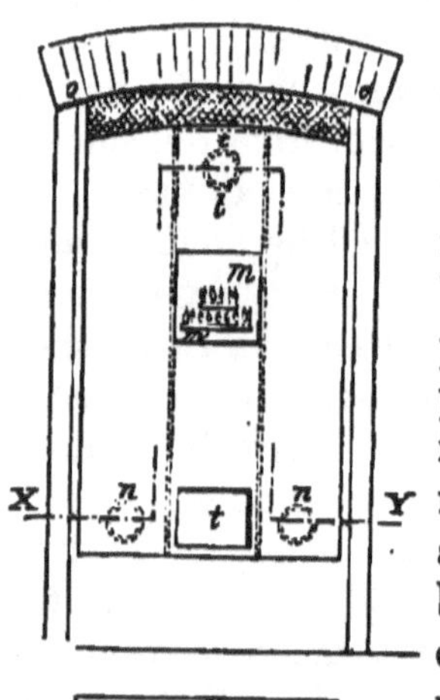
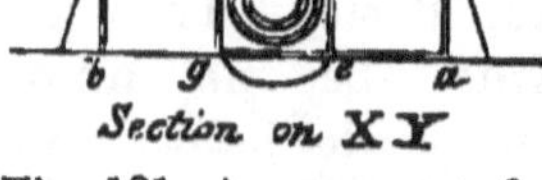

Fig. 131. Arrangement for Lighting and Ventilation.

compartment, the air of the room passing from *t* to the outside through the aperture   At the same time fresh air was allowed to enter by the two outer partitions, which were furnished with openings, *n n*, on the outside, which air, passing up through these two outer partitions, escaped into the room through the meshes of the wire gauze, *o o*, placed near the top.

During the day, when the pressure of gas was weak and variable, the results of the arrangement were variable; but as a general result it was found that the combustion of a cubic metre of gas, or 35 cubic feet, produced a discharge of 13,650 cubic feet of air at a mean temperature of 131° Fahr., thereby bringing in a supply of fresh air equal to from 14,000 to 15,400 cubic feet.

It is stated that a more powerful effect would have been produced if the gas had been divided into a number of separate jets enclosed within a larger number of ventilating openings; but under the conditions observed, from twelve to fifteen persons in the room during four or five hours in the evening were supplied each with more than 19 cubic feet of fresh air per minute.

APPENDIX.

HISTORICAL NOTE ON THE INVENTOR OF THE SO-CALLED POLIGNAC FIRE-PLACE.

WHEN this book was re-issued in 1858, a correction was made with respect to a statement in the First Edition, and although the interest that attaches to it is purely historical, it is right to repeat it here. Its effect is to restore to an old inventor the honour of which he has been most unjustly deprived. At pages 88 to 94 of this edition, the celebrated *Polignac fire-place*, which has served as the type of many modern inventions, is described. Having had to write an article a few years ago on "Warming and Ventilation" for the *Quarterly Review*, I had occasion to inquire under what circumstances so great a man as the Cardinal Polignac made this useful invention. Mr. Bernan states in his "History of Warming and Ventilating Rooms, &c.," that the Cardinal wrote the description of his fire-place under the assumed name of *Gauger*, and my description of the fire-place already referred to was taken from Gauger's book. Mr. Bernan opens the second volume of his work in the following manner :—

"The Cardinal Polignac is known as one of the most classic of modern Latin poets; and his biographers, in their admiration of his nervous versification, profound reasoning, and benevolence of sentiment, place him almost above the great Roman author whose opinions he combats and overthrows.

"A small work in a different style of composition, and on a somewhat unpoetical subject, that he composed in 1713, also possesses superlative merit. In this useful treatise the cleric prince observes, that persons who value a machine only from the apparently great effort of genius required to invent it, from the complexity of its parts, the difficulties encountered, and money spent in bringing it into notice, will find little to please their romantic taste in his performance. But those of a more correct judgment, who can see worth in a contrivance notwithstanding its simplicity of construction and easiness of execution, will perhaps prefer his apparatus to more ostentatious productions; and what, for instance, can be more pleasant, useful, economical, and necessary, than to know how to make a fire speedily, and make it burn vividly without the aid of bellows? to heat a capacious room with a small fire, and at the same time breathe an air fresh and pure, as well as healthily warm? In *Le Mécanique à Feu* he shows how these and other desirable comforts may be obtained by means of a very simple contrivance."—BERNAN, vol. ii. p. 1.

This statement of Mr. Bernan, repeated by subsequent writers, that the Cardinal de Polignac was the inventor of a new and greatly improved fire-place, and that he described it in a treatise published in 1713, induced me to examine more carefully the original treatise. I found two copies of the work in the Library of the British Museum, but these were reprints published at Amsterdam in 1714; and on the title-page the author's name appeared as "*Monsieur G* * * *." I also found in the same library an English translation of the treatise "set forth in French by Monsieur Gauger," published in 1716. I also found in the Library of the Royal Society a translation, or rather an adaptation of the work by Dr. Desaguliers.* To my surprise the learned doctor gave no hint as to the illustrious authorship of the book, a circumstance altogether unaccountable if he were aware of it; for what so likely to make his translation popular, or to favour the introduction of the stoves into England, which appears to have been his intention? To suppose ignorance in Desaguliers, would be to suppose what is scarcely possible, namely, that so eminent a personage as the Cardinal de Polignac should have caused the stove to be constructed, should have allowed his friends to see it

---

* "FIRES IMPROV'D: Being a New Method of Building Chimneys, so as to prevent their Smoking: in which A *Small* Fire shall warm a Room better than a much *Larger* made the *Common Way*. With the manner of altering such Chimneys as are already Built, so that they shall perform the same effects. Illustrated with Cuts. Written in *French*, by Monsieur Gauger: made *English*, and improved, by J. T. Desaguliers, M.A., F.R.S. By whom is added, The Manner of making COAL-FIRES, as useful this *New-Way*, as the WOOD FIRES propos'd by the *French* Author. Explain'd by an additional Plate. The whole being suited to the Capacity of the meanest Workman." London, 1715.

in action, and should have published an elaborate description of it, and yet should be able to prevent the authorship of the treatise from becoming speedily known all over Europe. I next consulted the biographical notices of the Cardinal for information on this point, but in vain; yet, meeting with a passage in Madame de Sevigné's letters, in which she said of Polignac, "Il sait tout, il parle de tout, il a toute la douceur, la vivacité, la complaisance, qu'on peut souhaiter dans le commerce," the probability again dawned upon me, that with talents so versatile, he might, after all, have been the inventor of the fire-place. Accordingly, I looked through a more copious life of the Cardinal, written by Père Faucher, and published in two volumes in 1780. This work supplied much that was amusing and interesting: it described its hero as an orator, a poet, a diplomatist, an antiquarian, and what was more to the purpose, a cultivator of the arts and sciences, but still not a word about the fire-place. Again, knowing that Dr. Franklin had taken this so-called Polignac fire-place as the basis of his improved Pennsylvanian fire-place, I consulted Dr. Franklin's works, and found him more than once referring to these stoves as the invention of a *Monsieur Gauger*, and not once ascribing them to the Cardinal. Anxious, if possible, to see the Paris editions of the treatise ascribed to Polignac, I repaired to the library of the Royal Society, where I found the edition published at Paris in 1749, with the name of the author, Monsieur Gauger, honestly looking one in the face. It then occurred to me—what, if after all, Gauger should have been a real personage, and not a mere *nom de plume?* Impressed with this idea, I consulted the *Biographie Universelle*, and in the sixteenth volume, published in 1816, I found the following entry, "GAUGER (Nicholas)," prefacing a notice of his life by M. Pataud, a few points of which it is of importance to state.

"Nicholas Gauger was born near Pithiviers, about the year 1680. He early devoted himself to the study of experimental philosophy, and supported himself by giving experimental lectures in Paris. His character and acquirements gained him the friendship of P. Desmolets of the Oratoire, and of the Chevalier de Louville. The latter said that Gauger, in repeating the experiments of Newton, arrived at more certain results than any of his competitors. Gauger died in 1730, after having published a work entitled 'Mécanique du Feu, ou l'Art d' en augmenter les effets

et d' en diminuer la depense.'   The first part of this work contained the 'Traité des nouvelles Cheminées qui échauffent plus que
les cheminées ordinaires, et qui ne sont point sujetes à fumer.'
Paris, 1713, 1749, in 12mo., embellished with twelve plates. This
work has been often reprinted, and translated into different languages, and includes a great part of the inventions of this description, which have since been published as new. It contains an
account of those healthful fire-places and stoves in which there is
a double current of air, invented by the same author, and described
in the *Collection des Machines* of the Academy of Sciences for the
year 1720, Nos. 218 to 222. Gauger's process having been followed
for the first time by his brother, a Chartreux monk, the fire-places
made after that principle came to be called fire-places *à la Char-
treuse.*"   I learn from the same memoir, that in 1728, Gauger
published an essay on the refrangibility of the rays of light, and
also an answer to the objections to Newton's Theory of the Composition of White Light. It appears from the title-page of an
essay on Thermometers and Barometers, published in 1722, that
Gauger was "Avocat au Parlement de Paris, et Censure Royale
des livres."

With this evidence before me, and more to which I shall
presently refer, I returned once more to the consideration of
Mr. Bernan's work, and found that he continued in the same
strain as the extract above given, to describe through fourteen
pages " the Cardinal's " invention, and to give us "the Cardinal's "
thoughts on the matter in " a style of composition " unlike enough
to the polished diction of Polignac. He repeatedly ascribes the
authorship of *Le Mécanique à Feu,* as he persists in calling *La
Mécanique du Feu,* to Cardinal Polignac; in one place saying,
patronisingly, " In his meritorious treatise, the Cardinal delineates
several complex varieties of his fire-place," vol. ii. p. 6. In
another, in *Le Mécanique à Feu,* the Cardinal describes one
" arrangement of his fire-place with the caliducts or meanders
perpendicular," &c., p. 7. " This arrangement was deservedly
recommended by the Cardinal as the best of the series described
in his treatise," p. 11. " And the whole arrangement, continues
the Cardinal, is so simple, so convenient, and easy of execution,
that it is best adapted for general use, and ' I myself at this
moment apply it to very good purpose,'" p. 12. . " In the course
of his experience the Cardinal found that his fire-place was a

perfect specific against the annoyance of smoke in rooms, which
destroyed the lungs of those who breathed it, and smutched the
finishings of the walls, furniture, and everything in the apartment,
' and particularly the lace, linen, skin, and eyes of the ladies,' "
p. 14. Mr. Bernan went a step too far for the most credulous of
readers when he ascribed to Polignac, the most polished gentleman
and finished orator of his age, any term which could be translated
into the " smutched eyes " of ladies. At p. 119 he returns to the
subject, and says that " Cardinal Polignac attempted to reflect the
radiant heat into the room from parabolic covings."

Could one suppose that Mr. Bernan's statements were made in
ignorance, or that they had arisen from some unaccountable
blunder, or from a too credulous following of previous writers,
one might be disposed to pardon, while we must continue to
deplore, an error which has led others astray. But when I
observe that he has consulted all the authorities where the truth
stands plainly revealed—that he has consulted Desaguliers' translation of Gauger's work, that he quotes from the " Experimental
Philosophy " of Desaguliers, and even from the very same postscript
in which the doctor says—" In the year 1715 I translated from
the French a book called *La Mécanique du Feu*, which I knew to
be written by Monsieur Gauger, a very ingenious gentleman of
Paris, though he concealed his name; "[*] when I find that Mr.
Bernan is aware of the engravings of Gauger's fire-place, in the
Memoirs of the French Academy of Sciences for 1720, where the
invention is fully described and imputed to its rightful author,
and where the question of the printed treatise is not left doubtful,
but is thus noticed:—" M. Gauger a fait un Traité sur cette
matière intitulé *La Mécanique du Feu* ou il s' etend beaucoup sur
cette sorte de cheminées, &c. ;"[†] when I find, moreover, that
Mr. Bernan has consulted Dr. Franklin's writings, where, in a list
of fire-places, mention is twice made of these of Gauger, and reference made to M. Gauger's tract, entitled *La Mécanique du Feu ;*"[‡]
when all these things are considered, with a knowledge of the
fact that both Gauger's Life in the *Biographie Universelle*,[§] and

[*] Desaguliers' " Experimental Philosophy," vol. ii. p. 557. London, 1763.
[†] *Machines et Inventions approuvées par L'Académie Royale des Sciences.
Tome quatrième. Depuis 1720, jusqu' 1726.* Published at Paris, 1735.
[‡] " The Works of Benjamin Franklin." By Jared Sparks. Boston, 1840.
Vol. vi. pp. 38 and 41.
[§] *Biographie Universelle.* Tome xvi. pp. 576, 577.

Polignac's Memoirs by Faucher,* were as open to Mr. Bernan as they were to any one, and that while in the latter there is not a syllable of any such invention being attributed or attributable to the Cardinal, in the former there is a distinct mention of Gauger's inventions, with the full title of the book which describes them (*Mécanique du Feu*, &c.), a notice of the parts into which the work was divided, its success, and translation into other languages, &c.,—considering this, my conclusion is, that Mr. Bernan has committed one of the most unaccountable blunders which has come under my notice for many a day.

* *Histoire du Cardinal de Polignac.*   By Père Faucher.   Paris, 1780.

THE END.

J. S Virtue, Printer, City Road, London.

INTRODUCTION TO THE STUDY

OF

NATURAL PHILOSOPHY;

FOR THE USE OF BEGINNERS.

Sixth Edition.   Price One Shilling.

"This little book is the first of a series of scientific treatises, which promise well.   Mr. Tomlinson's 'Introduction to Natural Philosophy' is broad and general, taking a summary review of the leading principles of those sciences, which are afterwards to be more fully expounded. Although dealing with striking examples in Natural Philosophy, the facts are made subservient to the principles they illustrate, and are used not for themselves, but the laws they establish.   Astronomy, and its geometrical proofs, the properties of matter, optics, sound, and other branches of Natural Philosophy, are exhibited in one or more remarkable examples of profound and conclusive discovery by man of the laws of nature, illustrated, where needful, by diagrams.   Although designed for popular circulation, and to stimulate the popular mind, there is no evasion of difficulties in Mr. Tomlinson's Introduction.   Having done an author's part in making the exposition as plain as he can, he calls upon the reader to do his, and to give attention to the task.   The book is remarkably cheap, looking at its kind; and such, we suppose, will be the character of the series."—*Spectator*, September 23, 1848.

"Mr. Tomlinson's Natural Philosophy is a very masterly performance; exact, lucid, and (beyond most works of the same class) interesting.   It has its 'Preface,' too; but one which is, happily, of the same grain with the work; and contains a piece of advice to 'the reader' of so just and sensible a character, and of such general application to the readers of all scientific works, that we beg to indorse it with our heartiest concurrence:—

"'But if scientific men are disposed to prepare popular treatises, and intelligent publishers to issue them, at a price sufficient to bring them within the reach of every one, it is not too much to expect the co-operation of the reader in carrying out so praiseworthy an object.   The reader must be prepared to bestow a higher effort of mind in the perusal of the work than is required for the appreciation of a romance, or even of a treatise on *popular science,* as this term is often understood.   He must be prepared to *study* the work, and not merely to glance over its pages. If he find it difficult on a first perusal, let him give it a second, or a third, and we may venture to assure him that his labour will not be misapplied.' "—*Mechanics' Magazine*, December 9, 1848.

"Carefully written, and amply illustrated."—*Athenæum*, December 30, 1848.

"Though there is no 'royal road' to science, yet it must be confessed that the paths which conduct the student to her temple have been so well macademised, and so many finger-posts have been erected by the way, that none but the incompetent or the indolent need despair of arriving at its threshold. The volume before us, *parva sed apta*, is one of these serviceable finger-posts erected by one who is thoroughly familiar with the road, and competent to offer valuable advice and assistance to younger and feebler wayfarers. 'To excite an interest in the study of principles, by making facts' and details subordinate to this higher aim,' was the object proposed to himself by the author in preparing this treatise for publication; and we should think that object will be found to have been generally accomplished with the most complete success. Taking the student by the hand, Mr. Tomlinson conducts him by a gradual ascent through all the stages of physical science, expounding the laws of nature in language clear, perspicuous, and intelligible to the most ordinary capacity, and offering at one compendious view the accumulated but simplified results—the facts and principles which have been established by the observations and experiments of generations of natural philosophers. As a class-book for schools, this work will be found of the utmost value; and the low price at which it is published is not the least among its recommendations to the favourable notice of the public. Mr. Tomlinson is, we believe, so well known in this neighbourhood, that his name upon the title-page will be accepted as a sufficient guarantee of the character of any scientific work he may put forth."—*Salisbury Journal*, December 1, 1849.

RUDIMENTARY MECHANICS;

BEING A

CONCISE EXPOSITION OF THE GENERAL PRINCIPLES OF MECHANICAL SCIENCE, AND THEIR APPLICATION.

Sixth Edition. Price One Shilling.

"The Rudiments of Mechanics is by the same able hand of whose execution of the part devoted to Natural Philosophy we felt called upon to speak in very high terms. The style of Mr. Tomlinson's lessons is altogether excellent, exact, and impressive, where principles are to be enunciated; copious, circumstantial, and yet clear, where the application of principles to practice has to be exemplified. . . . . We are not aware of any other treatise on mechanics with the same quantity of matter, and with so many engravings, which is to be had at so low a price."—*Mechanics' Magazine*, April 21, 1849.

PNEUMATICS;

FOR THE USE OF BEGINNERS.

Third Edition. Price One Shilling.

RUDIMENTARY TREATISE

ON

WARMING AND VENTILATION.

Third Edition, 1864.   *Price Two Shillings.*

"The student of science cannot commit himself to the guidance of a better teacher than Mr. Tomlinson, who is not merely thoroughly master of the subject on which he writes, but also possesses the faculty of communicating scientific knowledge in a clear and intelligible form, without involving the reader's mind in a maze of technicalities, or hurrying the student up to the higher results of science before he has removed the obstructions which crowd upon his path in the earlier stages of the pursuit. It would be superfluous to enlarge upon the importance of ventilation (the subject of the treatise before us). Mankind are beginning to perceive that to breathe is as perilous as to drink poison; and that no small portion of the sickness and suffering to which we are liable, is entirely referable to our ignorance or neglect of some of the simplest laws of nature. In fact, the ingenuity we display in perverting the wise and beautiful arrangements by which the operations of nature are made subservient to our health and enjoyment, and the whole economy of the physical world is subordinated to the sustentation of human life, borders closely on the marvellous. This consideration will often force itself upon the mind of the reader as he studies this treatise; a diligent perusal of which is not only essential to a thorough comprehension of the physical and chemical principles concerned in the art of warming and ventilation, but is also calculated to induce serious thoughts on the extreme importance of the subject, and so lead to practical results, prospectively affecting the health and longevity of the reader."—*Salisbury Journal.*

"Warming and Ventilation have now become essentials of house accommodation: it is strange, indeed, they should ever have been neglected, and that a chief labour now is in supplying the defects and remedying the mistakes of those who have gone before us. The subject, treated scientifically, is still new enough to justify any attempt at removing its difficulties, and we have therefore welcomed more than one work which have lately appeared. The present had a popular destination, and the author seems fully to have understood his mission, and in a small compass gives clear ideas, without neglecting the development of principles. Mr. Tomlinson begins at the beginning, and by explaining the physical and chemical principles on which the art of warming and ventilation is founded, he enables the student to understand the practical part of the subject."—*The Architect.*

EXPERIMENTAL ESSAYS.

I. ON THE MOTIONS OF CAMPHOR ON WATER.
II. ON THE MOTION OF CAMPHOR TOWARDS THE LIGHT.
III. ON THE MODERN THEORY OF DEW.

Price One Shilling.

The object of this Work is to show the amateur in science how to conduct a scientific inquiry, whether with a view to discover new facts, or to trace the progress of old ones up to a settled theory. The following notice of the book is from the *Athenæum* of September 19, 1863: —

"These Essays are accompanied by an Introduction, in which the author draws attention to the fact, that there are very few natural objects which have been studied so thoroughly that new investigations may not throw light on them. He then proceeds to show how researches on natural objects may be pursued, in such a manner as not only to afford the highest interest, but to enable the observer to enlarge the bounds of science; and this not with great expense, but by means at the command of everyone. In order to show what may be done, he records his own observations on the subjects of the first two essays. The facts that camphor moves on water, and when kept in a bottle has a tendency to crystallize on that side of the bottle which is towards the light, are familiar to most persons. But what are the causes of these phenomena? After recording all that has been written on the subject, the author gives his own researches, and shows on what these phenomena depend. We cannot here follow Mr. Tomlinson in his experiments, but we have no doubt of the correctness of his conclusions; and can recommend the study of the two essays as well calculated to lead persons interested in experimental research to follow his example in examining some of the simple phenomena of nature by which they are surrounded. The third essay is an examination of the claims of Dr. Wells to be considered the discoverer of the theory of dew. In this essay the author shows what great advances in a knowledge of radiant heat other observers had made, but claims for Dr. Wells the merit of having placed the true theory of dew in a position to demand universal assent."

"A delightful little book, evidently intended to find its way into the hands of young people, by whom most of the experiments may be performed without danger and with great advantage. The Author says truly, 'Nature speaks so lovingly to the young, and they respond so willingly, that we may well take advantage of this circumstance to gratify a taste which encourages the order, method, and exactness of science.' "— *The Builder*, April 11, 1863.

"Written with so much intelligibleness and pleasantness that they come within universal comprehension, and will certainly give to those who study them and are directed by them in personal experiment, not only much immediate knowledge, but the method of conducting scientific inquiry at little cost and with much easily appreciable result."—*Nonconformist*, May 26, 1863.

"The aim of this small volume appears to be to impress upon the scientific student the importance of the services which may be rendered to science, by the diligent investigation of the properties of many of the commonest objects, without the aid of any expensive or recondite apparatus."--*Spectator*, July, 1863.

CATALOGUE

OF

RUDIMENTARY, SCIENTIFIC, EDUCATIONAL, AND CLASSICAL WORKS,

FOR COLLEGES, HIGH AND ORDINARY SCHOOLS, AND SELF-INSTRUCTION;

ALSO FOR

MECHANICS' INSTITUTIONS, FREE LIBRARIES, &c. &c.,

PUBLISHED BY

VIRTUE BROTHERS & CO., 1, AMEN CORNER,

PATERNOSTER ROW, LONDON.

. THE ENTIRE SERIES IS FREELY ILLUSTRATED ON WOOD
AND STONE WHERE REQUISITE.

The Public are respectfully informed that the whole of the late MR. WEALE'S *Publications, contained in the following Catalogue, have been purchased by* VIRTUE BROTHERS & CO., *and that all future Orders will be supplied by them at* 1, AMEN CORNER.

. Additional Volumes, by Popular Authors, are in Preparation.

RUDIMENTARY SERIES.

2. NATURAL PHILOSOPHY, by Charles Tomlinson. 1s.

12. PNEUMATICS, by Charles Tomlinson. 1s.

20. PERSPECTIVE, by George Pyne. 2s.

27. PAINTING; or, A GRAMMAR OF COLOURING, by G. Field. 2s.

40. GLASS STAINING, by Dr. M. A. Gessert, With an Appendix on the Art of Enamelling. 1s.

December, 1865.

VIRTUE BROTHERS & CO., 1, AMEN CORNER.

151. A HANDY BOOK ON THE LAW OF FRIENDLY, IN-
     DUSTRIAL AND PROVIDENT, BUILDING AND LOAN
     SOCIETIES, by N. White. 1s.
152. PRACTICAL HINTS FOR INVESTING MONEY: with
     an Explanation of the Mode of Transacting Business on the
     Stock Exchange, by Francis Playford, Sworn Broker. 1s.
153. LOCKE ON THE CONDUCT OF THE HUMAN UNDER-
     STANDING, Selections from, by S. H. Emmens. 2s.
154. GENERAL HINTS TO EMIGRANTS. 2s.

PHYSICAL SCIENCE.

1. CHEMISTRY, by Prof. Fownes, including Agricultural Chemistry, for the use of Farmers. 1s.
3. GEOLOGY, by Major-Gen. Portlock. 1s. 6d.
4. MINERALOGY, with a Treatise on Mineral Rocks or Aggre-
   gates, by Dana. 2s.
7. ELECTRICITY, by Sir W. S. Harris. 1s. 6d.
7*. GALVANISM, ANIMAL AND VOLTAIC ELECTRICITY,
    by Sir W. S. Harris. 1s. 6d.
8. MAGNETISM, Exposition of, by Sir W. S. Harris. 3s. 6d.
11. ELECTRIC TELEGRAPH, History of, by E. Highton. 2s.
133. METALLURGY OF COPPER, by R. H. Lamborn. 2s.
134. METALLURGY OF SILVER AND LEAD, by R. H. Lam-
     born. 2s.
135. ELECTRO-METALLURGY, by A. Watt. 1s. 6d.
138. HANDBOOK OF THE TELEGRAPH, by R. Bond. 1s.
143. EXPERIMENTAL ESSAYS—On the Motion of Camphor
     and Modern Theory of Dew, by C. Tomlinson. 1s.

BUILDING AND ARCHITECTURE.

16. ARCHITECTURE, Orders of, by W. H. Leeds. 1s.
17. ——————————— Styles of, by T. Bury. 1s. 6d.
18. ——————————— Principles of Design, by E. L. Garbett. 2s.
22. BUILDING, the Art of, by E. Dobson. 1s.
23. BRICK AND TILE MAKING, by E. Dobson. 2s.
25. MASONRY AND STONE-CUTTING, by E. Dobson. 2s.
30. DRAINING AND SEWAGE OF TOWNS AND BUILD-
    INGS, by G. D. Dempsey. 2s.
    (With No. 29, DRAINAGE OF LAND, 2 vols. in 1, 3s.)

35. BLASTING AND QUARRYING OF STONE, AND BLOW-
ING UP OF BRIDGES, by Lt.-Gen. Sir J. Burgoyne. 1s. 6d.

36. DICTIONARY OF TERMS used by Architects, Builders,
Engineers, Surveyors, &c. 4s.
   In cloth boards, 5s.; half morocco, 6s.

42. COTTAGE BUILDING, by C. B. Allen. 1s.

44. FOUNDATIONS and CONCRETE WORKS, by E. Dobson. 1s.

45. LIMES, CEMENTS, MORTARS, CONCRETE, MASTICS,
&c., by G. R. Burnell. 1s.

57. WARMING AND VENTILATION, by C. Tomlinson. 3s.

83**. CONSTRUCTION OF DOOR LOCKS, by C. Tomlinson.
1s. 6d.

111. ARCHES, PIERS, AND BUTTRESSES, by W. Bland. 1s. 6d.

116. ACOUSTICS OF PUBLIC BUILDINGS, by T. R. Smith. 1s. 6d.

123. CARPENTRY AND JOINERY, founded on Robison and
Tredgold. 1s. 6d.

123*. ILLUSTRATIVE PLATES to the preceding. 4to. 4s. 6d.

124. ROOFS FOR PUBLIC AND PRIVATE BUILDINGS,
founded on Robison, Price, and Tredgold. 1s. 6d.

124*. IRON ROOFS of Recent Construction—Descriptive Plates.
4to. 4s. 6d.

127. ARCHITECTURAL MODELLING, Practical Instructions,
by T. A. Richardson. 1s. 6d.

128. VITRUVIUS'S ARCHITECTURE, translated by J. Gwilt,
with Plates. 5s.

130. GRECIAN ARCHITECTURE, Principles of Beauty in, by
the Earl of Aberdeen. 1s.

132. ERECTION OF DWELLING-HOUSES, with Specifications,
Quantities of Materials, &c., by S. H. Brooks, 27 Plates. 2s. 6d.

MACHINERY AND ENGINEERING.

33. CRANES AND MACHINERY FOR RAISING HEAVY
BODIES, the Art of Constructing, by J. Glynn. 1s.

34. STEAM ENGINE, by Dr. Lardner. 1s.

43. TUBULAR AND IRON GIRDER BRIDGES, including the
Britannia and Conway Bridges, by G. D. Dempsey. 1s.

47. LIGHTHOUSES, their Construction and Illumination, by Allan Stevenson. 3s.

59. STEAM BOILERS, their Construction and Management, by R. Armstrong. 1s. 6d.

62. RAILWAYS, Construction, by Sir M. Stephenson. 1s. 6d.

62*. RAILWAY CAPITAL AND DIVIDENDS, with Statistics of Working, by E. D. Chattaway. 1s.
(Vols. 62 and 62* bound in 1, 2s. 6d.)

67. CLOCK AND WATCH MAKING, and Church Clocks and Bells, by E. B. Denison. 3s. 6d.

78. STEAM AND LOCOMOTION, on the Principle of connecting Science with Practice, by J. Sewell. 2s.

78*. LOCOMOTIVE ENGINES, by G. D. Dempsey. 1s. 6d.

79*. ILLUSTRATIONS TO THE ABOVE. 4to. 4s. 6d.

98. MECHANISM AND CONSTRUCTION OF MACHINES, by T. Baker; and TOOLS AND MACHINES, by J. Nasmyth, with 220 Woodcuts. 2s. 6d.

114. MACHINERY, Construction and Working, by C. D. Abel. 1s. 6d.

115. PLATES TO THE ABOVE. 4to. 7s. 6d.

139. STEAM ENGINE, Mathematical Theory of, by T. Baker. 1s.

CIVIL ENGINEERING, &c.

13. CIVIL ENGINEERING, by H. Law and G. R. Burnell. 4s. 6d.

29. DRAINING DISTRICTS AND LANDS, by G. D. Dempsey. 1s.
(With No. 30, DRAINAGE AND SEWAGE OF TOWNS, 2 vols. in 1, 3s.)

31. WELL-SINKING, BORING, AND PUMP WORK, by J. G. Swindell, revised by G. R. Burnell. 1s.

46. ROAD-MAKING AND MAINTENANCE OF MACADA-MISED ROADS, by Gen. Sir J. Burgoyne. 1s. 6d.

60. LAND AND ENGINEERING SURVEYING, by T. Baker. 2s.

63. AGRICULTURAL ENGINEERING, BUILDINGS, MOTIVE POWERS, FIELD ENGINES, MACHINERY, AND IMPLEMENTS, by G. H. Andrews. 3s.

77*. ECONOMY OF FUEL, by T. S. Prideaux. 1s.

80*. EMBANKING LANDS FROM THE SEA, by J. Wiggins. 2s.

82. WATER POWER, as applied to Mills, &c., by J. Glynn. 2s.

82**. GAS WORKS AND MANUFACTURING COAL GAS, by S. Hughes. 3s.

82***. WATER-WORKS FOR CITIES AND TOWNS, by S. Hughes. 3s.

117. SUBTERRANEOUS SURVEYING, AND RANGING THE LINE without the Magnet, by T. Fenwick, with Additious by T. Baker. 2s. 6d.

118. CIVIL ENGINEERING OF NORTH AMERICA, by D. Stevenson. 3s.

120. HYDRAULIC ENGINEERING, by G. R. Burnell. 3s.

121. RIVERS AND TORRENTS, and a Treatise on NAVIGABLE CANALS AND RIVERS THAT CARRY SAND AND MUD, from the Italian of Paul Frisi. 2s. 6d.

125. COMBUSTION OF COAL, AND THE PREVENTION OF SMOKE, by C. Wye Williams, M.I.C.E. 3s.

SHIP-BUILDING AND NAVIGATION.

51. NAVAL ARCHITECTURE, by J. Peake. 3s.

53*. SHIPS FOR OCEAN AND RIVER SERVICE, Construction of, by Captain H. A. Sommerfeldt. 1s.

53**. ATLAS OF 15 PLATES TO THE ABOVE, Drawn for Practice. 4to. 7s. 6d.

54. MASTING, MAST-MAKING, and RIGGING OF SHIPS, by R. Kipping. 1s. 6d.

54*. IRON SHIP-BUILDING, by J. Grantham. 2s. 6d.

54**. ATLAS OF 24 PLATES to the preceding. 4to. 22s. 6d.

55. NAVIGATION; the Sailor's Sea Book: How to Keep the Log and Work it off, &c.; Law of Storms, and Explanation of Terms, by J. Greenwood. 2s.

80. MARINE ENGINES, AND STEAM VESSELS, AND THE SCREW, by R. Murray. 2s. 6d.

83 *bis*. SHIPS AND BOATS, Forms of, by W. Bland. 1s. 6d.

99. NAUTICAL ASTRONOMY AND NAVIGATION, by J. R. Young. 2s.

100*. NAVIGATION TABLES, for Use with the above. 1s. 6d.

106. SHIPS' ANCHORS for all SERVICES, by G. Cotsell. 1s. 6d.

149. SAILS AND SAIL-MAKING, by R. Kipping, N.A. 2s. 6d.

ARITHMETIC AND MATHEMATICS.

6. MECHANICS, by Charles Tomlinson. 1s.

32. MATHEMATICAL INSTRUMENTS, THEIR CONSTRUC-TION, USE, &c., by J. F. Heather. 1s.

61*. READY RECKONER for the Measurement of Land, Tables of Work at from 2s. 6d. to 20s. per acre, and valuation of Land from £1 to £1,000 per acre, by A. Arman. 1s. 6d.

76. GEOMETRY, DESCRIPTIVE, with a Theory of Shadows and Perspective, and a Description of the Principles and Practice of Isometrical Projection, by J. F. Heather. 2s.

83. BOOK-KEEPING AND COMMERCIAL PHRASEOLOGY, by James Haddon. 1s.

84. ARITHMETIC, with numerous Examples, by J. R. Young. 1s. 6d.

84*. KEY TO THE ABOVE, by J. R. Young. 1s. 6d.

85. EQUATIONAL ARITHMETIC: Tables for the Calculation of Simple Interest, with Logarithms for Compound Interest, and Annuities, by W. Hipsley. 2s.

86. ALGEBRA, by J. Haddon. 2s.

86*. KEY AND COMPANION TO THE ABOVE, by J. R. Young. 1s. 6d.

88. EUCLID'S GEOMETRY, with Essay on Logic, by H. Law. 2s.

90. GEOMETRY, ANALYTICAL AND CONIC SECTIONS, by J. Hann. 1s.

91. PLANE & SPHERICAL TRIGONOMETRY, by J. Hann. 2s.

93. MENSURATION, by T. Baker. 1s. 6d.

94. LOGARITHMS, Tables of; with Tables of Natural Sines, Cosines, and Tangents, by H. Law. 2s. 6d.

97. STATICS AND DYNAMICS, by T. Baker. 1s.

101. DIFFERENTIAL CALCULUS, by W. S. B. Woolhouse. 1s.

101*. WEIGHTS AND MEASURES OF ALL NATIONS; Weights of Coins, and Divisions of Time; with the Principles which determine the Rate of Exchange, by W. S. B. Woolhouse. 1s. 6d.

102. INTEGRAL CALCULUS, by H. Cox. 1s.

103. INTEGRAL CALCULUS, Examples of, by J. Hann. 1s.

104. DIFFERENTIAL CALCULUS, Examples of, with Solutions, by J. Haddon. 1s.

105. ALGEBRA, GEOMETRY, and TRIGONOMETRY, First Mnemonical Lessons in, by the Rev. T. P. Kirkman. 1s. 6d.

131. READY-RECKONER FOR MILLERS, FARMERS, AND MERCHANTS, showing the Value of any Quantity of Corn, with the Approximate Value of Mill-stones and Mill Work. 1s.

136. RUDIMENTARY ARITHMETIC, by J. Haddon, edited by A. Arman. 1s. 6d.

137. KEY TO THE ABOVE, by A. Arman. 1s. 6d.

147. STEPPING STONE TO ARITHMETIC, by Abraham Arman, Schoolmaster, Thurleigh, Beds. 1s.

148. KEY TO THE ABOVE, by A. Arman. 1s.

NEW SERIES OF EDUCATIONAL WORKS.

[This Series is kept in three styles of binding—the prices of each are given in columns at the end of the lines.]

HISTORIES, GRAMMARS, AND DICTIONARIES.	Limp.	Cloth Boards.	Half Morocco.
	s. d.	s. d.	s. d.
1. ENGLAND, History of, by W. D. Hamilton	4 0	5 0	5 6
5. GREECE, History of, by W. D. Hamilton and E. Levien	2 6	3 6	4 0
7. ROME, History of, by E. Levien . .	2 6	3 6	4 0
9. CHRONOLOGY OF CIVIL AND ECCLEsiastical History, Literature, Art, and Civilisation, from the earliest period to the present time	2 6	3 6	4 0
11. ENGLISH GRAMMAR, by Hyde Clarke .	1 0		
11*. HANDBOOK OF COMPARATIVE PHIlology, by Hyde Clarke	1 0		
12. ENGLISH DICTIONARY, above 100,000 words, or 50,000 more than in any existing work. By Hyde Clarke	3 6	4 6	5 0
———————————, with Grammar		5 6	6 0
14. GREEK GRAMMAR, by H. C. Hamilton .	1 0		
15. ——— DICTIONARY, by H. R. Hamilton. Vol. 1. Greek—English . . .	2 0		
17. ——————— Vol. 2. English — Greek	2 0		
——— Complete in 1 vol. . . .	4 0	5 0	5 6
————————————, with Grammar		6 0	6 6
19. LATIN GRAMMAR, by T. Goodwin . .	1 0		
20. ——— DICTIONARY, by T. Goodwin. Vol. 1. Latin—English	2 0		
22. ——————— Vol. 2. English—Latin	1 6		
——— Complete in 1 vol. . . .	3 6	4 6	5 0
———————————, with Grammar		5 6	6 0
24. FRENCH GRAMMAR, by G. L. Strauss .	1 0		

VIRTUE BROTHERS & CO., 1, AMEN CORNER.

HISTORIES, GRAMMARS, AND DICTIONARIES.	Limp.	Cloth Boards.	Half Morocco.
	s. d.	*s. d.*	*s. d.*
25. FRENCH DICTIONARY, by A. Elwes. Vol. 1. French—English	1 0		
26. ———————— Vol. 2. English—French	1 6		
———————— Complete in 1 vol. . . .	2 6	3 6	4 0
————————————————, with Grammar		4 6	5 0
27. ITALIAN GRAMMAR, by A. Elwes . .	1 0		
28. ———————— TRIGLOT DICTIONARY, by A. Elwes. Vol. 1. Italian — English — French	2 0		
30. ———————— Vol. 2. English—Italian—French	2 0		
32. ———————— Vol. 3. French—Italian—English	2 0		
———————— Complete in 1 vol. . . .		7 6	8 6
————————————————, with Grammar		8 6	9 6
34. SPANISH GRAMMAR, by A. Elwes . .	1 0		
35. ———————— ENGLISH AND ENGLISH-SPANISH DICTIONARY, by A. Elwes .	4 0	5 0	5 6
————————————————, with Grammar		6 0	6 6
39. GERMAN GRAMMAR, by G. L. Strauss .	1 0		
40. ———————— READER, from best Authors .	1 0		
41. ———————— TRIGLOT DICTIONARY, by N. E. Hamilton. Vol. 1. English—German—French	1 0		
42. ———————— Vol. 2. German—English—French	1 0		
43. ———————— Vol. 3. French—English—German	1 0		
———————— Complete in 1 vol. . . .	3 0	4 0	4 6
————————————————, with Grammar		5 0	5 6
44. HEBREW DICTIONARY, by Dr. Breslau. Vol. 1. Hebrew—English . . .	6 0		
————————————————, with Grammar	7 0		
46. ———————— Vol. 2. English—Hebrew	3 0		
———————— Complete, with Grammar, in 2 vols.		12 0	14 0
46*. ———————— GRAMMAR, by Dr. Breslau .	1 0		
47. FRENCH AND ENGLISH PHRASE BOOK	1 0		
48. COMPOSITION AND PUNCTUATION, by J. Brenan	1 0		
49. DERIVATIVE SPELLING BOOK, by J. Rowbotham	1 0		

GREEK AND LATIN CLASSICS,

With Explanatory Notes in English, principally selected from the best German Commentators.

LATIN SERIES.

1. LATIN DELECTUS, with Vocabularies and Notes, by H. Young . . . . 1*s.*

2. CÆSAR'S GALLIC WAR; Notes by H. Young . . 2*s.*

3. CORNELIUS NEPOS; Notes by H. Young . . . 1*s.*

4. VIRGIL. The Georgics, Bucolics; Notes by W. Rushton and H. Young . . . . 1*s.* 6*d.*

5. VIRGIL'S ÆNEID; Notes by H. Young . . . 2*s.*

6. HORACE. Odes and Epodes; Notes, Analysis and Explanation of Metres . . . . 1*s.*

7. HORACE. Satires and Epistles; Notes by W. B. Smith 1*s.* 6*d.*

8. SALLUST. Catiline, Jugurtha; Notes by W. M. Donne 1*s.* 6*d.*

9. TERENCE. Andria and Heautontimorumenos; Notes by J. Davies . . . . 1*s.* 6*d.*

10. TERENCE. Adelphi, Hecyra, and Phormio; Notes by J. Davies . . . . 2*s.*

14. CICERO. De Amicitia, de Senectute, and Brutus; Notes by W. B. Smith . . . . 2*s.*

16. LIVY. Part I. Books i., ii., by H. Young . . 1*s.* 6*d.*

16*.——— Part II. Books iii., iv., v., by H. Young . 1*s.* 6*d.*

17. ——— Part III. Books xxi., xxii., by W. B. Smith 1*s.* 6*d.*

19. CATULLUS, TIBULLUS, OVID, and PROPERTIUS, Selections from, by W. M. Donne . . . . . 2*s.*

20. SUETONIUS and the later Latin Writers, Selections from, by W. M. Donne . . . . 2*s.*

VIRTUE BROTHERS & CO., 1, AMEN CORNER.

GREEK SERIES,

ON A SIMILAR PLAN TO THE LATIN SERIES.

1. GREEK INTRODUCTORY READER, by H. Young.
   On the same plan as the Latin Reader . . . . 1s.
2. XENOPHON. Anabasis, i. ii. iii., by H. Young . . 1s.
3. XENOPHON. Anabasis, iv. v. vi. vii., by H. Young . 1s.
4. LUCIAN. Select Dialogues, by T. H. L. Leary . . 1s.
5. HOMER. Iliad, i. to vi., by T. H. L. Leary . . 1s. 6d.
6. HOMER. Iliad, vii. to xii., by T. H. L. Leary . 1s. 6d.
7. HOMER. Iliad, xiii. to xviii., by T. H. L. Leary . 1s. 6d.
8. HOMER. Iliad, xix. to xxiv., by T. H. L. Leary . 1s. 6d.
9. HOMER. Odyssey, i. to vi., by T. H. L. Leary . 1s. 6d.
10. HOMER. Odyssey, vii. to xii., by T. H. L. Leary . 1s. 6d.
11. HOMER. Odyssey, xiii. to xviii., by T. H. L. Leary 1s. 6d.
12. HOMER. Odyssey, xix. to xxiv.; and Hymns, by T. H.
    L. Leary . . . . 2s.
13. PLATO. Apology, Crito, and Phædo, by J. Davies . . 2s.
14. HERODOTUS, i. ii., by T. H. L. Leary . . . 1s. 6d.
15. HERODOTUS, iii. iv., by T. H. L. Leary . . 1s. 6d.
16. HERODOTUS, v. vi. vii., by T. H. L. Leary . . 1s. 6d.
17. HERODOTUS, viii. ix., and Index, by T. H. L. Leary 1s. 6d.
18. SOPHOCLES; Œdipus Tyrranus, by H. Young . . 1s.
20. SOPHOCLES; Antigone, by J. Milner . . . . 2s.
23. EURIPIDES; Hecuba and Medea, by W. B. Smith . 1s. 6d.
26. EURIPIDES; Alcestis, by J. Milner . . . . 1s.
30. ÆSCHYLUS; Prometheus Vinctus, by J. Davies . . 1s.
32. ÆSCHYLUS; Septem contra Thebas, by J. Davies . . 1s.
40. ARISTOPHANES; Acharnians, by C. S. D. Townshend 1s. 6d.
41. THUCYDIDES, i., by H. Young . . . . . 1s.